THE
KEY & THE FLAME

THE KEY & THE FLAME

CLAIRE M. CATERER

Margaret K. McElderry Books

New York London Toronto Sydney New Delhi

MARGARET K. McELDERRY BOOKS
An imprint of Simon & Schuster Children's Publishing Division
1230 Avenue of the Americas, New York, New York 10020
MARGARET K. MCELDERRY BOOKS
is a trademark of Simon & Schuster, Inc.
For information about special discounts for bulk purchases, please
contact Simon & Schuster Special Sales at 1-866-506-1949 or
business@simonandschuster.com.
The Simon & Schuster Speakers Bureau can bring authors to your
live event. For more information or to book an event, contact the
Simon & Schuster Speakers Bureau at 1-866-248-3049 or visit our
website at www.simonspeakers.com.
The text for this book is set in Impressum Std.
Manufactured in the United States of America
0313 FFG
2 4 6 8 10 9 7 5 3 1
Library of Congress Cataloging-in-Publication Data
Caterer, Claire.
The key & the flame / Claire Caterer.—1st ed.
p.   cm.
Summary: While visiting Hawkesbury, England, eleven-year-old
Holly Shepard, her younger brother, Ben, and new friend Everett
travel to a parallel universe where she learns that the adventures
she has always dreamed of can be messy and dangerous.
ISBN 978-1-4424-5741-6 (hardcover)
ISBN 978-1-4424-5743-0 (eBook)
[1. Adventure and adventurers—Fiction. 2. Space and time—Fiction.
3. Magic—Fiction. 4. Brothers and sisters—Fiction.
5. England—Fiction. 6. Science fiction.] I. Title.
PZ7.C2687916Key 2013
[Fic]—dc23
2012012658

FIRST
EDITION

*In loving memory of
Kenneth W. Caterer,
who was the first person
to read me fairy tales*

*and for Melanie,
who still believes in them*

Chapter 1

The Wish

Holly Shepard lived on a block of identical houses in the middle of the American Midwest. It might have been mildly interesting if she had lived in the *exact* middle, but when Holly looked it up, she saw that her suburb was off by a few hundred miles, so it lacked even that distinction. She attended a midsize school in a town that was neither bustling with glittering skyscrapers and dark alleyways nor quaint with eccentric musicians and Main Street bookshops. Everyone bought clothes at the same mall and saw movies at the thirty-theater megaplex and ate dinner at the same reasonably priced family dining establishment. Every June, the town put on a carnival with two inflatable rides and a Ferris wheel. It was the biggest event of the year.

If you were the sort who longed for more than that—if, for example, you interrupted Ms. Noring and said loud enough for everyone to hear that you didn't see how this week's spelling words were ever going to help you in the *real* world, like if you had to escape from a mountain lion or a shark—you would get a stern look and a tally mark next to your name and you would give up five minutes of recess because Ms. Noring was tired of being second-guessed every single day. You would sit at your desk during the five minutes and study the fake wood grain and wonder if anything in this school was *real*. You would remember, as Holly did, that the last social studies test you'd taken had earned a C because you didn't exactly answer the essay question at the end: *What was the significance of the Louisiana Purchase?* Holly was supposed to write four sentences, but instead she wrote fifteen and had to use the back of the page because she'd wandered off topic and described how Lewis and Clark had fought malaria and rattlesnakes and dysentery, and how their trip was kind of like exploring the Amazon, with lots of wild animals and sometimes unfriendly native people. Ms. Noring wrote at the bottom of the page (she had to squeeze it in): *Next time, answer the question. –5 points.*

Thinking about rattlesnakes had led to drawing three small but vicious Chinese dragons in the margins of her test paper. Holly worked very hard on them, creating thick bodies coiled like springs, and curly

CLAIRE M. CATERER

forked tongues. She spent so much time decorating the dragon's scales with alternating diamond patterns that she completely forgot to answer three of the test questions. Ms. Noring wrote: *Next time, work more on your test and less on your art. –3 points.*

It seemed unfair that this would be the test on which she forgot to write her name and date. Ms. Noring wrote: *Next time, follow the proper format for labeling your test. –2 points.*

Ms. Noring's minuses seemed to follow Holly closer than her shadow. Her classmates looked at her as though they were tallying them in their heads. She was known primarily for what she *didn't* do: She didn't play soccer or softball. She didn't join Girl Scouts or want a cell phone. She didn't buy the right blue jeans or listen to the right kind of music. Worse yet, she didn't *care* about any of those things. She didn't even know the names of most of the stores in the mall; she went there to climb rocks at the Monster Rockwall and sit in a corner of the bookstore with a stack of obscure tomes about Celtic kings or arctic explorers. When she wasn't reading she was outside, alone, wandering in the scraggly copse of trees that ran down the center of the town's five-acre Park & Wildlife Retreat.

No matter where she went, she thought about where she wanted to be, which was pretty much anywhere else. She thought of lives she didn't lead, fantastical lives fraught with danger and magic. Such visions played in her head on an endless loop so that she sometimes forgot just how much she yearned for something—anything—unusual to happen. Holly Shepard, age eleven, her life as dull as the peeling white paint on the back of her split-level house, wished for something extraordinary. And at last her wish—which had just been waiting for the right moment—was granted.

CLAIRE M. CATERER

Chapter 2

The Announcement

Almost two months before Holly was released from Ms. Noring's fifth-grade class at the end of May, her parents plucked Holly and her brother, Ben (thirteen months younger than she), from bed one Saturday morning to have their pictures taken. There were two unusual things about this: One, Holly's mother almost never got up earlier than Holly herself, and two, she didn't ask Holly to put on a dress or comb out her brown braids. It wasn't Christmas or a special birthday, when such things were normally done, and they didn't go to JCPenney, but to a dingy store in the strip mall called One-Hour Smile.

At first, Holly had assumed that they were taking a family portrait. But One-Hour Smile had no studio and no backgrounds of circus clowns or woodland settings. The man at the store didn't introduce himself or wave at Holly with a hand puppet. He sat her down in a straight-backed chair, frowned, and said to Holly's mother, "Glasses on or off?"

"On, I guess. They always are."

"On it is." *Snap*, the picture was done—one pose only. Then it was Ben's turn. He narrowed his eyes as if squinting through binoculars (which he never did, unlike Holly). "He doesn't have to smile, but he should have his eyes open," said Mr. One-Hour.

At that, Ben opened his eyes so wide he looked like toothpicks were propped under his lids. *Snap*. Then each of Holly's parents had the same perfunctory photos taken.

And then, a third unusual thing: After Mr. One-Hour handed them their pictures (tiny, and horrible), their parents took Holly and Ben next door to the Waffle Emporium for breakfast and let them order whatever they wanted. Ben ordered a pancake with a happy face drawn in whipped cream and sprinkled with chocolate chips. Holly had the Truckers' Deluxe, which was two eggs over easy and hash browns and toast and sausage with two buttermilk pancakes on the side. Holly's mother said, "You'll never eat all that."

"If you made breakfast for me at home, you'd know that this is not that unusual for me," said Holly. She knew she was short and skinny for her age. "I have a high metabolism."

CLAIRE M. CATERER

Mrs. Shepard shrugged.

Even though Ben shoveled in his food without noticing anything, Holly felt that crackle in the air when something important is about to happen. Her parents kept looking at each other and not saying much. Her mother drank two cups of black coffee and ate most of her egg-white omelet, then put her fork down. Holly sat up straighter, but her father said, "Let me get into this French toast first," and Holly waited some more. Finally, once her father had taken three bites of the French toast (he ate very slowly), her mother said, "I have an announcement to make." Everyone began talking at once.

"Are we getting divorced?" Ben asked.

"Don't be stupid," said Holly.

"Of course not," said Mr. Shepard.

"Kyle Langley's getting divorced," said Ben.

"*Who* is Kyle Langley?" asked his mother.

"He sits behind me in Mrs. Jenkins's class."

"But Mrs. Dade is your teacher."

"But I go to Mrs. Jenkins for math because I'm in the advanced class."

"You are?" Mrs. Shepard leaned in closer. "When did this happen?"

"Who *cares*?" Holly cried. "What's the announcement?"

"We're getting divorced," Ben repeated, scraping the whipped cream off his pancake.

"We're *not* getting divorced," said Mr. Shepard. "We're going to England."

It felt to Holly like the world stood still; even Ben stopped chewing for a moment. Then he said, "Will I be in advanced math there?"

"Oh, shut up," said Holly. "Are we really, Mom?"

"My law firm is sending me to Oxford in June for a month or so," said Mrs. Shepard. "And your dad will be writing a series of articles about the area."

"Do they have high-speed Internet access there?" Ben asked.

"Um, yes, I believe they do."

"*Please* shut up," Holly said, then turned red at her mother's look. "I meant Ben, not you, Mom."

"I still don't like it, Holly. In this family, no matter what the circumstance, we all show respect for one another, and that means . . ."

Holly knew that once her mother got on this topic, she'd have to be allowed to finish. About three minutes later, after Holly had apologized to Ben, who sniggered at her and then opened his mouth so everyone could see the pancake and whipped cream mushed together inside, Holly took a breath and said, "I would like to hear more about Oxford."

CLAIRE M. CATERER

"It's a very old city, famous for its university. We'll be renting a house in a lovely little town close by called Hawkesbury."

"Is that why we had our pictures taken?" Holly asked.

"Yes. We'll all need passports."

Passports. It was a lovely, mysterious word that sent a shiver across Holly's shoulders.

"Why do we need passports?" Ben asked.

"It's your identification," said Mr. Shepard. "It has your picture and your address. You carry it with you when you travel to a foreign country."

"Do we have to go on a boat?" Ben didn't like boats.

"No, on a plane," Holly said. "Right, Mom?"

"What?" Ben liked planes even less than boats.

"It will be a big plane, Ben," said Mrs. Shepard. "You won't even notice you're flying."

"And you can bring your laptop," added Holly, who was willing to say anything to change the panicky look on his face that might persuade her parents to cancel their trip.

"You'll love it, Ben," said his father, who didn't really know what Ben loved, but understood exactly what Holly loved. "A whole new place to explore, with little winding streets and old shops and bookstores. The countryside has woods and rivers. We can go to London and see the Tower and Buckingham Palace.

We can even take the train that goes under the English Channel and visit Paris."

"Does Paris have high-speed Internet access?" Ben asked.

Sometimes the best thing to do when your brother won't be quiet, and you've already been warned not to shut him up, is to think about something else. While Holly's parents assured Ben that high-speed Internet access would be available wherever they went, she let her mind wander to Paris and London and Oxford and Hawkesbury. A lightness filled her chest, as if something heavy that had long been sitting there had flown away. Suddenly Holly didn't care that she wouldn't make the honor roll this quarter. True, her mother would frown at her grade card and then make a huge fuss over Ben's straight As and advanced math and probably promise to send him to robotics camp. But none of that mattered now. Holly knew she was finally about to have an adventure.

What she didn't know was that adventures are never neat little affairs like a trip to the amusement park, from which you emerge tired but unaltered. They are messy. They are dangerous. They are hungry, and what they take from you can never be recovered.

The adventure that waited for Holly Shepard was hungrier than most.

CLAIRE M. CATERER

Chapter 3

The Gift

The journey finally began, eight days after school let out, with a series of waits: wait for the car to be loaded; wait for the luggage to be checked; wait for the plane to come; and the longest wait of all, inside the plane while it roared and hummed across the Atlantic. Once Holly's stomach had caught up with her—it dawdled behind when the plane swooped off the ground—her heart thrummed in time to the jet engines while Ben whined about finding an outlet for his laptop and his mother asked a dozen times if he had his inhaler and allergy pills in his pocket. Holly plugged her ears with earbuds that were connected to nothing and kept her eyes on her book. When they landed at Heathrow, the London airport, Holly stepped a pace away from her family and hoped she would be mistaken for a British girl.

In time they found the suitcases and their rental car. The steering wheel was on the wrong side, which looked very odd, but Holly said nothing because her father was trying to concentrate. He had to remember to drive on the left side of the road instead of the right and to follow the directions that Mrs. Shepard barked at him.

Nothing around Holly seemed especially British. She saw small family cars and large moving vans and gray overpasses and scrubby trees along the highway, and then came Ben's voice ("Mom, where's my Battleship game?") and her mother's voice ("You passed the turn *again*") and her father's voice ("I'm doing the best I can"). Holly wondered if this summer were going to be as fabulous as she'd thought.

But finally they shed the London traffic, and the buildings and roundabouts disappeared. The car pulled onto a curving, hilly two-lane road in the most beautiful place Holly could imagine.

"Are we there?" Ben asked, waking up.

"Not quite," said Mr. Shepard.

The land swelled around them in slopes of the greenest, dewiest grass Holly had ever seen. It looked like a giant had spilled his paint box over the hills until the colors had melted together—pine and Easter grass and fern and aquamarine. Long lines of flowering shrubs and stone walls bordered farmers' properties. Through stands of trees Holly glimpsed

CLAIRE M. CATERER

boxlike houses with thatched roofs and deep-set windows. A white-haired man with tall boots and a long stick hiked among clusters of grazing sheep. He dropped out of sight as they drove into the valley. Ahead of them, cloud shadows rolled across the land-swells. Even Ben, for once, was quiet.

A few minutes later the road straightened, and soon they passed a small wooden sign that read, WELCOME TO HAWKESBURY, HEART OF THE COTSWOLDS.

"That's our town!" Ben announced.

They passed the High Street and a small square of shops with a covered market. "Never mind that, we'll stop later," said Mrs. Shepard. Then to Mr. Shepard: "Now around the other side of the green, you'll see Charlton Road. And off that to the left is Chavenage Lane."

"The left?"

"Right. Sorry."

"You mean, 'Right, correct'?"

"No, I mean, 'Right, not left.'"

"What are we looking for again?"

Holly shut out the noise, and even Ben knew not to say anything during a discussion like this. Still, the roads were so narrow and twisty, and their car so slow and rumbling—and no drivers behind them honking or gesturing—that no one minded driving in circles for a few minutes. Eventually Mr. Shepard pulled down a quiet road called Hodges Close. It dead-ended abruptly at the top of a hill, and the car stopped with a little cough. In front of them was their house.

The cottage—that's what Holly's father called it. It was square and made of huge blocks of a softly silver stone that seemed to glow from within. The eaves hung low enough for Holly to reach up and touch the thin limestone tiles on the roof. The door was painted a glossy pine green and had a round knocker on it the size of Holly's fist. A large brass number 1 hung next to it. Sprays of wildflowers grew up around the front path.

Ben pushed past her, yelling, "Finally! An outlet!" and bolted inside.

"Holly, come back here and get your backpack," called Mrs. Shepard.

It isn't easy to look around a place properly when the ordinary things of life keep interrupting. But Holly grabbed her backpack and dodged around a corner while everyone else lugged suitcases upstairs. She glanced around. No front hall, no rec room, no family room, no mudroom; and yet the cottage seemed to be just big enough. The white plaster walls rippled under Holly's fingers. In the living room, she sank into a crimson sofa drawn close to an immense stone

CLAIRE M. CATERER

fireplace. She took a deep breath. The scent of a house was important to her. Lemon—that was the floor's dark, wide planks. Soot mixed with damp, flowery air—that was the open window and the smell from the woodstove in the hearth.

Holly shifted in her seat. Something was poking her. She reached behind her and found a small square box tied with a ribbon. A tag read: HOLLY.

For *her*? She groped around the sofa cushions and the two armchairs, but she didn't see presents for anyone else. It didn't seem fair, but then again, she was the only one bothering to get to know this place. The rest were busy upstairs, chatting and opening drawers. She heard Ben saying, "Which converter do I plug in the outlet?" and Mrs. Shepard saying, "Put that thing away and unpack first!" and Mr. Shepard saying, "I guess we'll have to go buy something to eat."

They'd be back downstairs soon. If Holly wanted to keep her present a secret, she'd need to open it now. She turned the box over in her hands. It was made of a smooth, fragrant wood. She untied the ribbon, undid a funny hooked clasp, and opened the hinged lid.

Inside was a heavy iron key. It was exactly as long as the box, about three inches, and one end was forged in a loop. The other was notched in three or four places. She had never seen a key like it.

Holly noticed something else tucked into a corner of the box—a folded piece of stiff paper. She opened it and read:

*Only the strong of heart take the
   circular path,
For to return from whence you came
Brings the ending back to the beginning.*

Holly stared, blinking, at the message. But no sooner had she read it than she heard Ben galumphing down the stairs. Behind him came the more orderly steps of her parents. She glared at the staircase; it was like she had opened an especially wonderful birthday present that her mother had put aside, saying, "Isn't that nice! Well, let's move on. What else have you got?" Holly didn't want to move on. But she grabbed her backpack and stuffed the wooden box deep into one of the zippered pockets before anyone else saw it.

The rest of the day was filled with things that ordinarily would have been interesting. They walked the streets of Hawkesbury and bought food with strange names like Weetabix and Typhoo. They stopped in a pub called The Willy Wicket and ordered fish and chips that came in paper-lined baskets (for everyone) and very dark beer (for Holly's parents).

Back at the cottage on Hodges Close, Mrs. Shepard herded everyone into the kitchen with bags of groceries, then up the stairs to finish unpacking. "Now, I don't want anyone going to sleep," she said. "We need to adjust to British time. Let's all hang in there until eight o'clock."

Holly heard her mother on the stairs behind her, but her voice was growing fainter and the call of her bedroom louder. She barely had time to notice which bed had Ben's backpack splayed across it before she fell, already asleep, onto the other.

Chapter 4

The Caretaker

Holly had traveled a very long way, slept scrunched in an airplane seat, and eaten odd-colored food wrapped in plastic; and so, when overtired from chatter and bickering, she arrived to a soft bed, she slept very well. She fell asleep at six o'clock in the evening and didn't wake up again until nearly five the next morning. The sun was already up. The first thing Holly remembered when she woke was the key.

She slipped out of bed, still dressed in the rumply jeans and T-shirt she'd worn on the plane. Slowly, so as not to wake Ben, she disentangled her backpack from the rest of the luggage. Then she cleaned her glasses extra thoroughly, so she wouldn't miss anything, and tiptoed downstairs, through the kitchen, and into the back garden.

A wrought iron table and two chairs sat on a tiny flagstone patio. Tall hedges of pink hollyhocks framed the garden, giving it a sweet, enclosed feeling. An ivy-covered arbor led out of the yard. Holly sat down at the table, unzipped her backpack, and took out the wooden box.

> *Only the strong of heart take the*
> *circular path,*
> *For to return from whence you came*
> *Brings the ending back to the beginning.*

What did that mean, *the circular path*? She hadn't ever been to England before, so how could she return from whence she'd come?

She shook her head and picked up the iron key, balancing it in her hand. It felt surprisingly warm. Someone who knew her name had entrusted her with a key to . . . what? It was too big to belong to a file cabinet or a padlock. Holly glanced back at the cottage. She walked around the garden path to the front door, but the lock was a tiny modern one that her key couldn't even fit in.

So it is *a mystery,* she thought with satisfaction as she sat down again in the backyard. Almost at once, she sprang back up.

Something was moving in the hollyhocks.

Holly stepped through the archway. The flagstones extended a few feet and then gave way to a much older path made of raised, uneven stones. Grass grew between them. She took a few steps and then gasped in surprise.

Spread out before her was a deep valley. The path in front of her edged down the hill in wide stone steps. Below, the land rippled like a green carpet sprinkled with a confetti of wildflowers. A dense forest spilled down the left side. A silvery snakelike thing—a river, Holly realized—poured down from another hill across the valley. Something large and dark loomed on the hill, but the thin morning mist hid it from sight.

A cluster of bluebells at Holly's feet shook in the breeze, each flower bent with the weight of a single dewdrop. Holly knelt down to touch her finger to one of the blooms.

"Looking for something, are we?"

The voice so startled Holly that her feet slipped on the wet stones. She fell, scraping her right elbow on the loose pebbles, and would have rolled right down the hill if a strong arm hadn't pulled her back. "You want to mind these steps. Not safe, I've always said."

Holly looked up to see a bent-over old man with a grizzled chin and deep-set, startlingly blue eyes. He wore a plaid flannel shirt and a linen cap over his crooked nose. When he pulled Holly to her feet, she saw he wasn't much taller than she was.

CLAIRE M. CATERER

Now Holly knew just as surely as you do never to talk to strangers, and certainly not to let them touch you. Had she behaved as she'd been taught, she would have screamed and stomped on the old man's fragile instep. And yet those rules seemed to belong to a place far away from this sunny morning in Hawkesbury. She brushed herself off, smiled, and held out her hand. "Thanks. I'm Holly Shepard."

"Splendid! I'm—"

"Holly!"

She dropped the man's hand in an instant. Her mother appeared through the arbor dressed in her bathrobe, her arms crossed in front of her. Holly had no doubt she could take out the old man if provoked.

But he stepped up to the garden, still smiling. "Mrs. Shepard? So sorry I wasn't here yesterday to greet you, ma'am. I'm Gallaway—the caretaker."

"Oh, of course, Mr. Gallaway. The rental agent mentioned you." Mrs. Shepard offered her hand. "Laura Shepard."

"Pleasure, ma'am. I trust you got settled in all right?"

"Everything's wonderful."

Mr. Gallaway held up a white paper bag Holly hadn't noticed before. "I brought some breakfast. I wasn't sure if you'd had a chance to do the marketing."

Mrs. Shepard raised one eyebrow, which Holly

knew meant, *What, at this hour?* But all Mrs. Shepard said was, "How nice of you! Please, come in."

Holly followed the grown-ups inside. Mr. Gallaway winked at her. Holly thought of her present.

"Were you in our house yesterday?"

"Just getting things ready. Wood for the fire and the like."

"Did you—"

"Holly, set out some plates, would you? I've just put the coffee on, Mr. Gallaway."

The old man sat down to share scones and coffee with them and proceeded to talk to Holly's mother about things like how crowded Heathrow Airport was and how to work the washing machine. Just when Holly was about to excuse herself, Mr. Gallaway turned to her and said, "And certainly you, Miss Holly, must go to school?"

"Um, yes. I'm going into middle school this fall."

"And are you excited about it?" asked Mr. Gallaway.

The old man's blue eyes prompted Holly to be honest. "Sure. Harder math and no recess, what's not to be excited about?"

"It must be quite tedious for you there," said Mr. Gallaway, his eyes very serious. Mrs. Shepard gave him the look that she usually reserved for Holly just before asking, "Why do you *say* things like that?" But now she said nothing.

CLAIRE M. CATERER

Mr. Gallaway picked up a scone and the butter, but instead of applying one to the other, he brandished the butter knife to emphasize his point. "Poor Miss Holly! I suppose you've been told you don't 'live up to your potential.' You're not to draw on your paper or natter on about kings and queens and lost princesses. They tell you not to read your storybooks when it's time for spelling, that you won't be learning about spelunking or falconry in your year, yes? Heavens!" His fist landed on the table, rattling the dishes. "Holly should be doing fieldwork, not sitting at a desk. Practice digging up a fossil instead of reading about it, eh, Holly?"

After a brief, stunned silence, Holly said, "Yes, that's exactly what I should be doing!"

"You could learn more about ancient Egypt in one trip to the pyramids than you could reading your entire history book."

"That's what I think too!"

"And what about applying your maths principles? Design a house, make blueprints—"

"I'd have to figure out dimensions and area—"

"Go snorkeling to learn about sea life—"

"On safari to learn about elephants—"

"Do real research instead of reading that tiresome Internet—"

"Excuse me." Mrs. Shepard had a way of halting

even a loud conversation while staying very quiet herself. "I suppose," she said, "that it would be fun to go on safari and design houses, but that's not what goes on at school, Mr. Gallaway. Holly needs to accept reality and apply herself to what's expected of her."

It was the sort of remark that is like the door slamming shut against a summer day. But before Holly could argue, her father came down the stairs saying, "Do I smell coffee?" And shortly thereafter Ben arrived, and a new argument began about whether he should have to eat breakfast before playing on the computer, and the whole morning became very ordinary. Holly slipped away from the table and out to the back garden.

By now the sun had dried the steps down the hill, and Holly found that they were not very steep. At the bottom, she could look up and see their cottage ringed with hollyhocks. At her feet, a worn path disappeared into the forest.

Holly had little experience in forests. She had gone camping exactly once, in what amounted to little more than a clump of trees. There was no getting lost in that wood; Holly had tried, and found her way out in ten minutes. The closest thing to a wilderness she'd experienced was climbing the Monster Rockwall in the mall. But this forest on the edge of Hawkesbury was *real* wilderness.

CLAIRE M. CATERER

The minute she stepped into the trees a curtain of silence dropped and the sunlight dimmed. She stood very still. The place was like one huge living body, its organs the trees and animals. She could almost feel giant lungs expanding and contracting. Then she did something very smart: She looked down at her watch, which was also a compass, and noticed that her toes were pointed due north. She started down the path.

Holly had an excellent sense of direction and easily remembered which way she took when the path forked. After a few minutes, the noise picked up. She heard scamperings nearby and squirrels chittering, and the songs of birds that made their homes deep within the wood. A gurgling sound told her she would soon come upon a stream. Underneath it all, she could hear a low hum, which grew louder as she walked.

At first Holly thought someone was running a leaf blower, which disappointed her, because she didn't want to meet anyone else. But the noise sounded more like fluorescent lights buzzing, or the static between radio stations. It was like a current, alive, reaching out.

In a moment she found the stream. She stepped across several flat rocks, then clambered up the far bank, where the path continued.

The humming immediately grew louder. Holly followed the path straight for a few minutes, then round another bend behind a dense cluster of trees. She stopped.

She stood in a sun-drenched glade. Several tall, skinny beech trees ringed the clearing like campers around a fire. Right in the center stood a single, ancient oak, twisted like a wrung-out cloth, and so broad that she and Ben easily could have hidden together on one side, and even by linking arms would not have been able to span it.

She walked up to it as if approaching a wild animal she wanted to feed. The humming grew louder. How strange that only one oak tree should spring up in the middle of a beech forest. But when she walked into its shade, she saw the strangest thing of all. Fitted right into the center of the tree's trunk was a rectangular iron plate, rather like a light switch. But where the switch would be was exactly what Holly had been looking for: a very large, odd-shaped keyhole.

CLAIRE M. CATERER

Chapter 5

Through the Glade

Holly drew the big iron key from her pocket and took a deep breath. Finding a keyhole in an oak tree was even stranger—and better—than finding a locked treasure chest. The gnarled, knotted trunk vibrated beneath her fingers; the humming she'd heard came from the tree itself. She knew, just as you do, that this was the beginning of something that would change everything.

The key fit; of course it did. The tumblers clicked together as if the lock had just been oiled. Then a rumbling began, deep in the earth.

If you've never been in an earthquake—and Holly had not—it can be unsettling. The earth beneath her feet rippled like a water bed. She stumbled to the ground. A beam of light shot out of the keyhole, and then the tree trunk cracked—first a short split crossways, about six feet above the keyhole, and then connecting to it, a crack down the right side, and another down the left. Holly recognized the shape at once.

It was a door.

The tremor stopped. The door opened.

Holly scrambled to her feet. For a split second she thought of running back to the cottage as fast as she could. But a split second is a very short time, and the fear passed into curiosity as she peeked through the doorway.

It's just the same place, she thought, and yet somehow it wasn't. She stepped across the door's threshold.

Yes, the same glade, the same ring of trees. But the trees were brighter, more distinct, and then she saw something else: Each one had a design on the trunk.

Holly stepped across the glade to one of the beeches. Odd wedge shapes had been cut into the trunk. It was some kind of ancient writing that she couldn't decipher. She traced the grooves with her finger. In fact, all the beech trees in the circle had runes carved into them—and they all were different. And then she noticed the most important thing: Each one had a keyhole, just like the oak tree.

"Oi! What're you doing?"

Holly spun around. Back in the wood where she'd come from stood a boy about her size with unruly brown hair and ruddy cheeks. His eyes were green with bristly long lashes, and when he stepped into the clearing the sun hit the streaks of red and gold in his hair.

CLAIRE M. CATERER

"Well?" The boy frowned and crossed his arms across his chest.

"I'm just walking." Holly knew how odd this sounded, considering that she had caused an earthquake and opened a door in an oak tree and now stood in front of about half a dozen different keyholes. But the boy didn't seem to think any of this unusual.

"I can see that. But this is my wood." He walked past the split oak without looking at it. "What are you doing with that?" He indicated the key, which Holly held out in front of her.

"I'm not really sure . . . and . . . well . . ." She glanced back at the oak. "I opened the tree with it."

The boy raised his eyebrows, then followed her glance. "Er . . . okay."

"See? Right here." Holly ran back to the oak. She waved her arm through the doorway in the tree.

"What are you on about?" The boy frowned at her hand. Then Holly realized: He couldn't see what she saw.

Watching him, Holly stepped back through the doorway in the tree. His eyes didn't follow her, but he said, "So now it's hide-and-seek, is it?"

The moment Holly cleared the doorway the rumbling began again. She clutched at the tree trunk and the door slid shut. The cracks around its frame vanished.

Holly walked around the oak. The ring of trees across the glade looked perfectly ordinary. No keyholes.

"Are all American girls as odd as you?" the boy asked, after her second time around the tree. Apparently he hadn't felt the rumbling when the oak tree closed, either.

"What? No. I just—I thought I saw something. It's not there now."

"Right," said the boy, smirking. "I'm Everett. You must be one of the family leasing the cottage from Mr. Gallaway."

"I'm Holly Shepard. How did you know?"

Everett shrugged. "Word gets round. What year are you?"

"You mean at school? I'm going into sixth grade. I'll be twelve in December."

"I'm already twelve. I live on Clement Lane, the other side of the close." He pointed down another path. "And this *is* my wood. So what's this rubbish about opening up a tree?"

Holly slid the key into her pocket. "Oh no, I was only kidding. It's just the key to our cottage."

"No, it isn't. It's too big for that."

"But it must be," said Holly, thinking fast. "Mr. Gallaway gave it to me. I just thought—"

"That it might naturally open a locked oak tree," Everett finished. "Clever idea, that. What d'you mean, he gave it to you? Like a present?"

Holly shrugged.

"He was walking round here too," said Everett. "I think your mum was missing you."

Holly's stomach jumped. "I'd better get back. I didn't tell anyone I was taking a walk."

"Suit yourself. You've a brother, haven't you?"

"Yes. Ben."

"I'll come by later then," Everett said, as if Ben were the only reason he might. "Did you know Hawkesbury's got a castle?"

Holly's heart fluttered. A *castle*?

"Course, nobody lives in it now, but it's fun to poke round in. I could show you sometime, if you're interested."

"Sure," said Holly. "That would be great."

"Right then, Holly Shepard." Everett gave her a half-smile. "You can walk in my wood if you want. It's all right."

I'll walk where I want anyway, Holly thought, but it seemed more polite to say, "Okay. Thanks."

"See you."

She waited for Everett to walk away, but he stood there, as if guarding the forest. Why didn't he go home? She could feel the shape of the key in her pocket.

Something incredible had happened, and only she had seen it. Everett half smiled again. "I thought you needed to get home."

And then, on cue, Holly heard her mother's shrill voice calling her name. She sighed. Well, she had all summer, and Everett couldn't stand there forever. She gave a little wave. "Yeah, I do. See you later." She headed back up the path, dragging her feet in the direction of her cottage.

It wasn't quite accurate to say that the wood in the valley north of Hawkesbury belonged to Everett Shaw, as he had told the American girl. But it might as well have. Hawkesbury was a small village with only a few thousand people—every one of whom he knew by sight—and there wasn't much to do apart from hanging round the shops or exploring the wood. Yet for all of that, Everett, who stood very confidently until Holly had disappeared round the path, shivered with a slight chill of unease as he stood in the glade.

It was the way Holly had acted—not like she was playing, and not like she was lying, but more like she'd really seen something odd and then tried to laugh it off. It was rubbish, of course, opening a tree with a key, even an ancient iron key like she'd had in her hand. So why even say so?

CLAIRE M. CATERER

He wouldn't have said as much to Holly, because he hadn't seen any such thing, but he had *heard* something—a kind of humming—and *felt* something—a sort of current. It reminded him of the time he had seen his neighbor's house struck by lightning, right on the telly's aerial, when he was out playing in mud puddles, which his mother strictly forbade during a thunderstorm. It was like that: the humming in the air, the fine hairs on his arms bristling, his heart thrumming as if plugged into a socket.

Trees, of course, don't have electrical currents, and Everett knew that. But there was no doubt that his own wood, which he knew as well as you know your own backyard, felt very different today.

Not that he hadn't felt something like it before.

To be sure, nothing *exactly* like it, but sometimes, hopping from rock to rock along the slopes, or swinging on the tire he'd strung up on the eastern end, he'd stop, panting, and listen.

He wasn't sure what he was listening for, but it was almost as if he could hear something, or if he waited a moment, he *would* hear something. He'd walk round a bend, catch an odd glimpse out of the corner of his eye, a light or reflection, feel a vibration on the path, just faint. And then nothing.

Until today.

And Mr. Gallaway had given Holly that key?

The old man lived on Hodges Close, where he leased several cottages, including Holly's. Everett supposed he made a bit of money that way, but Gallaway's own cottage was tiny, and he didn't even have a car. Everett had never seen any family come to visit him, though he noticed Mr. Gallaway posted a good number of letters, which almost no one did anymore. Everett had known him forever, and they were friendly enough, but Gallaway kept to himself and was sometimes gruff. Everett had been a bit frightened of him when he was a kid. The old man certainly had never given him anything. He didn't even know Holly. Why give *her* a present? Or at least, if he was giving out presents, why not to *him*? He must know that Everett and his mum struggled on a bit, ever since his dad had left, and it wouldn't kill him to be friendlier to them, would it?

Everett stepped out of the glade off the main path and started down a slope, following the meandering stream away from Hawkesbury to his favorite spot in the wood, where a fallen tree made a bridge over the water. He walked out to the very middle and sat down, dangling his feet over the stream. Holly seemed nice enough, for a girl. Plus, she had a brother. That right there would be enough reason to get to know them.

CLAIRE M. CATERER

It wasn't like he had loads of kids to hang out with. Most of his schoolmates lived in outlying towns, and Blake Worsley, his best mate, had moved to Bristol last year. He missed Blake; with him gone, that git Sean Fellowes had taken to making Everett's life miserable pretty much on a daily basis.

But why'd he have to mention Darton Castle to Holly straightaway? It was *his* place. Something about her, the way she kept walking round that oak tree, and then stood so straight frowning at him, made him want to show her the castle. Almost like he *had* to show it to her, for some reason.

Maybe there wasn't anything to Holly's present, but one thing Everett was sure about: She was hiding something.

And he was going to find out what.

Chapter 6

The Shaws

When Holly reached the creek, she started across and then hesitated. She hadn't heard her mother calling again. Maybe she could go back, just for a minute. Everett had probably gone home by now.

She started to clamber back up the creek bank.

"Miss Holly?"

Mr. Gallaway appeared out of a cluster of birch trees. Holly tried not to look disappointed. "Oh, hi."

"Your mum was a bit worried about you. She asked if I'd look for you, as I know the wood so well."

"Sorry. I was just out for a walk." Holly slid down the bank and stepped across the creek to join him. He held out a hand and helped her up the rise, and they started back down the path.

"Did you find anything interesting?" Mr. Gallaway asked after a moment.

Holly glanced at him sharply, but he had taken a pipe out of his pocket and was thumping it against his palm, then peering into it, hardly watching where he was going. "Is there something interesting to find?" she asked.

The old man shrugged. "I suppose. If you know where to look."

Holly thought of the oak tree she'd split open, and a very mundane and disappointing thought occurred to her. "Do you get earthquakes here very often?"

"Earthquakes? I should say not. Although technically, they can happen anywhere. But I don't recall one in all the time I've spent in Britain, which is considerable."

"What about power lines? Is there maybe an electrical plant somewhere nearby? Or wires buried underground?" Holly was thinking of the humming she'd heard.

"Not in this direction," said Mr. Gallaway. "On the south side of the village, yes. But this wood, the valley, the hills beyond—it's all quite primitive. Ancient, in fact."

Their path sloped upward over some fallen rocks, and Mr. Gallaway grasped a sapling to haul himself up, then turned to give Holly a hand. She wanted to ask him about the oak tree, and more especially, the beech trees that grew in a circle around it. She was quite sure that her key would fit those keyholes, but then what? What would those doors open up?

Grown-ups hated to hear kids talk about anything especially strange; she knew this from experience. Usually, they'd put one hand on your forehead and look at you oddly and ask if you needed to lie down for a while with the shades drawn. But Mr. Gallaway seemed a different sort of grown-up.

He glanced at her sideways. "Something on your mind?"

"Sort of, yeah. I was wondering . . . You *did* give me the key, didn't you, Mr. Gallaway? Where did you get it? Because it doesn't seem exactly normal, and I'm not sure what it's for—"

"It's for opening things," said the old man.

All of a sudden Holly found she had to walk rather fast to keep up with him. "Okay, I know *that*, but I mean, *what* is it supposed to open?"

"Things that are locked, naturally."

"But what kinds of things?"

"All kinds of things."

The terrain had gotten hilly, with lots of climbing and awkward passages around muddy, rutted paths. He was taking a different route than Holly had coming in, and it took some concentration to watch where she was going.

"But not trees, right? I mean, keys don't open trees."

"Certainly not in the usual course of events."

CLAIRE M. CATERER

"But they *could*? Is that what you mean?" Holly asked.

The old man had disappeared around a bend, and Holly had to push aside some overgrown shrubs to find the path. "Mr. Gallaway? Are you still here?"

"We're nearly out," he called ahead of her. "Just follow the path."

A moment later, Holly broke out of the trees and saw him just ahead, at the foot of the steps leading up to her cottage. She ran to catch up to him. "Mr. Gallaway, wait. Why did you give me that key? I mean, why *me*?"

His blue eyes looked watery, and he smiled at her briefly, then turned away. "That," he said, "is a story for another time."

Suddenly Mrs. Shepard appeared under the arbor at the top of the steps.

"Well, *there* you are! I had to send Mr. Gallaway after you, Holly! You need to apologize to him."

"I just went for a walk," Holly said.

"You should've told us. You could've fallen down a well for all I knew."

Holly climbed the stairs and stepped through the arbor. "Fallen down a well?"

"It happens." Her mother pursed her lips.

"Well," said Mr. Gallaway, "no harm done. Safe and sound. I had best be off. You do know where to find me,

Mrs. Shepard? Up the close, Number Seven. Come by if you need anything."

Mrs. Shepard relaxed a little. "Yes, thank you, Mr. Gallaway."

As he turned away, Mrs. Shepard added, "Oh, but let me give you my numbers." She pulled a notepad and pen from her bathrobe pocket. "This is the house phone and this is my cell number. Also, here's the office in Oxford, and the one in London, where I'll be occasionally . . . and of course my husband will be here most of the time, but if not, here's *his* cell. Oh, and our e-mail addresses." She tore off the note and handed it to Mr. Gallaway, then poised the pen over the notepad. "And how can I reach you?"

"Just come by if you need anything," the old man repeated. "I don't own a telephone."

Mrs. Shepard was too stunned to respond as he raised a hand and disappeared around the path.

Because it was Sunday, which her parents had long ago decreed as Family Day, Holly hardly had a chance to think about the strange happenings in the wood, let alone sneak off for another look. First there was a lengthy family meeting about rules, and then they all took turns in the shower, and everyone was given chores to do.

And just when they'd finally been dismissed (sometimes Holly's family was a little like the army), a sharp rapping came from the front door. Mr. Shepard opened it, and in breezed a slender, harried-looking woman bearing a covered dish and, behind her, the boy Holly had met in the wood.

"We're the Shaws, I'm Emily, and this is Everett," gushed the woman. "We thought you'd be ready for lunch. Everett told us he'd met your Holly in the wood. And you must be Steven, how lovely! Mr. Gallaway said you'd be arriving yesterday. You're a journalist, aren't you? And Laura, isn't it? These must be the children! Holly I've already heard about, and you are . . . ?"

Emily Shaw had already said all this before quite getting in the door, and she so startled Ben that he didn't realize it was his turn to speak until his mother cut in, "This is Ben," and motioned for the Shaws to sit down.

Now that company was here, Holly knew her chances of going back to the forest were slim. They had to sit at the table and eat politely and pretend to like the lunch, which was some kind of potpie. Once they'd had what Mrs. Shaw called the "pudding"—really a kind of blackberry crisp—Everett turned to Ben and said, "D'you have any video games?"

"Not a console or anything, but I have a bunch on the computer."

"Do you have Planeterra Four?"

"I have Planeterra *Five*," Ben said proudly. "There's a whole extra level on the sixth holodeck, and a bunch of new creatures on the space walk."

"Could I have a go?" Everett asked, and the boys jumped up and disappeared.

Mrs. Shaw turned to Holly. "Go along, love. Don't feel you have to sit here with the boring grown-ups."

"Can I go outside, Mom?" she asked.

"Nonsense," Mrs. Shaw cut in before her mother could answer. "Go on upstairs with the boys. Everett! Holly's coming up too!"

The look Holly's mother gave her said it would be rude not to do what Mrs. Shaw said, and Holly's look back said that sometimes boys go off together and she didn't really care, and Holly's mother's look said that *she* didn't care, Holly was to go upstairs, and Holly's father's look said couldn't Holly go on outside if she wanted, and Holly's look to her father said thank you. But in the end, without a word being exchanged, Holly trudged upstairs to see what the boys were doing.

She recognized the spacey music and little explosions of Ben's Planeterra Five game as she walked in the room. He and Everett had the laptop on the floor and were stretched out on their stomachs in front of it. They didn't notice Holly. She watched them for a

CLAIRE M. CATERER

moment, then reached into her pocket. She rubbed the key's cool, worn surface. It vibrated for a split second.

"Aw *man!*" cried Ben.

The laptop screen had flickered out.

"Is it just the monitor?" Everett asked.

"Naw. The whole thing's cut out. Gol *darn* it! The game's not even saved."

Holly turned her laugh into a cough.

Ben turned around. "What did you do?"

"Me? I'm just standing here."

Ben muttered something like "Girls" under his breath while he tried in vain to restart the computer, but Everett stood up.

"I could show you that castle, if you like," he said to Holly.

"Okay," she said in an offhand way, covering up the fact that as long as she was stuck with Everett, she wanted to see the castle more than anything.

"What? Where're you going?" Ben scrambled to his feet.

"There's an old castle across the valley. It's pretty cool," Everett said. "D'you want to come see?"

"Is it far?" Ben wasn't much of a walker.

"Not very. Come on, I'll show you."

"Maybe you should stay and work on getting that

computer going," Holly suggested. "It's not going to fix itself."

"It's just the weird power supply in this house," Ben said coolly. "I'm sure it'll be okay."

Downstairs, Everett explained to Mrs. Shepard where they were going and why it wasn't dangerous or far, and how he knew the area well, and he'd make sure they were back in a couple of hours. "Everett *loves* that old place," Mrs. Shaw bubbled. "He's rather a British history buff."

"Maybe we should all go," said Mrs. Shepard. "It sounds very interesting."

Holly caught her father's eye, and he said, "Let's leave it for today. You have all those files you wanted to go through before tomorrow."

"Oh well, *that's* true," her mother conceded, and looked as if her mind had already begun sorting papers. Holly smiled at Mr. Shepard and followed the boys outside. She could spare an afternoon to look at a castle. She thrust her hand into her pocket and ran her index finger over the iron key. The magic could wait.

What she did not realize, of course, was that she was carrying the magic with her.

Chapter 7

The Castle

The sun was high and warm now. Everett led the way down the hill, and behind her Holly could hear Ben stepping carefully, calling, "Hey! Wait up!"

At the bottom, Everett pointed across the valley at the hill that had been shrouded in mist earlier that morning. Nestled at the top was a high stone wall with a tower at either end. "That's Darton Castle," Everett said.

"Is that what you call 'not far'?" Ben asked.

"Oh, go home and play with your Planet Terror," Holly snapped.

"It's *Planeterra*. You know it is."

"It's closer than it looks," Everett told him. "And there's steps, like on our hill. Course"—he looked skeptically at Holly—"it might be a bit of a climb for a girl."

"I climb the rock wall at home all the time," Holly said, and stifled the urge to shove past him. "Let's go."

The tramp across the valley was longer than even Holly had expected, and the climb up the next hill—stairs or no stairs—was steep. She even felt a little sorry for Ben, who she could hear wheezing behind her. She turned to him and was considerate enough to whisper.

"Do you have your inhaler?"

"No," he whispered back fiercely. "And I don't"—*puff*—"need it. Quit treating me"—*puff*—"like I'm"—*puff*—"a baby."

"Okay, fine." She shrugged and pushed ahead.

"Almost there," Everett called over his shoulder. A moment later, the steps widened and they came upon the castle.

The hill was broad and springy with heather. A cold, stone cylinder topped with a toothlike edge rose a hundred feet in front of them. It was the sort Holly herself had made in the sand. The long wall stretched south to where the hill dropped off down a rocky precipice to the river. What had looked like a toy from the valley now seemed more like a prison. Holly shrugged off a chill. Silly, but she couldn't help glancing back at the green valley, as if it might have vanished. Seeing the castle up close unsettled her, like walking through a sunny meadow and coming upon a long-abandoned gallows.

"The main gatehouse is round the other side,"

Everett said, "but it's tricky to get to from here." He led them along the wall to a sudden break, where it looked as if a wrecking ball had pushed through it. "Easier to get in this way."

Holly stepped through into a wide, enclosed court- yard. Arched cloisters ran along two sides, and the remains of short stone stairways dotted the corners. "It's built sort of in layers," Everett said. "So that if invaders penetrated the outer walls, the family could retreat to the inner keep." He pointed to a massive, squarish structure in the center of the courtyard.

"It's all crumbly," said Ben. "Not like a real castle."

"Don't be rude," Holly told him.

"It's not like the one at Disney World," Everett said, "if that's what you mean."

Ben shrugged to show that *was* what he meant.

"Those posh manor houses were built later. Darton was built in the 1200s. It's a fortress, not a fairy tale." Everett led them across the courtyard. "Over that wall you can see the fields. There was a big peasant revolt there back in 1207, during one of the tournaments. The Great and Lesser Halls are in the keep."

"You know a lot about this castle," Holly said, to make up for Ben.

"I've read all sorts of books about the Darton family. They were lords of the castle and barons of

Hawkesbury from the eleventh through the sixteenth centuries." Everett led them through an open doorway into the keep.

At once, the sun blinked out and Holly shivered. She ran her fingers over the rough stone walls that yawned above her into the darkness. Deep-set window openings lit their way as Everett led them through a warren of small, empty rooms. The dank air settled like cold fingers on the back of Holly's neck, and she was relieved when they reached a broad set of stone steps that led into an airy space about the size of her classroom at school. "We know the most about Henry, the fifth Lord Darton. He kept lots of journals and things," Everett explained. "This was the Lesser Hall, where Darton received guests and so on—like a foyer." Even this hall, despite several tall windows, was rather dark. In one corner was a low, arched doorway. "That's one of the stairways up to the Great Hall."

"It's freezing! How'd they ever keep it warm enough?" Ben asked.

"I'll show you the fireplace." Everett started toward the far end of the Lesser Hall, but Holly wandered over to the little doorway. Light shone through it, and she saw when she went in that a deep window was set in the wall, overlooking the southern courtyard. Before her was a steep, tightly spiraled stone staircase.

CLAIRE M. CATERER

Holly took hold of a rusty handrail and started to climb. Each step was crescent-shaped, worn down in the center. It was strange to think how many thousands of feet had tread these stairs over the past eight hundred years.

After climbing several minutes, Holly thought she must have somehow passed the Great Hall. At the next landing, she looked out a window and saw the courtyard at least a hundred feet down. She turned to find her way back, and as she descended, she heard voices from below.

At first, Holly thought it was the boys, having entered the Great Hall from the main staircase. She followed the voices until she found a side doorway she'd missed on the way up. She walked through it into one end of a large hall.

But the boys weren't here. Somehow she had stumbled onto a private party—a costume party, by the look of it. The women wore long, high-waisted gowns, and the men wore capes draped over knee-length tunics and what looked like tights or hose.

She tiptoed inside, her palms tingling. It was a strange place to hold a party, and something about it sent a chain of goose bumps skittering down her arms. Unlike the empty caverns downstairs, this room was *alive*, as if real things happened in it every day, squabbles and music and boring dinners and loud banquets. The people clustered in the center of the room were too busy laughing and talking to notice her. Enormous firelit lamps were set in the wall every few feet, and beeswax candles lit the long tables, which stretched down the hall toward a raised dais, where a much grander table draped in red silk was set crosswise to the others. In the wall to her left a fire blazed in a hearth big enough to stand up in. Heavy scarlet and gold tapestries hung on every wall, and beneath her feet, something rustled. Holly bent down and picked up a long, dry stalk of something, like a reed or piece of hay.

What was going on?

Then she remembered something. A long time ago, her family had taken a trip to Colonial Williamsburg in Virginia. It was a whole town made up to look like it had in the 1600s, with people in costumes doing things like baking bread and making horseshoes. Her father had called it a living museum.

Of course, that's what this must be—a living museum. People had dressed in clothes from the Middle Ages and made up this room so that tourists could see what life was like back when the castle had a lord and lady to run it.

Holly shrugged off the goose bumps. Now she was

interested. She noticed the tables were really just long planks of wood set up on things that looked like sawhorses. Huge pewter serving platters with bones and half-eaten joints of meat covered each one. Holly turned away from the partly eaten pig's head. She walked closer to talk to one of the actors.

But an odd thing happened. The closer Holly got, the quieter the group of people became, as if she were walking in the wrong direction. They had been loud and boisterous, but now their voices were fading away.

And they looked different too. Something about the light? The people were nearly . . . transparent.

Holly's neck prickled. This room still didn't feel right, not even her idea about the living museum. Everett hadn't said anything about it, and shouldn't someone have been downstairs selling tickets? A faint buzzing vibrated in Holly's pocket, as if a bug were trapped inside. It was the key. She slipped her hand in and closed her fingers around the cold iron. It made her feel calmer—even warmer, oddly. She drew it out and held it in front of her.

Immediately the crowd grew louder, as if Holly had turned up the volume. And now, as she gazed at different people—a young woman in blond ringlets and a golden gown, a young man in a purple doublet—they solidified. The odd faintness was gone.

The next instant, a blast of heat billowed from the fireplace. The smell of roasting meat filled the air. The candles on the table blazed. The woman in the golden gown stared at her, open-mouthed. The man in the doublet followed her gaze. He reached out a hand and said something.

Was it like the oak tree in the forest? Was the key opening something, like Mr. Gallaway had said? Holly took a few steps toward the party, and now everyone was looking at her, pointing. Their excited murmurs grew louder, almost panicked. They pulled away from her, clustering toward the far end of the room, pushing one another against the walls, staring at her in horror. They cleared a path between the feast-laden tables, flooding onto the dais and crowding around the high table. Between them Holly could see a blond boy at the center, dressed in a heavily embroidered scarlet cloak. He paled at the sight of her.

Holly opened her mouth to speak, but her throat had gone dry.

At once a tall, bearded man leaped in front of the blond boy and pulled something from his belt. A sword? He jumped off the dais, advancing. Holly pulled back, afraid now, and glanced back at the high table. Through the crowd she could just see a small face next to the blond boy, but that *couldn't* be—*Ben?*

Then, behind her, a sharp voice. "There you are!"

Startled, Holly dropped the key to the stone floor with a clatter. A cold wind swept through the hall and the party in front of her vanished.

Everything was gone—the fire, the dais, the man with the sword. Her brother. The hall was empty and dark. She spun around.

Everett stood at the central staircase with Ben, who was puffing again. "We couldn't find you," Everett said. "You oughtn't wander off like that."

"What's this place?" Ben asked.

"It's the Great Hall," Everett said, "where the baron of Hawkesbury served meals. He also held big parties and banquets here."

Holly gazed back down the length of the room. The colorful tapestries had disappeared. She looked back at the boys. "What . . . What are you guys doing? Weren't you just . . . Didn't you see them?"

"See who?" asked Everett.

"The living-museum people. They were just here. And Ben was . . ." Even as she spoke, she knew how odd she sounded.

"The living what?"

"For the tourists." She ran to the fireplace, but the grate was swept clean. The dais was empty. Ben *couldn't* have been sitting there.

"There's nothing for tourists here," said Everett. "Did something scare you?"

Holly wasn't about to admit to *that*. "You must have seen them," she said, trying to steady her voice. "There was a whole party of people in costume, royalty or something, with a table and food and a big fire. Like Colonial Williamsburg."

Then Holly thought about the movie theaters at home. The projector was always set high up in the wall in the back. Above her head, in the wall where the narrow staircase was, she saw a tiny window. "Look! Someone was showing a movie from up there!"

"I'm quite sure no one else is here," Everett said calmly.

She didn't stop to listen to him. She dashed back up the spiraling staircase, even forgetting to grab the handrail. In a few moments, she'd found the small room at the top of the keep.

But the room was bare and cold. How *could* it be? She raced across to the window overlooking the Great Hall. Below, Everett and Ben were shrugging to each other. "There's nothing up here!" she called down.

"I told you," said Everett.

She started down the stairs, holding the railing tight to steady her wobbly knees. None of this made

CLAIRE M. CATERER

any sense. When she reached the Great Hall, still deep in thought, Ben said to her, "Hey, what's this?"

He had picked up the key where she had dropped it.

"That's mine!" She ran up and snatched it.

"Okay, chill. I just wondered. Where'd you get it?"

Holly didn't answer. The key, once back in her own hands, vibrated faintly. Far away, she heard excited shouts and talking. And lute music.

She raised her eyes to the Great Hall.

There they were—the lords and ladies and dresses and food and fire and roasted pig. But the shapes were dim, like a bleached-out photograph. She could barely hear them. The boy on the dais—Ben, it certainly was—stood up, pointing at her, shouting something, and the man with the sword bounded toward Holly down the aisle between the tables. "Stop! In the name of the crown!" he shouted. As he neared her, his form sharpened, and she heard the clinking of chain mail even above the frightened shouts of the crowd.

The man raised the sword above his head as he fought his way through the crush, barking at the people around her. Holly stumbled backward onto the floor; then she remembered the key and shoved it into her pocket. The man's beefy arm reached out to grab hers, but then the scene flickered before her eyes. In a moment, it winked out of existence altogether.

"What's wrong with you?" Ben asked. "And what's that big key for?"

"I want to go home," she said in a shaky voice. She turned to Everett. "I don't feel good."

"Course, no worries." He looked at her oddly. "Let's go."

Holly wasn't lying; her legs shook as they made their way back down the staircase to the ground floor, and her stomach churned with every step. Her hands felt cold and clammy. How could it be? How could she have seen *Ben*?

"Shall I call your mum to come get you?" Everett asked as they started down the hill. He pulled a phone out of his pocket.

"I'm okay. I can make it home," Holly said.

"Aw, man! Your parents let you have your own *phone*?" Ben forgot all about Holly and her key.

"Have a look. It even has games." Everett pushed a few buttons and handed the phone to Ben. He fell behind them, and Everett extended a hand to help Holly down the hill.

"You did see something there, didn't you?" he whispered.

"I—I don't know. Probably just something like, I don't know, the light."

"The light. The light made you see lords and ladies and a fire in the fireplace?"

CLAIRE M. CATERER

Holly didn't answer.

"And that key. That's the same one you had in the wood before."

"Yes! Got him!" shouted Ben, behind them.

"Holly?"

"So what if it is?" She knew she wasn't being very nice, but it was *her* key, after all.

"You saw something in the wood, too, didn't you?"

Holly pretended to watch her step as they reached the bottom of the hill, and then Ben provided the perfect diversion by tumbling headfirst off the steps behind them.

Holly saw at once that he had fallen into a soft mound of heather, but Everett helped him up and kept asking him if he was all right. "Where's the phone? Is it okay?" Ben asked.

"It's fine," Everett said, scooping it up from the grass. "But maybe I'd best put it away for now, yeah?"

"I guess. Thanks for letting me see it, though." Ben picked himself up without his usual whining, though as he walked past Holly he whispered, "That *really* hurt."

Holly stayed behind him in case of another fall as they climbed the hill to their cottage. Everett hung back with her but didn't say anything until they reached the top. He caught her arm before she went through the garden arbor.

"Look, Holly," he whispered, "I don't know what's going on with that key. But I know a lot about Darton Castle. It's a funny sort of place. Maybe because there's all those hundreds of years built up on each other. Sometimes, I almost think—"

He broke off as Holly's mother appeared in the back garden and greeted Ben.

"You think *what*?" Holly prompted.

Everett hesitated, then shook his head. "Sorry. Never mind. It's just—maybe I'd believe a lot more than you'd think." He let go of her. "If you ever want to tell me what's really going on."

"It's just that I don't feel well," she said, backing away from him. "Look, I have to go." She turned and stepped through the arbor. Holly knew Everett didn't believe her, and she didn't believe herself. But whatever had happened, it belonged to *her*, and Everett annoyed her anyway, with his smirking and refusing to mind his own business. The only person she could think of who she could really talk to about what had happened was Mr. Gallaway.

Chapter 8

Number Seven, Hodges Close

It wasn't easy to get permission to go and visit Mr. Gallaway. Mrs. Shepard was of the opinion that Holly "had done enough running around for one day," and she had pressed the back of her hand against Holly's forehead when she saw how pale Holly was. But Holly insisted she was fine, and then, feeling desperate, she told a very big lie about Mr. Gallaway's daughter visiting with her kids, and wouldn't it be good to get out and meet new people, and finally her mother said she supposed it would. She gave Holly her phone and told her to call as soon as she got to Mr. Gallaway's, so she could "touch base with his daughter."

Holly sprinted out of the house with the phone in her pocket. Her cheeks burned. She'd only ever told the garden-variety kind of lie about homework and missing cookies. She would talk to Mr. Gallaway very quickly, and then call her mother and say no one was home.

Mr. Gallaway said the key unlocked things, but to Holly it seemed more like the key made you *see* things—things that couldn't possibly be there. Why would he give her something like that? It was almost like he didn't mind if she were scared or hurt. What if the man in the castle had stayed solid enough to run his sword through her? She paused, not sure now that she was at his door if she really *did* want to talk to Mr. Gallaway.

And in any case, no one looked to be home, even when Holly knocked, just to be sure. She wandered around to the back of the house to see if he was in the garden. That seemed a less scary place to talk to him anyway, rather than inside his house.

A tiny screened-in porch extended from the back of the cottage. It was crowded with empty flowerpots and garden tools. Holly ventured inside and peered through the kitchen window. The house was deserted.

Disappointed, she turned to go, but something caught her eye. One long oak table on the porch held seedlings and a thick stack of garden catalogs, but another was bare except for a large iron box. It was perhaps the size of Holly's school backpack and it had a bowed top, like a treasure chest. Serious-faced suns and moons were etched all over it, and on the front was the figure of an oak tree inlaid with silver. The

CLAIRE M. CATERER

keyhole for the chest was right in the center of the tree's trunk.

Holly did not usually open things that were not hers, and what would Mr. Gallaway say if he found her here? But the oak tree with the keyhole . . . It had to have something to do with the present he had given her. She placed her fingers on the chest's cold lid and tried to lift it.

Locked, of course. Without thinking, Holly pulled the iron key out of her pocket and fitted it into the lock. The chest opened silently on well-oiled hinges.

Inside were dozens of keys, each in its own velvet-lined pigeonhole. Some were etched with strange scratchings, like the runes she'd seen on the trees in the glade. Her fingers tripped lightly over the pigeon-holes. One of them was empty. She was quite sure that her own key belonged in that spot.

"What've you got now?"

Holly was so startled she nearly dropped the key into the chest. She whirled around to find Everett standing just inside the screen door. "Oh—hi. What are you doing here?"

He walked in. "What are *you* doing here?"

"I was . . . returning something."

"That's the key Ben picked up at the castle. Did you pinch it from this box?"

"What? No—Mr. Gallaway gave it to me."

"And now you want to give it back. When he's not here." Everett reached a hand toward the chest.

Holly slapped his hand away. "Don't touch them! You don't know what they do."

"Oi, take it easy. I've got more business here than you. He's *my* neighbor." Everett looked at her keenly. "What *do* these keys do, anyway?"

"Nothing, it's just . . ." She sighed, wishing he'd go away, and knowing he wasn't going to. "I've seen some strange things since I got this key."

"Like at the castle. You saw something there."

"I told you—I just felt sick."

Everett smirked. "Are you afraid of something?"

"Why do you keep saying that? I'm no more scared than you!"

He shrugged, glancing away at the back garden as if he didn't even care about the chest of keys. "Look, if you don't want the key anymore, you don't have to give it back. I'll take it."

Holly looked down at Everett's small white hand, which he held out patiently. The key tingled in her palm. It was very quiet; Everett was holding his breath. His fingers twitched.

"No," she said finally. "It's mine." She assumed her Mom voice. "Come on, we shouldn't be here."

CLAIRE M. CATERER

Everett stood staring at the iron chest. Holly motioned to him. "Do you want him to come back and catch us in here?"

"Okay, I'm coming." He lingered behind while she stepped onto the garden path. And then Holly did spy Mr. Gallaway around the corner, walking up the road from town, a straw bag over one arm.

"*Everett!*" she whispered fiercely. "He's coming!"

The old man disappeared from view as he approached the front door. What would he do if he found them there? Take back his key?

"Come *on*," said Holly. "What are you doing?" She heard Mr. Gallaway in the house now, and he was heading for the kitchen—and the door to the screened-in porch. A moment later Everett appeared, slamming the screen door behind him. The two of them scurried out through the back gate and around the side of the neighboring cottage. Mr. Gallaway walked through his kitchen, humming, oblivious.

"Okay," Holly breathed, emerging with Everett on Hodges Close. She liked Mr. Gallaway, but she knew he wouldn't want them snooping in his private things. Her stomach calmed as they approached Number One.

"Why do you keep following me?" she asked Everett.

"Because I know you're hiding something." He paused at her front door. "I'd better get home. I'm glad you kept your key."

Holly watched him walk back down the lane. She liked Everett—mostly, when he wasn't being irritating—but he made her the tiniest bit uncomfortable, too. He was smart, and she couldn't put him off for long. If she wanted to talk to Mr. Gallaway and find out what was going on, she'd have to do it soon.

Everett tried his best to walk in his usual way back down the close to Clement Lane. He didn't want Holly to see him hurry, didn't want her to see how hot his face was nor how queasy he felt, didn't want her to hear the voice in his chest that drummed one thing over and over: *Hurry, hurry, hurry.*

The minute he was back in his bedroom, after passing his mother in the hall—"Yeah, Mum, castle was great, love the Shepards, see you later"—he sat down on his bed, took a deep breath, and pulled the key from his pocket.

He wasn't a thief by nature. Oh, once he'd found a five-pound note in the playground at school and kept it, even after he'd heard Sean Fellowes was hunting for it and was also looking to beat the head in of whoever took it. Fellowes was a bully anyway, and Everett was glad he'd kept it. He'd spent it on sweets and a comic book.

This was definitely different. He'd never seen the trunk of keys before, though he'd been to Mr. Gallaway's house loads of times to borrow gardening tools for his mother. Funny how it had appeared there just when Holly seemed to need it, wanting to give her key back. In fact, Everett thought, turning the key over in his hands, it had appeared just when he, Everett, had needed it too.

Because wasn't he just thinking about Holly's key and how Mr. Gallaway had never given him anything, certainly not anything as cool as this? He held it up to the light. He hadn't gotten a good look at Holly's, except to see that it was large and forged like the old keys had been, with a big loop and rough cuts. This one was very like it. Along the shaft Everett could see some tiny, pointed marks cut into the iron, like letters, or maybe teethmarks. If he took his key back to Darton Castle, could he see whatever Holly had seen? *People*, she'd said. People in fancy dress, so real she'd thought they were put there for tourists. But something about them had scared her. And what about the wood? Had she seen people there, too? Why wouldn't she *tell* him about it?

There was a reason Mr. Gallaway had left the trunk

out in the open, Everett decided. It was valuable, and the screened-in porch was never locked. He'd left it there for them to find—for *both* of them to find. Surely he'd meant for Everett to have a key too. It only made sense. So he hadn't really stolen anything at all. He'd just gotten his key in a different way.

He liked how it felt in his hand—warm, then cold, then warm—almost like it had a pulse. It made his heart tremble uncomfortably, but the tighter he gripped the key, the calmer he became. He had something incredibly special, he thought, something nobody else had (well, except Holly). Maybe the key opened all sorts of things. He could probably use it like a skeleton key and get into the headmaster's office or a locked shop after hours. Not that he *would*, he assured himself. Still . . .

He slid it into his back pocket. Holly was sure to go back to the wood soon, now that she'd decided to keep the key. She would show him exactly what to do to make the key work.

CLAIRE M. CATERER

Chapter 9

Holly's Choice

It was odd for Holly to wake up in England the next morning; but it was normal for Holly's mother to be searching for her briefcase and coffee and house keys. Holly's father lingered at the kitchen table with the paper and then drove her mother to the train station. When he got back, he took a shower and then announced he would be in his office if anyone needed him.

Having Mr. Shepard in charge was ideal. He wouldn't ask a lot of questions about where Holly was off to. She cleaned her glasses carefully with water instead of just the hem of her T-shirt. In her pile of clothes she found a bandana and tied it around her hair. Then she emptied her backpack of junk left over from the flight and filled it with two apples, a couple of blueberry scones, a bottle of water, and a book she was reading. Her Swiss Army pocketknife she shoved in her back pocket. Maybe she'd find a real rock wall to climb. Finally, thinking of rocks, she found a few

Band-Aids and packed them, too. She wasn't sure what she'd find in the forest, but it was best to be prepared. She planned to spend most of the day exploring it—as soon as she'd asked Mr. Gallaway a few questions.

Just as she had everything ready and had secured permission from her father, she opened the back door to find Everett there. Didn't he have anything else to do?

"What do you want now?" Holly asked.

"Are you going somewhere?" Everett stepped into the house, eyeing her backpack.

"Ben's awake, I think," said Holly. "He fixed his game."

"Yeah? Maybe I'll go up."

"Sure. He'd like that."

Holly waited until Everett was at the top of the stairs and she heard Ben greet him. Then she stole out the back door.

As she stepped through the garden, she glanced along the row of cottages next to hers. She saw Mr. Gallaway bent over the rosebushes of Number Three. He glanced up and smiled. She paused a moment; she *did* want to talk to him, and he couldn't dodge her in the wood this time. She walked down to Number Three and stood in the arbor.

"Pruning roses," he said, as if she'd asked him a question. "It is tricky work. Best not to be distracted."

He clipped a small branch and squinted at it. Holly wasn't sure what to say, or if she should leave him alone, but then he added, "Sit if you must. Did you not stop by my cottage yesterday, Miss Holly?"

Holly's face heated up. "I . . . You weren't home." Somehow he knew she'd been at his house. Did he know she'd opened the trunk? Holly sat down at the garden table, laying her backpack on the flagstones. The old man glanced at her with raised eyebrows. "Um . . . yeah," Holly started. "Everett Shaw took Ben and me to the castle on the hill yesterday, and some weird things happened. But just to me." She drew the key out of her pocket.

"Keys are forged for many purposes," said Mr. Gallaway, turning back to the roses. It was somehow easier to talk to him when he wasn't looking at her. "As I say, yours unlocks things."

"But it's just a key. . . . Isn't it?" Holly knew what her mother would say: The key was probably coated with some kind of substance that gave you hallucinations and stomachaches and vitamin deficiencies and high blood pressure. But some wild, caged-bird part of Holly's insides told her different. Something inside her whispered a word, a word forbidden by reason and mothers and Ms. Noring and Holly's entire fifth-grade curriculum.

Magic.

"I think," said Mr. Gallaway, snipping away at the roses, "the evidence suggests that what you have is not *just* a key, Miss Holly."

"But I saw *people*," said Holly, feeling breathless. "It was like I was there—not even like a movie. They were in different clothes—like costumes—and there was a table with food, and musicians, and a fire in the fireplace. But sort of faded. And then . . ." A shiver, like a trickle of ice water, fingered down her back. "I don't know. Ben was there too, Mr. Gallaway. With the ghost people. But how could he be? At first I thought it was just someone who looked like him, but then he saw me, too, and he was *scared*. And some guy with a sword came running at me. . . ."

The old man sat back on his heels and squinted up at Holly through the morning sun. "But you weren't hurt."

"No," said Holly. "I dropped the key and everything disappeared. But now I'm not sure he could've hurt me anyway. They weren't exactly *solid*, somehow. But I know it wasn't a dream or anything, even though Everett kept saying no one was there."

The old man sniffed and dabbed at his nose with a red handkerchief he pulled from his pocket. "Hmph. It seems to me you would know a good deal more

CLAIRE M. CATERER

about it than he. The key wasn't given to Everett." Mr. Gallaway coughed into the handkerchief and spat into the dirt. "A gift is a powerful thing, Miss Holly. That key knows who it belongs to. A theft, on the other hand, has power too, but of a different sort."

Holly laid the key on the table, her face feeling hot. "I would never, Mr. Gallaway."

His blue eyes softened. "I thought not."

"So I can see things other people can't?"

The old man put down the pruners and pulled his pipe from his pocket. "There's a sort of filter—a curtain, if you like. Some people can see through it."

Maybe that's what Everett had meant to say. "Like layers," Holly said half to herself. "Layers between times. Or—"

Or *places.*

"That oak tree in the forest," Holly said, talking fast now that she had his attention. "Where I was yesterday. The key *opened* the tree. And it wasn't like a curtain. It was a real door. The other trees have keyholes too. Are they doors too? Do they *go through* to somewhere?"

The old man shrugged, frowning at his pipe as he tapped it against his palm.

"I could get there, couldn't I? To where the lords and ladies were—where Ben was, or the Ben look-alike. I could really visit them, not just see them like ghosts."

"Now *that*," said Mr. Gallaway, holding the pipe up to the sun and squinting, "would be a real adventure."

Holly was sitting very still, but her heart galloped in her chest as if she'd just run a mile. Was he really saying the key was magic? That she wasn't sick or drugged or crazy? But then . . .

"Perhaps you've come to return your gift?"

Holly opened her mouth, but for a moment she had trouble saying anything. Sure, the idea of a magical journey was all very exciting, if it were true, but it wasn't all friendly and pleasant, either. *Did* she want to return the gift? "That other place," she said. "It looked dangerous. They were running at me with swords and everything. And that Ben clone . . . It was like he needed me to help him. But what could I do, even if I could get there? I'm just a kid. Do you think he's in trouble, Mr. Gallaway?"

"If you're asking me to guarantee your safety, or your brother's, I'm afraid I can't do that," said the old man. "Great opportunities involve great risk. Surely you know that. I believe you climb rocks at home?"

"Sure, at the mall," she said slowly. How could he know *that*? "But I have a harness and a belay. It's all safe and stuff. Or my mom would never let me do it."

"That's the difference, you see. No harness and helmets on a real adventure." The old man smiled.

CLAIRE M. CATERER

"There are no guarantees, but there *are* great rewards. You, Miss Holly, have something locked inside yourself that begs to be liberated. Opportunities come but rarely, and are never repeated." He pocketed the pipe and held out his hand. "Should you return that key, your biggest danger might be a stinging nettle or two."

Holly looked at Mr. Gallaway's hand. A hundred lines crisscrossed his palm. She knew that the line extending from between the thumb and forefinger down to the wrist was called the lifeline. But Mr. Gallaway seemed to have two lifelines. Maybe it was because he was such a very old man? She picked up the key from the table where she'd laid it. It tingled with warmth. She thought of that round-robin of activities at home—school, the mall, the park, the swimming pool—and how much she'd wanted to escape them. She had traveled almost five thousand miles from home— wasn't *that* an adventure? But even here, in Oxford, in London, there would be seat belts and looking both ways before crossing and synchronized watches and be back before dark. Going to this place—if she could get there—would be something else altogether. Anyplace you got to by magic had to have magic inside it, and she would never have the chance to see that again, not in her social studies textbook or on the top of the Eiffel

Tower. She had one chance. She'd have to take it or leave it.

"Once you give the key back, it's mine forever," said Mr. Gallaway.

"No," said Holly, and slipped it back into her pocket. "I'll take my chances."

Chapter 10

The Strongest Beech

Thanks to her compass, Holly knew the way quite well. At the edge of the forest, she pulled the bottle of water and one of the scones out of her backpack. The key, nestled in her pocket, hummed in tune with the forest. As she stepped farther in, a wood warbler trilled from the treetops.

It was on the bank of the stream that she first heard the crack of a twig. Somewhere nearby, leaves rustled. Her own feet made almost no noise in the wood. Holly stopped and listened; even the animals quieted.

She knew what the silence meant: She was being followed. She peered through the trees, but they were still. There was nothing to do but go on. Holly swallowed the last of her scone and jumped the rocks in the stream. As she turned the corner on the far bank, she heard a clumsy splash behind her, along with some fierce whispering. She hurried on to the glade, hoping to get there before she was caught. The footsteps pursuing her grew louder and more careless. Finally she stumbled into the glade and caught her breath, then sprinted to the oak tree and pulled out the key.

"Stop! You'd better tell us what you're doing!"

Her heart sank. She knew that whiny voice. And then another, accusingly: "Thought you said you were all out of scones."

Holly turned around, though she knew who was there. If she were going to handpick her companions, Everett might have made the cut; Ben, definitely not.

Holly thrust the key into her pocket and turned around to face them both. "What do you mean, what I'm doing? You mean walking in the woods?"

"That key!" said Ben, panting for breath. "She's doing something with the key, right, Everett?"

"I'm not surprised you wouldn't understand some-one wanting to explore the forest, *outside*, where there aren't any stupid computer games or electric outlets," said Holly, putting away the water bottle. This would be the perfect moment to shrug, the way big sisters are entitled to do, and wander off down another path. But it was also the moment she'd been waiting for, and hadn't Mr. Gallaway made it sound like *this* was the right time, as if there might be a wrong time?

"You can't just hog all the cool stuff for yourself," said Ben.

CLAIRE M. CATERER

"What cool stuff? It's just a key!" Holly said.

"So let's see it," said Everett. Then, more quickly than Holly would've thought possible, the boys flanked her. Ben was still panting, and Everett had his hand out, the way he had at Mr. Gallaway's cottage the day before.

"I told you, it's mine," she said, and then Everett's pale hand shot out and wrenched it from her.

"Hey!" She reached around to grab it back, but he cradled it against his chest, then darted back toward the path. Holly ran after him and grabbed one arm— the wrong one—and wrestled him to the ground. But his fingers closed so tightly around the key that she couldn't pry them apart. "Hand it over," she said through clenched teeth.

"Make her tell us what it does!" Ben said.

Everett twisted in the grass and stood up, breathing hard, his closed fist above his head. "Come on, Holly," Everett added. "We know something's up with your key."

Holly sighed. "All right, *fine*. If you want to know, I'll tell you. But you aren't going to believe me, and anyway, Mr. Gallaway gave *me* the key, for *me* to use."

"To use for *what*?" Ben asked.

"Well, it's sort of—sort of a magic key."

"Oh, *get real*."

"It's not just a key," said Everett. "Let her tell us."

Holly held out her hand and, after hesitating just a moment longer, Everett laid it in her palm. Ben plopped onto the grass and the others followed. "I know it sounds crazy," Holly began, "and the thing is, I don't think anyone else can see what I do, because the key only belongs to me."

"Like at the castle. You saw those people in fancy dress," Everett said.

"Right. And then they just vanished when I dropped the key. Mr. Gallaway says it unlocks things. It lets me see things from the past, or even from other places. At least, sometimes."

Ben rolled his eyes.

"But it also opens this oak tree, like a door. And those trees there"—Holly pointed at the far side of the glade—"those are all doors to different places. Or times. At least, I think so."

"And I guess we can't see the different places either?" Ben asked. "That's not even logical."

"Shut it," Everett told him.

Holly told them what she had seen at the castle— the lords and ladies, and Ben at the high table, and the knight with the sword. She explained about the trunkful of keys, and the few things Mr. Gallaway had said about them. "He knows exactly what's going on, but he won't tell me everything. It's like a test or something. I'm supposed to figure it out for myself, I guess."

"A test of what?" asked Ben. "To see if you'll go to a medieval party and get your head cut off by King Arthur?"

"He was in the Dark Ages," said Everett.

"I *mean*," said Ben, "what do we really know about this Gallaway guy?"

"He *knows* things," Holly said. "And he has these fantastic keys—lots of them! It's a once-in-a-lifetime kind of thing! He's not trying to hurt us."

"Sounds to me like he's playing a big joke on us. Or trying to get us killed."

"I don't think so, Ben," said Everett. "I mean, I've known him forever. He's mostly all right."

"So you believe this? That Holly's got a key to some kind of magic place?"

The boys exchanged glances. Holly knew Ben thought she was playing some kind of trick on him, but Everett seemed to be trying to convince himself that she was telling the truth. Finally Everett said, "Yeah, I do. Okay, Holly. Show us."

She walked over to the oak tree and brought the key to the lock. The hum of the forest grew, and the key vibrated in her fingers.

"What's that?" Ben asked. "Are you making that sound?"

"No, it's the key," Holly said. "Come here. You can see the keyhole."

Everett and Ben ran up behind her. "I don't see anything," Ben said.

"I *think* I see something—sort of," said Everett.

"Yeah, I see something *sort of*," Ben said at once.

"Here goes." Holly thrust the key into the trunk of the tree and turned it. With an earsplitting crack, the ground trembled and the trunk split apart like before. The doorway opened. "Do you see it?" Holly asked, desperately.

"What are we supposed to see?" Ben asked.

"Maybe if we held the key," Everett suggested.

"No," said Holly, afraid he would take it again. "It's mine."

"Come on, I'll give it back." Everett grabbed the hand that clutched the key. "Crikey! What's that?" He stared at the open tree trunk.

"What's *what*?" Ben whined.

Everett took Ben's hand and wrapped it around Holly's. "Whoa!" said Ben. "What did you do? Is that the door?"

"Come on, I'll show you the rest." She started through the doorway, but Ben tugged her back.

CLAIRE M. CATERER

"I don't think I want to do that."

"We're all here," Everett said. "There's nothing to be scared of."

"I didn't say I was *scared*. But you don't know what you'll run into," said Ben. "This isn't normal, Holly. We might find, I don't know, giant ogres with sea serpent heads or something."

"I'm just going to take my chances." Holly pulled her hand free from his. "You don't have to come if you don't want to."

For a moment, Ben looked at Holly and Everett, standing hand in hand. "If you're both going, I'm going too." He took Holly's hand again. Through the gap in the tree trunk, Holly could see the grass rippling, as if beckoning them. She closed her eyes, gripped both boys' hands tight, and led them through the oak doorway to the other side.

Holly let out a sigh. She realized she'd been afraid that it would be different this time, but the glade looked just as it had the day before. There was a glow about it, as if the sun had burst out of the clouds. The forest was humming again, but the vibration was louder this time, and it shot through all of them, the underbrush, the clusters of celandine and yellow primroses. The circle of beech trees quivered. The air thickened. Holly thought if she put out her tongue, she could taste it.

To be honest, she was relieved to have someone else along. "Can you guys see the keyholes in all the beech trees?" she said.

The boys nodded. "It's like they're, I don't know, brighter or something," said Everett softly. "And look." He pointed at their feet. They stood on a carpet of low, nodding purple flowers. "I've been in this glade a hundred times. There's never been bluebells before."

Holly took a deep breath. "Okay, so I'm thinking if we turn the key in one of these beech trees, it'll open up like the oak. And we can step into this other place. But, I mean, I'm just guessing." She would much rather have been a confident tour guide, to have already gone ahead and been able to say, "That's the way to the land of the unicorns" and "Steer clear of that monster pit." But as it was . . .

"So we just need to pick a tree," said Everett slowly, as if it were the most normal thing in the world.

"What about this one?" Ben walked over to a skinny tree, hardly more than a sapling. The others followed because no one had dropped hands. Holly was just as glad they hadn't.

"No," Holly said. "It doesn't look—I don't know—strong enough."

"Why's it have to be strong?" Everett asked.

"It's just a feeling, that's all."

"The *feeling* is that you want to be boss, like always," Ben said.

"Well, excuse me for being older than you!"

Everett cut in. "How about we just pick a really— er—*strong*-looking tree? Like . . ." He looked around the glade and pulled everyone over to an old, gnarled beech. "Like this one."

The tree Everett had chosen was the strangest Holly had ever seen. It looked like three trees growing together, as wide as the three children standing abreast. Each conjoined trunk had its own thick branches sprouting from it, every which way, each one as big around as Holly's waist. Green moss grew up its silvery roots. In the center, the keyhole glowed faintly.

Holly dropped Everett's hand and traced her fingers around the keyhole. Something answered her touch. It was almost like the key's vibration, but warmer. As if she were coming home after a very long time away, and her hand had just closed over the handle of her front door.

"We should vote on it," Ben said.

Holly turned to snap at him, but then the key vibrated in her fingers. Ben's damp hand clutched at hers. He didn't really look any different—still short and pudgy, with his annoying runny nose and his dorky stick-up hair—but now he *seemed* different. Like someone who needed her—as if straight-A-student Ben could need anybody. But then she remembered that day last year when she'd scared off some boys who were picking on him after school. She guessed he needed her sometimes. She had to lead, but something told her that they all had to be part of it. Even Ben.

"Are you okay?" Ben said. "You look weird."

"Yeah. Sorry." The feeling faded. "Anyway—what you said—we should vote."

Ben stared at her as if she'd spoken in Japanese, but then he raised his hand. "Okay. This tree looks good to me."

"Me too," Everett agreed.

"And me. So it's unanimous. Everett, hang on to my elbow." He did as she asked, and she pushed the key into the keyhole.

Chapter 11

The Wand

Holly imagined they would step through the beech tree as they had through the oak, but she was wrong. Just as she turned the key, a flash of light exploded along with an enormous thunderclap. Holly covered her eyes and stumbled. Ben's fingers crushed her own as the sharp scent of ozone and burning bark filled the air.

The three children tumbled to the ground. Holly opened her eyes. "It's all right," she said. "It looks fine."

The glade and the oak tree had disappeared. They stood up in the valley of an overgrown forest crowded with tall, thin trees and low shrubs. Their enormous beech tree looked out of place here. On a hill above them Holly could make out a little clearing. Tiny orange and yellow flowers carpeted the ground beside a broad path. The air was still, suffused with a deep, enduring quiet, as if sound had hardly been invented yet. They stood without moving for several moments. Finally a bird gave a raucous call and Holly startled, then relaxed. "Well, let's take a look around," she said.

Ben still held on to a branch of the beech tree they'd entered by. "But look at this forest," he said. "This path, all these trees—there's no landmarks. What if we get lost? How will we ever find our tree again? Maybe we should go back."

Holly took a breath. She couldn't even think of going back. Something about the air here, the sun filtered through the canopy, the speckled thrush that cocked an eye at her from a low branch above them. She *belonged* here.

Still, Ben had a point, as much as Holly hated to admit it. "Here, I'll mark our path." She rummaged in her backpack for a moment, then remembered the bandana and pulled it off her head.

"Hey, you've got food!" said Ben, peering in the backpack before she zipped it up. "And matches! What were you gonna do, camp out? I'm not staying here all night."

"Relax," said Holly. "We're just going to wander around a little and come right back."

"It feels primeval," Ben muttered. "There might be T. rexes or something."

"More like velociraptors," said Everett. "T. rexes were in North America."

"Gee, thanks. What a relief."

"Shut up and pay attention," said Holly. She flicked open her Swiss Army knife and poked it into the bandana, working the blade until she could tear off a strip of fabric. She tied it onto the branch of a nearby tree. "See? I'll tie one of these strips to a tree every time we make a turn. And we'll use my compass so we'll know which direction we go."

"But what about going *back*?" Ben asked.

"It looks pretty safe," Everett said. "And if it was dinosaur times, it would be tropical. It just feels like regular Britain." He cocked an eye toward the sky. "But later in the day, I think. Maybe afternoon."

"So we'll all stick together, right?" said Holly. "No going off on our own?"

"Agreed," Everett said.

"*Duh,*" said Ben.

"Okay then." Holly glanced around for other landmarks. The path in front of them was nearly wide enough for a car to drive through. Two low bushes framed their beech tree, and a fallen log lay behind it. It took only a moment for Holly to fix the picture in her mind like a photograph. She would easily find this place again.

The path rose along a slight incline to their left. "Let's go that way," Ben said.

Holly held out the compass. "Northwest. Sounds good to me."

They had taken only three or four steps before Everett said, "Holly, what's that you're holding?"

"Oh, the key. I'd better put it in my pocket."

"That's not the key," said Everett. Holly stopped walking and held it up.

He was right. What she held was no longer a key, but a carved stick, perhaps a foot long. Wound around it were carvings of vines and flowers. It tapered to a narrow tip at one end, where a tiny, faceted crystal was fixed into the wood. Holly dropped it. "Oh no! Where's the key?"

"I think this *is* the key," said Everett, picking it up. "It's changed."

"What do you mean, changed?" Ben asked sharply. "It's got to stay a key, or we can't get back home."

Holly took the stick from Everett and darted back to the beech tree. She pointed the narrow end at the knot in the trunk's center. It glowed. The keyhole had changed too—it was exactly the size and shape of the crystal at the tip of Holly's stick.

"Everett's right. It's still the key. But what's happened to it?"

"It looks like a magic wand," Ben said, shrugging.

The other two stared at him. "He's right," Everett said. "That's exactly what it is."

Holly turned the stick over. It had the same strong, heavy feel to it as the key, as if it were hers—as if she'd found something she'd lost long ago. What could it do? she wondered. What could *she* do?

It tingled in her hands and she pushed it into her back pocket. "I'd better put it away," she said, shaking off a shiver. "What if I accidentally turn one of you into a frog?"

"Oh, right. By *accident*," said Ben. "Let's go. It's too quiet here."

They set off on the path again. It *was* too quiet, despite the occasional trill of birds and the rustling of chipmunks through the dead leaves. Every twig they stepped on echoed like a rifle shot. Though the trees grew dense, the path was wide and well kept. *Someone must live near here,* Holly thought.

They walked in a straight line for perhaps five minutes, not saying much, which only increased the oppressive silence. And then Holly, who was somewhat in the lead, although they were walking abreast, halted.

Ben bumped into her; he'd been holding on to her backpack strap. "Why're we stopping?"

His voice rang out as if they were in a library. "Shhh!" Holly and Everett whispered together. "I hear something," Holly added.

It wasn't so much that she heard something as that she *felt* something. A vibration shook the ground beneath her feet in a steady rhythm, like a drumming. And it was getting stronger. The three of them stood, frozen.

"I feel it too," Everett said finally.

Ben said, "What are we supposed to feel?"

Everett pulled him off the path. "Get out of the way! It's a horse!"

Holly knew at once Everett was right, and she dodged into the trees on the other side of the path. She signaled to the boys to hide, but Everett didn't need any advice. He pulled Ben in among a clump of bushes. Holly crouched behind a tree. The ground shook as the rhythm grew. More than one horse.

Around the bend in the path the first horse bounded into view. It was twice Holly's height, thickly muscled and shiny black. On its back sat a skinny blond-haired boy a bit older than she, dressed in a bright tunic of purple and gold. A broad scarlet cape billowed behind him. Holly squinted, sure she had seen him somewhere before. As he approached the rise, a sliver of sunlight caught a thin gold circlet on his head. The horse slowed, and a smaller chestnut appeared behind it. The man astride it was a grown-up, and his clothes weren't quite as fine as the boy's.

CLAIRE M. CATERER

"The theves," the boy said to his companion. *"Hie beth nere. The hors smelleth hem."*

The older man glanced around. *"Nis non here, Sire."*

The boy frowned and peered through the trees. He said something else to his friend, sounding irritated. Holly wished she could understand them. She pulled the key—now wand—from her pocket, worrying her fingers over the carvings. For some reason, holding it made her feel calmer. Almost without meaning to, she pointed it at the blond-haired boy. His speech hummed and crackled like a distant radio signal, and then all at once she understood him perfectly, though his accent was British.

"I tell thee, Pagett saw them in this wood, and I shall have their heads when I find them!"

"My lord," said the older man patiently, "their heads you shall have, but they have not been seen these three days."

"My informants tell me otherwise."

"Do you mean the horse, Your Highness?" The dark-haired man pursed his lips. Holly guessed he was trying not to smile.

The boy turned his mount, searching the trees, and Holly crouched lower. She looked down at the wand. *Your Highness . . .* Had she cast a spell on a *prince*?

Then, above the blowing of the horses, Holly heard a familiar sound: snuffling.

It was Ben, on the opposite side of the path. She could just make out his face between two shrubs. The tail of the older man's horse swished in and out of the brush, inches from Ben's nose. Holly knew why he was snuffling: He was fiercely allergic to horses.

Hold it in, Ben, come on.

"Dost hear?" The boy stilled his horse.

Another rustle told Holly that Everett was trying to hold Ben still, but it was no use. She recognized the gasping that meant Ben was trying not to sneeze.

"Someone is here, Clement," the boy whispered.

For a long moment, everyone, even the horses, was still. Then a loud, messy sneeze exploded in the wood.

"There, my lord!"

The man called Clement pointed, the boy wheeled on his horse, and then several confusing things happened. Everett broke from the underbrush and, dragging Ben by one hand (he was in the middle of another sneeze), he crashed through the forest, off the path. The boy on horseback uttered some kind of curse and jumped off his mount, then took off after Everett and Ben. He called behind him, "Follow on the path!" At that, his companion caught the free horse by the bridle and galloped down the path in the general direction the boys had gone.

CLAIRE M. CATERER

But before man and horses had gotten too far, a triumphant cry (and a frightened kind of squeak) emerged from the woods. "I have them at swordpoint!" called the prince.

The other man dismounted and took off into the brush. Holly crouched lower, silently making promises as one will do, things like, *I swear I'll study harder, just let them be okay.* But in a few minutes, they reappeared. The boys' hands were tied in front of them, and Clement and the prince held them securely with thick ropes.

"I should run thee through right here," the prince observed, pressing the flat of a broad sword against Ben's neck.

"Stop! Leave him alone!" Holly sprang from her hiding place and brandished the only thing she had— the wand.

"What! Is there a third?" The prince sounded surprised, but his sword never moved.

"'Tis but a maid, Your Highness," said Clement.

"But mind!" The boy stepped back, his wide eyes trained on Holly's wand. "Clement," he whispered. "Look there!"

Clement's glance lowered to the wand, and his face whitened. He swallowed. "She cannot be, surely," he said. "They are dead, all."

Holly gripped the wand tighter. What could she not be? *Who* was dead?

Clement tossed the rope to the prince. "Take the prisoners, Your Highness, and stay you clear." He crept closer to Holly, pointing his sword at her. The blade trembled. Was he frightened of her? Her face grew hot, as if she'd been caught stealing. She thought of Mr. Gallaway.

"Take heed!" cried the prince, his voice breaking as he clutched the rope that held Everett and Ben.

Clement's voice rose. "I shall make short work of her."

Holly looked down the etched blade, her mouth going dry. He was going to take her head off. "No, wait, I'm—"

"Take her alive!" said the prince.

"Please—" she started.

"But wound her if it pleases thee." The prince's blue eyes glittered at her; Holly thought that if he had a long spear, he would poke her with it to hear her scream. Clement advanced, swishing his blade in a figure-eight motion, locking his eyes with Holly's, his jaw white and hard. She stood, frozen, the wand out-stretched, as he crept toward her.

"Holly, *run!*" Everett shouted.

Of course, she would have, a second later; but for

CLAIRE M. CATERER

the very long moment that stretched between her and Clement, she was transfixed. His eyes, so dark she could not see his pupils, bore into hers. Suddenly his sword flashed in front of her. A whiplike sting tore across her right palm, and the wand was flicked from her grasp. She heard a soft thump as it landed somewhere nearby. Clement had disarmed her of her only weapon.

Holly's glance darted around the forest. She *had* to find the wand, but if she took too long at it, she would feel the sword at her neck. In the midst of her indecision came the thundering of more hooves—heavier, and more urgent.

Clement halted, glancing back at the prince. "Hark, Sire! The Mounted!"

Clement raced back to his horse. He threw Ben like a sack of potatoes into the saddle and leaped up behind him. The prince had already secured Everett on his own horse.

"Ben!" Holly cried.

The hoofbeats grew louder just as Holly darted across the path. She had no clear idea what to do, but she couldn't let them take the boys. She grabbed at Ben's leg, even as the stallion was stomping in fright at the approaching sound. Then three things happened just together: Holly pulled on Ben's ankle; Clement raised his sword and brought it down toward her wrist; and a pair of strong arms snatched her from the ground a moment before the blade made contact.

She hung upside down over a horse's flank. Its hooves flashed by in a blur a few inches from her eyes, wheeling on the woodland path. What did he want her for? And where were the boys?

She managed to look up just in time to see Clement and the prince disappear around the bend, their horses kicking up a cloud of dust.

In a moment they were gone, and Ben and Everett with them.

CLAIRE M. CATERER

Chapter 12

A Safe Haven

"Ben!"

Holly hoped her horseman would ride after Clement and the prince, but instead he whirled and took off in the opposite direction.

"Wait! Stop! My key!"

But no one stopped, or spoke, and Holly hung off the side of the horse like a saddlebag. The horse's hooves raced over the ground in a blur. She tried to jump, but a strong hand was planted in the small of her back, holding her down.

Holly reached up and grasped the rider's wrist. The horse slowed to a canter and the rider curled his arm around Holly's waist and hoisted her upright. "Can't you just *stop*?" she cried, but either the horseman didn't hear her or didn't care. As soon as she was sitting up (and with a dizzy headache), they sped off again. Holly threw her arms around the rider's waist and hugged him tight. He was riding shirtless—and bareback.

Holly's rib cage rattled as the horse bounded sure-footed up and down the hilly path, around bends, over fallen logs and under low-hanging branches. It took all her attention to duck around the shrubbery that clutched at her from either side; she forgot about noticing which direction they were headed or how many turns they had taken. Her heart hammered against the horseman's back nearly as loudly as the hooves drumming beneath them. She would never find her way back to the beech tree.

She didn't dare change position, but kept tight hold of the horseman, her face pressed against him. Her cheeks were damp with his sweat, and a little sore from something scratchy that fell down the center of his back. Overhead, the canopy thickened as they rode deeper into the forest. The path narrowed, and brambles tore at Holly's jeans as they flew past. The birdsong she'd heard earlier quieted; creatures on their path scurried under rotted logs and into their burrows, silenced. Holly held tighter than ever.

At last, before they'd been traveling quite an hour, more light began to filter through the trees and Holly could see a clearing ahead. The horseman began to slow down, and his right hand shot down to her ankle and held it fast. The other clamped down on her left

CLAIRE M. CATERER

wrist, which still encircled his waist. The grip was like granite; she had no chance of jumping off now.

They came at a trot to a large glade and stopped at its far end. The rider did not dismount; he merely reached behind him with a very long, strong arm and grabbed Holly around the waist. He swung her onto the ground, still clenching one wrist so tightly that she couldn't break free. She landed on her feet, which nearly collapsed beneath her, she was so sore; and when she looked up at her captor, all thought of escape deserted her.

He wasn't a man on horseback at all.

He was a centaur.

Most people have only seen pictures of centaurs in books; Holly was one of those people. She might have expected to see a handsome man's torso growing out of a horse's body. And while this was essentially true, the man didn't look as she would have imagined. He was wild, with large, brown, horselike eyes nearly on the sides of his head. His chest was massive and powerful, and covered with chestnut-colored hair and a broad beard. His long, free hair extended down his back. Holly touched her cheek; his *mane* had been scratching her face. Her legs weakened, as much from the sight of him as from their gallop through the wood. She knew she should try to run, but she couldn't stop staring at him. When he spoke at last, a deep whinny ran under his words.

"Almaric!" The centaur spoke not to her, but to the edge of the clearing.

Holly saw they were standing at what looked to be an enormously thick, twisted elm tree. But then she saw it was *two* trees, one on each side of a low arched wooden door. Holly couldn't decide if it was a tree grown around a house or a house inside a tree.

The centaur raised a front hoof and kicked gently on the door by way of a knock, and bellowed again, "Almaric!"

After a moment, during which the centaur pawed the ground impatiently, the funny little door opened and a man stepped into the glade.

He was the smallest man Holly had ever seen, hardly taller than she, with bones as thin as a boy's. But he looked ancient, with shoulder-length white hair that blended into his beard, and so many wrinkles on his face that his deep-set blue eyes looked like two more. He wore a simple buff-colored robe edged in leaves and vines embroidered in green thread. One gnarled hand leaned on a crooked, highly polished staff. He tottered forward and glanced in confusion from the centaur to Holly and back again.

"And who is this?" he asked.

"I leave that to you, Lord Magician," the centaur replied. Their voices lilted in a kind of Gaelic accent, but Holly could understand them.

The centaur turned to Holly suddenly, as if just remembering something. He released her wrist and extended one foreleg, bending the other. He bowed his head and torso low, nearly touching the ground, and from a pouch slung around his waist he pulled a long stick. It looked quite like a wand. *Do centaurs cast spells?* she wondered. She backed away, but the centaur laid the wand flat on his palm, presenting it.

Holly gave a small cry. It was *her* wand, the key that she'd thought lost in the forest. She snatched it up, thinking too late that she was being a bit rude.

"Your Ladyship," the centaur said gravely, still speaking to the ground. Holly realized she was pointing the wand at him.

"Ranulf! She is an Adept?" the old man asked, breathless. Holly turned toward him, the wand still outstretched. He flinched, then bowed. "My lady."

She lowered her arm. "I'm not a lady—just Holly." What else had he called her? Her head still throbbed from the ride. Maybe she'd been knocked out and was having a very odd dream. She turned to the centaur. "You don't have to—um—bow."

The centaur raised his head. "You honor me, Lady.

I am Ranulf of the Mounted, at your humble service." He bowed again, not quite so deeply.

At once the old man sprang to life. He clapped his hands together and rubbed them vigorously, smiling wide. The wrinkles in his face condensed into dimples, and his voice strengthened, making him sound like a young man. "Almaric of the Elm, if it please Your Ladyship. Imagine, Ranulf! An Adept amongst us again!"

"An Adept who narrowly escaped capture by His Highness not this hour gone," said the centaur. "She cannot bide in the open, Almaric."

"Gracious me!" The old man's eyes darted frantically around the glade as he threw open the door to his odd little house. "Quite right! Inside, my lady, if you please!" He waved his hand in front of Holly. "Quickly, now. 'Tis humble, but safe within."

Holly hung back. Her mother's warnings about entering strange houses echoed in her head. "But—"

"No time for discussion, my lady!" Almaric grabbed her arm and bustled her into the house ahead of him while the centaur disappeared around the back.

It was like walking inside the tree itself. The snug room was round, like the hollow of a great trunk, with smooth branches supporting a low roof hung with ivy. Two broad chairs made of pliable branches grew out of the floor and huddled around a low table set with

CLAIRE M. CATERER

a tea tray. Opposite the table an iron pot hung in a generous hearth.

Almaric breathed a sigh and smiled again. "My apologies, Your Ladyship, but even this deep in the wood, your safety may not be guaranteed. Yes, Ranulf, come in, just there." He motioned to the centaur, who had appeared at a deep-set window opening beside the hearth. Ranulf ducked his head and shoulders inside.

"Heavens, Lady Holly," said Almaric, blushing, "do not stand on ceremony here! Take your ease." He patted a chair next to her and began pouring the tea, chuckling. "A narrow escape from His Highness, was it? And Your Ladyship summoned Ranulf? Fine work!"

She glanced from Almaric to the centaur. Her heart made a fluttery jump in her chest. Who were these people? Were they even people at all? Holly had hardly moved from the doorway, and she glanced back with a brief idea of bolting back into the wood, but her legs wobbled beneath her, and Almaric's chair, piled with flowered cushions, did look soft. Had she been saved? Or captured?

Almost against her will, her body sank into the soft chintz and her sore muscles eased. "I . . . Well . . . It *was* pretty great that you came by just then," she said to the centaur.

"At your summons, Lady," said Ranulf, inclining his head.

"But I didn't do anything. I just . . ." What exactly *had* happened? "I pulled out the key—wand—"

"I came on my fleetest hoof, my lady."

"Uh . . . right." Holly put a hand to her head, trying to still the pounding in her temples.

"Ranulf!" the old man exclaimed. "Our guest is exhausted. Did you fling her over your back like a bag of barley?"

"Your Ladyship's pardon, I beg you," said the centaur. "Your safety was of the essence."

"It's okay, really. I mean, thank you," said Holly weakly. She grasped the cup of tea that Almaric poured for her. Its warmth calmed her. What kind of place had she come to? She had thought the key would take them back in time, like what she'd seen at Darton Castle, but this place was somewhere else altogether. She glanced at the window, where Ranulf's horsey face poked through. The steeping tea had a sweet, wild scent. Holly's mother would not approve of her drinking it, but it seemed the only ordinary thing in a world of very extraordinary things. Before she knew it, Holly had nearly drained the cup, and she saw with relief that Almaric had poured cups for himself and Ranulf from the same bulbous teapot. So at least it wasn't poisoned.

CLAIRE M. CATERER

"It is to your liking, my lady?" Almaric asked.

"Thanks, it's great," Holly said.

The old man smiled and sat down opposite her. "'Tisn't much, Lady Adept. But now, to hear your tale. Ranulf and I would know from whence you came."

"Oh!" Holly cried—because now she remembered, having just gotten comfortable—"My brother! Everett!"

At their blank looks, she continued, "That prince rode off with them. I have to find them! It sounded like he was—I don't know—maybe going to kill them." Her voice caught.

"The boy is your kinsman? Is he the Elder?" Ranulf asked from the window.

"No, I'm the oldest," said Holly, wondering what difference it made. "The other boy is a friend of ours."

She heard a sharp scraping sound and saw with alarm that the centaur had drawn a sword. "We shall avenge them, my lady."

"Now, Ranulf," Almaric said, looking as nervous as Holly felt, "there's no need to ride off to battle. The prince has been on the hunt for poachers these seven days. He has no reason to think these lads are any more than that." He patted Holly's knee. "Prince Avery does not kill poachers. At worst, he might cut off a hand."

"What!" Holly sprang up from her seat.

"Patience, my lady. There is time enough to keep

our heads. His Highness will want to feast and toast his success. He shan't deal with his prisoners until daybreak, unless he has too much wine and waits till midday."

"But are you *sure*?" she prodded.

"Better to work with a plan in mind than to charge into a volley of arrows, eh?" He glanced at the centaur, who sheathed the sword reluctantly.

"Okay," Holly said, "so we make a plan. You guys are great and all"—she tried to swallow her doubt, looking at Almaric's thin frame—"but I think we need more help. I mean, the longer the boys stay there, wherever it is—"

"The tyrant's castle," said Ranulf. "It cannot be breached on a whim. We shall need aid and, aye"—he glanced at Almaric—"swords."

"I see no need for swords," the magician insisted. He took Holly's hand gently, pulling her back to her chair. "My lady, you have the magic of an Adept! We have not seen one of your kind for nigh on forty years, nor has the king."

"If we make a show of force, the king may release the prisoners in fear of Her Ladyship's power," said Ranulf.

"What are you talking about?" Holly asked, sitting down again. The conversation was getting more confusing by the minute. "I don't *have* any power. And why are you calling me that—adept?"

The centaur and the old man exchanged a surprised look. "Your wand, my lady," Ranulf said. "Only a true Adept can wield it."

Holly pulled the wand out of her pocket. Her two companions winced. "But I'm no one special. It was just a present. It could belong to anybody—like you, Ranulf. You picked it up."

The centaur blushed a deep scarlet. "Oh no, my lady. I claim no such power. 'Twas *you* who summoned *me*."

"But I *didn't*," said Holly.

"You were in peril. Did you not desire aid?"

"Well . . . I guess I did."

Almaric beamed at her.

"So it was *this*?" She twirled the wand, and the centaur's eyes followed it, one hand on the hilt of his sword. *They're afraid of me,* she realized. *They think I'm going to cast some kind of spell.*

"Please, my lady," urged Ranulf. "How can you not know your own people? Tell us whence you came."

"Over the sea, was it? From the Island of Exile?" asked Almaric. "Perhaps a shipwreck," he added, turning to the centaur. "If she hit her head, she may not recall—"

"It *wasn't* a shipwreck," cried Holly. "You don't

understand, I don't even come from here." She stopped herself just in time, before the words tumbled out. How could she trust them? They were strangers—certainly stranger than anyone she'd ever met. She held the wand upright, gazing at the carved vines and flowers that encircled it. Almaric and Ranulf were frightened of it, and they had just *given* it to her. That would have to be reason enough to trust them, right? And anyway, how would she find the boys without them?

The old magician and the centaur stayed very still, staring at her.

"Look," Holly said slowly, turning the wand to let the crystal catch the light. "I know this sounds pretty weird, but Ben and Everett and I came from a different place altogether. Like another world, maybe. It looks a lot like this one, but we don't have a king or prince or thingies—Adepts—there. Someone there gave me the wand—I mean, it *was* a key—and then I used it to take us here through the forest. But I didn't even know where we were going, or where we are now."

"Gracious me," Almaric whispered, one hand over his heart.

"If it please Your Ladyship," said Ranulf, "you have come to the Northern Wood, in the kingdom of Anglielle, which extends many leagues from here. Do you know naught of King Reynard's realm?"

"I've never heard of him," Holly admitted.

"He is a beast of a man," Almaric said in a low voice. "He has long hunted the Adepts, and those of us who are in league with them, since first he took the throne."

"He's . . . hunted them?" Holly's heart beat faster.

"Aye. Killed or banished every one he could find." The old man poured more tea all around. "You see, Lady Holly, the kings of this land are mortalfolk—they always have been. Before Reynard took the throne, magic- and mortalfolk lived harmoniously together. The Adepts even advised the king from time to time— some are quite gifted with Sight, and they are scholars of many things apart from magic. But when Reynard was born, everything changed."

"But why?" Holly asked.

"The kingdom fell apart," Almaric said, his forehead creasing with wrinkles. "The prince heir was taken— snatched from his cradle in the middle of the night. Naturally, his parents were grief-stricken. Reynard's father, King Lancet, took to his bed and died shortly thereafter. Queen Priscelle was left to rule alone, and she spent all her energies searching the kingdom for her son."

"How did she find him?"

Almaric shrugged. "She didn't. Oh, she consulted with all manner of creatures—the Adepts themselves as well as dark sorcerers and other beings. The Mounted"—Almaric nodded at Ranulf—"rode in search over the moors and to the sea. But the prince was nowhere to be found. The kingdom plunged into chaos. The queen's knights went missing, warring tribes invaded. Drought and famine spread across the land. It was brutal."

The old man wiped his eyes with one hand, and even Ranulf bowed his head. Holly waited for Almaric to continue, but when he didn't, she said, "But . . . what happened? It doesn't seem so bad now. At least," she said, wanting to sound respectful, "from what I've seen."

Almaric nodded. "Nay, my lady, you're quite right. You see, at last Reynard did return to the castle. By that time, he was in his sixteenth year, a strong and cruel man. He struck down the queen and took the throne for himself."

"You mean"—Holly swallowed—"he *killed* his mother?"

"Aye. And some say for the better. In a way, it was like a miracle—Reynard became king, and suddenly the drought was gone. The fields were fertile. He organized armies, crushed the invaders. Even invaded other lands himself and extended the borders of Anglielle to the sea on all sides."

CLAIRE M. CATERER

"And enslaved the people," the centaur spoke up, his tail switching. "Let us not forget that."

"He is a ruthless man," Almaric agreed. "Those that cross him are never heard from again."

Like Ben and Everett, Holly thought. "But what about your magic?" she asked. "What happened to all the Adepts you talked about? And the rest of you?"

"That," said Almaric, "is the sticking point. Reynard fears all magic and those we call the Exiles—those beings of magical lineage. He knew he would never rule the land absolutely unless he crushed them. Many are dead, and the rest are scattered through the moors and the woodland. Their magic hides them, for the most part, though the Mounted have to be careful. The king rarely ventures this deep into the wood. Of course, the Adepts are all gone. They were never really under the king's rule, and Reynard couldn't have that. So he exiled them—your people—to a far-off island. No one knows where they are now." The old man smiled sadly. "Perhaps they even found their way to your own world."

"But I told you, they're not my people," Holly protested.

Almaric shrugged. "Whether you know it or not, my lady, a wand such as yours can only belong to an Adept—one of great magical power. A shaper of spells.

A sorcerer, if you may excuse the term. They are the most powerful beings in Anglielle."

"But how could I be one of those? I've never heard of Adepts in my world. They aren't even in the history books."

"Do your books tell no tales of magic and sorcery?"

Holly thought a moment. "I guess they *do*. But they're just stories."

"How else did Your Ladyship acquire the wand? Was it not forged for you by a Wandwright?"

"Well, I . . . He's more of a gardener."

Almaric glanced at the centaur, who snorted.

"So, that prince, the one who made off with the boys," Holly said, shuddering off a chill, "that's the king's son?"

"Aye, the prince Avery," said Ranulf. He turned his head and spat into the old man's garden. "He too is arrogant and cruel, even at thirteen years."

"And he has Ben," said Holly. Pudgy little Ben, who didn't like planes or boats, Ben with his asthma and his allergies. Her heart rose in her throat. "Don't you see, I have to *do* something. I have to get them back. It's my fault that they're here in the first place."

The centaur shifted from one hoof to the other, as if deep in thought. "If Your Ladyship is not of this land, perhaps you have not been schooled in the arts of the wand?" he said at last.

Holly shook her head. "I don't really know how to use it."

"Then to free your kinsman, we must use conventional means." Ranulf drew his sword again. "Almaric speaks truth. Much as I would storm the gatehouse in all due haste, our plan is best executed under cover of dark. Now, until such time is upon us—" The centaur suddenly broke off his speech. Holly saw his pointed ears swivel back toward the dark wood, and he looked to the sky. "Hark! Almaric, a moment. 'Tis Hornbeak." He withdrew from the window into the wood.

"No, wait!" said Holly. She ran to the window with Almaric behind her. Together, they peered into the clearing.

A moment later, the centaur galloped out of the trees on the far side. His brown eyes were wide and his ears laid flat against his head. "She has been discovered!" he shouted. "The counsel is assembling. She must be protected, and we must go to them." Then, without another word, he bolted back into the forest, clutching his sword in his fist.

"No, Ranulf! Come back!" Holly called.

But the centaur was gone.

"It must be terribly important," Almaric was muttering, scooping the teacups and sugar tongs onto the wooden tray. "The counsel must be dealt with, Lady

Holly. We cannot delay. Come, this way . . . quickly . . ."

Before Holly could say anything else, Almaric had gripped her hand and pulled her through a low doorway in one corner of the room. It led to an even smaller round room, dense with flowered vines that grew up the walls and across the ceiling.

"'Tis the safest place in the forest, this room," Almaric was saying as he fluttered across to a window and fastened the shutter. "My talents are nothing to your own, Lady Holly, but this elm does have certain protective properties—shadowed from mortalfolk, you see—no, I don't suppose you do," he added at her bewildered look. "You must bide here a time, all will be well."

The old man's trembling hands and furtive glances at his back did nothing to reassure Holly. "But I can't," she said, trying to push past Almaric. "The boys—"

"Are precisely the point, Your Ladyship," said the magician, gripping her arm. At her surprised look, he softened, trying to smile. "I shall go and consult with Hornbeak and the others. You must remain. No more arguments."

And with that, the old man backed out of the room and shut the wooden door behind him. Holly heard the sturdy click of a key turning. She yanked on the door handle, but it was no use.

She was locked in.

Chapter 13

What Happened to the Boys

Everett had little time to think about what had happened to Holly or where her captor had taken her. He was quite good at horseback riding, but even he had never been on a ride like this one. For one thing, the prince, astride the horse behind him, held the reins, giving Everett nothing to grasp but the horse's mane. For another, this was a much finer and more spirited horse than Everett was used to. The prince pushed the horse to a near full gallop along the winding, hilly path through the woods. Occasionally the saplings on either side whipped branches across Everett's face. At one point the horse leaped a fallen tree and Everett nearly went over its head. Finally he found himself doubled over the horse's neck, clinging to its mane. The pounding of the hooves gave him a headache, and the dust blowing up from the path caught in his eyes and throat. He tried to look ahead to quell the dizziness but couldn't see much. It was like being on an amusement-park ride without the amusement.

At last—less than half an hour later, though it seemed like a lot longer—the horse slowed abruptly as the path widened and emerged from the forest. Everett could hear the other horse blowing behind them. He tried to turn around to see Ben, but the prince's pointy elbow cracked his temple. "Be still, poacher," he muttered, as they crested the hill.

For a moment Everett forgot that he was a prisoner on horseback and would probably be killed shortly. In front of him was the most magnificent castle he had ever seen—and he had seen several.

They trotted up to a long drawbridge over a wide moat that surrounded the castle. Two massive octagonal towers flanked its wide, stone face. He counted five stories of narrow windows. Above him sentries armed with crossbows paced the crenellated battlements. Masses of flowering trees and manicured beds lined the graveled drive.

The horses slowed as they approached an imposing gatehouse, where stood two guards in chain mail. The lord of this castle apparently feared no one; his fortress was wide open to visitors. The prince paused his horse, waiting for the guards to bow.

Lord Clement's horse came up abreast and Everett

got a look at Ben, thrown face-first into the horse's mane. His eyes were pink and swollen like Ping-Pong balls, and his face was smeared with snot. Hives spread down his neck. While the horsemen spoke to the guards, Everett whispered, "Are you all right?"

"Allergic," Ben whispered back in a thick voice. "To horses." He sneezed.

Everett could only hope it wasn't the sort of allergy that made your throat close up. As it was, Ben's breathing had a thin, wheezy sound to it. But then again, thought Everett, that was likely the least of their problems.

The horses walked through the gatehouse into a vast courtyard enclosed by the castle walls on all sides. It was a busy place. A group of ladies sat in one corner doing some kind of needlework. Men carried barrels and drove sheep in and out of open storage areas, shouting orders; barefoot boys scuttled back and forth. Then all at once the courtyard fell silent and every knee bowed.

The prince dismounted, drawing his sword in the same motion. He held its point at Everett's neck and shouted, "Gervase!"

A young knight dressed in chain mail, like the castle guards, appeared from the far side of the courtyard. "Your Highness."

"Lord Clement believes he has seen an Adept in the Northern Wood," said the prince.

"An Adept, Sire!" Gervase breathed, his eyes wide.

The prince snorted as if he didn't believe it himself. "She looked to be a lass with a stick, if truth be known. But best send two of your fellows along the main path to search for her. Follow the stream a few leagues in. A horseman rode off with her—mayhap they can discover his trail."

"'Twas the Mounted," Clement muttered, turning red.

"And these," said the prince, nudging Everett, "be poachers. We shall try their case on the morrow. Confine them until then."

The knight bowed and motioned to another man. Gervase reached up and unhooked Everett's bound hands from the saddle's pommel and pulled him to the ground. His legs, numb from the ride, fell in a sort of puddle, but he was kicked roughly to his feet. The other knight lifted Ben down.

"Sire!" exclaimed Gervase. "What manner of beast is this?"

Ben did look beastly, with his blotchy face and his eyes swollen nearly shut. He was crying, too, which didn't do his appearance any favors.

The prince shrugged. "He was a good sight more

　　　　CLAIRE M. CATERER

comely when we caught him. Take them to the North Tower."

"As you wish, Your Highness." Gervase grabbed Everett from behind by the elbow, laying his sword flat across Everett's chest. The other knight took hold of Ben, and together the knights marched them through a colonnade on the far side of the courtyard.

"This lad has need of a healer," said Ben's knight to Gervase as they passed out of the prince's earshot.

"He is for the gallows in any case, Pagett."

Ben began to howl.

Pagett gasped. "Not such a youngling as this?"

They covered steps and passageways until Everett had lost count, but at some point they approached an open basin with a pump next to it.

"Excuse me, Sir—knight," Everett said.

"Aye, lad?"

"I was wondering, would it be all right if my friend at least washed his face?"

The knight shrugged and nodded at Pagett, who shoved Ben in front of the basin. He moved the sword to rest against the back of Ben's neck. "Make a false move, friend," he said, "and your head shall part company with your shoulders."

While Ben sobbed quietly and pumped water into the basin, Pagett turned to Gervase. "Did you hear

Lord Clement in the courtyard, Gervase? News of an Adept?"

Everett's ears perked up. They were talking about Holly.

Gervase shrugged. "A tall tale from an old woman. There be no Adepts in this land since my father's time, or longer."

Pagett lowered his voice. "Mayhap it be unwise to hold the king's tournament at Midsummer. 'Tis said to be a time of . . . of their power."

"Will children's tales be your excuse for not besting Bertran of the Oak?"

"'Tis he who should fear me, I should wager."

"Take no offense if I lay no coins to that score. Aye, lad! That serves well enough." Gervase jerked Ben away from the basin.

A moment later, they came to a steep, winding stone staircase. The knights prodded the boys up it at swordpoint.

"Fie upon the prince's tower," said Pagett, sounding winded after several minutes. "Can we not run them through? We might tell His Highness they turned on us and essayed to do battle, then perished in the attempt."

"Are you not a knight of the realm? They may yet be spared. 'Tis not ours to judge."

"We didn't know the wood belonged to anyone,"

Everett said. "Besides, if we were poachers, where're our . . ." He paused, about to say *guns*, and then substituted, "Bows and arrows?"

"They were found unarmed," Pagett agreed. "Perchance His Highness will be merciful."

And that was the last word on the subject.

After about ten minutes of climbing, the silence broken only by Ben's gasps and wheezing, they reached a heavy door. Gervase took a key ring from somewhere on his person and opened it.

The room was small and round—Everett guessed they were in one of the tall, skinny towers at the back of the castle—and had a single high window. Otherwise, it was bare and dry, except for a few iron rings set into the stone wall.

"Ye shall stay fast enough unshackled," said Gervase, following his gaze.

Ben collapsed on the floor, and Everett sat down next to him. The knights backed out of the chamber with swords raised. The door slammed shut behind them.

As soon as they were gone, Everett took off his jacket and rolled it into a ball. He lifted Ben's head and laid it on the jacket, then peered at his puffy face anxiously. Ben's breathing was thin, as if he were trying to suck air through a straw.

After a few moments, Ben managed to say, "In . . . my . . . pocket. Pock . . . et."

Everett rummaged around in Ben's jacket until he found an inhaler. Ben seized it and pumped it into his mouth, then gestured at the jacket again. Everett probed deeper into the pocket and found a flat foil pack of pills. "This?"

"For all . . . er . . . gies," Ben panted, and Everett at once punched two pills out of the foil. He helped Ben sit up so he could take them. In Ben's other pocket he found a packet of tissues and some Tylenol. Weakly, Ben blew his nose several times and littered one corner of the tower with used tissues. Gradually the wheezing eased, and Ben's eyes began to look more human.

"Are you sure you're okay?" Everett asked at last.

"*Okay?*" Ben's breath hiccupped, then found its footing. "Let's see. First, Holly drags us into this place, then gets us captured by I-Don't-Know-Who. I'm practically dying of horse allergies and now we're locked in a tower and people are talking about trials and hanging. Sure, Everett, I'm great." His eyes teared up.

"Yeah, all right. I admit things are a bit sticky, but there's no use panicking." Everett was trying to sound more grown-up than he felt. His own throat was a little thick, and he could feel his eyes stinging from tears he was trying to keep down. He distracted himself by looking around the tower. "I wonder where this place is."

"Who cares? How're we gonna get *out*?" said Ben.

Everett got up and walked to the window, which was a bare opening without glass. He gazed down. The ground, a wide grassy area, was a sheer drop, more than a hundred feet. "I don't know," he admitted, coming back to sit by Ben. "But we've got a little time. We need to play along with his lot, make them think that we at least respect the king and his authority."

"That kid is a king?" said Ben.

"Prince, the knights said. The lord with him, Clement, he's some kind of nobleman or adviser or something. Anyway, poaching's a serious crime. If we want to get out of here, we've got to get our story straight. We were just wandering, lost; we hadn't any weapons. . . ."

"My sister magicked us here from some other world. . . ."

"I don't think we'd best mention Holly. They didn't like her for some reason."

"And she got caught too." Ben collapsed again, his head on Everett's jacket. "Do you think that guy was from some other kingdom? Like a rival?"

Everett sat up suddenly, his heart racing. It was as if, through all their trials, he had only now recalled what he'd seen. Or what he *thought* he'd seen. "That wasn't a guy, Ben. Didn't you see?" It couldn't be right; they were in England, weren't they, in the Middle Ages sometime? Everett glanced at Ben. He had collapsed, exhausted, on the cold floor. Everett whispered to himself. "It wasn't a man at all. It was a centaur."

Chapter 14

Holly's Resolve

Holly spent a good deal of time pounding on the little wooden door and jerking the handle and calling Almaric's name before she kicked the door for good measure and slumped against the wall. "Let me out!" she tried once more, but her words echoed through the little house. She sensed it was empty.

She opened the porthole-shaped shutter that Almaric had fastened, but the opening was too small for her to fit through. She peered into the forest, straining her ears, but all she heard was the distant scream of a hawk. "Ranulf?" she called, but even his hoofbeats had faded.

What an idiot she had been. Now it seemed so clear, how the prince had captured Ben and Everett, and Ranulf had captured Holly herself. She couldn't imagine why anyone would want her, unless they had been telling the truth about these Adepts and intended to use her somehow.

But then why would they leave her with her greatest weapon?

Holly pulled the wand from her back pocket. *Weapon.* Sure it was. She grasped the wand at its broad end, the wood smooth and warm beneath her fingers. Like the key, it seemed to belong there, molded to her touch. A trembly warmth spread down her fingers into her arm, then to her heart. The feeling was like drinking hot chocolate on a snowy day.

Holly stood up and circled the room, holding the wand out in front of her. Above the chest of drawers hung a round, convex mirror. She pointed the wand at the cloudy glass.

Her dim reflection brightened, then wavered. The wand in the mirror glowed like a lit match, though the one in Holly's hand merely trembled before the glass. What good was a mirror? If only it would show her Ben and Everett . . .

Just as these thoughts flitted through her mind, her reflection dissolved and other faint shapes crowded into the round glass. Holly spun around to see what was behind her, but it was only the empty room. When she looked back at the glass, one of the shapes solidified.

Ben?

Now she could see him quite clearly, curled up against a stone wall, Everett next to him. She held her breath; were they dead? But no—Ben's arm twitched. He was asleep.

Holly stretched out her fingers toward the image, but it blinked out like the picture on an old television set. She tapped the wand against the wavy glass. "Come back! Bring him back!" she said aloud, but the mirror was blank.

The wand trembled in her hand, warming up again. She leaned forward, peering into the glass.

A black shape flew across her vision, and then, just as fast, a face flickered by—a pale, pointed face with sharp teeth, which turned and grimaced at her for a split second.

Holly dropped the wand with a cry, and the figure vanished.

What was *that*? Were the boys all right?

Yes.

She couldn't say how she knew. She picked up the wand gingerly, refusing to look at the mirror again. She had seen that the boys were safe; that was all that was important. That other thing, whatever it was, might just be some property of the mirror, a kind of defense mechanism. Whatever else was going on, somehow she knew the wand wouldn't lie to her. She had to believe the boys were safe—for now.

The wand did have power, but did she? Holly

crossed the room to the locked door and tried waving the wand at it. Nothing happened, not even when she said aloud, "Open sesame!" (and immediately felt silly for doing so). She couldn't make the wand do what she wanted it to, at least not all the time, so what kind of power was that? *Pretty lame, if you ask me,* Ben would say, and Holly almost laughed before she remembered where he was.

She sank onto a funny round bed in the center of the room and sighed. Suddenly she felt so very tired, as if all her energy had flowed from the wand into the mirror. Her thoughts tumbled one on top of the next in no coherent order. If she rested on the soft goose down, she would certainly feel better in a few minutes.

Maybe it was what she had done with the wand or the warm tea she had drunk or her long ride through the forest, but whatever the reason, Holly fell asleep before another thought entered her head.

She awoke with a start. The light coming through the window was reddish now; it must be late. She dashed to the door and pulled on the handle, but it was still locked.

Then she heard a great amount of noise—honking and squawking and animated voices—coming from outside. She ran to the window.

Outdoors in the gathering dusk several strange creatures were fighting to make themselves heard. Holly recognized Ranulf; a few other centaurs circled the clearing, stamping impatiently. Several large falcons wheeled above their heads. Other animals seemed to be part of the meeting as well—two great stags and a large black cat. A very short, burly man with a long beard was showing a small ax to one of the female centaurs. Something else that Holly took to be a raccoon faded out before her eyes. An enormous snake took its place. Had the creature changed? Holly's heart skipped a beat. The animal blurred out again and turned into a gorilla. Then suddenly it was a bat.

"Be still!" someone snapped, in a sort of half yowl. Holly peered closer; was it the *cat*?

"I can't help it," cried the changing creature, which was now a large parrot. "It happens when I get excited."

Holly drew back a little so the strange, noisy group couldn't see her. Almost without realizing it, she pulled the wand from her pocket. At once, a glow like a gentle flame washed through her from her fingers through her body and back again, like a completed circuit. The wand was starting to feel familiar, as if it were greeting her when she picked it up, the way a computer turns on with a musical sound. Holly peeked through the window again.

Centaurs, changelings, talking cats—there was real magic here, just as Ranulf had said, not just card tricks and fancy stage nonsense like she'd seen at home. Holly glanced around for Almaric, and then spied him in the middle of the half circle.

"Listen, all of you!" he called. "It is true what you've heard. We have seen the Adept, Ranulf and I."

"Where is she? Can we meet her?" cried the change-ling, whose azure wings started to blur. The cat glared at him, and he solidified again.

"All in good time," said Almaric.

"How did she escape the Island of Exile?" asked the female centaur.

"She came farther than that. She was spirited here from another world."

"To help us?" cried the changeling.

"It is she who begs help," snorted one of the other centaurs. His mane was white like a palomino. "And Ranulf says she is untrained. What good is she to us?"

"Her Ladyship is not your mercenary, Hoofstone," said Ranulf.

"Very noble, to be sure," said the little man in a gruff voice, shouldering his ax. "But times is changed, an't they? There might've been a time when we'd be obliged to serve such a lass as this, but where be the Adepts this forty year? Holed away on some comfy island? They's got no tyrant king to fash 'em, has they? If they's as all-powerful as they always was, why an't they come back, eh?"

"I say it is marvelous to have an Adept amongst us again!" squawked the changeling. "Surely she will come to our aid."

Holly bit her lip. What kind of aid could she give these creatures?

"Our battle is not hers," said a deep voice, which Holly thought came from one of the stags. "And hers is not ours."

"Fools!" snorted Ranulf. "She is an Adept. We are pledged to serve her." He glared at the burly little man. "You know that better than most, Bittenbender."

"And I say any such pact is far expired," growled Bittenbender. "That balance you always talk of, Ranulf, that's long been tipped. And not in our favor, neither."

"And where is Fleetwing?" the stag added. "If he is not willing to join us, why should the rest of us risk a visit to the castle?"

"He has been called," Ranulf said. "He answers a summons in his own time."

"Hmmph," snorted Bittenbender, as if he thought the rest of them should have been as wise. The other creatures all started talking at once.

"Hearken all!" bellowed Ranulf above the din. "We

may each have our own score to settle, but we have a common enemy. If you would desire Her Ladyship's aid—"

"Hey!" Holly shouted, almost before she realized it. The group fell silent. Holly blushed, and thought of pulling her head back through the window, but why should she stay quiet while the rest of them decided what to do with her? "I'm not doing anything for any-body until someone lets me out of here."

Almaric gave a little jump and glared at the others as if to say, *Now look what you've done.* He scurried into his little house. In a moment, he was at the bed-room door.

"A thousand pardons, my lady," he said nervously, as he pulled the door open. "It was for your own safety, I assure you."

"You could've just told me to stay here," Holly said, feeling angry all over again.

Almaric inclined his head in a sort of half bow, following her into the sitting room. "I *am* sorry, Lady Holly. But I couldn't chance your trying to find your kinsman on your own. The prince has no doubt sent his knights in search of you." Almaric shuddered. "If they had found you—"

"Okay, okay." Holly took a breath and tightened her grip on the wand, which she still held at her side.

She *did* trust Almaric and Ranulf, even if the other creatures didn't seem as friendly. "What's going on out there, anyway? Did you and Ranulf get all these—people—together to help me rescue Ben and Everett?"

"Of course, Your Ladyship," said the old man, blushing. "Er . . . that is, primarily."

"What do you mean, *primarily*?"

"Lady Holly, Ranulf and I went to gather a few of the stronger magicfolk, but word spread of your arrival even before we summoned anyone. The Mounted all heard your summons, and once it was known that an Adept had appeared . . ." Almaric cast a worried glance at the side window, where the group's argument was still rumbling.

"They want something from me," Holly said, following his glance.

Almaric shrugged his white, bushy eyebrows. "In a manner of speaking. It was a sort of unspoken pact, you see, with the Adepts of old. They were a solitary lot, but they did use their powerful magicks to protect the rest of us from all manner of dark creatures from the Gloamlands and beyond. In turn, those with other sorts of powers extended their own protection."

"Like an alliance, you mean?"

"Precisely, my lady."

"But the Adepts are all gone now," Holly said, feeling small. "There's just me."

"Quite so," said Almaric. "And . . . to be honest . . . these good folk have gathered to help you, but more than that, they have assembled because the appearance of an Adept may mean deliverance from the king's tyranny."

"But . . ." A shiver ran across Holly's shoulders. "They don't expect me to lead an army against the king, right? I mean, they're the fighters, I'm not."

Almaric had found a very absorbing ember in the fireplace, which he prodded with a long iron poker.

"Almaric!"

"Well . . . there's a bit more to it, Lady Holly," said the old man absently. He rearranged the teakettle on the hob, then pulled a linen cloth from a hook and wiped his hands. "The important thing is that they are willing to help you."

"But they're right, you know," said Holly. "I don't have any training. Even if I was an—an—"

"An Adept—"

"Right, even if I was, and I don't think I *am*—"

"A wand is not given lightly, my lady. You have crossed the veil between worlds, and that is no small feat," said the magician.

Holly sighed. How could she explain it? Anyone might have done what she had, if they'd had the key.

But the key was given to *her*.

And why was that, anyway? Mr. Gallaway didn't even know her, yet he seemed to be waiting for her, as if she were someone special. He didn't seem to realize that Holly's greatest power was her invisibility. She didn't have a cloak, nor a magic box to crawl into, but she was invisible all the same. She was the one sitting in the back of the classroom, sketching dragons because no one noticed her doing it. She snuck along the edges of the playground looking for fossils and arrowheads while the other girls jumped rope and played soccer. What use was it knowing how to tie a dozen different knots and reading scads of books? What could she *do*? She had potential, her mother said, usually with a sigh. Why hadn't Ben gotten the key? He was the smart one, the one the teachers liked and their mother praised, who had plans and ambitions, even if they *were* dorky.

And now he was in trouble.

Holly twirled the wand between her fingers. "But what good is this thing anyway, Almaric? I couldn't even unlock your bedroom door with it. How could I storm a castle?"

Almaric winced as she waved the wand helplessly in the air. "Yes, yes . . . I see what you mean, my lady. But . . . if you would lower it, please . . ." She stopped waving it and laid it on Almaric's little table. "Quite.

Now, if you will beg an old magician's pardon, you are not exactly correct. Even an Adept with no training has power. It is simply a matter of finding it."

"Simply?"

"In days past, even those younger than Your Ladyship were able to make—well, demonstrations, shall we say—"

"But they expect something real from me, Almaric! Like—I don't know—magical leadership or whatever. That isn't me. It's just . . . I'm not who you think I am."

"And I would wager," said the old man, "that you are not who *you* think you are, Your Ladyship." He smiled at her. "Do you suppose the Adepts of old were born with great knowledge and power? Nay, they *learnt*. They were schooled. They uncovered what was buried deep within themselves. Our friends the Exiles may indeed require some show of—how did you put it? Magical leadership? But if you search within yourself, you will find it, Lady Holly. Betimes, a great need must arise before we see our true calling. What greater need might there be than the safety of your kinsman?"

Holly swallowed, her throat thickening. "It's my fault they're here," she said, her voice quavering. "Him and Everett. I've got to do something to help them. I'm—I'm not usually that nice to Ben. He probably doesn't even think I'll *try* to rescue him. And what's going to happen to him if I don't? What if he has an asthma attack? What if they feed him strawberries? He probably doesn't even have his EpiPen with him!"

"Er . . . quite so, Your Ladyship," said Almaric, frowning. "But whilst I cannot speak to those things, I do know this: You must be strong in your resolve. Or you shall persuade none else." He gestured to the door.

The old man had a point. Holly's army, if that's what they were, might not believe in her, but she needed them. She would just have to try and win them over. She couldn't leave the boys here, even if she didn't have any magical powers, even if she wasn't very good at anything in particular and "didn't apply herself" and was a little on the scrawny side. *There's no one to do this but me,* she told herself. With this thought in mind, and barring all others (*But how?* and *What if I get caught?* and *What if they won't do what I say?*), Holly picked up her wand and stepped out into the twilit glade.

Chapter 15

The Test

The creatures quieted at once at the sight of Holly standing in Almaric's doorway. She wasn't sure what to say, so she merely held the wand out in front of her. The creatures backed away, the ones with hooves shuffling and snorting as if about to bolt.

Almaric ran up from behind her and smiled nervously. "May I present Her Ladyship the Adept, Holly of the Northern Wood."

Holly continued to stare down the little group until Ranulf, muttering to the others, dropped his head and bowed. Everyone followed suit—that is, everyone except (for Holly took close note) the cat, one of the stags, and the small man.

The changeling, its head still lowered, glanced up at the cat and whispered loudly, "What are you doing?"

"I am assessing the situation." The cat stepped forward and looked Holly in the eye over her wand. Holly lowered it and put it away. "You come not to threaten us, then."

"Of course not," said Holly.

The cat blinked his bright-green eyes and wrapped his tail around his feet. "I am called Jade," he said, then added, not exactly respectfully, "Your Ladyship."

"I . . . ah . . . nice to meet you."

The others rose and watched Jade nervously.

"It is much you ask of us," said the cat.

The stag wheeled to face Ranulf. "This Adept is naught but a child! You would have her lead us into battle?"

"Peace, Fortimus! I ask Her Ladyship to lead us nowhere."

That was a relief. She *couldn't* lead anyone into battle.

"Yet we are to lay down our lives for her!" said Fortimus.

"The Earthfolk have more quarrels with the king than the lot of you," said Bittenbender. "Whose magic d'ye think it was what pulled the gems from the earth, what gives these Adepts their power? And what's it got us? Enslaved, is what!"

The palomino centaur snorted. "The Mounted have been hunted to near extinction. Some would say the Dvergar are more collaborators than slaves!"

"Silence!" shouted Ranulf. "Will we war against each other or the tyrant in the castle? What plagues you, Bittenbender? Hoofstone? And you!" He reared to face the cat so abruptly that Jade's fur stood on end. "A familiar renders service, not judgment! Aye, Her Ladyship is untrained. So much the better! She is willing to learn. We have all suffered under the tyrant's rule. But we know naught of magic. Not compared to what may yet be achieved by this youngling."

Holly couldn't think what Ranulf meant; what did he expect her to achieve, anyway? She glanced around nervously. Fortimus and Bittenbender were looking at the ground; the small man's face was red right up into the roots of his hair, and even the stag's brown cheeks looked a bit pink. Hoofstone the centaur pawed the earth. Jade alone met Ranulf's glance.

"Very well," said the cat. "Ranulf, you speak truth. We are fools to waste such a chance as this." He extended one black paw to Holly, inclining his head. "I am willing to render my service as your familiar, Your Ladyship. Provided . . ."

The other creatures all raised their eyes.

"Provided there is a test."

Holly's heart sank to her stomach.

Ranulf stepped closer. "Do you dare require such a thing?"

"I am not alone in wanting proof beyond a wooden stick."

"Do I speak to the wind? Her Ladyship is untrained."

"Yet if she be genuine, she will have some innate power."

"Oooh!" cried the changeling, popping into the shape of a hedgehog. "Let's see some magic then! Her Ladyship will show you up, Jade, and no mistake!"

Holly's heart beat harder and she glanced at Almaric. The old man nudged her forward.

"But I can't *do* anything," she whispered to him.

"Courage, my lady," he said. "Envision what you desire."

"Surely this lady does not expect us to take her on faith?" said the cat. "Come now. A saucer of cream. That should prove simple for a true Adept."

Cream? It didn't seem the kind of spell that would do much good against a king. But the cat said it would be simple.

Simple to make something out of nothing?

Holly drew the wand from her pocket. Everyone but Jade pulled back into the trees. She raised the wand; the cat flinched, ever so slightly.

Now what? An incantation? She wasn't about to say *Abracadabra*. She closed her eyes a moment and heard the faint humming from within the wand.

It vibrated in her palm. She thought of what she had seen in the mirror: Ben and Everett huddled on the stone floor. Again the warmth, like blood, surged through her body and down her arm into her fingers. Was this what Almaric was talking about? The magic within her? Was this the great need that would show her true calling? She pointed the wand at the ground, just in front of the black cat. What had happened in the cottage bedroom? She had thought about Ben, and then the mirror showed him to her. Surely if she pictured what Jade had asked of her—a saucer of cream—in her mind, she could create it. One thing seemed sure: If she couldn't, her little band would never risk their lives to help her. *A saucer of cream. Think about nothing else.*

But as soon as she told her brain what to do, *two* images flashed through her mind. They fought with each other, first one dominating, then the other: the boys in the king's tower and the saucer of cream. She tried to push away the picture of Ben looking so cold and small, and tugged on the saucer, trying to bring it to the surface of her thoughts.

Clearly, that wasn't going to work. The harder she tried not to think about Ben, the stronger his image became, and she felt the wand's power fade as she struggled. She took a deep breath. Rescuing the boys was what this was all about; *that's* why she needed to show this magic. It was the only way to gain the help she needed. She thought about how Mr. Gallaway had trusted her with the key, how Almaric trusted her now to demonstrate her power. Something in her, perhaps, knew better than she.

So she let the images come, and with them, her fear, a clutching, acidic feeling in her throat that told her Ben was in danger, that he might even now already be hurt, that she might never bring him back home; and then, on top of her fear, came a fiery will, because she *had* to bring him home. And like the sun shooting from behind a dark cloud, the current gathered in her chest and burst out of her fingers, down through the wood and into the crystal, and bloomed into the open air. Holly's eyes flew open.

A dim spark lit the darkening ground, and then the grass seemed to bubble up from below. It rounded, forming a bowl, and the dirt within it swirled, lightening in color. Holly gasped. There it was: a shallow clay bowl, filled with—

"Buttermilk," the cat muttered in a low tone to her. "But close enough, Lady Holly."

Chapter 16

The Leogryff

Every creature was quiet, as if everyone, including Holly, were holding a collective breath. Even the changeling stood still. Holly locked eyes with the cat, the wand shaking in her hand. She couldn't believe she had done it—Holly Shepard, who could do almost nothing right at home, had created something out of thin air. She stepped back, feeling the buzz of a slight headache. Almaric and Ranulf looked at each other and nodded. Finally the stag called Fortimus stepped forward. "You shall have my help, Your Ladyship," he said, bowing his great antlers. One of the falcons flapped noisily, saying, "And I too!" Even Hoofstone bowed, and Holly's heart lifted.

But Bittenbender, the little man of the Dvergar, snorted. "There's a fine army, Lady Adept. But I for one need more than a cat's dinner to stake my life upon."

The other creatures muttered among themselves. The cat Jade looked sharply at the changeling, who popped into the shape of a starling and flitted off into the trees.

"You dare ask for a test, and then scoff at the results?" Ranulf asked, glaring at Bittenbender.

"Nay, she's Adept, true enough," said the little man grudgingly. "Tha's all very fine. But we an't heard her tell us what she'll do fer us, have we?"

Holly felt the blood leave her face. She had thought once she showed them what she could do—true, a saucer of cream wasn't much against a bunch of castle guards, but still . . .

"What . . . What exactly do you want?" she asked.

Bittenbender stepped forward, grinning in a not very nice way. "How's about a promise, then? The promise of a Banishment?"

A low murmur circled the clearing, and the little man cocked an eyebrow at her. "Eh? Seems only fair, nae?"

Ranulf stepped in front of Holly before she could ask what a Banishment was or why the little man demanded it. "It is not the proper time for a Banishment. Even the stars say as much."

"The *stars*? Pah!" The Dvergar spat on the ground again. "The Earthfolk likes results, we do, not predictions and prophecies. Own up, my lady. Can ye or can't ye perform a Banishment?"

Holly looked, bewildered, at Almaric and then at Ranulf. "Well . . . I . . . To banish *what*?"

"Nae *what*," said the little man darkly. "*Who.*" He narrowed his eyes at her. "Do ye not ken my meaning, lass?"

Holly shrugged. "You mean the king? He's the one who—"

"Faugh on this king!" spat Bittenbender. "Enough brawn and he'd be done for! We all ken who the real problem is. And my question to the lady is, would she be willin' to help us with *him*?"

"I'm sorry," Holly said, her breath constricting in her throat. What could be a bigger problem than the tyrant king? "I don't know who you're talking about."

"Raethius," said the little man. "Raethius of the Source."

The forest fell silent, as if a heavy, dark blanket had fallen over them all. Every face looked away, most at the ground, some fearfully at the skies. The stags huddled closer to one another, and the centaur called Hoofstone glanced at his mate, his chest heaving as if he'd come in from a long gallop. Jade's green eyes went cold.

"Aye," said the Dvergar in a low, brittle voice. "So ye've been told only half the tale, of our wicked mortal who slaughtered the magicfolk and exiled the Adepts.

Well, now." He brought his ax down and held it in his two hands, running one thumb over the curving blade. "How d'ye suppose *that* were possible, eh? He's naught but a man, an't he? But who d'ye think it was what snatched him as a babe from his cradle in the castle? A being come from the Gloamlands, may be, or somewheres else altogether, who kenned magic beyond the Adepts, beyond all of us! And he hid that bairn with his enchantments, raised him up in the ways of darkness, and returned him to us, his sorcerer's foot still on his neck. Reynard." Bittenbender snorted, throwing his ax into the earth, where it stuck fast. "Wot's he but a lot of bluster? Raethius of the Source holds this kingdom by the throat, Lady! It's *him* what keeps us all in chains, and the king besides! No one here'll deny that."

Holly felt like someone had scooped out her insides, leaving her heart to flutter helplessly alone inside her body. "But . . . But I don't know what you think I could do about someone like that." Holly paused as the truth began to sink in. Why hadn't Almaric and Ranulf told her about this sorcerer? A king was one thing, but . . . "I don't know that kind of magic," she said in a small voice.

"As I thought!" crowed Bittenbender to the others. "We're to help her storm the castle, take on Reynard's guards, open ourself to the slaughter, but what's she doin' for us, eh?"

All the creatures began speaking at once, some quite loudly. Those with hooves began to stamp and scuffle the ground until it shook; Almaric tried to reason with them, dodging the stags' antlers; Jade argued with Bittenbender, who waved his ax in the air, crying, "Banishment! A pledge is a pledge!" Glancing around the darkening clearing, Holly saw that some of the creatures had already disappeared into the wood. She would lose them all if she didn't do something. She pulled out the wand and held it above her head.

"Quiet!" she shouted.

The loud discussion eased, every eye on the wand.

"Look," said Holly, "I don't blame you guys for being upset. But we're wasting time. This king you all hate has my brother locked up somewhere in that castle, and I've got to get him out—and Everett, too. I don't know what do about the—the Sorcerer. I want to help you, but right now I have to think about my brother. I brought him and Everett to this place, and I need to get them out. And"—she glanced at Ranulf and shrugged—"if I have to do it by myself, then I guess I will."

At once everyone clamored to be heard again. Ranulf's voice rose above the rest. "Will you see our last hope, the only Adept left in the kingdom, go to her certain doom? Who of you will stand with us and defend her?"

A long, uncomfortable silence stretched out while the group glanced at one another. Bittenbender shouldered his ax and waved a thick forearm. Several of the creatures walked ahead of him, heads bent low, into the forest. Holly started to speak, but the little man pointed his blade at her and growled: "When ye're trained, when ye're ready, *then's* may be a time to talk. We'll be pledgin' our service when we get a pledge of our own." He stalked off into the woods after the others.

They were a sorry lot now. Only two stags, Hoofstone the centaur, and a few falcons remained. One minute she was their hero, she was making things appear out of the twilight, and the next they were turning on her. What good was magic if it didn't get her what she wanted?

Holly sighed, then blinked. The cat still stood in front of her; that was something, though she couldn't see what help he would be. She slipped the wand into her back pocket and looked at Ranulf. "I'm sorry," she said. "I should have managed to do something more amazing, I guess. Thanks, everybody. I know you're trying to help."

"Do not despair, Your Ladyship," Ranulf said, coming forward. "We are few, but I believe enough. We await still another who shall turn the tables to our favor."

Hoofstone spoke up. "Ranulf! Then Fleetwing will come?"

"Fleetwing?" said Holly. "Who's that?"

"Hark!" cried the centaur. "He is here!"

All eyes turned to the sky, and Holly's glance followed. She could hear the beating of a huge pair of wings, but she could see nothing. And then, at her feet, the ground shook. The other creatures scattered. Then suddenly, right in front of her, a figure solidified.

It was Holly's turn to step back toward Almaric's cottage. The thing approaching her looked like an enormous black panther. Its paws were like manhole covers, and the shoulders towered over the centaur's. It had no mane, only sleek, black fur and a long, tapered head like an otter's. Extending from its dark shoulders, an enormous pair of batlike wings spread and flapped, making a breeze.

"Almaric, what is that?" Holly whispered.

"Fleetwing is a leogryff, and Your Ladyship's best hope of rescuing your kinsman." Almaric scooted behind her. "Show no fear, my lady."

Holly willed her voice to be steady. She looked up at the centaur. "Is Fleetwing . . . Is he yours, Ranulf?"

CLAIRE M. CATERER

A gasp whispered through the group, and the leo-gryff threw back its head and screamed like a hawk (if the hawk were the size of a small elephant). It strode toward her. "I belong to neither beast nor man," it cried in a windswept voice, fixing one of its fathom-less black eyes on Holly. When the leogryff was close enough to tickle her ear with its hot breath, it whis-pered, "I belong only to the sky . . . *human*."

It took all Holly's courage to gaze into the leogryff's eye. *Almaric's right; I have to be strong.* "I'm . . . I'm sorry if I was rude," she said. "I'm a stranger here."

The leogryff raised its great head from her shoul-der. "So we are told—an Adept from a faraway land."

"You have to help me," Holly blurted. "It's my brother, at the castle. I don't know what the prince might be doing to him, and I have to get him out of there. Please."

Almaric and Ranulf exchanged an alarmed look. "My lady," Almaric whispered, "you must *ease* into an agreement with Fleetwing, he isn't the type to—"

The leogryff bounded into the air, its great wings spreading out thirty feet or more. It circled the clear-ing and roared like a lion, ending in the long, lonely cry it had made before. The other creatures stampeded back to the safety of the trees; even Jade backed up to Holly's legs. "Show him your strength," Almaric whis-pered.

Holly rooted her feet into the ground. Above her head, the leogryff swooped above the trees, dove toward the ground, and grazed Holly's shoulder with his powerful tail. She flinched, breathing hard. *Don't move, don't move, don't move.* One hand strayed to the wand in her pocket, reminding her of the way Ranulf grasped the hilt of his sword in its scabbard. The leogryff's claws brushed the top of her head as it screamed and shot back into the sky. At last the creature landed lightly before her.

"The Lady Adept is fearless," said the leogryff, inclining his head. "I have watched and listened to this counsel this past hour, cloaked in the night sky."

It was an uncomfortable thought. Holly hoped no one else could hear her heart rattling inside her rib cage. "I . . . I *want* to help," she said, remembering Bittenbender. Fleetwing was clearly the strongest creature she had seen, and she would need him. "With the . . . the Sorcerer, I mean." She tried to look the leogryff in the eye, which was as broad as her forehead.

"Ye know naught of what ye speak," said the creature, hissing.

"No, I know that, but maybe I could learn." Learn what, though? She couldn't take on that Sorcerer, but maybe if she got quite good with the wand . . .

The great black eye narrowed, gazing into hers,

gauging her sincerity. "You speak truth, Lady. You would come to our aid." The leogryff's glance swiveled to Ranulf. "The skies tell of it?"

The centaur nodded. "They do."

Fleetwing raised his head, as if catching a scent on the wind. "I pledge my service now," he said, "and expect more of this Adept in times to come."

Holly bowed in response. She didn't know what he meant, exactly, or what Ranulf had meant either. They made her a bit nervous, as if she'd promised something without quite realizing it. But there was only one way to breach a castle wall, and that was with a beast like this. "Thank you, Fleetwing," she said.

Almaric beamed and sighed with relief. "Well now, isn't that wonderful . . . Of course we knew Fleetwing would help. Very good. Now, Ranulf, what do you suggest?"

The centaur drew his sword and swept it over the grass. Holly jumped back as sparks flew from it and it sheared the grass like a lawn mower. "My sword, Claeve-Bryna, has never failed me in battle before. She shall not fail me this night. Do not fear, my lady. We shall likely find the lads stowed in the North Tower, where others of us have been taken. We are fortunate in that: the prison is far from the gatehouse, and so tall that the castle guards do not expect it to be breached."

He glanced up as if the tower had sprouted in the wood before them.

"How tall is it, exactly?" asked Holly, who had been thinking the boys would be in a lower dungeon somewhere.

"Twice the height of Almaric's Elm, at the least," said Hoofstone. Holly gulped; the Elm stretched fifty feet or more into the sky.

Almaric gave her a tremulous smile. He patted her shoulder and cast a sneaking glance at Fleetwing. "Not to worry, my lady. Such a tower is no match for a leogryff."

Chapter 17

Flight

It was only a few minutes later that Holly watched as the stag and centaurs galloped away with a rallying cry, Ranulf holding the weapon he called Claeve-Bryna high over his head. The falcons disappeared ahead of them into the gathering dusk. Holly stood with Almaric, Jade, and Fleetwing for a few moments in an awkward silence. Ranulf had explained his plan to rescue the boys, and while Holly had felt quite brave in demanding help from the Exiles, suddenly the whole project looked impossible. And this was the worst part: waiting. Ranulf had pointed to the moon, near full above the cottage, and instructed her to stay put until it cleared the treetops.

Almaric wrung his hands nervously for a few moments, then gave a little jump as if remembering something. "But of course! Your Ladyship must be armed. One moment," he said, dashing back into his cottage.

"But—" Holly called after him. "What for?"

The leogryff glanced at her and paced the clearing, flapping his leathery wings.

The magician returned with a longbow and a quiver of arrows. "These should do, Lady Holly."

Was he expecting her to shoot something? She picked up the bow, which was made of a smooth yellow wood anchored by a leather grip in the center. It was taller than Holly by a foot or more, and the quiver, a leather bag with straps to go across her back, was heavy and loaded with long, straight, barbed arrows. These weren't toys; they were meant to kill. Her stomach felt weak. She had tried archery exactly once, in Girl Scouts. It hadn't gone well.

Almaric helped her take off her backpack, which he laid on the grass, and then looped the quiver of arrows over Holly's shoulder. Quickly he strung the bow and handed it to her.

Holly nocked an arrow and squinted at one of the trees that framed Almaric's cottage. She pinched the bowstring between her fingers. "Not that way, my lady," said Almaric, adding with a blush, "if you'll beg pardon." He stood behind her and half wrapped her fingers around the string as if she were playing the harp. "Now draw straight back, along the jaw . . . Good . . . And loose!" The tight string thrummed forward and the barbed arrow whizzed through the air before sticking in the clump of English ivy that climbed the jamb of Almaric's front door.

"A bit low," the old man said, shrugging.

"And a bit wide," added the cat, who was washing his face nearby.

By about three feet, in fact. Holly frowned at Jade, her spine tingling in a cold sweat. "Almaric," she said, "I don't know if I—I mean, I'm not going to be hurting anyone, am I?"

The old man gave her a blank look. "But why else bring weapons, my lady?"

Holly swallowed. She had never shot anyone—any*thing*, not even a target—before.

Jade gave her a shrewd look. "'Tis wise to be armed, Your Ladyship. The castle wall is sheer, and there is naught to land on save the battlements above. A leogryff is not a hummingbird, like to hover at a window."

This was the part of Ranulf's plan that made Holly feel as if her stomach were climbing up through her throat. The ground shook as the leogryff paced restlessly back and forth. Almaric was right: There was only one who could breach the castle walls, and only one who could reach the top of the North Tower. But Fleetwing wouldn't fly alone.

"Wait," said Holly. "Do you mean we're landing on *top* of the castle?"

Jade shrugged. "The upper chamber of the tower is but twenty feet below."

"Oh, is *that* all?"

"Now, now, my lady," said the magician, patting her shoulder. "We simply have to find a way to hoist the lads up to the battlements, and all shall be well."

The cat smirked.

"Wait! Almaric, do you have some rope?"

"A good quantity, Lady Holly. One moment." He dashed back into the cottage and returned bearing a heavy coil of rope.

Holly studied it a minute, trying to remember what her survival guide had told her about makeshift harnesses. She looped the rope around her waist, around her seat, and between her legs, tying two half-hitch knots and one square knot. "See?" she said to the others. "I can rappel from the top of the castle wall and pull the boys out one at a time." She hesitated, picturing Ben on her back, flailing and probably screaming. "I mean, it *could* work."

"An admirable tool," the cat admitted as Holly yanked on the harness. "Her Ladyship is fit to use it?"

"I've done five-point-two-level climbs at the Monster Rockwall," Holly said. "That is . . . I mean, I'm pretty good." She had no helmet and no carabiner, but that couldn't be helped. "See, I'll just sort of sit in the rope seat here and walk down the wall, and the other end will have to be attached . . . I don't know . . ."

"To me."

The three of them jumped, startled to find Fleetwing's black whiskers only inches from Holly's ear, peering at the climbing rope.

"Um . . . yeah." Holly pictured struggling down a sheer wall with no belay, attached to a leogryff. She knelt beside Fleetwing and took a breath. His panther paws, which ended in curved talons, were nearly a yard across. She threaded the rope across the palm of one paw, as if helping the creature to make a cat's cradle. Once it was knotted securely, the great beast flexed its foot, testing its strength.

Fleetwing nudged Holly's shoulder. "The moon, my lady," he whispered, giving a soft cry.

Holly looked up and saw that the moon had passed over the elm tree as Ranulf had predicted. "Right. We need to go. Almaric . . ."

"The blessing of Lunetia be upon you, Lady Holly." He bowed to her, oddly formal.

"The blessing of what?"

"Make haste!" cried Fleetwing. He crouched so Holly could climb on his back, and Jade jumped up in front of her, right behind the creature's head. With a great bound, they were airborne.

In an instant Fleetwing had taken them above the trees, and Almaric and his cottage shrank below them. Holly felt as if her stomach had stayed behind with the old man. The night air was cold and windy, and she had a horrible feeling of emptiness around her, with nothing to cling to. At least during her wild ride on Ranulf's back, she'd been close to the ground; now, she was a couple of hundred feet up. She desperately wanted to close her eyes, but she would have to stay alert if she were actually to rescue Ben and Everett. Her head swam as they climbed. She gripped Fleetwing's flanks with her knees and dug her hands into the short fur at the base of his neck. His leathery wings beat with a horrible rhythm. They were getting higher, and she could see nothing but blackness.

Jade the cat kept his balance perfectly in front of her. He seemed to read her thoughts. "Take heart, Lady Holly," he said, the stiff wind blowing his words back to her ears. "Even the bravest of us fear something. Imagine you are safe."

She tried not to look down, tried not to think about the empty air around them, the ground so far below. Climbing was one thing: She controlled that, pulled with each hand, pushed with her toes, flexed her muscles, knowing they would propel her to the top of the wall. But with each dive and swoop that Fleetwing made, Holly felt smaller, like a leaf blown on the wind.

She took a deep, full breath. The cold air stung her throat. *I'm safe, I'm safe, I'm safe,* she thought. *I'm in my own bed at home.* The beat of the leogryff's wings was steady. They would hold her aloft. "Okay," she whispered, even as a line of cold sweat trickled down her back. "I can do this."

"In a few moments you will see the castle," said Jade. "Together we shall rescue your kinsman, and all will be well."

The cat's reassurance surprised Holly. He glanced back at her. "'Tis an honor to be an Adept's familiar, my lady, however untrained she may be. It has been too long since I had the privilege. Henceforth am I bound to you by choice and oath."

Holly swallowed. So Jade *did* think she was an Adept. He had stood with her while most of the creatures had deserted her. And now she'd have to prove herself worthy. "Thank you, Jade."

"It is not an occasion for thanks. You have my loyalty unto death."

"I just hope that won't be coming too soon," Holly whispered.

Fleetwing took another steep dive and a sharp turn to the east. The castle loomed into view below them, gray against the black sky. Holly had never seen the night so dark, despite the moon.

"Look fast," Fleetwing whispered. "The North Tower."

The leogryff had flown to a back corner of the castle, hovering not far above a skinny, crenellated stone cylinder that extended higher than any of the other turrets. The castle was massive and complicated, with several shorter towers, some topped with what looked like steel dunce caps, others ringed with battlements. Short stone staircases and walkways linked them together. Below the castle, a wide moat shone silver in the moonlight.

"I don't see the others," Holly whispered.

"The drawbridge is on the east side of the castle," said Fleetwing. "They will divert the guards there."

"But what if they need help?"

"'Tis they who must help *you*, Your Ladyship," Jade reminded her.

The castle looked deserted. It seemed too easy.

But then the noise erupted below them. A clash of steel followed a great roar, then, frightened shouts and urgent footsteps. The battle had begun. "Time grows short!" Fleetwing cried to her. "Arrow on the string!"

Holly clenched one fist around a handful of the

leogryff's sleek fur and reached behind to pull an arrow from the quiver. Her palms were damp, and to make matters worse, Fleetwing dove just as she nocked the arrow to the longbow. She lurched forward and the arrow fell useless to the ground.

One lost! A real Adept could probably shoot in a thunderstorm with a dozen knights at her back, and Holly couldn't even fit an arrow to the string. She reached for a second and gasped. She'd stabbed her own palm with it; she could already feel the blood spilling down her wrist. *Never mind that, keep going,* she told herself. She yanked the arrow from the quiver and fitted it to the string, wincing as she flexed her wounded palm. She held the bow to her shoulder, sighting for a target along her left wrist.

Below, two archers were already running along the battlements toward the North Tower.

"They have seen us!" Jade shouted, and Holly released the bowstring.

It was a miserable attempt. She'd shot on instinct, without aiming well, and the missile flew well to the west of the tower. *At least I didn't hurt anyone,* she thought, and then, *But wasn't that the point?* She pulled another arrow from the quiver.

Now aiming was even more difficult. Fleetwing was climbing and diving from side to side, trying to create a hard-to-hit target. Though the archers hid behind the battlements, they were unprotected from above, so the leogryff climbed higher and wheeled to give Holly room to shoot. She aimed the longbow down, but it was an awkward stance, and the archers were hard to see in the darkness. "Hold still a moment!" she yelled at Fleetwing, and then took her best aim.

This arrow was more true; Holly heard it clatter on the stone. At once, she seized another. But before she could aim, a *whoosh* near her right ear gave her a nasty shock. The men on the tower were shooting back, and they were better archers than she.

"A direct fight it must be," the leogryff cried, and took a steep dive.

Holly's stomach lurched as they dropped to the tower. Fleetwing curled his paw into a fist and knocked one archer down. The other gaped at the creature and wheeled at once. He scampered along the battlements to the next tower and down into the depths of the castle.

"Quick! To your plan!" Jade shouted above the wind.

It didn't seem so brilliant now that Holly was standing on top of the tower. She snuck a peek below. The lawn shone silver as the moon slipped in and out of the clouds. She remembered her last climb at the Monster Rockwall, thirty-five feet up, her dad holding the belay below her. Now the ground, swallowed in the inky night, was three times as far down. Holly ran a hand over the crenellations. The stone was rough, but she could see no footholds.

Fleetwing held the line taut as Holly backed down between two crenellations at a steep angle. She gripped the rope, her palms burning. Below, she heard shouts and roars from the unseen battle on the other side of the castle. *Don't think about it. I have to take my time.* The rope of her makeshift harness pulled and burned against her thighs and the breeze whipped through her hair. She missed her helmet.

One foot out. Then the other. The rope shuddered as Fleetwing fed it out. How far down to the window? It seemed forever.

"Ben, look! It's Holly!" someone yelled.

She chanced a look down.

A small, white face appeared at the window, not ten feet below her. And then, next to it, an even smaller, whiter face, and Holly nearly burst into tears. Ben was all right. They both were.

"Hang on! I'm going to pull you up!"

Ben's skinny arms poked out the window like a baby who wants to be picked up. Just a few more inches and she would be inside the tower.

She was nearly even with the window when it

happened. A sudden tugging at her waist shook her loose from the castle wall. Then she heard them: "Archers to the North Tower! To the tower!"

Holly swayed away from the wall. "No, wait! I've almost got him!" she cried, but then she came crashing back to the wall, dangling at the end of the rope.

"Holly!" Ben yelled.

The harness pulled against her thighs. For an awful moment, she was splayed out like a fish on a line, and she heard a *thwump* and *zing* as an arrow flew past her ear. She gathered her limbs, hugging the rope. She swayed farther from the stone wall.

Ben screamed.

"Fleetwing! Pull me back!"

She strained her neck upward and at once understood the problem.

More archers had gained the tower. The leogryff hovered just above them, striking out with his free paw and occasionally with the one tied to Holly. As he swooped, he bore Holly farther and farther from the castle. "Cut the rope!" one knight hollered, and the leogryff pulled back toward the forest, Holly wrapped around the rope, praying the harness would hold.

"Leave her alone!" Ben's voice floated across the sky in between the archers' cries.

Arrows flew through the sky, and Holly swayed

and swung as the leogryff dodged them. She reached behind her, straining to reach one of her own arrows, but they dove sideways and she nearly lost her grip on the rope. She wobbled, rocking back and forth, hugging the line, straining to see the leogryff's black body against the inky sky. The rope shone white beneath the moon as she swung back and forth like a giant pendulum. The leogryff dove, nearly clearing the outer castle wall.

But then Holly swung wide, dangling in the cold air. She heard the clean *thwump* of an arrow finding its mark, and Fleetwing let out a long, high cry. The rope went slack. Holly peered up and saw the leogryff bearing down on her, three arrows sunk deep into one shoulder. At once they plummeted together, spiraling, to the ground below.

Chapter 18

In the Tower

All that had happened down at the tower window, on the archers' battlement, and in the night sky had looked quite a bit different to Everett and Ben, trapped as they were in the king's North Tower.

The boys had dozed on and off since arriving in the tower that afternoon, but they were startled awake by shouts coming from the other end of the castle. The moon was up by then, and it was past nine o'clock by Ben's watch. Everett had seen it first, the great winged panther swooping through the sky, but once it landed on the tower he couldn't see anything until Holly started rappelling down the wall. Ben bounded to the window and very nearly fell out making a mad grab for her. But his sister and the flying beast were far out of his reach, and it was only Everett's firm hold on his waistband that kept him from hurtling to his death. He screamed her name as she dangled in midair, and then again as both beast and girl tumbled to the earth.

"They've shot her down! We have to help her!"

Everett yanked him back into the tower. "And just how, do you think? If you'd grabbed the rope when she'd been closer—"

"Like I could've climbed up that thing!"

"You could've done something besides scream!"

"I *didn't* scream! It was more like a holler—"

"That's what alerted the archers. That's why she got shot down."

Ben opened his mouth, but no sound came out. Instead his eyes brimmed over and he collapsed on the floor at the other end of the room.

It's very hard, when you've said something awful, to know how to make it right. Escape had nearly been in their grasp, and now Holly was probably dead, and Everett didn't know what to say, but even *sorry* seemed more than he could manage. He threw himself down against the opposite wall.

After a minute, he heard shouting below. He ran to the window and leaned out.

"What's going on?" Ben asked, sniffling. "Is it Holly?"

"I can't see properly. . . . Shut up a minute."

Ben joined him at the window, and the two of them hung out, straining their eyes through the dark.

They could hear angry voices, but nothing that told them whether Holly was all right. At length, the sounds faded around the corner of the tower, and the night was silent again.

"Maybe they found her," Ben said quietly.

"It can't be any good for her if they did."

After a moment Everett came away from the window. Awkwardly, he approached Ben, who had curled up on the floor into the smallest possible ball he could manage.

"Look, Ben, it wasn't your fault. They'd already seen her."

Ben refused to uncurl.

"I'm sure I heard them shouting before you said anything. Honestly."

Ben pulled his head from underneath one arm. His face was wet and blotchy. "So . . . she's either dead or captured."

"Maybe."

"They'll kill her! That one guy tried to in the forest."

"We don't know anything about it. Maybe not."

"And what about us? How long do you think we've got?"

Everett sat down next to him. It didn't look good for any of them.

"You know, this doesn't make sense," he said finally.

CLAIRE M. CATERER

"This castle . . . You know what it reminds me of?"

"A prison?"

"No. Well, yes. But also . . ." He raised his eyebrows. "Darton Castle. In Hawkesbury."

Ben sniffled and pulled the tissues out of his pocket again. "How could that be? Holly said we were in some different world, not back in time."

"What does she know about it? I know that castle inside and out. This is it."

Ben thought a minute. "Okay, even if it does look like it, was there a prince and stuff back then? And weird flying things as big as horses?"

"Maybe not. But I know where we are. I've even been in this tower before." Everett stood up and walked around the small room, examining the masonry. "At Darton, there's an irregular stone in the northern tower, right near the window. . . . See? Here it is!"

Ben got up despite himself and peered at the wall. One of the stones jutted out the tiniest bit. "So you must know the secret passageways and stuff! Like you can open the wall by tapping three times on the rocks." Ben rapped his knuckles along the wall.

"Well, no," said Everett. "This tower's pretty secure."

"So how does that help us?"

"I don't know!" Everett said. "Give me some time to think about it, all right?"

Ben plopped down again and closed his eyes. "I wish Holly was here."

Everett gazed up at the moon, hoping to see the giant winged beast silhouetted against it. He'd seen pictures of gryphons and pegasuses in mythology books; this beast had to be something like those. How had Holly managed to find one? And who had rescued her in the forest? It had happened so quickly; he *thought* he'd seen a centaur. Maybe it was just a man on horseback. A man who was friends with a flying panther.

Ben was right. This place, however much it felt like home, was very different. Like England, like Darton Castle, but . . . not. And what about the rest of the world?

He had to give Holly credit. Somehow she'd found a way to rescue them—well, *try* to—only hours after their capture. It was that key of hers; it had to be. But then, he thought glumly, she didn't have it anymore. Lord Clement had seen to that.

Still, if Holly could stage a rescue, surely *he* could, knowing the castle as well as he did. He remembered a passageway between the curtain wall and the Great Hall. If he and Ben could somehow overpower a guard and make it as far as the passageway, they could shortcut to the courtyard . . .

And then what? How were they supposed to find Holly, if in fact she wasn't already dead? Everett sank down next to Ben, gazing out the window high above. Slowly the moon moved across the sky. Everett watched it until he fell asleep.

Chapter 19

The Audience

The last things Holly heard as she was hurtling to the earth were the horrible screeches and cries of Jade and Fleetwing as the ground rushed toward them. Fleetwing managed to keep his good wing spinning to slow their descent, but they hit hard. Holly passed out.

As a result, she didn't hear the shouting and stampeding; she didn't see Fleetwing vanish or Jade streak into the woods. And, as often happens, Holly came to before her eyes decided to open. What she heard was this:

"Whence did it go? We had it in our sights!"

"'Tis a beast in the service of the Adept. Of course it can vanish."

"We shall never find the familiar."

"And what of this maid?"

Quiet footsteps around her, in a circle.

"Run her through. 'Twould be the king's wish."

"Do you speak for the king now, Grandor?"

"Do you not recall the law, Loverian? Adepts are to be executed!"

Holly's eyes sprang open.

She was lying on the ground. Every muscle throbbed. Her thighs burned from straining against the rope harness, but the rope itself was gone. Her right elbow felt wobbly and when she tried to move, a bolt of pain shot through it. She was sure it was broken.

Three men stood over her, dressed in knee-length tunics and vests made of iron rings. One of them had slung Almaric's longbow and quiver over his shoulder. Moonlight glinted off the swords pointed at her throat.

"I—" she began.

"Silence," advised one of them. He was young, hardly twenty, with long, curling dark hair and a stubbly beard. He glanced at one of the other knights as they circled Holly. "She is but a child, Grandor."

"And nearly killed the king's archer," sneered a shorter, more muscular knight. Holly guessed this was Grandor. "It seems she be old enough for the sword."

"Peace," said the third, older knight, whose eyes crinkled at the edges the way her father's did. "Your thirst for blood is boundless."

"As befits a king's knight, Tullian." Grandor held the other knight's gaze so long, Holly wondered if she should try to break away. But then he stepped back. "On your own head be it, then."

Tullian withdrew his sword. "On your feet, lass."

Holly glanced around, but Fleetwing and the others had deserted her. She struggled to her feet, her knees wobbly. As soon as she stood up, Grandor snatched her by the broken arm. A shock of pain tore through her shoulder and she cried out. Bright spots danced in front of her eyes.

"Art a brute?" Loverian pushed Grandor out of the way. He steadied Holly, his arm around her shoulder. "Come, lass, 'tisn't far."

"She would not be hurt had she not attacked the castle," Grandor muttered.

The four of them trudged along the dark side of the castle below the tower. Holly glanced up, hoping to see Fleetwing circling, but all she saw was the mist-covered moon. Even the window where she had seen the boys was dark.

It was like being caught cheating on a very important test and having not one but three of the less friendly teachers prod you along to the principal's office, except that Holly felt about ten times worse. And she could hardly help but mentally replay all her mistakes. Holly thought she should have practiced more with the longbow before they left for the castle;

she shouldn't have panicked and sent arrows flying wildly; she should have clambered down the wall more quickly. She should have done *better*, period. She'd managed to live through it, but Ben and Everett were as good as dead.

Adding to this misery was the fact that her torso was bruised and her palms scraped; her thighs ached; her right elbow was purple and puffy. All things considered, she might be excused for the few tears that stung her eyes.

Then suddenly Grandor, whose sword was pressed flat against Holly's shoulder, seized something from her back pocket. "Aye, now *this* shall interest the king indeed!"

"There be the lass's wand, by the king's beard," said Tullian in a hushed voice.

"Mayhap the king will allow me to keep it as a token of my catch."

"His Majesty will need to see it first," Tullian said sharply.

"I say no different."

At these words, their small group came in sight of the enormous arched doors to the castle. This was the gatehouse, and beyond it stretched the drawbridge that Ranulf and the others must have tried to breach.

Four knights now stood at either side of the

gatehouse, still on high alert, with swords drawn. "Halt, in the king's name!" one shouted.

"Peace, Gervase. 'Tis I, Tullian, with Grandor and Loverian. We have the Adept as our prisoner. How fared you at the gatehouse?"

"They swam under stealth of night, as merfolk," said the other knight, who was the young Pagett. "Two of the man-horses, and stags as well. 'Twasn't until they burst onto the bridge that we engaged."

"We surprised them by our number," said a third, shorter guard. "By chance Gervase and Pagett had but just arrived to relieve Gregory and myself."

"Then how is it we see no leavings of the battle, Bryce?" Grandor asked.

The young guard reddened, and the one called Gregory said, "We slew none. Their falcons flew at our eyes—it was near impossible to see—"

Holly's heart lightened a little. Ranulf and the others were all right!

"They did not essay to breach the castle," Gervase explained. "They were only the four—"

"And the falcons!" Gregory added.

"Aye, and the falcons. By the time the archers were alerted, they had fled, cowards all, leaving their lady to the king's mercy. We did not give chase—we had the castle to defend."

Holly hadn't thought of that. Couldn't they have stayed? Hadn't they seen Fleetwing fall? And what about him, and Jade?

"His Highness has been told?" Tullian was saying.

"Aye, my lord, but 'twas finished in such short order, it hardly put pause to the feasting. His Highness is within, at the Great Hall."

"Ye have done well, Sir Gervase," said Tullian. "The castle is not breached, and the prisoners are fast in the North Tower."

"And this fine trophy be ours." Grandor shoved Holly ahead with his sword hilt.

They led her through a wide moonlit courtyard to a massive octagonal tower, connected through a passageway to the interior castle. Inside, they walked up three or four stairs and found themselves at one end of the Great Hall.

It looked like a cathedral, with its arched timbered ceiling and long, stained-glass windows. Someone was playing a lute. Although four long tables steamed with platters of roasted meat and tureens of soup, the large crowd of people were not seated, but standing in clusters, talking and whispering, gesturing excitedly. Everyone was dressed splendidly, the men in embroidered tunics with puffed sleeves, the women in long gowns and complicated headdresses. At the far end, on the dais, Holly could see the prince, who looked much more relaxed than anyone else. Holly couldn't help staring; the party looked very much like the one she had seen in Darton Castle only the day before. In fact—she gulped—the prince looked *exactly* like the blond boy she'd seen at Darton. No wonder he had looked so familiar to her in the wood. The whole scene looked familiar, actually—except, of course, Ben wasn't sitting at the high table.

At their approach, the lute music stopped. The room fell into awed whispers as the knights prodded Holly closer to the dais at the far end of the hall. The people pulled away from her, crowding against the walls; the men's hands clasped the hilts of their swords, and the ladies clustered near to them, hiding their eyes. Holly heard mutterings like "But she's just a child" and "*She's* the Adept?" and "Such strange garments she wears." But none would look her in the eye.

"Sir Tullian!" boomed a voice from the high table. "What have your knights brought us this evening?"

"If it please Your Highness, this is the lass captured in the outer bailey. She fell from the sky."

Holly took a deep breath. Maybe she still had a chance to help the boys. The prince smiled and strutted off the dais with a sneer on his face. His guests gasped as he approached Holly, but he silenced them with a wave of his hand. She spied Lord Clement, sitting at the high table with a piece of bread poised near his mouth.

"His Royal Highness, Prince Avery," Tullian said to Holly.

She got a better look at the prince now than she'd had in the forest. He was thirteen, Ranulf had said, though not much taller than she. His blond hair curled near his collar, and his eyes were a deep blue. She didn't pay much attention to boys, but this one might have piqued her interest if he didn't have the look of someone very rich who looked down on everyone who wasn't. He had changed from his hunting clothes into a short royal blue tunic, embroidered in gold. A scabbard was slung casually around his waist.

Loverian nudged her. "Bow, lass, if you value your life."

Holly bent from the waist. The prince snorted at her, but the arrogant smile faded when she raised her eyes to his and shrugged. "We don't have princes where I come from," she said.

"Is that so?" he said. "Nor proper attire?"

Holly didn't know what to say to this.

The prince circled her as if thinking of buying her at auction. "Fascinating," he muttered. "Where is thy wand?"

"If it please Your Highness." Grandor drew it from his belt and held it out to the prince. The huddled crowd muttered, craning their necks to see.

Holly saw the glint in Avery's eyes as he twirled it, observing the torchlight playing over the facets of the crystal. He glanced sharply at Holly. "Whence camest by this, Adept?"

"My name is Holly."

A small gasp traveled the room. She had not used a tone her mother would be proud of.

"I think you are called the *Lady* Holly, am I right?" the prince asked.

"If you say so."

"She has a sharp tongue, Your Highness," Grandor snarled. "Might I not dull it?"

"Peace, Grandor. Go and find a rabbit to frighten if needs must."

The knight's face darkened to a purplish color as he sheathed the sword.

"She is injured?" The prince glanced at Loverian.

"Aye, Your Highness."

"In the fall from the sky." The prince raised an eyebrow. "Why not fly away now, Your Ladyship? These good knights could not follow you to the heavens, I'll warrant."

Holly swallowed. "I—I can't fly by myself."

"'Twas a flying beast, sire," Loverian offered. "A leo-gryff, the myths call it."

Avery snorted. "A flying beast! Man-horses! Wands and magic! Enough of this nonsense. Ye knights may be prisoner to such tales, but not I. She has powers, but cannot escape? Canst not vanish before our eyes, *Lady* Adept? Show us!"

The prince thrust the wand at her, and another low cry circled the room. Holly's resolve faltered. "I . . . I just want to take my brother and our friend and go home." Her throat thickened, closing up.

"As I thought." Avery snatched back the wand. "My Lord Clement would have had thy head earlier today. So be it. Suffer the same fate as thy kinsman, if thou wouldst have it so. All three, for the sword, at daybreak."

"No, please!" cried Holly. "We haven't done anything wrong!"

"Your Highness!" gasped Loverian. "Would not His Majesty wish to question her when he returns? Lord Raethius has said we must hold any Adept we might find. Or mayhap Her Majesty—"

"Lord Raethius," the prince broke in, "has been traveling since Beltane and will not return until long past Midsummer. As for my mother, she begs our royal pardon as she is indisposed this evening." The prince drew himself up to his full height—not nearly as tall as Loverian—and looked him in the eye. "Well, sir knight? Hast further instructions for our royal court?"

Loverian's face turned scarlet. "Nay, Your Highness."

Grandor tried to pull Holly away, but she broke free. The prince had already turned back toward the high table.

"Please, Your Highness! You can't kill Ben! He didn't steal anything, I swear! We were lost, we were trying to find our way out of the woods! He's just a kid!"

Avery waved his hand behind his head, not looking back. Grandor tugged at her again.

Holly turned to Loverian. "You've got to help me! You can have anything you want—I can even show you, in the woods, where we came from—you don't understand . . ."

What Holly actually meant was that she herself was only beginning to understand. From the moment she had arrived, everything had happened very quickly, but she had been free to do as she wished. Now she was a prisoner too. All the faith that Almaric and the others had placed in her meant nothing. Without the wand, she was surely no Adept, and they would never help her now, even if she could escape. The prince had the wand, the only thing that could get her and the boys back home. "Your Highness, wait!" she called after the prince. "Just listen to me!"

CLAIRE M. CATERER

"What has happened to the music, lute player?" boomed the prince. "Stay the noise in this hall!"

At once, the music started again, and Holly was led out of the Great Hall.

She had started to cry, and Loverian took her arm. "I shall take her to the tower," he said.

"Very well, Loverian," said Tullian, as the other knight glared at him. "Sir Grandor, I need your assistance with another matter."

Grandor shoved Holly away. "Mind Her *Ladyship* doesn't vanish from your grasp."

Loverian waited until the other two disappeared into the courtyard. He took Holly up a narrow staircase on the right side.

"I don't want to get you in trouble," Holly said, choking back tears.

The knight fumbled in his tunic and pulled out a silk scarf. He tied it into a sling and cradled her right arm in it.

"It's just that we really didn't do anything, and I—"

"You wounded the king's archer," said Loverian shortly.

"Well, okay, I did do that. But I was only trying to save Ben and Everett. You don't understand—I wasn't trying to hurt anyone with the wand. If there's anything you could do to help us—"

They had reached a small landing next to a mullioned window. Loverian stopped and turned to her. "My lady, 'tis my sacred duty to serve my king."

"But . . . but it's wrong."

"I regret that you find yourself in these circumstances. But the prince has decreed your death."

"But if any of you would just listen for a *minute*—"

"Sir Loverian!"

A boy about Ben's age came bounding up the stairs behind them.

"I am occupied, Dart, what is it?"

"The prisoner, my lord. Her Majesty says to take her to the western chamber." The boy gaped at Holly, scanning her blue jeans and T-shirt.

"Not the tower?" asked Loverian.

"Nay, my lord, Her Majesty was very clear. *Not* the tower, but the western chamber."

"Very well. Come." Loverian led Holly back down the steps, the page just ahead of them.

"Mayn't I help, my lord? I have no sword, but . . ." The boy drew a small dagger, which he brandished at Holly's face.

"Away to your duties at once," Loverian said, frowning at him.

"Aye, my lord." The boy scampered off, chancing a glance back.

"I cannot think why Her Majesty wants you enclosed in the western chamber," Loverian muttered.

"Is that bad?" Holly looked back up the tower steps. She had hoped she would be imprisoned with the boys, that they could figure out some plan together, but the knight descended the staircase without answering her.

When they reached the landing, Loverian led her down a wide corridor, open on one side to another courtyard.

Holly wasn't a girl to go on crying when it wouldn't do any good. She fell silent, afraid of making the knight angry. He seemed to like her; why wouldn't he help her?

"The prince . . ." Holly began. "He doesn't believe in magic, does he?"

"The prince fears magic. He feigns disbelief. He has been taught to do so."

"Taught by who?"

"Everyone. 'Tis the king's wish that his son knows naught of the Other World."

"But he must know that the Adepts were exiled, and that some of those—other creatures are still around." Holly was careful not to say too much. Even if Ranulf and the others had deserted her, she didn't want them hunted.

"Naught but legend feeds his knowledge. Thus 'tis not very accurate. He considers you a fanciful magician, nothing more."

"But I know *you* believe me, Loverian. That I came from a different place—a different world."

"My lady." He stopped a moment and held her at arm's length. "Do you know why it be unwise to give names to the hogs in the sty?"

"The . . . What?"

"Because the hog will be slaughtered, and your heart grieve for what was named."

"I . . . Okay."

"I am the king's knight," Loverian said. "And you are his condemned."

"Oh. I get it." Holly swallowed hard as Loverian prodded her forward. She was doomed, and he didn't want to make a friend of someone he was sworn to execute.

CLAIRE M. CATERER

Chapter 20

A Nighttime Visitor

It was about this same time, as Holly was being led to the western chamber and facing the grim prospect of a morning execution, that a loud clatter startled Everett, waking him after a brief sleep. Ben gasped beside him. "What? What?"

At the far end of the tower was a floating, golden light. Ben scooted closer to Everett. The light drifted toward them. "Who's there?" Everett called, trying to sound bold.

"Just me." The light danced lower, and Everett saw it was a boy holding a lantern below his face. He was perhaps ten years old, dressed in a colorless tunic, his feet bare. In his other hand he held a dagger.

"Well?" Everett said, standing up. "What do you want?"

The boy's voice came out in a squeak. "I answer not to you."

"Fine, then. Don't."

Ben eyed the dagger. "Don't make him mad, Everett."

"Why not? He can't do anything to us. Did you bring us something to eat?"

"I . . . Look here, I mean to see ye are held fast. And . . . aye. Leavings from the feast."

Everett peered at the floor and saw the platter the boy had dropped there. That was the noise that had wakened them. "What is it?"

"Ye shall be glad enough of it, no matter what it be."

Everett sat down again near the platter. "I guess that's true enough. Come on, Ben, tuck in." He was glad of the poor light, because he was able to feign looking indifferent, when in truth even a scrawny boy was frightening enough when holding a dagger.

He picked over the platter. A hard, flat piece of bread was covered with dried gravy, and the bits of roast pork looked like they'd been chewed on.

"I can't eat that," said Ben, gagging. "Isn't there anything else?"

"No," Everett said, "so quit whinging about it." The food on the platter turned his stomach too, but neither of them had eaten for several hours, so Everett gave half the bread to Ben and scooped up some limp greens with the other half. The page stared at them.

"Did you want some? There's plenty," Everett said.

"There's not *that* much," Ben muttered.

"My thanks." The boy set the lantern near the platter,

so that it was almost like sitting around a campfire. He picked up a piece of meat, and shrugged under Ben's scowl. "This *was* to be my supper. Sir Grandor said it was foolish to feed doomed men. I only wished . . ."

"To see what we were like," Everett suggested.

"'Twas all the talk at the feast: the prisoners, their strange garb, the Adept. Be ye truly poachers, then? Brave on the king's land?"

"No, we aren't. Look here, I'm Everett, and this is Ben. What's your name again?"

"I am called Darton. Dart, that is. And I shall be a squire soon. Sir Loverian has promised, at the tournament."

Darton . . . Like the castle in Hawkesbury? Everett's mind spun a little thinking about it. "Right. okay. Anyway, we came from . . . I don't know, exactly. Another time, I think."

"Another *time*?"

"Like in a machine," Ben said. "You know, like if you could go back to, I don't know, Caesar's time or something."

"He's not exactly read sci-fi, Ben."

"Okay, so you explain it."

It wasn't that easy. "Right, then. Well, just as you're in England, we came from—"

"I be in the king's castle."

"Yes, right, but the castle's in England, and we—"

"This castle is in Anglielle," said Dart.

Everett stopped chewing. "What? It's where?"

"Holly was right," said Ben. "This isn't England at all."

"Don't you think I know my own village?" Everett said.

"The king's realm is called Anglielle," Dart said, setting his chin. "It extends to the sea on every side, even unto the Gloamlands."

But it *was* England, Everett's mind told him stubbornly, circling the same thoughts as before. Some things were different, he supposed—the roads weren't built and the forest was overgrown—but the castle and the valley looked as they always had. Even the grass in the courtyard seemed familiar. Of course, there was the business about the flying lion thing. *That* was different.

"So you live on a big island," Everett said.

Dart shrugged. "'Tis a vast land, but there be open sea, I am told, within a few days' ride."

"And what about the rest of the world? You know, beyond the sea? Your king doesn't rule all that bit, does he?"

"He may as well," said Dart loftily. "My father has told of a mighty battle with lands off the southern coast, but that was many a year past. A great pestilence has since swept that land, and we do not dare cross the water for fear of it."

Maybe it's like the European continent, Everett was thinking with some excitement. *Everything's here, just . . . different.* "Tell me about the king," he said.

The page sat up, as if the king were a personal friend. "King Reynard, may he reign forever. He has ruled near forty year."

"I never heard of a King Reynard," Ben put in.

"Nor me," said Everett.

"And who's that prince guy?" asked Ben.

"His Royal Highness Prince Avery. And of course Queen Elianne rules at the king's side."

"Are they any good? As rulers, I mean?"

"Ben!" Everett elbowed him.

"What? It's a fair question."

Dart clenched his jaw. "The king and queen be the finest rulers Anglielle has ever known. But then ye be thieves and poachers, how could ye agree?"

"We're *not* poachers. We just don't know this place," said Ben.

"But the king's realm is all there is. Once, there existed all manner of horrid creatures, great flying beasts and demons, and the greatest of all evils, the Adepts—"

"Yes," Everett said. "The Adepts. Tell us about them."

Darton's face glowed in the lantern light. "They are

a race unto themselves, powerful sorcerers who once lived in the western cliffs."

"So they're not human? I mean, like regular people?" asked Ben.

"They appear as we do, but how can they be? 'Tis said they charmed the beasts of earth, sky, and water, and could command the very trees to do their bidding. 'Twas a terrible time. Some call it the Veiled Times; others, the Eternal Night. Wherever the Adepts traveled, they spread mayhem and despair, wielding their wands like swords. Then at last King Reynard took the throne and exiled them. From that day forward, peace has reigned over Anglielle. His Majesty is our savior."

The prince's companion in the forest had called Holly that—an Adept. Everett glanced at Ben, who looked confused. Clearly, he didn't remember what Lord Clement had said.

"So there aren't any of these Adepts left?" Everett said carefully.

"It was thought they had all been destroyed. But did ye not hear of the lass this day? In the wood? When . . ." The page, who had been chewing cheerfully on his food, suddenly went white. "Came ye with *her*, over the sea?"

"We came through a forest," said Ben. "By magic."

Everett kicked him. "Are you an idiot?"

But it was too late. Dart had scrambled to his feet. "'Tis truth, what was said," he whispered.

"Look, we didn't mean to trespass on anyone's land," said Everett. "We came here by accident."

"By magic! Ye came with the Adept!"

"She's my sister," Ben blurted. "What happened to her? Is she okay?"

"She has been captured," Dart said. "She is a traitor. All Adepts are."

"But Holly hasn't done anything wrong," said Ben. "She's not—one of those things—"

"His Highness the prince took her wand himself, at the feast. I saw it with mine own eyes. They say she came on a great flying beast. Ye be like her! Stay back!" Dart brandished his dagger.

"But what *happened* to her?" asked Ben.

Never taking his eyes off them, Dart backed up slowly, then reached behind and knocked frantically at the tower door. "What think ye?" he whispered. "She is an Adept. All Adepts are traitors to the realm." The door creaked open and he stepped halfway through. "What befalls a traitor? Even a stranger knows this. Death to the Adepts. Death by the sword."

A moment later the door slammed shut with a hollow boom that shook the tower walls, and the boys were left alone.

Chapter 21

Everett's Secret

Carrying a very big secret is not so different from carry-ing a large television set, or a backpack crammed with more schoolbooks than should be allowed. It makes you short-tempered. The bigger the secret is, and the longer you bear it, the more it weighs on your shoul-ders. Everett was carrying just such a secret, and so perhaps can be excused for snapping, "Shut it, will you!" when Ben began to cry.

"But Holly's *dead*!" Ben wailed.

"You don't know that. Just because Dart said it doesn't make it so. He's just a page."

"A what?"

Everett shrugged. "You know, like he runs errands and stuff. And I guess he's training to be a squire, which means eventually he'd be a knight—"

"I don't care."

"Ben, the point is, he's nobody. Even if he knew any-thing, what makes you think he'd tell us the truth?"

Ben sniffled. "Why did he keep calling her that—Adept?"

"It's got something to do with the wand. You saw how Dart acted. They're all terrified of magic. I hate to say it, but when Holly tried to rescue us, it linked her to us. Now they think *we're* magic too."

"But if the king kills all the Adepts, then she's already dead!"

"Or maybe she's still here in the castle. Maybe they'll bring her up here until morning, then execute us all together."

"Oh, great. At least we'll be *together*." Ben picked at the leavings on the platter.

"What I mean is, we'll have time to think up a plan. And we can all escape."

"Then where *is* she?"

Everett had no answer to this, and it made him irritable. "If you hadn't started blathering on about magic, I might've been able to make friends with Dart. I was trying to get some information. Now he won't come anywhere near us."

"Everything's my fault, isn't it?" Ben pulled his jacket toward him across the stone floor. Everett heard a clatter.

"Hang on, what's that?"

"Hey, I forgot I had this! I was using it on the plane."

Ben produced a handheld electronic Battleship game.

"Does it go?"

Ben pushed some buttons and the game emitted a few *beep boops*.

"Brilliant!"

"It's okay. I've been on Mom to get me one of those new Rigel GA handheld systems, but she won't cave till I'm twelve. But by then, the technology's gonna be that much better. I think Planeterra Five's already available for Rigel, and when it comes out in 3-D—"

"Never mind that. Don't you see? To these people, that game's just as much magic as Holly's wand."

"And how does that help? They're going to *kill* her."

"But they're also scared of her. Maybe we can scare them too. Use it as kind of a fake weapon or something."

"You mean one Battleship handheld against an army of knights with swords," Ben said.

Put like that, it didn't sound promising. Everett's secret knocked on his brain, asking to be let out. But he wasn't ready to share it yet, even seeing the naked fear on Ben's face. Maybe he wouldn't need to risk it. They might still be able to talk their way out of execution. But then there was Holly to think of. If she'd been taken somewhere else, how would they find her?

Everett slipped his hand into his jacket. Through

CLAIRE M. CATERER

the lining of the breast pocket he could feel a wand—
the wand that had once been a key.

Because of course once he had taken one of Mr.
Gallaway's keys, he hadn't let it out of his sight. In fact,
the day before—it seemed like forever ago now—he'd
gone to the wood himself. He had meant to wait for
Holly, and show her that he had a key too and ask her
how it worked, but he had been too eager, and there
had still been a good bit of daylight left after tea.

He'd found the clearing in the forest easily and
pulled the key out of his pocket. Again that trembly
feeling stirred in his heart, but he crushed his palm
against the iron until something swelled in his chest,
like he could take on anybody who crossed him. He
held it out in front of him as he'd seen Holly do, waiting. But although the key pulsed a couple of times in
its odd way—warm-cold, warm-cold—nothing else
happened. He circled the tree, peering at it, laying his
hand against the rough bark of its trunk, but it looked
as it always had. After a while, he gave up and went
home.

And then this morning, when the three of them had
stood at the oak tree, Holly producing her key like she
was some kind of expert, lording it over him and Ben
the way she had, well . . . Everett hadn't felt the need
to pull out *his* key. He'd keep his secret, then whip it

out and show her up, he'd thought. Except that once they'd actually stepped through the beech tree, he'd forgotten all about it. And everything else had happened so fast.

Now he realized that having a key—or now a wand, as he assumed it must be—wasn't exactly a bonus, not as far as this King Whatsis was concerned. It would just mark Everett as one of those evil sorcerer Adepts who the king had gotten rid of. If the knights found out Everett had a wand, he and Ben would be strung up this very night if Dart was telling the truth. But what if it were their only chance at escape? Dart had said the prince himself had taken Holly's wand.

Everett glanced at Ben, who had started playing a Battleship game halfheartedly. He might be a bit immature, but he wasn't stupid, and if Everett was smart, he'd work with Ben instead of insisting on taking the lead in everything. Still, once the secret was out . . .

"Oh, hang it, all right," he said finally, unzipping the jacket pocket.

"What?" said Ben. "Have you got more food?"

"No. It's just . . . this." Everett pulled out a long, wooden stick.

"Holly's wand!"

"It isn't Holly's. It's mine. It was a key before, like

CLAIRE M. CATERER

hers." Everett knew it must have become a wand, but he still turned it over in his hands in wonder. The wood was darker than Holly's, and the carvings were different—tiny faces with sharp teeth. He followed the carvings around the base of the wand and saw the nasty faces were all attached to one long, spiky tail that curled around the tip, which was affixed with a dark red stone.

"Mr. Gallaway gave you one too? Let me see it."

"No. It's mine."

Ben shrugged, sulking. "When did he give it to you?"

"I got it yesterday." An uncomfortable knot of guilt played in Everett's stomach at the implied lie, but he fought it down. The main thing was that now he had a wand. And he could use it to get them out of here.

"You should've told me," Ben said. "How long were you going to hang on to that?"

"I couldn't very well let everyone know, could I? You saw what happened to Holly."

"We've been in here for *hours*! You could've used it to help us get out when Holly came for us!"

"I don't know how to use it, okay?"

"So let's figure it out. Holly didn't do anything special with hers. Bring it over to the lantern."

It was a piece of luck that in his haste Dart had forgotten to take the lantern with him. Everett brought the wand into the light, gazing at the carvings around the handle. "What did Holly do? Wave it around?" Ben asked.

"She just pointed it at things."

"Try the door! Holly said her wand unlocks stuff," said Ben.

Everett picked up the lantern and tiptoed to the great wooden door with its iron handle. "There must be a guard outside," he whispered. He pointed the wand at the keyhole.

He definitely felt something, a kind of humming from the wand that shook his hand until he forced it still. The wood warmed inside his palm. At first it was a pleasant feeling, but quickly the wand grew hotter until he was forced to drop it.

"What happened? Is the door open?"

"I don't think so. The wand got too hot for me to hold."

Ben bent down and picked it up before Everett could stop him. "Feels like it's been in the freezer to me." He aimed it at the keyhole.

"Ben, don't!"

But Ben shrugged. "It's not doing anything. It's just a stick."

Everett grabbed the wand back. It did feel cold. But it knew him, somehow. As he held it in his palm, the warmth spread through it. He pointed it at the key-hole again.

"So *you're* allowed to do it," said Ben.

The wand thrummed in Everett's grasp. This time he wrapped the sleeve of his jacket around the wood. But even through the denim he could feel the heat rising, faster than before, until a flame exploded from the wand's tip. Everett struggled to control the wand, but it wrenched itself from his hand. The flame grew into a lick of fire the size of Ben's torso, and like a giant Catherine wheel, it whipped in a circle, scorching the tower walls. It struck Dart's lantern and exploded it, throwing shards of glass everywhere. Everett grabbed Ben and crouched on the floor, watching as the ring of fire ascended. It paused like a bird at the window, then flew into the night with a muffled roar.

The room was dark and still. Slowly, Everett disentangled himself from Ben. "Whoa, that was—"

A boom erupted from the opposite side of the room as the door flew open. A knight strode into the tower, holding a lantern of his own. He was dark and thickset, with a long scar down one cheek. In his other hand he held a sword. "What devilry be this?" he thundered. "Have ye been lighting fires? Do you mean to burn down the castle?"

"It was an accident," Ben said in a small voice.

The knight turned his blade with a flick of his wrist and rested it against Ben's neck. "You shall address me as Sir Grandor or my lord, or not again, I'll warrant."

Everett still had an arm around Ben's shoulders and could feel him trembling. "Sorry. My lord."

Grandor shined his lantern around the small room, taking in the broken glass and the boys' singed clothes. "I saw fire," he whispered. "It came through the key-hole. This lantern—how came ye by it?" He directed the sword to Everett.

"It was left here. My lord."

"By whom?"

Everett hesitated. He knew Dart would get in trouble. "One of the pages. I don't know who."

"'Tis but a candle," murmured Grandor.

"It fell and broke, my lord," Everett went on. "We didn't mean to start any fire."

"But what be this?" Grandor cleared some of the glass away with the tip of his sword and held his own lantern above it. The wand glittered in the refuse. The knight fell silent, so entranced that if Everett had thought of it, he and Ben might have bolted through the open door behind him. But as soon as the idea occurred to him, the tip of the sword rose swiftly to his face. "You are an Adept as well," whispered the knight.

"I . . . No, we just found it."

Grandor turned and pushed the heavy door shut. He whirled round, pointing his sword at Everett. "Go on then, Adept. Wield your wand."

Everett released Ben, who grabbed at his sleeve. "Don't, Everett. He'll kill you."

Grandor held his gaze. His chain mail glittered in the lantern light and the sword showed a near perfect reflection of the moon through the window. "Take up your wand."

"You can have it," Everett said. "I don't want anyone to get hurt."

But the knight began to circle him now. "A cursed race, the Adepts," he said softly. "Traitors to the king and to all who serve him."

"But I promise, I'm not one. I'm just a stranger."

"A stranger indeed. From the Realm of the Wee Folk, perhaps? Traitors all. Placing themselves above the king's rule. He has decreed it. Decreed that you be hunted, like the fox and the hare."

Grandor's boots crunched the broken glass as he sidestepped around them, his dark eyes fixed on Everett's.

Next to him, close enough that he could feel every move, Ben stirred. His hand was creeping forward, inching toward the wand.

"Once the king hears that I have dispatched an Adept, I shall be lauded," Grandor went on. "His Highness is partial to the drama of daybreak. But I prefer the cover of night."

Ben's fingers stretched over the broken glass.

"Would you really kill us?" Everett asked. "Defenseless prisoners?"

"Do you dare say the word *coward*, young master?"

"No, no—it's just that, well, fair fight and all—"

"Tell me." Grandor slowed in his circling, but he didn't stop. Beside him, Ben stretched, his muscles trembling. "Tell me how you conjured the fire. Tell me, and you might yet live to see the dawn."

"It was the lantern. You must have seen it flare through the keyhole. That's all I can think of."

"And yet my notion is different." Grandor circled to face Everett, his back to Ben, who took the chance to make a mighty grab for the wand and point it at the knight.

"L-leave us alone, you," Ben said unsteadily, sitting up. A thin line of blood trickled down his wrist; he must have snatched up a shard of glass as well. "Or I'll blast you in the name of—of—Planeterra Five!"

"You have not the authority of that weapon, lad," whispered Grandor, though he backed away a little. "'Tis best not to meddle with magic beyond your ken."

Everett could feel the wand's vibration through Ben's arm, still touching his own. "Ben, be careful."

Then two things happened nearly at once. Grandor charged forward, brandishing the sword, and Ben made a wide sweep with the wand, as if shooting a machine gun. A thin flame shot from the wand's tip, illuminating the tower but inflicting no damage; it struck the sword, glancing off, and Grandor dropped it in surprise. Then, recovering himself, the knight snatched up his weapon and sidestepped the range of the wand, whose flame was feeble and blue now. Then, suddenly, Grandor leaped behind Ben, seized him around his neck, and forced the wand from his grip. It clattered to the stone floor. He grabbed a handful of Ben's hair and pulled his head back, bringing the sword to Ben's throat. The blade shone white in the moonlight against Ben's bare skin. The knight grinned at Everett.

"There be honor in fair judgment and a hearing before the throne," he whispered. "But when a knight is attacked, the only fair judgment is death. You have chosen poorly, lad."

Chapter 22

The Queen

Holly was just like anyone else: Any complaints her body might have had earlier that evening had been drowned out by the excitement of an attempted rescue of captives by leogryff under cover of night. But now that she was alone in her captivity, her adrenaline spent, Holly's body could at last be heard, and it told her several things. One was that she was very tired; another was that she was very hungry; and the last was that her right arm throbbed constantly.

But even these thoughts were fleeting, for the western chamber was nothing like she'd expected.

It was hardly a cell. By the lantern Loverian had lit Holly could see that the walls were lined with gold tapestries and shelves of books. A canopied bed sat at the far end. A green woven rug covered most of the stone floor.

Holly wandered to a writing table crowded with quills and inkpots. Tiny carvings covered its curved legs. She knelt to get a better look at them. Winged humans, gryphons, and centaurs with longbows scampered down the length of the table legs. It was a strange design indeed to find in the castle of a king who despised magic. Holly touched one of the centaurs with a fingertip and it vanished. She blinked in the lantern light. The table leg was smooth and plain now.

"Rise, Adept," said a voice behind her.

Holly turned around, nearly knocking over the lantern. Standing before her was a lady who could be none other than the queen.

She was taller than Loverian, Holly guessed, and slender, with very pale skin. Her auburn hair was gathered in an elaborate arrangement of knots and curls, atop which sat a thin gold circlet. Ranulf had said the prince was thirteen, yet his mother looked hardly ten years older.

Holly scrambled to her feet.

The woman's deep green eyes gazed into Holly's with something like sadness, but her face was set in its high cheekbones like a carved statue. "Thou hast come far, my lady," she said in a cold voice.

"Yes, Your . . . Highness," said Holly.

"Your Majesty," said the queen.

"Oh . . . I'm sorry." Holly made a clumsy attempt at a curtsy.

The queen pulled a high-backed chair from behind the writing table and sat down. "I am Elianne, Queen of Anglielle. Thou hast met His Highness, the prince Avery?"

"Yes."

The queen raised her eyebrows.

"Your Majesty," Holly added hastily. She felt her face go red. Her brain flipped through the catalog of rules her mother had tried to teach her—sit up straight, shake hands with adults, speak when spoken to, use the right fork.

"Thy garb is strange," said the queen. "What age art thou?"

"Eleven. Your Majesty."

"And not yet betrothed?"

"Hardly!" Holly blurted without thinking.

"In Anglielle, thou mayest by this age have a husband."

Holly made a face, then caught herself. The queen gave a hint of a smile. "Some customs are strange even to the natives. Have things changed so much among the Adepts?"

"Please, Your Majesty, I'm not an Adept."

"Only a lass who travels the skies as easily as the earth? Who commands the beasts? Who wields the wand?"

CLAIRE M. CATERER

"Yes, I did those things, but I'm not from here. I came from another world. That's where I got the wand."

The queen's voice fell to a hush. "Dost speak of the Realm of the Good Folk?"

"I . . . I don't think everyone's good, exactly. But I didn't mean to trespass on anyone's land. My brother and Everett came with me."

"But they have no magic?"

"No, Your Majesty. They just kind of . . . hitched a ride."

Queen Elianne leaned back in the chair, absently twirling an auburn curl around one finger. "Sit, Lady Adept. Tell me of the wand. What can it do?"

Holly sank onto a cushion at the queen's feet. "I'm not sure. It got me here, through the forest."

"And what hast thou learnt of our land?"

Holly opened her mouth, then closed it again. It might not be a good idea to let on that she'd heard the king was a tyrant. "That . . . That things have been very peaceful here, since King Reynard has been ruling."

"And the Adepts have been exiled."

"Yes. I've heard that, too."

The queen reached behind the table and drew out a tray set with a silver teapot and several heart-shaped cakes. A warm, spicy scent filled the room. She poured Holly a cup of something frothy.

"Eat," said the queen, and there was no question of disobeying.

The drink tasted of ginger and cinnamon. Holly took a bite of one of the cakes, only to have it dissolve in her mouth. It was like eating air, yet her stomach was full. "Thank you, Your Majesty," she said at last, remembering her manners. So far, the queen was the only person in the castle who hadn't mentioned execution, which Holly took to be a good sign. This might be her last chance to help Ben and Everett.

Holly finished her drink. "Excuse me, Your Majesty? My brother . . ."

The queen turned her gaze from the fire. "Thou wouldst seek clemency for him? The prince does not change his orders on a whim."

"But maybe if you talked to him, he'd see he made a mistake—"

"He is heir to the throne. A king cannot appear weak."

"But they're innocent!"

"That is regrettable."

"Regrettable?" Holly stood up, hardly noticing that the queen's face had whitened. "You're going to kill a ten-year-old who never hurt anybody, someone who's never going to see his mother again! He's miles from home and he's scared! The only reason he came with

me is because for once he wanted to be part of something, not just be some computer geek off by himself.
He was counting on me to keep him safe, and now my
dad has probably called the police and my mom thinks
we've fallen down a well, and the prince took my wand
and we've got no way back. And all you can do is call it
regrettable? It's murder, that's what it is!"

Holly ran out of words because her tears were
finally overflowing. She wiped them away but more
kept gathering.

The queen held up a slender hand. "Peace, child.
All may not yet be lost. Come."

Holly sniffled a bit, then followed Elianne to a set of
tall mullioned windows at the other end of the room.
Elianne turned a handle. They were doors, not windows.

Holly ventured out onto a narrow balcony. The
queen gestured at the stars. "Dost thou know these
lights?"

"They're planets and suns," Holly said. "And they
make constellations, like pictures. I can always find
the Big Dipper. It's . . ."

She scanned the sky. She had never seen stars so
bright, undimmed by city lights. But something else
was different about them. "That . . . that looks like
the Chained Princess. But she's in the wrong place."
Hercules and the Swan were missing, along with a lot

of the other constellations she had learned from her father.

"The Chained Princess. Such tales are not my province," said the queen softly. "But not every light in the sky is a star, Lady Holly."

"It isn't?"

"Some are thy guides and thy salvation. Mark me." The queen's deep green eyes looked directly into Holly's. "They shall not lead thee astray. And mark thy bedchamber, for the coverlet is long, as the ground is to the sky."

"I'm sorry, I don't understand what you—"

"I am able to do but one thing for thee," said the queen loudly, turning back to the chamber. She guided Holly through the doors and closed them. "The events of this day have not yet been made known to His Majesty the king. He will not return for three days. It is in my power to stay thy kinsman's execution until that time. This I have done."

"And Everett's, too?" Holly asked quickly. She felt guilty that she hadn't spoken up for him as well.

"Three days. It is all I have to give." The queen's voice fell to a hush. "What may happen in that time, I know not. Take care. Be wise, with one ear to the ground and the other to the skies."

She glided to the door of the chamber. "We shall

meet again, thou and I," she said. "May Lunetia preserve thee."

The door opened at her touch, and the queen slipped through, closing it behind her.

Holly stared after her, trying to make sense of the queen's words. She had gained them all three days—that was something. The queen seemed to want to help her, but why? She hadn't condemned the Adepts like the prince and the knights. Maybe she had some sympathy for Holly's plight. But why bother showing her the balcony? Did she think Holly could fly off the tower?

She walked back outside. The tower dropped several stories below, outside the castle's curtain wall onto a tiny square of lawn. It was hardly more than a foothold. Below that, the chalky cliffs tumbled into the river that fed the moat. The balustrade was solid. She could certainly climb over it, but then—what? Drop to her death?

Holly leaned against the stone tower. The queen wasn't making the escape very easy. Maybe she thought Fleetwing would fly in and rescue Holly. She was supposed to be some kind of hero; wouldn't he and the others try to free her?

But no. The leogryff had to have been badly hurt, maybe killed. She had let them all down. She hadn't defended Fleetwing, and some of the others were probably hurt too, all for nothing. Whatever respect they'd had for her had surely vanished. They must think she wasn't worth saving.

Holly wandered back inside and climbed onto the high bed. She sank into the deep, down-filled mattress and very nearly fell asleep. But her broken arm ached, and the room was chilly. She reached to pull the blankets closer, and Elianne's words suddenly came back to her.

Mark thy bedchamber, for the coverlet is long, as the ground is to the sky.

The queen had said a few things like this—nonsense things that Holly didn't understand. Something about the ground and her ears . . .

The coverlet. That was the blanket, or maybe the sheets.

Holly's hand glided over the sheets. They were made of a thin, shimmery fabric. They could easily be . . .

"Tied together," Holly whispered aloud. The balcony!

That's what the queen was talking about. Maybe she'd been so mysterious because she feared being overheard. Holly jumped out of bed (and fell, forgetting how high up she was) and started pulling the sheets off the bed.

Often, when a good idea comes, the brilliance of

CLAIRE M. CATERER

it so amazes you that you act very fast, before the thought fades and your brain returns to its usual state of torpor. But no matter how grand the plan, injury is not an asset. Holly became so frustrated tugging with her one good arm that she shook off the sling and tried to use the broken one. At once the pain shot up to her shoulder and she collapsed on the floor, biting her lip to keep from crying. Three full minutes passed before she could get up and try again.

Pulling the sheets from the bed was the easiest part of her job. To make her rope longer, she had to rip the two sheets in half and knot the four pieces together. The ripping was hard enough—the fabric was very tough—but tying a knot with one hand was not her custom. And then she had to stop and think, because it would not do to tie a knot that would pull apart when she put her weight on it.

She fetched more sheets from a wardrobe to lengthen her rope. She was so busy with this project, and so pleased at her own cleverness, that she was positive she would overcome any problems. She would climb down the makeshift rope with one hand—surely she could manage it, even through the pain—and sneak away from the castle. She'd find her friends somehow (they had certainly been planning to rescue her, she thought now), and come up with a way to free the boys. They had three days, didn't they? And still the fatal flaw did not occur to her.

She grabbed the sheet-rope, double-checked the knots, and dragged it out to the balcony. Holly peered over the balustrade in the moonlight. Her landing pad was no more than a few square feet. She would have to climb all the way down—no wild jumping.

Holly tied one end to the balustrade, then gathered the sheets and tossed them over the balcony, confident they would pool on the ground below.

The awful truth came all at once, like a hose dousing a candle.

Her makeshift rope was too short.

Chapter 23

Her Majesty's Order

Everett's thoughts ran a split track as he crouched in the tower. In the first moment, he admired Ben for the brave thing he'd done, threatening Grandor with the wand, and he wondered if he himself would have been able to do it; and then less than a second later, he realized how stupid Ben had been and how awful it would feel to be trapped without him, that Ben would soon be skewered on the tip of the knight's sword while Everett, feeling worse than useless, sat by watching.

"Don't!" was all he could think of to say.

"Observe, lad, and learn," said Grandor, drawing the sword back. Ben whimpered.

Behind them, the tower door sprang open with a resounding boom. A young knight burst into the room.

"Grandor!"

"These lads attacked me, Loverian," growled Grandor.

"Release him," said the other knight. "I bring the queen's order. The both are to be spared for three days."

Grandor glared back, still holding Ben by the hair.

Loverian charged forward, sword drawn. "Now, I say, in the name of the crown."

Everett held his breath, glancing at the open door.

Grandor shoved Ben onto the glass-strewn floor, where he lay sobbing quietly. Loverian swung his sword toward Everett, following his glance. "Do not think on it, lad."

Everett, not knowing what else to do, held his hands up, the way you're supposed to do when surrendering.

Grandor turned his head and spat. "The queen's order! Did she deliver it to you in person?"

"It was . . . conveyed to me."

"And the king?"

"He has not yet returned from the hunting party."

"He shall have interest in this." Grandor strode to the other end of the tower, slammed the door, and picked up the wand. "Here be the lad's weapon. He made fire with it."

Loverian reached out a gloved hand, but Grandor snatched his back. "Spoils of war."

"War? Your opponents be but lately off their mother's breast."

The older knight's face reddened. "They have power!"

"Then the king will want to know of it. You will hand your spoils to His Highness, nay?"

"Of . . . Of course."

Grandor's sword was still drawn. He pointed it not an inch from Everett's nose. "Mind me, thief. Your life was spared tonight, but three days hence, luck shall not be with you."

Grandor strode out of the tower. Loverian turned to follow, but Everett said, "Excuse me . . . my lord?"

"Aye?"

"Holly . . . the girl . . . Do you know what's happened to her?"

Ben sat up too, his face grimy and bloody from where he'd wiped it with his hands.

"'Tis not your affair."

"Please, my . . . lordship. She's my sister," Ben said, his voice catching. "Is she okay?"

From somewhere in his chain mail, the knight pulled a handkerchief. He leaned forward, wiping Ben's face. "You are injured."

"I don't care! What about Holly?"

Loverian leaned forward, his voice low. "She was captured. She be safe for now."

"For now?"

"You're going to kill her, too," Everett said in a low voice.

"No, you're not!" Ben cried.

"Peace, lad." Loverian stood up. "The queen has decreed three days' clemency for all of you. Be glad of it."

"But where is Holly?" Everett asked.

The knight smiled. "Dost think me a traitor to my king?" He walked to the tower door, drawing out a key ring. "Take care, young master. Whatever you think, you have no friend here."

The door closed with a bang, and the boys were alone again.

Chapter 24

The Elemental

Holly's rope was not just a little bit short. It didn't reach more than halfway down. Holly raced back inside. She circled the chamber, rifling through the wardrobe, feeling under the bed, looking for anything, even a hand towel, to extend the sheet-rope. But the room was bare.

Holly sprinted back to the balcony and peered over the edge. She couldn't jump the last sixty feet, that was sure. All that work for nothing. Her eyes swam as she gazed up at the unfamiliar stars. Maybe if she looked long enough she'd see Fleetwing through the trees. But there was no one.

Except for the very brightest star, which winked at her.

And then it began to move across the sky.

Holly's first thought was that it was an airplane. But of course it couldn't be. The light swelled as it approached. The funny thing was, it grew even less distinct the closer it got, so that it looked just like a star until the moment it landed on the balustrade in front of her.

Though small enough to fit inside Holly's fist, it burned so white-hot that she could hardly look at it. It bounced about the balustrade like a crazy, flaming rubber ball. Finally it leaped up in front of her face. By now Holly's eyes had adjusted to the light, and she gasped.

It was a tiny, white-hot *person*.

Its pale face and wild, crackly white hair glowed at the center of a white flame. It wore some kind of robe or feathers that were too bright to look at for long. Holly couldn't decide if it was male or female.

Its voice was faint and high-pitched, but Holly, standing very still, could hear it now. "Thee hath ears without hearing! It needs quiet! Silence!"

"I . . ."

"Art sure an Adept?" The little person peered at Holly skeptically.

"I'm Holly. Are you . . . I don't know . . . A fairy?"

The creature's white cheeks burned blue. "Thee speakest blasphemy! I be of the Elements! I is the flaming brilliance! I is the power of the flame! I is—"

"Okay, sorry." Holly sighed. "I'm not from around here."

CLAIRE M. CATERER

"So I be told." The creature's flames cooled. "Be thee the Lady Holly?"

"I guess so."

"What be this meaning? Ist thee the lady? Or—or an agent of the winged man? Hims of the Source?" The little person drew away, its eyes wide.

"No," said Holly quickly. "I am . . . the Lady Holly. The Adept."

The creature, who had been hovering above the balustrade, came to rest on it. Its light faded to gold and it blinked tiny, bright eyes. "Then I be sent for thee."

"I'm sorry for not knowing," said Holly carefully, "but who are you? Are you a friend of Queen Elianne's?"

"Her Majestyness be not queen of the Elements, whether or no hast she numberous friends. I be an Elemental—Ignata, of the Cináed, of the Kingdom of the Good Folk."

The creature's cheeks burned blue and then back to yellow-gold. Holly decided the impish face was female. She could see iridescent wings folded along the Elemental's shoulders as she strode back and forth along the balcony railing. She stopped when she reached the tied sheet-rope.

"Ah!" Ignata said, burning white. "Thee hast forgot thee magic!"

"I don't have my key—that is, my wand."

"Hast need of wands? Funny little mortal." Ignata smirked.

"Are you going to help me or not?" Holly said crossly.

"Raise not thee voice to loudness! Thou be not friend to the Elementals! It is duly noted! It is duly noted!" Ignata jumped up and down in her fury until she became airborne and buzzed like a wasp around Holly's head.

"Fine!" Holly said. Too many incomprehensible things in a single day can be tiring, and suddenly she was exhausted again. She turned back to the chamber. "Duly note whatever you want."

"Wait! Wait! Wait!" The creature's voice rose to a near inaudible pitch. "Thee must be aided! Thy be Adept! Wait wait wait!"

The voice trailed off and broke into a string of high-pitched squeaks and trills. Her light burned very bright, and sparks showered onto the balcony like fireworks.

Holly was afraid she was having some kind of fit. "Are you all right? It's okay—I'm staying right here, see?"

Gradually Ignata's fire condensed back into the ball around her body. Her voice returned. "Ignata begs pardonest of His Ladyship," she said, still sounding a bit squeaky. "His Majestyness. She be not accustomed to speaking with Adeptest—Adpets—Apdets—"

"It's all right. Just calm down."

"I be sent to help thee," she said at last, settling back onto the balcony. She peered over the edge at Holly's inadequate rope and gave her a sidelong glance. "This be not much aid."

"No kidding."

"But Ignata be of aid. Observe, Lady."

The Elemental floated into the air and lighted on the knotted sheet. It burst into flame.

"Hey! What are you doing?" Holly shouted.

"Dost desire aid or no?" asked the Elemental. "Adpets be an impatient lot. Work of Elementals be elegant but slow." With these words, the creature floated down the tower, following the flames. Holly squinted up at the battlements, expecting an archer to appear over the edge. But no one seemed to have noticed what was going on.

And then a strange thing happened. Something appeared in the center of the flames even as the sheets shriveled. Holly couldn't make out what it was, but it was growing, stretching out like a great burning snake toward the grass. Holly couldn't see the Elemental anymore, but after a few moments, she appeared back on the balcony. The fire dwindled, then disappeared; and what had once been a length of knotted bedsheets was now a thick ivy stalk, hugging the wall of the castle all the way to the ground, where it looked rooted. Ignata crossed her arms and smiled.

"Now, Lady Adept, seeth the handiwork of the Elementals."

"You—you *did* do something!"

Holly realized that she sounded not quite gracious, but Ignata only glowed brighter. "It suiteth, my lady."

"It does—suiteth." Holly searched the ground, but she didn't see any sentries. "This is my chance," she said. "I might still be able to save Ben and Everett if I get going."

The Elemental sat down and preened her wings. "Thee ist near correct."

"What do you mean, 'near correct'?"

"Thee canst save one mortal, not two."

"What?" Holly said. "Why can't I save both of them?"

The little creature studied her nails. "One be dead, my lady."

Holly's heart stopped in her chest. "No."

"Aye, 'tis truth. The mortals in the tower. One hast the magic stick, and didst attempt to overwhelm the knight. He is dead. The other livest," Ignata added brightly.

"They didn't have a stick—a wand. Neither one of them. You must be wrong. They're alive."

"You!" Ignata flew from her perch and pointed a

thin finger in Holly's face. "Thee darest to doubt the word of the Elemental! Thee Adpet! Thee Apdet! The Elements see all! Knowst all!" Flames billowed out from her chest. "Thee hast not yet escaped! Fire giveth life, and fire taketh life!" The creature raised up a blazing arm as if to curse the vine she had planted.

"No, please!" Tears choked Holly's voice. "I'm sorry! I just . . . Which one? Which one is dead?"

"The firesight is limited," the Elemental muttered. "One is dead. One liveth. Such be the news the Elements bring."

Holly sank onto the balcony. "I can't believe it."

How could one of the boys have a wand like hers? Or did they threaten one of the knights with something stupid, like a pencil? Ben might have a pencil in his pocket. No, it couldn't be Ben. What would she tell her parents? Well, what did it matter, because when was she likely ever to see them again anyway?

A great sob rose in her throat.

"'Tis the same with all mortals," said the Elemental, sounding bored. "Once the wine be spilt, tears be useless. My lady, comest thee away to the wood! The Elementals shall hide thou well protected! Then mayest thou free the remaining mortal!"

The Elemental's words brought her up short. She didn't know *who* was left alive; it might be Ben. Of course she wanted Everett to be alive too, but if she couldn't have them both . . .

Holly pulled herself up and leaned over the balcony, tugging on the vine. Its twisted trunk was nearly as thick around as her waist, with plenty of sturdy branches and neat little footholds. It would be the sort of thing one would love to climb *up*, if not going very high; but climbing down a hundred feet or more, with a sharp cliff face shining white below in the moonlight, seemed a bit more tricky. She didn't even have a rope this time.

And she would have to manage it one-handed.

Somehow, she had forgotten this, even through the throbbing in her right arm. "How am I supposed to climb down with *this*?" she asked.

Ignata heaved an extravagant sigh. "Adpets be difficult beings. Needst thee further aid, Lady? It be dull magic."

"Can you help me? Dull is fine."

Ignata shrugged and flew up to Holly's right shoulder. "May thee be lit by fire within," she said, then squeaked as she flew down the injured arm.

At once the heat erupted in Holly's muscles as if her arm was aflame from shoulder to wrist. It glowed white and Holly screamed.

But the pain lasted only an instant. The skin cooled,

CLAIRE M. CATERER

and cautiously, Holly took off the makeshift sling and tried to bend her elbow.

The arm was perfect. Even the bruises were gone. She flexed the muscles; they were stronger than before.

"That's amazing! Thank you!"

"'Tis not fitting to give thanks," the fiery creature said, but she glowed.

"So now," Holly said, turning her attention back to the vine that wound its way to the ground. "This thing."

Keep your eyes straight ahead; don't look down. A horrid untethered freedom surrounded her as she put one foot over the balustrade. For the second time tonight, she missed her helmet and now, the tension of the belay. She concentrated on the balcony door in front of her and took hold of two branches. A cool breeze blew by her and she heard the river roaring below the chalky cliffs. The other foot came over the side.

She never was sure how she managed it. She watched her knuckles, as white as the moon, as with each step she scrambled for a foothold. At one point she flailed, her foot finding nothing but air; she took a nasty slide down a few feet, her palms burning. "'Tis just beneath thee feet!" the Elemental urged her. "Now to the left! Nay, right! Nay! Left!"

Holly had to tune out the creature's advice. Hand under hand, foot below foot, she advanced. The balcony above her receded. Her knuckles scraped against the cool stone of the tower. She panted, feeling faint. She forced herself to breathe in slow, measured rhythms.

But after about two minutes of climbing, another problem emerged—one greater even than her fear and the sound of the river crashing below. Above her head, following her descent, the vine's branches began to fade. It was disappearing. "What's happening?" Holly cried.

Ignata, floating near her face, shrugged. "'Tis impermanent magic. Thy musteth make haste afore it vanish."

Now looking up was as awful as looking down. Holly climbed faster. "Can't you do something? Bring it back?"

"Spells be not callest forth again and anon! Thee must fly if needs must."

"If I could fly, I wouldn't need it at all!" Holly said. Only a few feet of the vine remained above her head. And it was still too far to jump.

From there it became a race: Holly against the disappearing vine. Sweat poured down her back. Her palms stung with blisters. Her ankle had a deep gash from her slide down the vine. But still she climbed, hands and feet chasing each other, until at last she felt the earth beneath her feet. The vine in her hands disappeared, and Holly collapsed on the ground.

She sat panting for a moment, leaning against the cold, sheer wall of the western tower. The grass was soft and wet beneath her, and a few yards away, the cliff face dropped into the river. She had made it.

A rustling sound, not far from her right hand. Holly stopped breathing, willing herself to blend into the wall. Then voices.

"Round round round! This way! At once!" squeaked the Elemental, circling to the other side of the tower.

Holly pulled herself up and plunged ahead after the little creature, who lit her way like a firefly.

The voices behind her grew louder, then urgent. Shouts came from the balcony above. They knew she had escaped.

How stupid of her! She'd left the door wide open. Whoever checked the room had seen right away that she was gone.

Ahead, the Elemental flew north along the long wall that framed the back of the castle. The land leveled a bit, though the hill down into the valley was rocky, and Holly stumbled. Ignata darted into the forest, then turned and shot a lick of flame at Holly that burned her body for a moment, much as her arm had burned before. She cried out and a large, armor-clad man bowled into her.

"By the crown!" he cried. It was Grandor.

"Lady Adept!" squeaked a voice. Just through the trees, Holly glimpsed a flicker of light. She sprinted after it.

"This way! 'Tis the Adept!" Grandor shouted, and a horde of footsteps and hoofbeats thundered after her.

Holly kept her eyes on the bobbing light in front of her, winking in and out of the trees. She stumbled through a creek, then along the path, which grew darker as she penetrated the forest. But she was no match for the horses, which she could feel now, panting and blowing behind her. "She be not in the wood," someone shouted.

"Aye, she is! Do you think me blind?" Grandor shouted back.

One of the knights on horseback came galloping around the bend. Holly had to throw herself off the path to avoid being trampled. She landed in a low shrub in a very uncomfortable position, but she didn't dare cry out.

The horseman drew up even with her and turned this way and that. "I tell you, she is not here." He was carrying a small torch, which he raised above his head. The wood was bathed in firelight. The knight looked

CLAIRE M. CATERER

straight into Holly's face where she crouched. "She has escaped," he pronounced.

Holly looked down at herself, puzzled. The knight had moved his torch, but somehow she was still glowing. How had he missed her? She looked like a giant light bulb.

Grandor appeared on his horse behind the other. "'Tis part of her craft, fool. I shall search myself." He snatched the torch and walked the horse up and down the path, peering into the woods. He too looked at Holly but didn't seem to see her. "Very well, Gervase," he conceded finally. "'Twould seem you are right. These creatures have ways of hiding themselves. We must loose the dogs. His Highness will not be pleased to hear that she has vanished."

"Grandor," said the other, drawing closer and lowering his voice, "how *did* she escape? Two guards were posted outside the chamber door."

"Perchance she flew. What knowledge have we of black magic? The prince ought to have killed her at once. Come."

The two knights turned their horses back through the wood and, when they were clear of it, pushed them at a canter toward the castle. Holly wouldn't have much time before the dogs came after her.

"My lady," squeaked the Elemental, near her ear.

"Ignata! Why couldn't they see me?" Holly asked.

"A gift of the Elements." The little creature flew in front of Holly's face and put out a hand. A wave like a splash of cold water washed over Holly from the inside out, and the glow around her condensed into a finger of flame that shot back into the Elemental's palm. Holly shivered.

"You made me invisible," she said.

"It would not last, my lady, but still, 'tis best to nothing."

"Thank you."

"My duty." Ignata glowed proudly. "Now, this way!"

Chapter 25

The Enemy of the Good Folk

Holly pulled herself up out of the shrub she'd been crouching in. She didn't feel much like an Adept, with no wand and dependent on temperamental fireflies for help, but at least she was free. The Elemental bobbed ahead of her along the forest path, and more than once Holly thought she could hear the distant barking of dogs. Why didn't she feel more grateful, instead of low and tired? She'd gotten away, and yet the knowledge that one of the boys was dead—*please, let it not be Ben, but how awful, please let it not be Everett, either*—gave her a cold, hollow feeling in her chest. She had failed them. Both of them. She wanted nothing more than to sleep.

"'Tis not much farther, my lady," came the fiery creature's voice through the dark. "Then thee must eat and drink, take rest."

"I don't even care about food. Just bed."

"Nay nay!" The Elemental zoomed back in front of

her face, burning very bright. "Her Ladyship needseth food and drink! Eat eat eat! Else she be died!"

"Okay, I'll eat. Let's just get there."

"Follow, my lady! 'Tis not far!" The creature turned and led the way again, this time faster. Holly sighed. Her legs trembled beneath her.

There is a kind of desperate exhaustion that takes over when one is forced to trust strangers in a hostile place. Holly's limbs ached from the climb down the vine, and any moment she expected to feel the hot breath of hounds on the back of her neck. And she couldn't shake the nagging feeling that something wasn't quite right. Even now.

Holly strained her ears against the cricket song in the woods. The knights had been in a hurry; where were the dogs? Then she had a thought.

"Ignata, you're so small and . . . well, smart . . ."

"Aye, mistress, truth ye speakest."

"Maybe . . . I know this is a big favor. . . . But couldn't you maybe get into the castle and get my wand back for me?"

The little creature turned and stared at Holly, her mouth agape.

"I know it would be dangerous, but that wand, it's more than just a stick, it's a key that can get me back where I came from, and—"

"An Elemental touchest not the stick of magic! 'Tis of the Adpets! Apdets! We touches it for only the briefest of moments or we burn!"

"Okay, okay. It was just an idea."

Ignata let out a long sigh, then turned around. "Ahead, my lady! We be arrived!"

Holly peered through the trees. The Elemental was heading for a small clearing in the wood. Maybe here at last was a bed.

In this she was disappointed. All she found were a few spindly trees and something that looked like an enormous anthill. It was nearly three feet high, mostly dirt, though grass grew on one side. Nearby were small rings of stones, as might surround a doll's campfire. The mound had a hole near the bottom on one side, and another in the top, like a chimney. A warm glow came from within, and Holly could hear the titter of squeaking voices, like the Elemental's own language.

"This be our home, my lady," said Ignata, landing on the top of the little hill. The mound burst into flames.

Holly jumped back. The fire was contained, and very clear and bright. As her eyes adjusted, Holly could see movement in the flames, little balls of light even brighter than the fire itself.

"Come inside, my lady, and find thee bed."

"But I can't go in there!"

"Aye, thee musteth!" cried Ignata.

"I'll burn up! Can't you see that? I'm not one of you!"

"This have we consideredeth." The little creature darted into the flames and returned with what looked like a small live coal, which it placed on a nearby tree stump. Gradually the offering cooled. Holly blinked; it had become a little slice of cake.

It must be said in Holly's defense that everyone has a weakness, and lemon chiffon cake was hers. It was so light that she could see the perfectly formed pockets of air in the texture. Buttercream frosting and sugared violets decorated the top. It was the loveliest cake Holly had ever seen.

"'Tis food of the Good Folk," the Elemental whispered in her ear. "Eat. It allowest thee to take refuge in our home, to become as us."

"But not forever, right?"

Ignata fluttered around her head. "Affirmatious, my lady! Sadly, these effect be but temporaneous!"

"And I'll be hidden from the knights?"

Ignata landed on the tree stump. "Mortals see nothing. If they sight our home, it be only from the edges of eyes, and when they looketh straight, all be invisibiliousness to them."

"Then how can I see it?"

"Thee beest Adept!" scoffed the creature. "Thee be differentious."

"Everyone keeps saying that," Holly muttered. "I don't even have the wand anymore."

"But nay, Lady." Ignata's voice lowered to a whisper. "'Tis not the wand that maketh ye the Adept. Adeptishness be in the blood, the blood of Anglielle. The wand cannot be givish to others." Ignata took a breath, struggling to calm the tiny popping flames that flickered around her body. Her smile looked forced. "Now. Eat."

Holly wanted to argue, but her words died in her throat. She looked at the cake, and her stomach felt strangely empty, although she'd eaten her fill of the queen's food. Ignata was right; she should get a good night's rest and make her plans tomorrow. She reached out and picked up the cake. It was like lifting air. Ignata leaned forward, glowing.

A black streak tore through the trees. The cake was knocked out of Holly's hand, and the Elemental tumbled from the tree stump. Above the little creature's shrieks rose the growls of the thing that had taken her. They rolled on the ground, fire and darkness; Holly noticed the firenest's light growing dimmer.

"Stop! Leave her alone! Get off!" Holly followed the rolling pair to the edge of the clearing. The black beast tore at the Elemental and her light dimmed to a sickly yellow. The firenest extinguished. When Holly glanced back, it looked like an anthill again. Her eyes took a few moments to adjust to the darkness.

"Hang on, Ignata! I'll help you!" Holly pulled out her Swiss Army knife and opened the blade. The Elemental's screams filled the night air.

Holly had some idea of slashing at the black creature, but it was moving too fast, rolling around and around on the ground, first on top, then on its back, clawing at the translucent wings. Finally Ignata broke free and fluttered out of reach. Her light looked like a dying candle flame. Holly glanced back at the ground.

Ignata's attacker was a large cat. He circled the clearing, glaring up at the hovering Elemental. His teeth glowed as if he had ripped hot coals from the creature. Holly startled, recognizing him.

"Jade!" she cried. "What are you doing? Leave Ignata alone! She's helping me!"

The cat kept his eyes trained on the tiny creature. "Her Ladyship must beware of help from such a beast as this. Did you take food from it?"

"I didn't get the chance."

"If you would be an Elemental forever, then by all means, eat."

"But you've hurt her." Holly's voice caught, and

the Elemental flew to her feebly, landing on her out-stretched hand.

"Who wouldst Lady Adept trusteth?" Holly could barely hear the creature's weak voice. "Taketh ye the word of a betrayer? One who delivered thou to her catchers?"

"Fool! Would I have risked my life to have an Adept captured?" the cat snarled.

"Thy . . . didst not . . . save her."

"Oh no!" cried Holly. "She's dying!"

The creature's light faded. Only her chest, where her heart might have been, still glowed, but the outer edges of the body grew gray and cold.

"I hast done my best for thou, my lady," whispered the Elemental.

"No, don't!"

But the little creature laid her head down in Holly's palm, and all at once, her light blinked out like an extinguished light bulb.

"Now look what you've done!" cried Holly, feeling heartsick. "And she helped me escape!"

Jade stopped pacing, sat down, and began to wash his face. He winced as he shook the embers from his jowls.

"Set that creature on top of its home, my lady," said the cat, stretching. "Come with me. Time grows short."

"I'm not going anywhere with you. You *killed* her."
Holly cradled the little winged body.

"It sought to entrap you, not save you. Her Ladyship
does not know the Elementals. Put it down. It lives."
Jade tensed his body, ready to spring.

The creature in her hands looked quite dead. Holly
didn't really trust Jade, but an uncomfortable warmth
was spreading along her palm. She laid the little body
on top of the grassy mound.

Jade relaxed. "My thanks."

"Don't touch her," Holly warned.

"Watch, my lady."

Holly was in no mood to do anything the cat asked
her to, but she couldn't help paying attention to what
happened next. The mound in front of her gradually
became brighter, like a lantern lit from within. The
Elemental's body rose straight up, riding a current of
hot air, and her filmy clothing stirred about her. The
mound burst into flames. Once again Holly spied the
tiny fireballs whizzing about inside. After a moment,
one of them flew out of the flames, snatched the body,
and bore it back into the nest.

Holly blinked, trying to see what happened next,
but the mound was too bright to look at properly.
Suddenly another ball of flame licked out from the
nest and flew into her face.

CLAIRE M. CATERER

"Ignata! Are you all right?"

If anything, the Elemental looked brighter than before. Tiny flames licked out from her feet. She flew past Holly and hovered over the cat's head, hissing and popping like logs on a hearth. "Thee hast made an enemy of the Elementals!" she spat. "It be mosteth unwise!"

Jade yawned.

"The Adepts will foreverest be friends of the Elements, but thee hast incurred our wrathest!"

"Wait a second," said Holly, turning to the Elemental. "So you weren't dying?"

The winged creature shrugged in midair. "Fire ist rebirthed from within, Ladyness. The Elements be not mortalish."

Holly glanced at Jade, wavering. "And that cake you gave me—"

"It be given to hidest thou in the flames of the firenest! A giftest of the Elementals!" Ignata glowed more fiercely.

"But I could come out again, right?"

"Comest out, fly within, what matters this? Adpets be reverest! Apdets be forever!" The little creature's pitch grew higher, disappearing into squeaks and hisses. Holly looked at Jade.

"While the Good Folk mislead, they find it difficult

to lie outright, especially to those they wish to endear," said the cat.

"Enemy!" cried Ignata. "Fierceth black beast who knowsest naught of the Realm! Thy be traitors to the Adepts! Thy gives her to her captors with all willing!"

"How do you know that?" Holly turned to the Elemental. "Fleetwing got shot down too, you know! And Ranulf fought with the castle guards."

"But such cannot protectoreth Her Ladyness! These be mortalish! Comest to us, who keepeth thou safetest forevermore!"

"Waste no more energy on this creature, my lady," said the cat, turning away. "We must join the others."

Holly heard a dog bark far away. And then another.

"It's the knights! I've got to get out of here!"

"Who helpeth thee when thee need it most?" whispered the flying creature, lighting on her shoulder. "Come with me, little magician, we will hideth thee in the flames."

Jade turned and crouched beneath Ignata, growling.

Holly glanced from one to the other. The dogs' barking was louder, deeper.

Jade took a step closer.

"As you wish!" the flying creature cried. "Farewell, enemy of the Elementals!" She gave a great hissing shriek and threw herself into the firenest.

"Ignata!"

But the fire blinked out, leaving the cold grassy mound behind.

"Now look what you've done!" Holly cried, turning on Jade. "I don't need any more enemies!"

"'Tis I who be their enemy," said the cat. "Now! This way!"

Jade bounded out of the clearing and into the brambles. Holly lost sight of him in the darkness, but in a moment, he turned, and his green eyes glowed in the moonlight. "You must follow or be captured," the cat said. "What is your choice, Lady Holly?"

Somewhere in the distance, the hungry, desperate howls echoed. Holly had no choice. She followed.

Chapter 26

Morning's Plan

No matter how many dogs are after you, cutting a path through old-growth forest with a pocketknife is slow work. Each time a young sapling whipped her in the face or she stumbled over a fallen tree trunk, Holly became more convinced she should have followed the Elemental. At least she'd be safe there. And what made Jade so trustworthy, anyway? Hadn't he abandoned her?

She had nearly made up her mind to turn back when Jade bounded into another clearing. Standing beside him was Ranulf.

Holly stumbled into the glade, stood panting before the centaur, and started to say, "I don't see why I should—"

"No time, my lady!" Ranulf reached down a long, burly arm and snatched her from the ground, throwing her onto his back.

He thundered away to the opposite side of the

CLAIRE M. CATERER

clearing onto a path. At once, a pack of dogs met them from the other side and bounded after them, leaping at the centaur's flanks.

"You've led them straight to us!" said Holly.

Ranulf galloped faster, drawing his sword at the same time, and glanced backward. Hunched against his back, Holly saw the sword flash in the moonlight, and a bright light shot from it. One of the dogs yelped.

"What are you doing?" Holly shouted.

"Protecting Her Ladyship!" The centaur brandished the sword again and a fireball exploded on the ground. The dogs hung back. The knights, not far behind on horseback, nearly trampled them. Ranulf pointed the sword above his head and a shower of sparks erupted into the sky. The knights hollered at one another; the dogs howled and barked; and the ground trembled with stampeding hooves. The horses reared and turned back to the castle, the dogs at their heels. A moment later they had disappeared into the wood.

Ranulf turned back to the path. Once again Holly found herself clinging to his sweaty torso as he galloped away. Within twenty minutes he had pulled up short in front of Almaric's cottage.

She was back where she had started, and now so tired she could hardly stand. She was vaguely aware of Almaric fussing over her ("Her Ladyship is cold. . . .

Bring her here. . . . That's right. . . ."). Then she was herded to a soft bed and made to lie down. And before she had another thought, she had fallen asleep.

Holly's room was already bright when she stirred. She was momentarily confused by where she was: It was not her room in America, nor her bedroom in Hawkesbury, nor the western chamber of the king's castle. Each of these discoveries brought a mixture of relief and fear, but it wasn't long before all the events of the day before tumbled through her mind. She was in Almaric's tiny round bedroom. With a sharp pang, she remembered what Ignata had said about the boys.

Holly pulled herself out of the bed, wincing at a dozen different muscle aches. She peered into Almaric's glass. She couldn't see the boys now, just her own reflection. It would not be an overstatement to say that she looked a fright. Her disheveled braids were matted with leaves and dirt, her face covered with scrapes and bruises. She wore a long nightdress that Almaric had given her. Her jeans, caked with mud, were folded over a chair. She could hardly put them back on. She found her glasses sitting on the chest of drawers. At least they weren't broken.

Holly turned the bedroom door handle, relieved

CLAIRE M. CATERER

it wasn't locked. She found Almaric and Jade sitting at the little table, drinking something hot from bowl-shaped cups.

"Ah! The Lady Holly!" Almaric said, standing up at once and beaming at her.

"Sorry I'm such a mess," she said.

"Perhaps a bath," said the cat.

"Jade, manners! Do not mind him, my lady. Come with me, if you please."

Almaric led Holly out to an ivy-covered wooden shed behind the cottage. He opened the door, and inside, Holly found a large iron tub full of water. A towel hung nearby next to something that looked suspiciously like a dress.

"The water is heated," Almaric said. "'Tis one of my small talents, but it comes in handy. And the clothing . . . I'm afraid we don't have anything quite like what you arrived in."

"No, it's fine," Holly said quickly. "Thank you."

Almaric smiled and bowed, backing out.

It was a long while before Holly was satisfied with her wash. She scrubbed her hair as best she could and scraped the mud from her skin. In the end, she was a good deal cleaner than when she'd begun. She slipped the white cotton dress over her head and combed through her hair with her fingers. She glanced down at herself. If she were going to rescue anyone, she'd prefer her jeans and tennis shoes.

Back at the cottage, Almaric sat Holly at the table and loaded up her plate with hot fried fish and bread. He pushed a tureen of porridge toward her and passed her cream and butter and honey and jam tarts. Holly hardly paused between bites. "I hope we shan't run out," Jade observed dryly.

Holly glanced at him. "My mother doesn't let animals eat at the table."

"Nor do we."

Almaric stacked the empty platters. "Jade! Such a way to speak to Her Ladyship!"

When the plates had been cleared, Almaric brought Holly a cup of tea. "Now, my lady, you must tell us the exciting tale of your escape."

You mean after the others left me behind? Holly thought. But that wasn't Almaric's fault. "When Fleetwing and I fell, the king's knights captured me and took me to see the prince. I'm lucky he didn't kill me right then."

"Yes, quite!"

"But then they locked me in a room and told me I'd be executed this morning."

"My goodness!" Almaric leaned forward eagerly.

"I kept expecting someone to come help me—Ranulf

CLAIRE M. CATERER

or Fleetwing or *somebody*—because they didn't know what was going to happen to me—"

"How dreadful!"

"And then . . . Then . . ."

"Yes? Then what?"

But Holly dissolved in tears. Almaric sprang up and rummaged in a nearby sideboard for a handkerchief. "My word, Your Ladyship . . . Goodness gracious me. Jade . . . ?"

"I believe," said the cat, from his place in front of the fire, "that Her Ladyship feels herself ill used because the rest of us neglected to stay and be captured as well."

"But you didn't even come back for me! And . . ." *One of the boys is dead.* She couldn't even bring herself to say it.

"Do you imply cowardice?" The cat stood up, his back bristling. "Do you realize the risk taken on your behalf by creatures who have no reason to trust you, save their own desperate hopes? Have you no concern for *their* welfare?"

"Fleetwing!" Holly said, remembering the fall. "Is he all right?"

"Gravely wounded, and Fortimus the stag as well," said Jade, switching his tail. "A leogryff, as fortune has it, heals quickly. His magic grants him this. I cannot say the same for the stag, but I do know they shall be hunted now and slaughtered, unless you prove to be of some use to them."

"Jade! Her Ladyship!"

"Should earn her title, Almaric." The cat settled back into the cushion. "'Twas an Elemental who rescued her, before our own plan could be realized at daybreak."

"An Elemental!"

Holly wiped her face. "So there *was* a plan?"

"Of course," said the cat. "Before the execution, when you would be brought into the open air, and escape was possible. Not when you were locked in the North Tower with no means of egress."

"I wasn't there. They took me to the western chamber. It was the queen's order."

"The *queen's* order?" Almaric's voice fell to a hush.

Holly described Elianne's visit and how Ignata had helped her. "And you tried to kill her!" She turned to the cat, angry all over again.

"Jade!" Almaric beamed at him. "What bravery! You are too modest!"

"But aren't you listening? She was helping me," said Holly.

"Oh no, my lady, certainly not," Almaric said. "Jade saved you from a prison from whence escape would be impossible, queens or no queens."

"I don't understand."

"Did the Elemental not offer you a firecake?" asked Jade. Almaric gasped.

"Well . . . yes. She said I couldn't get into their little house otherwise."

"Exactly. What it failed to mention was that you would never again be as you are."

Almaric nodded. "'Tis true, my lady. When the king banished magic from the kingdom, the Elementals retreated into their invisible homes and refused to show themselves except to those who proved useful to them. With an Adept at their side, they would gain great power. They would never have released you."

"She . . . She said that one of the boys was dead," said Holly.

"Quite possible," said Jade.

"But just as possibly not," Almaric countered. "These creatures always pretend to know more than they do."

Holly held the warm cup of tea close to her. Maybe there was hope that both boys were still alive. Queen Elianne hadn't said anything about one being dead. "The queen said she would delay the boys' execution for three days."

"Her Majesty is a recluse. She has no power," Jade said quietly.

"But she's pretty equal to the king, right?" asked Holly.

Almaric snorted. "She is more the king's prisoner than his wife. Since the birth of the prince, she has rarely been seen in public."

"But she must be able to make some decisions," Holly insisted. "She said she wanted to wait until the king got home. Maybe he'd want to question Everett and Ben himself."

"Still, she could not have meant to aid your escape, my lady," said the cat.

"'Twould be treason," Almaric agreed.

"Who here speaks of treason?" boomed a voice. Ranulf's face appeared through the open window.

"What a start you gave us! Put that silly thing away!" Almaric waved at the sword the centaur had drawn. "I wager you unsheathe it in your sleep, Ranulf."

"'Tis best to come prepared," the centaur said, though he did as asked. "I came to see that all was well with Her Ladyship, and to discover what plans have been made."

It took a few minutes to catch Ranulf up with all that had happened so far. Holly still thought Ignata wasn't as bad as Jade had said, but at least she was convinced that everyone had tried to act in her best interest. The question was what to do next.

"I too would be loathe to believe that the queen had meant to aid the lady Holly," Ranulf said at last. "Did not the knights come swift on our heels?"

"We cannot tell what the queen is playing at," said Jade. "But we can at least discover if the prisoners are still alive. Send Hornbeak the falcon to the castle. He will find out."

"'Tis already done. I await him here," said the centaur.

"I don't even have any way of getting home," said Holly in a small voice. "Even if I do get them—him—back. Whoever's left. I need the wand."

Ranulf and the cat had no answer to this dilemma, but Almaric's eyes brightened. "Ah yes. I have been thinking on this since daybreak. Your wand, my lady, is likely lost forever. But perhaps another could be forged."

The cat snorted, and Ranulf said, "I would wager an Adept's wand has not been forged these hundred years."

"But why should it not be possible? 'Tis not a long journey from here—"

"And who has seen her since the Last Days, Almaric? She has no apprentice, she is likely dead—"

"Her race are long-lived, Jade."

"We must act at once, not waste two days on a fool's errand. I say we attack."

"Typical of your race, Ranulf, I daresay!"

"An untrained Adept without her wand is little more than a lost child."

"The proper respect to Her Ladyship, if you please, Jade!"

"Her *Ladyship*, Almaric, is not one of us."

"Hey!" shouted Holly. The three of them looked up, startled. Holly cleared her throat. "Are you saying I could get another wand somewhere?"

Ranulf shifted from one hoof to another, then grunted, "Possibly."

"How?"

Almaric leaned forward. "The same way Adepts have always obtained their wands, my lady. You cannot simply go to market and buy one with a few coins. A wand must be forged, and only one is able to do so."

"Who is it?"

"She is of an ancient race, my lady, one even more reclusive than the Adepts. Only one in a generation of her kind becomes the Wandwright, and once anointed, she lives a life twice that of ordinary mortals. Her chosen apprentice lives equally long, until the Wandwright chooses her time to die, and the apprentice takes over."

"So you're saying only two people in Anglielle can make a wand?"

"Nay, only one, my lady. The race of the Wandwright

was hunted to near extinction. It is likely the Wand-wright has no apprentice."

"It is a fact she has not," Ranulf said shortly. "I saw the king himself murder the Wandwright's apprentice unarmed at the Battle of the Wastelands. A child of seven years, she was."

The little group fell silent.

"I did not realize you fought at the Battle of the Wastelands," Almaric said at last. "But the Wandwright herself survived, did she not?"

"I cannot say. My brother and I drove the king from her home that day, but I have not heard tell of her since. She was not young those many years ago."

"I tell you, she is not far. My crystal says that her home lies beyond the woods on the distant moors."

"Are not crystals influenced by wishful thinking?" asked the cat.

"I don't care," Holly broke in. "I have to try and find her. How else can I ever get the boys out of the castle and get us all home?"

A sudden breeze interrupted her. With a great flourish of his wings, one of the falcons Holly had met the night before landed on the cottage windowsill.

"What news, Hornbeak?"

The falcon bowed to Holly, ignoring the centaur. "Greetings, Lady Holly. I bring gladsome tidings."

"Is my brother okay?"

"Both youths live, my lady. I have visited the royal falconry and heard the falconers' talk. They say the prince has stayed the executions three days, until the tournament to come."

The group gave a general cheer, and relief washed over Holly. The queen hadn't lied to her after all.

"What tournament be this?" Ranulf asked when they had calmed down.

"One of the king's follies. In these times of peace, he must encourage his knights to competition, and treat his nobles to feasting and games."

"This may be to our advantage, my lady," Almaric said. "With everyone in the castle busied about the tournament, your kinsman will have greater chance of escape. Eh, Ranulf?"

"It would seem so," the centaur admitted.

"That's it, then," Holly said. Suddenly she felt lighter than at any time since their botched rescue attempt. "I can go see this Wandwright, get a new wand, and use it to help rescue the boys. Right?"

Ranulf and the others glanced at each other uncomfortably.

"Well?"

"Lady Holly," said Almaric gently, "consider that no one has forged a wand for a generation or more. It is not the work of a moment. The Wandwright must develop an affinity with the Adept; she must have the right herbs in season; the phase of the moon also makes a great difference. And that is not all. The Wandwright herself may not agree."

"But why wouldn't she? She must be an enemy of the king. He tried to have her killed, didn't he?"

"The Wandwrights are a race like none other. Even in the face of brutality, she is enemy to none—but in kind, friend to none as well. She will not happily forge a wand for battle."

"Your Ladyship's plan be sound," Ranulf said, "if the Wandwright be still alive. And if we are able to find her. *If* she yet has materials to forge a new wand. *If* she be willing to help Her Ladyship. *If* she is able to forge a wand so quickly. *If*—pardon me—Your Ladyship can be schooled to a new wand. And *if*—"

"All the king's horses and all the king's men. I know how it goes," said Holly. She stood up. "So we'd better get going, don't you think?"

Chapter 27

Sol

To say that the rest of the boys' night was cold and uncomfortable—that Everett at first couldn't sleep and then started up, heart racing, only to sink back into the darkness; that Ben cried himself to sleep and then jolted awake to escape a dream-death by sword-point; that they both cut themselves on the scattered glass; that the stone floor grew harder by the minute, no matter how they tried to soften it with their jackets; that at any moment they expected a knight to burst in and kill them outright—to say all these things would be a fair account of the boys' evening, and no exaggeration. Exhausted and cranky, they spoke very little. And so passed a long night that at last brightened into dawn.

The news of their execution's delay didn't cheer them as much as you might think. It's fine to sit in a soft chair and hear someone else's tale and feel a stirring of hope, but for Everett, it was just putting off the

CLAIRE M. CATERER

inevitable. As their cold room brightened, he glanced around at the shattered glass, Ben's bloodstained face (he was still asleep), and the sheer stone walls, and felt about as low as he ever had. He looked out the window at what appeared to be a very English morning. On the other side of the outer castle walls, the stream that fed the moat meandered into the dense wood. He heard sheep bleating and cows lowing to be milked. From somewhere nearby, the smell of baking bread and smoke from a cook fire wafted up. The steep hill rolled into the valley, and on the opposite rise, he could just make out Holly's cottage—or where it ought to have been.

Just as he was working this out, a bright butterfly landed on the ledge of the stone window. It emitted a shrill squeak.

Everett jumped, and then peered at the butterfly— which wasn't a butterfly at all.

Its doubled wings were a transparent magenta, and its body humanoid, though the legs and arms were very long and its face pointed. The skin was a faded yellow hue and its golden eyes so bright he could hardly look at them. The creature seemed clothed, but whatever it wore clung so tightly to its body as to be nearly invisible.

"It's like a fairy," Everett whispered.

The creature flew up to his face and bared tiny, pointed teeth. "I come from the Realm of the Good Folk, mortal." Its voice was shrill, like steel being welded.

"Who are you?"

The creature backed up, hovering. "I am born in the heart of the sun, and ride its rays each day to Earth. I am called Sol."

"Ohhh-kay. I'm Everett Shaw."

"And the other? Hath he the Blood as well?"

"The . . . blood?"

"Are you kin?"

"Oh no. Ben's just a mate. But who *are* you? I mean, what are you doing here?"

Sol descended gently onto the windowsill. "We are drawn to the wand, like moths to the candle. It has been used in this place not long ago. Only true Adepts may wield it, youngling of the wood. You are gifted."

There was that word again—*Adepts*. Everett remembered how Dart had reacted when he thought Everett was one.

"So . . . do you want me to conjure up bigger wings or something?"

"You are ignorant," said the fairy. "Aid comes to you and you scoff at it."

"Hang on. No one's scoffing. We're in real trouble, and Holly, too. If you can help us—"

CLAIRE M. CATERER

"Holly." The fairy expelled a long, hissing breath. Its golden eyes gazed into Everett's, burning until he was forced to look away.

"Have you seen her? Where're they keeping her?"

"Silence. I too have power. Observe." Sol gestured toward the ground and Everett leaned his head out to see. Unfolding from the window, at first wavy and transparent, but then quite solid, was a spiral staircase made of stone. "Would this not be of some use to you?" Sol asked.

"Are you kidding? It's brilliant!" He turned to wake up Ben, but the fairy laid its tiny hand on his arm.

"The Good Folk do not grant favors without payment in return. This egress is yours only if you share your knowledge and power." Sol released him and Everett uttered a low curse. A tiny hand-shaped burn appeared on his arm.

"The wand," said Sol.

"The knights took it," Everett said.

"And the maid's?"

"I don't know what's happened to Holly. I was asking you."

The fairy flew up to Everett's cheek, extending its white-hot fingers.

"Don't!" he cried in a panic. Somehow he had to keep the fairy here, and happy. It was their only chance of escape. "The knights said she was captured. I think she's somewhere in the castle, and we're to be executed in three days. There, is that enough?"

"Tell me," said the fairy, flying close enough to singe Everett's hair, "of her power."

"She doesn't *have* any power. I mean, she did use the wand to open a tree in the wood. That's how we came here—from some other place. But she doesn't know spells or anything."

The fairy settled on the ledge and smiled. "She is untrained, this Adept."

"Yes!" Everett said. "She's untrained."

"That is easily remedied."

Everett's stomach shifted uncomfortably. Why did Sol—why did *everyone*—want to know about Holly? No one ever asked about him. Something in the fairy's smile seemed cold, even . . . wrong. "Look, I'm sure Holly's keen to get trained up, but we really need to get back to the wood, back to our own place."

"Is this tree the only way to return to your land?"

"I guess. I don't know how else we'd do it."

"Would you be able to find it again?"

The fairy was leaning forward, listening to him very closely now. Everett hesitated again; it seemed to want an awful lot of information, and he didn't know if it could be trusted. Still, Holly had made friends with all sorts of magic creatures, and where was he? Stuck in a tower with rubbishy food and a stone floor for a bed. Sol could be *his* friend. A powerful friend.

"I think I could find it," he offered at last, though he wasn't at all sure this was true. "Holly was—I mean, we were both keeping track of where we were going, but then the prince came and took us, so . . ."

"Yes, yes," said the fairy impatiently. "But what of you, young master?" It was then that Everett realized she was female. Her voice was soft, her legs long, her tiny body perfectly formed. Funny how he hadn't quite seen all this before.

She flew onto his shoulder, and a shiver whispered down his back. "You too had a wand. You too are of the Blood, are you not?"

"I'm . . . well . . ." Everett cast a desperate glance at Ben, who, impossibly, was still asleep. "I *did* make the wand spit out fire. That's pretty good, isn't it?"

"Fire? That is most unusual. Art of Elemental blood as well?"

He wanted to be of *some* kind of blood, but he couldn't quite lie to Sol. "I don't think so. I'm just telling you what it did."

"Then how did you fail to escape, with a wand of such strength?"

"It . . . sort of backfired. It got so hot I couldn't hold it."

"I see," said Sol, flying back to the window ledge. She paced back and forth along it. "A wand protects itself against thieves. You have taken what is not yours."

Everett's cheeks warmed. "It was like he *wanted* me to have one! Why else would he leave them lying about? Anyone could've nicked one!"

"You are a thief. And you are not of the Blood."

The knot of guilt in Everett's stomach hardened. Somehow, losing the respect of this tiny, fiery creature made everything worse.

"What is more," Sol continued, "you will never have the power of the wand. Do not doubt me," she added, when Everett tried to speak. "I know more of magic and fire and darkness than you could learn in a thousand lifetimes. But perhaps . . ."

She stood still several moments, as if thinking. Then Everett heard her whisper in his ear as she lighted there. "Perhaps I was hasty. A thief may be contemptible in your world, but not so in this. You have cunning and a lust for power. Therein lies nobility. You are great magic in the making, my lord."

Everett's heart swelled. Great magic . . . like Holly had. "But I thought you said I couldn't have any power? I'm not—whatever—bloody."

"There are other ways of attaining power. 'Twill be your task to find them. Make, shall we say, the proper friends?" She blew against Everett's ear with the quietest touch, as if a dandelion puff had brushed past.

Sol flew from his shoulder and swept one arm in a wide arc behind her. The stone staircase disappeared.

"Oi!" cried Everett. So much for escape.

"I cannot help you at present, young lord. I had hoped the wand would yet be in your possession. But we shall meet again."

"But—but—"

"Soon. On the wings of the wind."

As she spoke, a breeze touched with sun sprang up like a golden cyclone and swallowed her. She vanished before Everett could call out to her again.

He stole another glance at Ben, who turned over. How had he managed to sleep through Everett's entire conversation? Or had he just imagined Sol?

As the thought crossed his mind, a tiny golden feather fluttered in through the window on the breeze. One of *hers*.

He felt a keen ache in his chest, wanting to see her again. But she said she'd be back. And he, Everett, was *great magic in the making*. That could change everything, even back home. If he could learn to use the wand, maybe his mum wouldn't have to work all the time, maybe he could show Sean Fellowes a thing or two. With real magic, he might do *anything*. . . .

He suddenly wished that he hadn't admitted to stealing the wand—well, *taking* it. That wasn't the same thing, not at all. He wasn't a thief, more of an . . . opportunist. Sol seemed to understand that.

But Ben wouldn't.

Whatever the fiery little creature was offering Everett, he wasn't ready to share it. *He* had the power, she had said. Ben would only ask a lot of questions and want the power for himself, whatever it was. Sol had chosen him, Everett. He was special. And he would guard her secret.

Chapter 28

The Agreement

Just as these thoughts crossed his mind, Ben's voice piped up behind him.

"Were you talking to someone? Is it morning yet? Where's breakfast?"

Everett blinked and sighed as the image of the fairy faded. Whatever Sol had said, he was still stuck in the tower with Ben. He couldn't help wincing at his friend. Ben had wiped his bloody hands on his grimy face, and his hair stood up at odd ends all over, and his eyes were red and puffy. The smell was nothing pretty either, and that was both of them.

"They haven't brought anything," Everett said in answer to Ben's question.

"I thought I heard someone come in."

"No, I was just . . . thinking out loud. Trying to see if there's some way out this window."

"If we could just get a message to Holly somehow,"

said Ben. "We should make that Arrow kid help us. He owes us, after saying she was dead and all."

Before Everett could remind Ben that the page's name was Dart, not Arrow, the knight Pagett opened the tower door. "Come with me, lads," he said. "His Highness wishes to see you." He unhooked from his chain mail a set of iron cuffs and chains, which he locked around their wrists and ankles. Pagett drew his sword and led them out of the tower.

"This can't be good," Ben whispered.

The stairway seemed even longer going down than it had going up, but at least they had left the tower. Everett's mind spun with foolish ideas: He could loop his chain around the knight's neck or maybe jab him in the eye and seize his sword. Or he could break their chains with a swift kick and then leg it out a window. And while these sound good from an action-film standpoint, they are much less believable when you're actually shackled and shuffling down a narrow stairway with a sword against your back.

They reached the bottom of the steps and started down one long passageway after another. They crossed in front of the Great Hall, through a courtyard, then up a short staircase to a door where another knight stood.

"The prisoners, to see His Highness," Pagett announced.

The other knight used his sword's hilt to rap on the door. Then he opened it and let them through.

They entered a large chamber filled with short, armless couches and poufed ottomans. Everything was covered in dazzling red and gold fabrics, and large leaded windows let in the sun.

The prince himself sat on a carved wooden throne at the far end of the room. Flanking him were a few large potted trees where several ravens nested. A low table held the leavings of his breakfast. Everett's stomach growled. He could hear Ben wheezing. He needed his inhaler again.

"Leave us," said the prince to Pagett and the other guards.

Pagett hesitated. "Does His Highness not wish protection?" he ventured.

The prince glared at him. "I have no need of it. And take away these fetters." He waved a hand, which spurred Pagett to action. He unlocked the boys' shackles, whispering fiercely, "Mind yourself, I shall be outside the door." The knight bowed to Prince Avery and left with the others.

It was the first time Everett had gotten a proper look at the prince without bumping along on horseback or being threatened in some way. He wasn't much taller than Everett himself. He wore an embroidered silk tunic and a long overcloak, but even the extra clothes couldn't hide the fact that Avery was just a kid, and kind of a scrawny one at that.

"Ye be a sight, the pair of you," said the prince finally. He grimaced as if Ben were something a cat had coughed up. "What ails thee?"

"He needs his medicine." Everett rummaged in Ben's jacket pocket until he found the inhaler. Ben pumped it into his mouth and his breathing eased.

"Give that to me," Avery ordered.

"You can't keep it," said Everett.

"I shan't *keep* it." Avery snatched up the inhaler, turning it over in his hands. "'Tis a strange device. Yet it seems effective."

"Give it back."

"Very well." The prince tossed it to Everett, and for a moment they were just three ordinary boys, looking at one another's trinkets.

"Now then. Whence do ye come? I have never seen garments such as yours."

"It's all been a mistake, Your Highness," said Everett. "We were lost. We just wandered into the wood. We didn't know it was yours. And anyway, we had no weapons, so how could we poach anything?"

"I would have had your heads at daybreak, but my mother the queen has stayed your execution. Why?"

CLAIRE M. CATERER

"Maybe she wants more evidence."

"Or she has been bewitched," said Avery. "I have not forgotten, ye were in the company of an Adept, who has since escaped the castle."

"Yes!" Ben shouted.

"I told you!" cried Everett. He slapped Ben a high five.

"She can do anything!" Ben gushed, swiping at his eyes. "Even at home, when she's in a ton of trouble and she's grounded to her room, she can *always* get out, through a window or—"

"Silence!" said the prince. "How are ye called?"

"I'm Everett Shaw," said Everett, shushing Ben. "And this is Ben Shepard. We're not Adepts. We don't even know what they are."

"Then how came ye by this?" The prince picked up a stick from the table and twirled it in his fingers.

"Everett! That's your wand," Ben said.

"Sir Grandor said thou didst make fire with it." Prince Avery's voice dropped to a hush. "Do it again." He stretched his hand out, the wand flat in his palm.

"Don't, Everett!" Ben cried.

"I can't control it, Your Highness. What happened last night was an accident."

"Take it."

This sounded more like an order than a request. Everett took the wand. Ben winced. The wood felt cool and ordinary, but when Everett closed his fist around the broad end, the vibration tingled in his fingers. He swept the wand away from the prince and aimed it at the floor, where he thought it would do the least damage.

But it didn't spin out of control like before. He was able to steady it as the vibration thrummed through his body. A thin, orange spark shot from the wand's tip.

Everett was sure something would catch fire, but instead, the flame rebounded from the floor and flew up to the ceiling, where it exploded in a shower of sparks like fireworks. Everett pointed the wand at them and they changed color from orange to yellow to blue, twirling in Catherine wheels before falling harmlessly to the floor.

Was this the great magic the fairy had talked about? Maybe now he could use the wand to get them out of here. But then he remembered the knights just outside the door. Everett laid the wand on the table.

Only then was he conscious of having heard the prince gasp and Ben utter a sound like "Ooooh!" Avery looked Everett in the eye. "Tell me how it was done."

"I honestly don't know, Your Highness."

"Nonsense." The prince snatched up the wand. "What men call magic is but illusion. Why does it not make fire for me?" He lowered his voice, leaning close

CLAIRE M. CATERER

to the boys. "Can it be that thou hast *real* power? That thy magic be true?"

"It belongs to him," Ben spoke up. "That's why it works."

The prince glanced at him.

"See, it's like Holly's wand—my sister's. She could do all this stuff with it, but when I picked it up, it wouldn't do a thing."

"This one worked for you last night," said Everett. "Why's that, then?"

"Well . . . I don't know. But it was nothing like what Holly can do. I think it's because Mr. Gallaway gave that wand to her, like it's meant for her. And he gave you that one, right?" Everett glanced away. "Only this one doesn't work right, for some reason. Maybe it's defective."

Prince Avery turned the wand over in his hand. He seemed not to hear them. "I do feel something," he whispered. "A sort of . . . *rightness*. A power."

He lay down the wand and shivered, lost in thought; then, abruptly, he stood up. He walked around the two boys. "How many years hast thou?" he asked Everett.

"Twelve, Your Highness. Ben, you're . . . ?"

"Ten."

"And I, nearly fourteen. Still, thou be not too young. . . ." An exotic perfume came from the silks

Avery was wearing. "An idea has occurred to me. Hast competed before?"

"Competed, Your Highness?"

"His Majesty is hosting a tournament anon. Knights from all corners of the kingdom will come to shew their talents. I should like my personal champion to win, naturally. Grandor has served me well enough in the past, but none has seen power like thine before, whether real or no. Thou shalt joust, Everett, wand in one hand, lance in the other."

"Joust? Isn't that the thing where the knights fight?" Ben asked.

"'Tis a contest of strength," the prince explained, "and skill. Mounted knights essay to unseat one another with the lance."

"I can't do that. I'll get killed," Everett said.

"But not if thou wieldest the wand, nay? Besides, I have trained in the joust myself. We have three days afore the tournament; it will amuse me to train thee."

"Can you really learn to joust in three days?"

"No, Ben, you can't. He's just playing with us."

"A serious game," said Avery. "I shall spare your lives if thou be victorious."

Victorious? The prince couldn't be serious. Everett's stomach lurched as if he were already on horseback.

"What about Holly?" asked Ben.

"She is an Adept," said Avery. "She must be captured and executed."

"Then forget it! No deal."

"Wait, Ben—" Everett put his hand on Ben's shoulder.

"Maybe *you* don't care about Holly, but in case you forgot, we can't even get back to our world without her," Ben said, throwing his arm off.

"What is thy meaning?" said the prince, giving him a sharp look.

Everett nudged Ben, pushing him off balance. "Hey!" Ben said, scowling. Everett raised his eyebrows at him, trying to project his thoughts into Ben's head. *We can't just tell him everything. He already thinks we're outlaws. Now we're going to look mental as well.*

Ben stared at him blankly. "*What* is your deal?"

"Speak, poacher! Or I shall rethink my offer of clemency," said Prince Avery.

"All right, listen," said Everett. "We're not poachers, and we're not those Adept things, because we come from somewhere else altogether. This whole country— we've never been here before. We came through the wood with Holly's wand from, I don't know, another place. I mean, the land is pretty much the same. Except the river runs a rather different course. Like you said, the clothes are different. It's . . . I don't know . . . *later.*"

"It's more advanced," Ben cut in. "Like, we've got cars and planes and computers . . ."

"Like a carriage, only it goes on its own, without horses. . . ."

"And big metal birds that fly, and you can sit in them. . . ."

"Running water! You can take a hot bath whenever you like. . . ."

Avery's face whitened, his eyes large and round. *And . . . greedy*, Everett thought. *He wants to see this world.*

"And you don't have to burn candles," Ben was saying. "You just turn a switch, and it's bright as day. . . ."

"You can talk to people far away, using a kind of speaker thing. . . ."

"There aren't any knights, though there used to be. . . ."

Avery collapsed back onto his throne, his mouth open. "What . . . What *is* this place you speak of? Is it truly a magic realm?"

"It's real," said Everett. "But only Holly knows how to get there. She can take anyone she likes, you know. Maybe . . ." He pretended to think, but in fact he had been thinking very quickly for some time now. "Maybe you could come back with us."

"He could *what*?" said Ben.

"Just for a visit, just to see what it's like."

Avery's eyes glittered. "Truly, men can fly in your world?"

"You could come and see," Everett said softly. "It wouldn't take much time. But we need Holly."

"And when you got back, you could tell everybody how you chased us all into our world and left us there," Ben offered.

The prince's voice dropped to a whisper. "To release an Adept . . . 'Tis treachery."

"Not if you sent us back to our world."

"But how're we supposed to find Holly, anyway?" Ben asked. "Haven't the knights been looking for her?"

Avery smiled. "She shalt come to us, nay?"

"She . . . shalt?" asked Ben uncertainly.

"She essayed rescue before. She will do so again, most likely during the king's tournament. We must make pretense to fight against her. Then I shall ride after you into the wood, and ye shall transport me to your land."

"Well, *maybe*—" Everett said.

"And I will be the only man ever to glimpse another world!"

"Well, *boy*, anyway," Ben muttered. "Now we just have to hope Everett doesn't get killed in this tournament."

"So let me get this straight," said Everett. "You want to train me for the joust, put me in a tournament against trained knights, pray I don't get killed and even *win*, make a proper show of magic with this wand—which is illegal, as far as I've been able to figure—and then you'll just let Holly rescue us?"

"I would see thy mastery of magic—in this world and thine."

"What about Ben? I won't do it unless he does too."

"He is too young and . . . infirm. Still," said Avery, "a knight needs a squire."

"Hey, isn't that like a servant?" asked Ben.

"Thou shalt attend the needs of thy knight," said the prince. "Groom his mount, carry his lance—"

"Sounds like a servant. Or a golf caddie."

"Shut it." Everett nudged him. "He'll be happy to do it, Your Highness. We both will."

"Then we are in accord. We shall begin training this morning." The prince yanked on a bellpull, and one of the knights entered the room.

"Your Highness?"

"Take these two to the servants' quarters. They shall need a proper bath if they are to remain in our royal presence. And find them some fresh attire." He twirled Everett's wand between two fingers, watching as it caught the sunlight. "Then return them to me."

Chapter 29

Knights Rest

Holly thought that now they had decided what to do, they'd pack up a lunch and be on their way. But Almaric fussed over how much food to take, and how best to fashion a bedroll, and which of his magical instruments would prove most useful. Eventually he settled on something he called a firestarter and an expanding jelly pot. "A pity we have no pavilion, never mind the vanishing sort, but it can't be helped," he said.

It was Ranulf who pointed out that while Her Ladyship's dress was comely, it wasn't practical for traveling. Hornbeak the falcon was dispensed to snatch something from a peasant's clothesline. He brought Holly a boy's tunic and some kind of trousers (the legs were cut apart and had to be joined by tying them to something that looked suspiciously like boxer shorts). Around her waist she tightened a leather belt and she tied the close-fitting hood under her chin.

With her hair covered, she would easily be mistaken for a boy.

She was determined to take her backpack, too, over the objections of the others. Almaric spent several minutes debating about it until Holly pointed out that she could carry food and supplies as well as the others. "Plus, it's olive drab, so it'll blend into the landscape," she said. Almaric glanced at Ranulf and shrugged—olive drab meant little to them—and Holly strapped it on.

The sun was high and warm before they finally set out. At first the ground was flat and easy to walk on. They kept to a path until they left the wood, and then tramped along through a meadow, vaguely northwest by Holly's compass, toward some distant brown hills. The shoes Hornbeak had brought were little more than thick pieces of leather sewn together, and they were too big for her. It was tough going, if you can imagine trudging through tall grass with floppy slippers on. But at least they were *doing* something.

Once they had found their path, Holly broke the silence. "Almaric, there's something I don't understand about all this Adept stuff. Ignata said I was an Adept by blood, but wouldn't the wand work for anyone? Why couldn't I just give it to someone else and make them an Adept?"

Almaric reddened as if Holly had said he had food stuck in his beard. "Nay, my lady. You were given the wand because you were *recognized* as an Adept. Your wand, once lost, is almost useless to another, unless he had some innate power of his own. But even then, a wand that is not given freely can be a dangerous thing."

"But, Almaric, you don't have a wand, and you do magic too, don't you?"

The old man picked a handful of purple wildflowers and placed them in a leather pouch around his neck. "Nothing very impressive, I daresay. Once I had friends among the Adepts, and certain objects were entrusted to me when the king's rampage began. My minor magician tricks I learnt from my nurse, an outcast from the Realm herself."

"The Realm—that's where Ignata comes from? I've heard stories in my world about fairies. I guess that's the same thing."

"Take care, my lady," said Almaric, his voice falling to a whisper. "The Good Folk take offense easily. We never speak of them as . . ." He winked, then mouthed the word *fairies*. "They are the Good or Gentle Folk, we call them."

"Ignata said she was an Elemental."

"The Realm is its own kingdom under no man's dominion. The Elementals are an especially powerful race within the Realm. The Cináed are the fire tribe. I imagine the being you speak of is one of them, judging by the state of Jade's whiskers."

The cat glared back at them. Holly hadn't noticed how crinkly his whiskers were, as if he'd gotten too close to a candle flame.

"She *did* help me. The Elementals can't be all bad."

"Not *bad*, my lady," Almaric said, glancing around as if afraid of being overheard. "I should think *independent* is more the word."

Holly was less afraid of the Good Folk than she was of the king. "It's so quiet. We're just out here in broad daylight. Won't the knights come looking for me?"

Ranulf turned to her. "Had we the time to tarry until sunset, I would have preferred it. But this path is safer than most. The king's men will not gladly traverse the forest to the northern end. It is my hope his knights will give you up for lost."

"Some of them, maybe," Holly murmured. But she was sure that others would be willing to brave the forest to bring back the head of an Adept.

As they progressed, the grasses grew high and wild, slowing their pace. The little party had left the flat meadow and were obliged to climb steep hills thick with gorse and heather. Holly bounded up the first few easily and enjoyed the view from above, but going down was less fun. Occasionally she startled a flock of grouse, small brownish birds that Almaric said made fine hunting. She had to watch her feet carefully to keep from sliding down the gravelly slope, and her toes began to hurt as they pushed into the tips of her shoes. Every pebble poked her through the thin soles. But none of the others complained, so Holly said nothing.

Conversation died as the hills got steeper and the sun climbed. Just as Holly thought she could walk no farther, Almaric announced that his old bones could do with a rest and lunch.

Ranulf made do with a bit of grass and a jug of wine he had strapped across his back. Jade wandered off into the wood to stalk a rodent. Almaric pulled a woven blanket from his pack. He set out his expanding jelly pot (which, though it grew no larger, never ran out of jelly) along with a large loaf of bread and a funny kind of crock that kept the butter quite cold.

They ate their fill, and Almaric stretched out on the blanket, his fingers knitted behind his head.

The centaur brushed a fly from his flank. "Nap if needs must, Almaric. I will keep watch."

"Yes, a fine idea," Almaric agreed.

"I'll go refill this," Holly said, picking up the waterskin.

She could hear water gurgling nearby. She stepped carefully into the wood, listening for the stream, but instead she heard a distinct rustling. She froze. "Jade? Are you here?"

Suddenly the black cat streaked through the forest and landed at her feet. "Be quick!" he whispered. Ranulf broke through the trees and grabbed Holly by one arm. Almaric took the other and they herded her deeper into the forest. "In here, my lady," said Jade. He crawled under the skirt of an enormous pine tree and beckoned to her.

"Farther in!" Almaric whispered.

"No time," said Ranulf.

Holly followed the cat. The tree's branches hung nearly to the ground. She knelt on the soft nest of pine needles. On either side of the tree she could just make out Almaric and Ranulf.

"Jade, what is it?" she whispered.

"Knights, my lady." He huddled closer to her.

Now she heard them. Two or three on horseback, just outside the wood—right where they had been resting. Holly held her breath.

The horses stopped. Holly could see one of the riders through the trees as he dismounted; he wore a chain-mail shirt and a belt with scabbard. He sat down in the grass with the other knight. Two younger boys

                                CLAIRE M. CATERER

appeared and walked the horses some distance away, where they unsaddled and brushed them. Were those the squires? Food was passed around and the party ate while the horses grazed. "'Tis sure to be a fine tournament, Bertran," said one of the knights.

"I shall welcome the diversion," answered the other. "I grow weary of the countryside's unending quiet."

"The talk is that you have brought your own diversion to your manor."

Bertran laughed. "My squire brought me one of the Earthfolk who had escaped Lord Raethius. We made fine sport of him."

"Earthfolk! Had he magic?"

"One of the Dvergar. Naught of great consequence. We let the villagers have their own sport, then left him to the ravens."

"A good example you have made of him."

"Aye—but hark! Be still." Bertran paused, peering right at Holly in the little stand of trees. She held her breath. "Do you see something, Jordain? Just there?"

Both knights stood up, tensed, hands on their sword hilts. They took a step toward the wood.

"Do not move," Ranulf said in the quietest of whispers.

But Holly made a sudden decision, one that might have looked very foolish. She straightened up and walked straight out of the trees to the clearing where they stood.

"Greetings!" said Jordain, relaxing as he saw her. "And how are you called, lad?"

It was a moment like none other Holly had ever experienced. It was like being a thief, with one hand in the cash box, as the policeman strolled up. She had no chance to run, or if she did, she'd quickly be caught. She couldn't risk exposing the others, but if she could think on her feet, she might not have to. Holly swallowed. "I am . . ." She groped for a name, then thought of her father. "I am Steven. My lord." Belatedly, she bowed.

The knight inclined his head. "I am Sir Jordain of the North. Here be Sir Bertran of the Oak." Bertran smiled tightly, his hand still resting on his sword hilt. "Where is your master, young Steven?"

Holly's face grew hot. Her master? She could hardly trot out Almaric and call him a knight. "He's . . . He's just over that hill in the wood. We were hunting. His name is Sir Gallaway." She pointed away from where Ranulf and Almaric were hiding, up the rise. "And I was . . ." She glanced around, then remembered the grouse. "Oh! I was going ahead to, you know, startle the birds."

Jordain raised his eyebrows as if impressed.

"Bringing feast to the feast, is it? You are en route to the king's tournament?"

"Yes!" Holly said eagerly, remembering Hornbeak's news. What exactly had the falcon said? "In these times of peace, the king must encourage his knights to competition."

Jordain's eyes searched hers for a moment. She held his gaze, swallowing. "Aye," he said at last. "Well spake, squire."

"Jordain!" shouted the other knight. Bertran was standing some distance away at the edge of the wood, his sword drawn, his face taut. Holly's heart stopped. With one boot heel he had Jade pinned to the ground by the throat. The cat thrashed in the dirt, but he was held fast.

"Stop!" Holly cried, running to Bertran. "Don't hurt him!"

Jordain followed, sword drawn. "Stand aside, lad. Creatures of that hue once acted as familiars to the Adepts of old. This one has the look of an Intelligent Beast."

"But he's mine!"

Holly blurted the words before thinking, and the two knights stared at her, openmouthed. She had said something horrid, and now had to fix it. "I . . . I mean, he belongs to Sir Gallaway."

Jordain's lips curled in disgust. "Why would a knight of the realm befriend such a creature?"

Her throat went dry as Jade's struggles grew feebler. She heard Ranulf stomping impatiently back in the trees; at any moment he would charge out, but then he would be fighting both knights and their squires. They'd kill him. Holly held her hand out to the trees in a gesture that she hoped Ranulf would understand as *Wait, I've got this*. "Here's the truth," she said to Jordain. "We found him in the woods, and we're taking him to the castle as an—an enemy of the king. So he can be questioned. Or—or executed. Anyway, he's *our* prisoner."

Bertran stared long at her, as if trying to work out whether she was telling the truth. Jade's body grew still. Not knowing what else to do, Holly lurched at Bertran, shoving him off balance. At the same time, something bright and hot erupted from the grass, and the knight cursed, brandishing his sword. Jade sprang up, hissing, his back bristling. Holly scooped him up in her arms, skittering back from what had looked like a brushfire. But it was gone now. She turned back to Bertran, whose face was red. "Please, I'm very sorry, sir knight. But my master . . . See, it would be my fault if he didn't get credit for taking this cat alive to the castle. He'd beat me for sure."

Bertran raised his sword. "I ought thrash you myself!" he cried, but Jordain held him back and shrugged. Bertran broke away, muttering. Jordain gave Holly a pointed look. "Perhaps you and your master ought move along, if ye are to make the castle afore nightfall."

"Yes, thank you! I'll just go and find him." Holly darted off into the woods, jostling Jade in her arms. Behind her, she heard the knights call their squires to bring the horses. In a few moments, the party had moved on.

Holly watched them until their hoofbeats died away. Finally she let out her breath. Then, remembering Jade, she placed him gently on the ground. Almaric and Ranulf came out of the stand of pines where they had hidden, and everyone began to speak at once. Almaric beamed like a proud grandfather and told her how brave she was; but Ranulf was grave and said she ought not have risked it.

"But what else could I do? They were coming right for us," said Holly.

"It is *my* duty to defend *you*, my lady," the centaur insisted.

"And it is I," Jade broke in, "who owe Her Ladyship the greatest debt."

Holly looked down at him in surprise.

"I was foolish," the cat admitted. "I had hoped to

follow Your Ladyship and protect you if 'twas needed, until that beast caught me and threw me to the ground." He bowed very low.

"Anyway, at least you're okay." Holly blushed. Her knees felt a bit shaky now that it was all over. "Did you start that fire?" she asked, suddenly remembering.

Jade raised his whiskered eyebrows. "It was Your Ladyship, surely?"

"Not me." She explained what had happened to the others, but at Ranulf's serious face, she tried to laugh it off. "It was the knights, probably. They dropped a match, I guess. Right?"

The centaur said nothing, only looked at her strangely, and Almaric stepped between them, clapping his hands and beckoning. "Onward, I think, yes?" he said.

They walked on, and Jade stayed quite close to Holly's feet and seemed more respectful after their close call. Occasionally he even nuzzled her ankles, though when she tried to scratch his head, he darted away and preened himself to rearrange the fur. Mostly, the group remained silent as they climbed hill after hill. The late-afternoon sun was hot, and Holly's rough-woven tunic was itchy. She checked her compass frequently to see that they were still moving in a northwesterly direction, toward the high moors.

She wanted to ask Ranulf and Almaric about Raethius. The Sorcerer was the one subject they hadn't seemed eager to talk to her about. She shivered; even thinking about him put a chill in the air. But no, that was silly. She remembered Bittenbender, the little man of the Dvergar, and the bitterness on his face. His people had been enslaved, he'd said, and even talking about Raethius had divided the magicfolk. As if he had power beyond his very presence.

Whatever Bittenbender thought, Almaric and the others were convinced of her magic. And she *had* produced the saucer of cream—well, buttermilk—out of thin air. Could they be right, that she had some innate power? And how did Mr. Gallaway know it if she did? Maybe just possessing the wand had changed her somehow.

But even though her wand was gone—maybe even destroyed—Holly felt different. Or perhaps not different so much as *discovered*. As if something had been slumbering just under the surface of her heart. She could feel the wand's warmth even now, a kind of glow inside her, although faint. Ignata had thought it funny that she couldn't fly or escape by herself. Why? *Was* she able to do magic, even without the wand? Had the wand recognized her, as Almaric had said?

Maybe it was the air of the place. Even with

everything horrible that had happened, there was a rhythm in Anglielle that she almost *knew*. It was like searching for a melody that someone had asked her to sing, a song that she could hear in her mind but that seemed just out of reach. Everything was different here. *She* was different here.

The sun was low when they stopped at last. The distant moors loomed closer. "Let us bide here, Almaric," said the centaur. "We shall reach the Wandwright in the morning."

They chose a spot at the edge of the forest, where Holly would be sheltered beneath a tall rowan. Jade disappeared into the forest to hunt. Almaric gathered firewood, which he arranged in the center of a ring of stones that Holly had helped him collect. Then he took from his rucksack an egg-shaped object about half the size of a football. From either narrow end sprouted a tuft of gold metallic material like very bright tinsel. Almaric donned some gloves that looked like oven mitts, held the firestarter over the kindling, and pulled hard on the tinseled ends, as if trying to break open a Christmas cracker.

The egg exploded with a loud *bang* and a ball of fire shot into the sky. The flame gathered itself and fell straight into the ring of stones, igniting the kindling.

CLAIRE M. CATERER

Ranulf glanced up. "You have announced our position well."

Almaric shrugged. "I am a bit out of practice. I should have held it lower, perhaps."

"Perhaps."

Holly huddled close to the fire. The temperature was quickly falling. In a few minutes the cat returned bearing a net of fat, troutlike fish ("Jade has his own talents," Almaric said when he saw Holly's surprised face). Within an hour, the fish were cleaned, roasted, and eaten, and Holly helped Almaric make up beds from the rolls of blankets he had brought. Two minutes later, she was sound asleep.

Chapter 30

The Lesson

Everett guessed that the court of King Reynard was normally a rather dull place, for he could think of no other reason for the news of their change of status to spread so quickly. If he hadn't known better, he'd have said courtiers were texting one another on their mobiles. Everyone treated Everett and Ben very differently now. Pagett did not lock the chains around them again, but merely led them out of Avery's chamber and beckoned to Dart. Pagett brought them into a small room and said to the page, "Attend these youth. They shall need baths and fresh attire."

"Aye, Sir Pagett." Dart bustled about the room as the knight walked out. He built up the fire and settled a huge cauldron on hooks above it.

Ben watched him darkly as he went about his duties. "You shouldn't have lied to us about Holly getting killed," he said, when Dart turned back to them.

The page paled. "I—I merely said what was surely to happen."

"Still, it was a pretty awful thing to say. She's my sister."

Ben's face was turning red, and Everett stepped between them. No point in getting them in more trouble. "It's all right, no harm done. Holly's escaped, hasn't she? Thanks for the bath, Dart."

"I shall speak to Laundress about clothes for you. Mind the fire," he said, eyeing Ben, and walked out.

"You're making friends pretty fast," said Ben, scowling as he trailed his fingers along the stone hearth.

"Well, oughtn't I? We're trying to stay alive, remember?"

"I know. I just don't trust this prince guy. First he's like, 'We're gonna kill you,' and then it's, 'You're gonna joust with a wand.' And you're all ready to just dump him in downtown Hawkesbury—"

Everett sighed. "So what if he mucks about a bit in our world? He won't want to stay there."

"You hope," said Ben. "Meantime, you get to do all the fun stuff with magic, and I'm stuck being your servant. And I bet the clothes will be itchy."

"Probably," said Everett, trying to be agreeable. "But at least we'll both be wearing them, yeah?"

Their bath was not nearly so nice as Holly's. Dart

filled a wooden barrel with well water, but even when he had tempered it with the heated cauldronful, it was much colder than the boys were used to. They scrubbed as best they could with a rough towel and a strong-smelling soap. Eventually they were reasonably clean and dressed in clothes very much like the ones Hornbeak had found for Holly. (Although instead of leggings, they wore knitted hose, which looked like pantyhose cut apart. It was lucky for them Holly couldn't see them.) They buckled drawstring pouches to their belts. Ben stashed his inhaler and packets of pills in his.

It wasn't long before Pagett returned. He walked around them, nodding. "'Tis an improvement, to be sure. Come."

Despite a more or less friendly manner, the knight kept his sword drawn. He grasped Ben's elbow and prodded Everett ahead of him. They walked out of the castle and across the drawbridge to a large field near the east tower. Several rows of seats, like bleachers, had been built upon high platforms around it, forming a sort of arena. The center was cleared of grass. The prince, astride his black stallion, had exchanged his bright silks for sturdier riding clothes, but they were still quite a bit finer (and more comfortable, Everett assumed) than anything the boys were wearing. Avery trotted his horse to where they stood.

"Release them, Sir Pagett. They be not fools enough to bolt." The prince glanced up, and both Everett and Ben followed his gaze. A few spectators were scattered among the seats—Everett recognized Lord Clement—along with at least ten archers, crossbows at the ready. "Their aim is excellent."

So much for running, Everett thought.

"A horse for my champion!" commanded the prince, and in a few moments, Dart appeared from behind the stands leading a fat yellow mare. With the other hand, he pulled a wooden cart loaded with supplies. "Thou hast some knowledge of horsemanship, I presume?"

"Some, Your Highness," Everett answered.

"Squire! Help thy knight to his mount."

Everett glanced at Ben, who was pulling fretfully at his tunic. "That's you!" he whispered.

"What? What do I do?"

"Take the horse."

"Are you crazy? I can't touch horses! You didn't notice yesterday?"

Avery paced his stallion back and forth impatiently. "Squire! Perform thy duties!"

"That leather thing is covered with horsehair! I'm already getting congested." Ben found a handkerchief in his pouch and blew his nose.

"Ben, if you don't, they won't have any use for you," said Everett. "Here, take this."

Everett handed his own handkerchief to Ben, who wrapped it around his hand. He turned his face away from the horse as he took the lead from Dart. "Okay, now what?"

"Steady," said the page. "Await your master's mount."

"My *master*?"

"Just hold her still." Everett shoved one foot into the stirrup. The mare was so docile she hardly noticed Everett climbing aboard.

The prince walked his own horse alongside. "A worthy steed for my champion!"

"Just how do you expect me to win with a horse like this?"

Dart whispered something to Ben, who called up, "Her name's Buttercup, Everett." And then, after some more furious whispering, he added, "I mean, *my lord.*"

"Behold, 'tis what she fancies," said Avery, as Buttercup wandered over to nibble a patch of wildflowers.

"You're not serious! I'll never get her into a trot, let alone a gallop at full tilt." Everett tugged at the reins, but the horse ignored him.

"A true horseman will conquer any steed."

Everett considered this, and remembered what his riding teacher had told him. He sat up tall. The saddle was little more than a shaped blanket of leather thrown over the mare's back. A wooden cantle reinforced with an iron plate supported most of his lower back. A rectangular piece of wood was built into the front. He ran his fingers along its edges. It looked like a painful thing to fall against if he were unseated.

"What's that thing?" Ben asked, pointing to where Everett's hand rested.

"'Tis the pommel," said Avery. "It shall protect thy knight like naught else."

"If it doesn't slice him open."

"Thou knowest little of jousting, or wouldst not speak so. Should an opponent's lance hit there, it will do little harm. Else the danger would be grave indeed."

Everett glanced down at the area the pommel covered. The prince had a point.

"Of course, thou wilt have full armor as well," the prince continued. "In training this is not vital. But look there! Some of thy opponents!"

Everett glanced behind him and saw a few of the castle knights walking horses out to the pitch, followed by boys he took to be their squires. Two of the knights dismounted and drew swords.

"Fencing is another tournament contest," Avery said. "But we shall not have thee essay it. The danger be too great for the inexperienced."

"And this isn't?" Everett's mare backed away as Dart handed him a long stick like a broom handle.

"Whilst thine is not a proper lance, 'twill do for training purposes. I shall show thee how to wield it, but the knights of the realm, Sir Everett, are highly skilled. The task shall not be simple. Squire, my shield!"

Dart handed Avery an armored shield painted scarlet with a wide gold stripe across the top. Below the stripe was the image of a black bird, its wings outstretched, holding crossed swords in its talons.

"Well, squire?" Everett nudged Ben with his stirrupped foot. "Have I got a shield, or what?"

"Let me look." Ben sorted through the items on the wooden cart. "I guess this is it." He held up something that looked like the lid from a garbage can.

Everett glanced at the prince. "I know. 'Twill do for training purposes."

"Quite so. Now, to the lists!" Avery turned his horse and cantered to the center of the pitch in front of the grandstand, which Everett knew was called the berfrois. He prodded Buttercup with his heel until she followed.

Down the center of the area stretched a wooden fence about three feet high. "This barrier be called the tilt," said the prince. "At the tournament it will be covered with banners and rich decor, but for now—"

"'Twill do for training purposes?" Ben suggested.

"Don't interrupt," Everett said.

"*You* said it before."

"Look sharp," said the prince. "Sir Loverian!"

One of the fencing knights fended off a blow and nodded to his opponent, then walked over to join them. Avery called to the boy attending him. "Squire, fetch thy lord's lance and horse."

"Aye, Your Highness." The boy sprinted away.

"Thou art acquainted with the prisoners, my lord?" the prince asked.

"To a degree, sire." Everett recognized him as the knight who had saved Ben's life the night before.

"For our royal amusement, we have dubbed the prisoner Sir Everett. And his squire . . ."

"Ben Shepard," said Ben.

"The Adept's kinsman," said the knight.

"Yes, sir. My lord."

"You be a bit improved from the evening."

"Thanks for—"

"*Anyway*," Everett interrupted loudly, "I'm learning to joust." He didn't want to get the knight in trouble.

"Too true! Loverian, thou and I shall give a demonstration."

Loverian's squire returned, leading a tall piebald gelding. He helped Loverian mount it, then handed him his jousting tools.

"Sir Everett, mind what we do," said the prince. "In the *joust à plaisance*, we seek merely to disarm or unseat the opponent, never to kill. Elsewise there should be no knights left to defend His Majesty. Pray, how many tournaments hast thou won, Loverian?"

"Seven, Your Highness."

The prince beamed. "One of His Majesty's finest knights."

"Sir Grandor has won eight, I believe, Highness."

"Grandor does have a fierce nature. He has also been cited for unchivalrous conduct, else he might have won ten by this time."

"What's that?" Ben asked. "Unchivalrous conduct?"

"A knight above all must be a man of honor," Loverian said, glancing at Ben but looking harder at Everett. "A knight does not strike an unarmed opponent. A knight does not steal, nor resort to trickery. A knight does not, in short, dishonor his king."

Everett shifted in his saddle, and Buttercup snorted. He refrained from saying that he hadn't seen much chivalry from the king's knights, one of whom had been ready to slit the throat of a ten-year-old the night before. Still, Loverian seemed all right, or better than the others, anyway. He didn't like Everett, and that made him uneasy. He was sure the knight would not hurt him, but he wanted Loverian's respect.

The prince noticed nothing. "Well said, Loverian. And now clear the path, Sir Everett. Squires!"

The boys leaped to their jobs as Everett walked his pitiful mare to the edge of the lists, where she found some clover to chew on. Avery trotted his horse to the far end of the tilt. Loverian walked around it to the opposite side, so that the two were facing each other with the tilt between them on their left sides. Loverian's horse snuffled and hoofed the ground, eager to get going. Loverian patted its neck and whispered to it.

Everett watched closely. He'd seen jousting demonstrations before, but nothing so realistic as this. Loverian was using only a practice lance, padded at one end with a bit of cloth tied around it. He hugged his shield to his left side, and held the lance upright like a flag. He sat tall and focused his dark eyes directly on the prince.

"*Prêt!*" shouted Avery from the opposite end.

"*Prêt!*" repeated Loverian.

The horses took off at a healthy canter. Loverian's jaw was tight, his eyes unblinking, and Everett remembered that Avery was just a kid, and Loverian a full-grown knight.

The horses drew closer.

Just before they met, Loverian brought his lance down across the horse's left shoulder. It pointed just across the tilt, square at Avery's chest. The prince lowered his lance as well. The two collided.

Avery's lance glanced off the pommel of Loverian's saddle, but Loverian's hit the prince full in the chest. Avery lurched, but righted himself as the knight flew by him. In a moment he had arrived at Everett's end of the barrier, whirled his horse around, and made another run. Loverian was coming toward them now, his dark hair flying. The lances came down. Everett could see now how well Loverian was using his shield—he fended off Avery's blow easily—but he couldn't see from his angle exactly what kind of thrust jolted Avery out of the saddle and into the dirt, where he rolled over and groaned.

Loverian dismounted and sprinted to the prince's side. Everett jumped off his own horse and ran over too, with Ben and Dart. "Your Highness!"

"No matter, sir knight." Avery rolled over again. "'Tis nothing."

"Take care, sire." Loverian spoke gently and cradled the prince's head in his lap. He glanced up at Dart. "His Highness is hurt."

"I am *not*! I be perfectly fit." Avery tried to stand, but limped and stumbled.

Loverian caught him. "Allow me to be of aid." He led the prince to the shade of a broad poplar tree at the edge of the tournament lists. "Squire, fetch your liege a cushion or chair."

"I must train the prisoner," Avery said, sounding whiny. "I have no need of a nursemaid."

"Leave it to me, Highness. In time you can rejoin us."

Even as he spoke, Dart was scurrying back from the castle with a cushion.

"It's his ankle. You need to ice it," Ben said. Everyone looked at him. "To keep the swelling down. Believe me, I've fallen a lot."

"Where're they going to get *ice*?" Everett asked.

"Well, they—oh. Right."

"'Tis hardly the season," Loverian said.

"At least elevate it. You could make a compress. The well water's pretty cold." Ben glanced around and then pulled over a short log. "Get a cloth or something, soak it in cold water, and wrap it around his ankle. Here, I'll show you."

Several arms eased Avery onto the cushion, and Ben lifted the ankle carefully, setting it on the log. "You'll want something soft to lay it on. And a bucket of water, so you can keep changing the wrapping and keep it cold." When no one moved, he barked, "Well? Get going!"

Dart sprang into action, running toward a well, which Everett could just make out on the edge of the grounds. Loverian pulled a handkerchief from somewhere on his person. "Will this do as a wrap?"

"Something thicker would be better, but it should be okay."

In a few minutes, Dart returned with a bucket of well water. Ben dunked the handkerchief in and wrung it out, then wrapped it around the injured ankle.

"Ah! By the king's beard, 'tis cold!" Avery exclaimed. "But soothing. Well done, squire! From here shall we watch the proceedings until such time as our royal person be restored. Carry on, Loverian!"

"As you wish, Your Highness."

Everett returned to Buttercup, who had used her spare time to gather more breakfast. He gazed off toward the Northern Wood. The prince's injury would've been the perfect time to bolt. Avery himself couldn't have followed them, and the archers were distracted. They might've gotten away safely.

Loverian brought his horse across Buttercup's path, breaking Everett's line of sight. "You would have broken His Highness's trust," he said in a low voice, "and been captured all the same. Your best chance is here, young knight. Pray it not go to waste."

Chapter 31

Into the Fire

A high-pitched scream jolted Holly awake.

She sat up in a panic. Above her head, a flock of black birds had startled out of the treetop and wheeled above her, screeching. Holly sighed; for a moment she'd thought it might be Fleetwing. Jade had said he healed fast. Peering into the canopy, she caught a glint of something else—a burst of flame, she thought. It had frightened the birds. But it was gone now, like the grass fire she'd seen yesterday. Whatever it was, it hadn't hurt her. She didn't mention it to the others.

The group ate a quick breakfast of bread and jam, along with some berries Ranulf had gathered in the forest. Holly didn't feel much like talking as they resumed their journey. Her back was sore from sleeping on the hard ground, and her feet ached from all the walking they had done the day before. She fetched two Band-Aids from her backpack to cover a blister on her left heel. Almaric was intensely interested in the Band-Aids, and asked if he couldn't have one to add to his collection, or were they very dear where she came from?

After about an hour of walking, Almaric pointed between the two moors they were approaching. "Just over these hills, my lady. Not an hour's walk more, and we shall be at the Wandwright's doorstep."

Holly doubted they could be over the moors in an hour's time. They were considerably higher than any they'd hiked the day before, and covered in slippery moss and large stones. At times Holly bent nearly to the ground, grasping rocks to haul herself up. Even Almaric, who seemed to mind nothing, huffed and blew, driving his walking staff deep into the ground with every step.

The woods disappeared. The landscape grew harsh. The rocky hills were covered with a coarse, spiky grass. Even the tiny white flowers of heather were gone. Overhead, clouds hung low and dark. The wind picked up.

At the summit Holly pulled off her flimsy leather shoes to massage her feet. Almaric sat down too.

"See there, Lady Holly," he said, pointing into the valley. Off to the north another bleak hill loomed. "Just near the foot, on the eastern side of the moor. That is the Wandwright's home."

"Are you certain, Almaric?" Ranulf said. "The crystal shows this very spot?"

"Oh, I am sure of it."

"But how can you tell?" Holly asked. "All these hills look the same. Why couldn't it be farther on, over another rise, in another valley?"

"Well . . ."

"The crystal must mark the way," Holly prompted. "Right? Like on a map?"

"Not . . . not *exactly*."

The others stared at the old man. Ranulf swished his tail.

"That is, certain points, landmarks, were indicated. . . . For example, the wood where we spent the night . . . and then not much more after that. This does *look* like the spot. . . ."

"As could a dozen others. Her Ladyship speaks rightly," said Jade. "We will waste time traversing the east side of the moor if the Wandwright is not there. I propose that I make haste to the far rise alone and seek her out. *If* her home be there."

"It's not a bad plan," Almaric admitted.

"But how will you signal us if she's there?" Holly asked. "We need a flare gun or something."

"Take the firestarter," Almaric suggested, digging through his rucksack.

"He can't use that," said Holly. "His paws can't pull those tinsel things."

"Humans have their ways of manipulating magic," said Jade. "We cats have our own." He took the little gray egg in his mouth (being careful to avoid touching the bright ends with his whiskers) and bowed to her. Then, in a flash of black fur, he was gone over the rise and across the open moorland. After a moment, Holly couldn't see him anymore.

She picked up her shoes to lace them on again, but when Ranulf noticed the cuts and blisters on her heels, he insisted that she ride. She felt guilty—a centaur hardly seemed the same as a regular horse—but Holly didn't see how she could refuse. She gripped Ranulf's flanks with her knees and leaned back to help him balance on the steep hill.

The descent took all their attention, Ranulf zigzagging this way and that to find the safest path. Almaric followed their steps, sometimes grabbing on to a scrubby tree to steady himself. At one point, his foot found a rock that tumbled loose, and he slid several yards in front of them. Holly cried out, but he righted himself and smiled back at her. "No fear, Lady Holly! It would appear I found the fleetest route!"

It was just as the ground began to level out, with

CLAIRE M. CATERER

the vast moorland stretched before them, that Holly saw something bright and orange against the far hill on the right side, just barely grazing its top.

"Was that the signal? Ranulf, did you see?"

"Aye, my lady." The centaur sounded skeptical. "It appears Jade has found the Wandwright."

"Splendid!" said Almaric. "I was certain this was the right way."

Holly squinted. "But didn't you say she was on the other side of the hill? That signal came from *this* side, near the south end."

"No doubt Jade came back round to cast the signal, in case it carried not high enough. Eh, Ranulf?"

"If in fact it was the signal."

"Of course it was! What else could it be? We must press on. Flat land ahead—we shall make good time."

Jade had streaked through the valley, but it was slower going for the rest of them, for parts of the ground were marshy and Ranulf had to divert them a good bit to the east. After half an hour they had gotten no closer, but at least the ground had dried out. Almaric sighed and said, "There now, I think we're coming to the end of it."

Another orange spark flared against the moor's mud-colored sides. Holly remembered the firebursts she had seen that morning and the day before, with the knights. "Could someone be making camp over there?" Holly asked.

"There is no smoke," said Ranulf.

Holly wrapped her arms around her chest. The sun had faded behind the clouds, and a stiff breeze whipped around the stark moorland. She kept her eyes on the hillside as they approached it. Soon they were within a ten-minute hike of its base, and again she saw two bursts of flame, just together.

"That can't be Jade," she said in a low voice in Ranulf's ear.

"Aye, my lady, it appears to be something else altogether."

"Then what's happened to him?"

"That was not the firestarter, by the crystal," Almaric exclaimed as another fireball erupted.

"It is perchance an enemy. Lady Adept, pray—"

"Right behind you." Holly slipped from Ranulf's back and pulled the bow from her shoulder. She fitted an arrow to the string.

"We are too exposed here," said Ranulf.

Almaric moved closer to them, shielding Holly from the other side. "Whoever it is, they've seen us by now," she said. She glanced around. There was no cover, no woods to run to.

"Then we have no choice but to face them. Lady Holly, you should ride, for if we need flee—"

"I'm an easy target if I do," she said, crouching low. Her dun-colored clothes blended—she hoped—into the high grasses.

They crept stealthily now, though nothing could shield the centaur from plain view. Holly walked behind the others, her bow aimed between them. Her hands grew stiff holding it steady, but she didn't dare relax. The fireballs shot into the air like small, silent explosions every minute or two. And still, even within fifty yards, they couldn't tell what was making them.

"It *is* a campfire," Holly said doubtfully as they came upon it.

But it was no ordinary fire. The stones ringing it were large and smooth, like river rocks, each marked with a rune like those carved into the trees back in Hawkesbury. The flames fed on some invisible fuel, changing color from amber to red to indigo. Occasionally, a lick of flame geysered into the air. These were the fireballs they had seen from across the valley.

The three stood silent for a moment, though it felt like much longer. It was hard to look away from the flames. They were so bright they stung Holly's eyes, but after a little bit she adjusted to them. The next moment, she thought she saw . . .

"Something moved in there! Did you see?"

"What is it, Almaric?" Ranulf whispered. "A firenest? The Cináed?"

"It doesn't look like the one Ignata tried to take me to," said Holly.

"They are always concealed in the wood," said Almaric. "This is . . . *meant* for us, I think."

"Then the more care be taken," said Ranulf.

Holly gazed into the center of the flames. "I'm sure I can see something moving. And can't you hear that?"

The others quieted, listening to the roar as the fire devoured the air around it. They glanced at each other and shrugged, but Holly *could* hear something more—a song. The longer she stared into the ring of stones, the louder the song grew. The mournful notes sounded like Uilleann pipes. She walked closer.

"My lady! Take care!" Ranulf called sharply.

The urgency in his voice seemed unimportant. The song was so beautiful. Holly stared into the fire's white-hot center. There, as the music swelled, she saw it quite clearly: a creature.

It looked like a gecko, perhaps six inches long, with a whiplike tail. As Holly watched, its sparkly white scales blossomed to a deep gold. The lizard faded to white again, then gold, like a pulse, or no: like breath.

CLAIRE M. CATERER

The creature was changing color in rhythm to Holly's own lungs.

It crawled about in the flames as naturally as a dog turning around in its bed. Holly leaned in closer. The gecko turned its triangular head toward her. Its bulbous eyes glittered in a hundred different variants of gold and amber. It wanted something from her.

Holly had the vague notion that both Ranulf and Almaric were shouting now, but they sounded far away. She heard the words *test* and *magic* and *Adept*, then *help* and *aid*. The five words circled her ears, but after a moment, a strange thing happened: She forgot what they meant.

The firesong changed. The notes became a kind of language, more ancient than the ground she stood upon, and they called to Holly. As she stared at it, the fire creature's eyes started to grow. They expanded to fill her entire field of vision. Nothing was left in the world but the stones and the flame and the song and the great eyes of the creature. Holly reached out her hands, though she couldn't see them in front of her.

The breeze, the gray moorland, the others' voices all vanished. She had walked into the fire, she supposed, but the thought didn't frighten her. The dancing flames rose in a great circle around her in violet and gold. A pleasant warm wind blew back her hood.

The creature was the size of a small dog now. Its iridescent scales pulsed white-hot to gold in time to her breathing, deep and slow, as if she were asleep.

Somewhere in her brain buzzed the idea that she should be afraid, but the warm air spread through her like summer sun, soothing her. Still, the song was asking for something. The creature needed her. She crouched and held out her arms. The lizard crawled into her lap and she stood up, cradling it. At once the song grew louder, triumphant, and Holly closed her eyes. The glow deep inside her, the warmth that seemed to be waiting for a wand, intensified. It was like being bathed in the sun. She took a few steps forward.

A chill, harsh breeze washed over her, and her eyes flew open. She stood again on the open moorland. Her arms were empty; the creature had disappeared. What was worse, so had everyone else.

CLAIRE M. CATERER

Chapter 32

The Wandwright

Holly whirled around. "Ranulf? Almaric? Is anyone here?" Her voice bounced off the nearby hills. The valley was deserted.

The fire had gone out. Not even a whisper of ash remained. Holly knelt and touched one of the stones. It felt cold, and when she drew back, it vanished. The other stones followed, each disappearing in turn. Soon nothing remained but dust.

You might think Holly would begin running around in hysterics, screaming for help. But the moorland had an odd effect on her. She was quite tired from all the walking and the fire and now the desolate feeling of being alone; so she sat down on the coarse grass and pulled off her thin shoes to inspect her feet.

The soles of her feet were smooth and pink. She peeled off the bloody bandages, but the skin was perfect underneath. *The fire did it*, she thought, though that made no sense.

"What's happened here?"

She spoke this aloud, and at the same instant, something grabbed onto her right shoulder. She yelped and spun around, but no one was there.

Then she felt it: a weight clinging to her shoulder blade. Something huge, bigger than a bee or a spider, but she couldn't quite see it. "Get off me!" she cried, batting at it. Finally she heard a thump as it hit the ground behind her. She whirled around.

It was the creature from the fire.

Quite small now, and harmless looking, its amber scales glittered as if covered in sequins. It blinked enormous, golden eyes at her. And—Holly blinked back—could those be *tears*?

A pang of remorse stung Holly. She sat down, and the creature immediately crawled onto her lap. Gingerly, she touched its smooth back. One of its feet splayed its long, sticky toes on her upturned palm.

"You came from the fire," she said. "I know what you are. You're a salamander."

The creature flicked out its thin, orange tongue.

"Do you understand me? Show me. Walk in a circle."

The creature bowed its head, stepped out of Holly's lap, and traced a circle in the dust.

Holly picked it up and stood, finally considering her situation. She spoke aloud to the salamander. "All right, I was standing right here, with Almaric and Ranulf. We saw you in the fire, and I guess I walked *into* the fire, but I can't see how. . . . But then what happened? Did I go through to some other place?"

It wasn't as strange an idea as you might think, since Holly had come into Anglielle through a kind of doorway, and she thought the fire might be a portal as well. But the fire was gone. She shivered in the cold breeze. The salamander crawled up and perched on her shoulder, warming her neck. The sun was a thin silver disk behind the clouds. It was clearly still morning, yet it felt like hours had passed.

She tightened the leather lacings of her shoes. Almaric had said the Wandwright lived on the other side of the moor. Holly would have to find her.

She had not taken two steps before the ground trembled with hoofbeats. She tensed. There wasn't a tree or even a shrub to hide behind. The salamander tightened its grip on her shoulder. Holly flattened herself against the swell of the hillside, not making a noise.

A moment later relief flooded through her as Ranulf galloped up through the valley. But before she could call out to him, something jolted her shoulder. She glanced at the salamander. It extended a foreleg toward the centaur, and at once flames sprung up in front of Holly. She whirled around. They enclosed her on every side.

"Lady Holly!"

"I think it's all right, Ranulf," she said. She realized what the creature was trying to do. "He's a friend," she told the salamander. "Let me go."

The flames shot into the sky with a roar, fused into a ball, and fell straight toward her. She staggered as the fireball flew back into the creature. It glowed brightly for a moment, then faded.

"Lady Holly!" Ranulf stepped closer. "Are you well?"

"Yes, I'm fine. I'm so glad to see you! I went into the fire, and when I came out, you were all gone." She hugged the centaur around his waist.

"Apologies, my lady. We essayed to call you out, and when we could not, we went for aid. Come and see."

Holly's knees trembled a little. She hadn't realized how frightened she'd been, finding herself alone. She took Ranulf's hand and followed him around the slope into a deep valley on the other side. The centaur turned her to face the moor.

Holly knew right away that this was the home of the Wandwright. The thatched cottage nestled against the slope above a steep drop into the valley below, where a river had cut a shallow gorge. But while the moorland was gray and cold, the Wandwright's cottage glowed

CLAIRE M. CATERER

on a carpet of bluebells and soft green grass. Gentle wisps of pink rosebay willowherb grew on either side of the arched wooden door. Though well kept, the house had an air of being long abandoned; yet smoke rose from the thick stone chimney, and the path was swept.

"Is . . . Is anyone here?" Holly asked, confused.

"'Tis a trick of the mind. Most who pass here scarce take note of this cottage, for it seems a part of the moor itself."

Holly dropped the centaur's hand and stepped around the stone path, following the gentle cataract. She glanced behind her. "We didn't see a river on our way here. Where's it coming from?" she asked.

"The land itself is a servant of the Wandwright," Ranulf said, as if that explained it.

"The Lady Holly at last! We had near given up hope for you!" Almaric scurried out of the cottage with Jade in his wake. "By the king's beard!" Almaric blinked at the creature on Holly's shoulder. "You have captured it! Well done, Lady!"

"Do you know what it is, Almaric?"

"It is an ancient creature, much sought after. Very rare indeed. It is called . . . A moment now, I shall think of it. . . . "

"It is the Golden Salamander."

The voice that spoke was soft, but it silenced

everyone. The air itself became still, and even the river was quiet. At the door of the cottage stood the Wandwright.

She was at least seven feet tall, and very thin. She wore a long gown that looked like liquid silver poured over her head. Holly blinked. However regal, the Wandwright seemed not quite present, like a hologram. Her silver hair was wound on top of her head, and though her face was smooth, her gray eyes were ancient.

Without thinking, Holly dropped to one knee.

"Rise, Adept."

"I'm Holly," she said, wishing her voice didn't sound so small.

"Welcome. I am the Lady Belisanne, called the Wandwright." The lady inclined her head. She spoke in a soft, measured tone, treating each word with care. "Curious," she said. "You have knowledge outside this realm, yet you are of this realm."

"But I'm not," Holly blurted, then blushed. "I mean, I came from somewhere else."

"And yet not," the Wandwright insisted. "Come. I would hear the tale of this Adept." The Wandwright passed under an arbor that stood on one side of the cottage. She glided rather than walked, as if her feet hardly needed to touch the ground.

"Have no fear, my lady," Jade said in a low voice, following Holly. "The Wandwright is not an enemy."

But as Almaric had said, she wasn't exactly a friend, either. On the other side of the arbor Holly was surprised to find a garden ringed by trees. A small table set with a tea service sat on a stone patio. "Sit," Belisanne told her, pouring a cup of tea. "Tell your tale."

Holly settled on one of the benches with Jade at her feet. She hardly knew how to begin.

"You require a wand," Belisanne prompted.

"Yes, Your . . . Ladyship. The prince took mine, and my brother and friend are prisoners in the castle. I don't know how else to get them out or how to get home. The wand was how I got here in the first place."

Holly sensed the inadequacy of her story, and glanced at Ranulf, standing behind her.

"We have told Her Ladyship of your arrival and our meeting," he said. "In fact, all the events as far as we know them."

"Oh."

"Tell me of the Beyond, Lady Adept," said Belisanne. "Beyond the end of the world, from whence you come."

"Well . . . it's sort of like this. I mean, this place, Anglielle, looks a lot like my world did centuries back, I think."

"Much has changed." The Wandwright gazed deeply into Holly's eyes.

"Yes. It's very . . . different."

At her feet, Holly felt a growl rumble through the cat's body.

"Peace, Jade," said the centaur sharply.

"It is different there, in the Beyond. All is fire and smoke and iron, noise and blinding light."

The Wandwright was speaking softly. The surrounding garden faded as Holly's eyes locked with the Wandwright's. She felt something inside her head— a nudging, an opening.

"I don't . . ."

"The rage and war, a million words, cataracts of figures, the dwindling silence. The spaces are filled; the wild emptiness closed. Time itself is compressed, hurtling, suffocating . . ."

The voice caught, as if choked with tears. Holly's mind poured forth pictures unbidden. She saw the immensity of her world in a moment's time—bright screens and neon lights, vast cities, green strings of binary code, stripped mountains, burning seas, and the noise of seven billion souls crying.

And then, other voices crying.

Even as Holly's head came close to bursting, somehow her mind pushed the other way, and the pressure was relieved a tiny bit. And her vision changed.

It wasn't her world, she realized. She saw a high cliff teeming with black birds, ravens and crows, and in the midst of them, a tall, thin figure in a winged cloak, arms thrown up, commanding the heavens. From this horribly high, open vantage point, Holly could see armored knights below swarming like insects over the land, and before them fell the Mounted with their swords and the Dvergar with their axes, the Adepts huddled in their cliffside homes, slaughtered in their beds. Lightning broke from the heavens and set the verdant hills aflame, and everywhere that magic was raised as a feeble weapon it was struck down by a greater and darker power, the one who stood on the cliff, whispering to the elements.

Raethius of the Source.

A searing pain exploded in Holly's head.

And then, a pinch in her thighs, and her mind snapped shut. Jade had leaped onto her lap, claws dug in. He bared his teeth at the Wandwright.

"Peace, friend," said the lady softly. "I mean Her Ladyship no harm."

Jade's fur bristled. "To invade an Adept's mind is to steal her power."

"I merely wish to see."

"Then ask it of her!"

"Jade, you speak out of turn," Ranulf said.

"Nay, the familiar speaks truth. Her Ladyship is untrained. And I am uninvited." Belisanne inclined her head toward Jade, who relaxed.

The pain in Holly's head eased. "You saw everything in my mind?"

"Not everything, child. But much. Your world is a strange one. And, as you have seen, so is this." The Wandwright smiled faintly, as if she and Holly shared a secret. "But this bridge has been crossed before. Strange that you do not know of it."

Did Belisanne mean that someone else had come to Anglielle before Holly? "No, I'm sorry, I never heard of . . . the bridge being crossed. I'd be happy to tell you all about my world, but we don't have much time." She thought of Ben, and her stomach twisted. "Look, we've come a long way, and I just need to know. *Can* you make me another wand? It's the only way I can help Ben and Everett."

Almaric's face went scarlet. "Lady Belisanne, forgive Her Ladyship. She is not schooled in our ways—"

"Our new Adept is untamed, but the better for it, I think. And she has chosen her familiar well." The Wandwright rose, poured another cup of tea, then walked back to her seat. She arranged her gown and

CLAIRE M. CATERER

sipped the tea. "I have not forged a wand for many an age. I am the last of my kind, and I am not young. I have guarded my powers in secret, hoping to find another of my race to apprentice. Yet I fear they have all been vanquished."

"I'm sorry," said Holly. "Ranulf told me about your apprentice."

"The king himself ran his sword through her. An unarmed child." The Wandwright's face was still and peaceful.

"That's awful!"

"He did what he thought needful. Without a Wand-wright, the Adepts lose the power of the wand. 'Tis not their only power, but it is considerable." Belisanne peered keenly at Holly. "How will you wield your wand, Lady Adept? With fire and war?"

"I just want to take the boys home. I don't want to hurt anybody."

"But there is one who would bring war."

"You mean another Adept?" Holly asked.

"Perhaps. I have seen him in the movements of the river. But a ripple does not always become a wave." Lady Belisanne shifted her gaze to the salamander perched on Holly's shoulder. Again the faint smile lit her face. "Now this shows true promise." She held out a pale hand to the creature. It backed away, its sticky feet tickling Holly's neck. "Come." She spoke softly, but with such command that the salamander crept onto her palm. It turned back to Holly with a desperate look.

"You won't hurt it?"

The Wandwright held the creature up for all of them to see. "The Golden Salamander guards my home. Only those of great power are able to walk into the flames and release it. For this you will be rewarded. It shall never leave your side, and offer you protection always. In fact, it sensed you from far away, and sent its protection ahead, did it not?"

"You mean those fireballs I kept seeing? With the birds, and the knights yesterday?" Holly asked. The salamander blinked its bulbous eyes at her longingly.

"It is one of only three that I know of, the one called Áedán. The name comes from the Old Tongue, meaning 'fire.'"

Belisanne extended her hand, and Áedán scampered up to Holly's shoulder, shuddering. "Once freed, the salamander can never part from its liberator, lest it die."

"That doesn't sound very free," Holly said. She caught a glance from Almaric and closed her mouth.

"It may hibernate for a time until its keeper returns, but if she does not, the creature will die.

CLAIRE M. CATERER

The salamander's freedom is not measured in life or death. You are chosen most carefully. Áedán could not be bound to one who does not come from this land, whose blood does not flow in the very earth and water of Anglielle. And this creature was bound to you by something else. A destiny."

"You mean like fate? My future already laid out?"

"No future is predetermined. The choice is always yours."

"But the choice to do what?" asked Holly.

"That is to be seen. It is enough to know that the salamander sees greatness in you."

The Wandwright picked up her teacup and sipped slowly. Several moments of silence slipped by. Holly sighed, then finally said, "But what's this got to do with getting another wand? Can you help me?"

The Wandwright took a deep breath and let it out slowly. "Many things must be considered in the forging of a wand. The first is the cycle of the moon. In this you are fortunate. The moon is waxing, and thus it is a fortuitous time to forge a wand. The second is the movement of the stars. Ranulf, tell us of the dance of the heavens."

"The Wand may be seen, my lady, in the hour before daybreak, on the western horizon."

"Another boon for thee, Lady Adept. Now. The

season of the year: 'Tis the season of fire; Midsummer approaches. A wand is best forged in the season of the winds, but this shall do, before the sun circles back to the time of earth and death."

Holly held her breath.

"Finally, the necessary materials. The time of blooming is upon us. I believe we shall find what is needed. And it is your great fortune that I have preserved a very few of the crystals that the Earthfolk mined long ago. Thus, Lady Adept, a wand may indeed be forged. You have told me it is to be put to noble purpose."

"Yes, Your Ladyship. I swear I won't hurt anyone, not even the king."

"And what of Raethius, who holds the king in his grasp?"

Holly glanced at Ranulf, who sighed. "No, not even him. I wouldn't be strong enough anyway."

"It is well," said Belisanne, "if true. But how will you train? A wand must learn its mistress, else it be like a venomous serpent in the hands of a child."

"I guess that'll be the hard part. But I have to try, Your Ladyship. I don't know what else to do." Holly swallowed hard, willing herself to look Belisanne in the eye. "Please?"

The Wandwright stood suddenly. "Our time grows short, Lady Adept. We shall begin."

Chapter 33

The Stolen Wand

The same morning the Wandwright agreed to forge Holly's wand found Everett and Ben waking up to another day on the tournament lists.

Their circumstances had changed considerably for the better. Prince Avery had ordered them to be moved from the North Tower to a lower chamber on the east side of the castle. It was still little better than a cell, but Dart had brought them thin pallets to sleep on. Ben complained that the straw poked through the mattress and made him sneeze, but when Everett laid his jacket over it, even Ben admitted it was better than the stone floor.

When they woke up, the boys were summoned to Avery's chamber. They found him sitting in front of enough food to feed ten boys. "A knight—and even a squire—must build his strength," he explained, passing them platters of eggs, bread, and thickly sliced meats. Lord Clement, standing in a corner of the room with a tankard of ale, scowled as Everett seized a piece of venison. Everett fought the urge to make a face at him. Avery was their friend, whatever Clement thought. He and Ben were starting to think of him as just another boy, albeit a stiff and oddly dressed one.

As soon as they had eaten their fill, they returned to the lists. Everett mounted his horse gingerly. He had trained several hours the day before with Loverian. His shoulder and chest ached with bruises from the pummeling he had endured. And he wasn't used to riding for quite so long.

Though Avery insisted his ankle had healed, Everett noticed the prince was limping, and he called Loverian to help them all the same. "He is a boon to Sir Everett's training."

"He'd better be," Ben muttered. "You've only got two more days to get this down."

Loverian brought his horse alongside Everett's. "His Highness tells me you will be using magic during this tournament. Do you think it fair?"

"I'm just doing what I'm told," said Everett.

"It be less than chivalrous."

"I haven't much choice, have I?"

Loverian clenched his jaw. "Perhaps not. But I know a rogue when I see one." Loverian turned his horse away. "Your Highness. How would you have me aid this young knight?"

"Allow that he should practice the joust again, Sir Loverian. I shall ride alongside, and we shall consult on how best to use the wand."

"As Your Highness commands."

Avery rode with Everett to the far end of the tilt and pulled the wand carefully from a pouch at his side.

"I hope I don't hurt him," Everett said. "I'd rather stay on his good side." At the far end, Loverian's horse pawed the ground.

"Let us essay a practice. Aim the wand at the jousting target . . . there." Avery pointed away from them. A long stick wrapped in rags and affixed with a shield was planted in the grass. A couple of boys were running at it and pummeling it with lances. Avery called to Ben. "Pray tell the squires to be gone from that space. Sir Everett will be using the wand."

Ben scampered onto the open field, waving his arms wildly. "Clear the area! Clear the area!" Everett positioned the lance Ben had handed him, awkwardly palming the wand in his left hand. He had no hand free to rein the horse.

Avery signaled Loverian that they were ready. Everett gripped the wand, but it pulsed unevenly, cold to warm, and he had a hard time holding it steady. Loverian spurred his horse and came at him.

He and Avery started off as well. It was awkward; he would have to reach the wand across his body to point it at the target, and he wasn't sure at what point in the run to do it.

The knight was twenty yards away. Now ten.

"Strike!" Avery shouted, and Everett flung his wand arm across to the right, missing Avery's nose by inches, and aimed at the target.

Loverian's lance came down.

A blue flame hissed from the end of Everett's wand and sizzled, harmless, in the grass. The lance caught Everett in the chest, quite off guard, and jolted him sideways. He clung briefly to the horse's back with his thighs, but a moment later he tumbled onto the dirt.

He had fallen from horses before, but the lance's blow had knocked the breath out of him.

"Ev! You okay?" Ben asked, bending over him.

It took a few moments before Everett could breathe again. "It's too hard, Avery," he panted. "I can't do both. I wasn't ready for the lance. I never even got my shield up."

Loverian reached out a gloved hand to help him up. "'Twas a bold attempt."

"It was a *stupid* attempt!" Ben said. "There's no way he can do this. Just forget the wand."

"He lacks naught but practice," said the prince. "Though, in truth, the wand's display was less than impressive."

"That's just it. I don't have control over it," said Everett, still panting out every word.

"That," Avery said, "will change."

After two more falls in the dirt, it became apparent that the training was moving too fast. Even the prince saw the wisdom of putting aside the jousting for the moment and concentrating on Everett's wand work.

"Maybe if you flick your wrist more," Ben suggested. He was standing with Everett on the edge of the tournament pitch. Everett waved the wand with a jerky motion. A small blue flame dribbled out.

"It may be a bit like swordplay," said the prince, taking the wand from him. He swung it in an arc as if brandishing a rapier. A solid yellow beam like a laser shot from it and ignited the grass. Everett leaped up and stamped it out.

"Hey, that was good!" Ben said.

The prince blushed. "I knew not what it would do."

"Nor me." Everett took the wand and imitated Avery's move, but all he got was the same tepid blue spark as before. He couldn't even get the wand to warm up in his hand now; it seemed to actually dislike him. Maybe the little fairy Sol had been right. He certainly wasn't seeing the great magic she'd talked about.

"Are you concentrating?" Ben asked. "I'm sure you're supposed to transfer your power to it mentally."

"Listen . . . Lissssten."

"I *am* listening. I'm doing the best I can!" Everett said.

"Okay, I'm just suggesting."

"Inhale the powers of the sun."

"I don't see what the sun has to do with it," said Everett.

"What sun?" Ben squinted up into the cloud cover. "Everett, are you okay?"

"Perchance he hit his head in the fall," Avery said.

"I'm fine," said Everett. "Just let me concentrate."

He inhaled, took his stance, then heard something, very close to his ear: *"I would speak to you alone."*

Sol?

Everett stood up straight. "You know, I think you're right, Your Highness. Maybe I should rest a bit before I go on."

The prince, who was squinting at him strangely, relaxed. "Of course. Squire, secure thy knight's horse and allow that he rest beneath yon poplar for a time."

Ben grumbled, but he went to do as he was told, and Avery returned to the lists to practice with Loverian.

"Sol?" Everett whispered. "Where are you?"

A featherlike touch brushed down his jawline. He blinked as a beam of light darted into his eyes. He sat with his back against the tree trunk and drew one knee up. The winged creature settled onto it and smiled.

"Won't the others see you?" he asked.

"They have not the Sight. But send yon squire away so that we may speak freely."

She spoke as Ben approached, sniffling.

"You should rest too," said Everett to him. "Take your allergy medicine."

"Am I all blotchy?" Ben brushed his cheeks with his fingers. "Once the hives start, I'm done for."

"Why don't you go and wash up? Stay at the well for a bit, away from the horses. It'll do you good."

"What about the prince?"

"I'll cover for you. He's busy anyway."

"Okay. Tell him I'll be right back." Ben walked toward the well, fumbling in his pouch for his pills.

Everett waited until he was out of earshot, then turned back to the tiny creature on his knee. "I'm so glad you came back."

Sol bowed her head, looking up at him through a veil of eyelashes. "You have acquired the wand, I see."

"Yeah, how about that? Avery just gave it to me. He says he wants to go to our world, but I can't figure out why, really."

"You are fated to master it. And how goes your training?"

"Pretty miserable, actually. I'm rubbish at this. Even Avery can make it do things."

"You are a thief, but I shall teach you to master your power."

"I told you, I'm *not* a thief—" Everett began.

"You are as the wand perceives you," said the fairy coolly.

Everett started to argue, then remembered the staircase that Sol had conjured from the tower window. "You can help us escape, you said. And find Holly?"

"All in good time. I fly shielded by fire and have seen the Adept on her journeys. She will attempt to forge another wand this day, in the company of allies. If she be successful, she will essay to rescue you as hath been foretold."

"Hang on. Holly's got *another* wand now?" Everett bristled a little. No matter where Holly went, people just gave her whatever she wanted. But it didn't really matter, he thought; after all, he would be learning magic too. "Does she know about the tournament?" he asked.

"'Tis at that very hour she will strike."

"But that's brilliant!" Everett said. "Holly can use her new wand to take us home. She's the one who's so clever with it."

"But take heed, my lord," said the fairy. "You have promised the prince a journey to your world. This vow you must not break."

Everett cleared his throat, remembering how sensitive she was. "But I'll need your help . . . please? I would be honored to have someone so beautiful as a teacher."

She flew from his knee and hovered again by his ear. "You have learnt well the art of flattery. Take this token of your lady's favor, my lord." From the air, the fairy produced a long scarf of red silk. "This you must keep with you always. It will grant you the power you seek over the wand."

Everett caught the fabric as it wafted through the air. "What do I do with it?"

"Wrap it round the hand that wields the wand, and you shall be guided in all your endeavors, as I guided you in the prince's chamber."

"*You* helped me make those fireworks?"

"Alas, I cannot touch the wand," said the fairy. "I only grant power to others."

Everett's heart beat faster. He could make this

whole thing work—the magic, the joust, Holly's rescue, getting them home.

"But there is a price, my lord."

In the distance, he saw Ben at the well, rubbing his runny nose on his sleeve. Ben would be dead if Everett couldn't manage to pull this off. "Anything, I'll do anything," he said.

Sol's pointed face broke into a wide smile, but her eyes were cold. "I require the Adept."

"Hang on, what's this?" said Everett, suddenly afraid. "You *require* her?"

"She has power. And soon, a newly forged wand. She has a destiny to fulfill with the Good Folk. Deliver her to me, and all you desire shall be yours."

The little fairy's eyes locked on to Everett's own. He struggled to speak. In his head floated the words: *Forget it, that's rubbish, I won't do it. Holly's my friend, and Ben's sister, and . . .*

The sounds around him faded—the chatter of Avery and Loverian; the rhythmic thumping of horses' hooves; the clash of swords as the knights practiced their skills—a thousand summer noises silenced. Sol's golden eyes filled his, and her hair swam through his fingers, soft as gossamer.

In his hands, he could feel the power she had offered him. It would be so easy to accept. She only wanted a promise. They were just words, that's all. One word, really, a word that slipped through his lips, sighing into the air almost before he realized it, before he recoiled, horrified at himself: "Yes," he whispered.

Something cold and wet splashed on Everett's foot. He blinked and glanced around. Sol had vanished.

"Sorry," Ben said, putting down the sloshing bucket. "I figured we'd want something to drink."

"You were supposed to stay there awhile," Everett said.

"I was gone fifteen minutes." Ben checked his watch, then frowned, pointing at the red scarf Everett was winding around his hand. "Is that a bandage? Did you get hurt?"

"It's nothing—I'm fine. I just found it in my pouch, is all." But he felt strange, like a wild animal was caged deep in his chest. He tucked the end of the scarf into his sleeve. Already he felt different. Stronger. Something brushed his earlobe. He stayed very still, held his breath, and then he heard it, soft as a baby's whisper:

"The power is yours."

Everett sat up straight on Buttercup's back at one end of the tilt. He held the wand in his right hand, wrapped in the red scarf. A warm strength flowered in his chest, as if he had drunk something hot on a very cold day. It snaked down to the hand that held the wand. He would trust his instincts. He knew they would lead him right.

"I want to try it with just the wand, no lance," said Everett to Ben. "Oh, and I won't need this." He handed him the shield.

Ben gaped at him. "You'll get creamed!"

Everett shrugged.

"Everett, think on thy squire's advice," Avery said, glancing from Everett to Loverian, whose horse pawed the ground at the other end of the tilt.

"I know what I'm doing."

Everett took a deep breath. His whole body tingled. Loverian leaned forward in the saddle, taller, stronger, and better trained. "Please don't let me get knocked off," Everett whispered.

He swallowed and nodded to his opponent. Loverian spurred his horse, his lance held high in his right hand.

Everett kicked Buttercup. She tensed, then broke into a gallop. He heard Ben and Avery gasp. No one had ever seen the little mare run like this.

He could almost hear instructions in his head, coming from somewhere in that fire in his chest. *Raise the wand. Strike the shield.*

He raised the wand high above his head. Loverian lowered his lance, his horse at a full gallop. Only ten yards away. His horse's flanks glistened.

Everett's heart thundered in his chest.

Now!

He swung the wand in an arc like a lasso, then flung his wrist out, aiming the wand at the knight's shield.

The tip of Loverian's lance sparked, and flames blazed down its length. The knight dropped it; his horse reared, its eyes rolling back. The flames billowed against the shield, then rebounded into the air, turning blue, then amber, trickling down in a shower of sparks. The knight's horse threw its rider and galloped toward the stables.

Through all of this, Everett was calm, as if watching someone else wield the wand. He wasn't surprised when Loverian fell, but it was still alarming. Everett leaped off Buttercup and jumped over the tilt to where Loverian lay, not moving.

Ben had run up too, his face very white. "What did you do to him?"

"Is he all right?"

"Hardly." Ben patted the knight's white face. "Can you hear me, Loverian? Wake up!"

The other squires and knights gathered nearby, eyeing Everett. "Get me the bucket," Ben said, and when Everett returned, Ben splashed the knight with cold water. "Come on, come on . . ."

After a moment, a groan came from Loverian's chest. His eyelids fluttered.

"You're okay. You just got knocked out," Ben said. "Careful, now. Not so fast."

But the knight was already sitting up. "My thanks, squire. I am not ill." But he grimaced as he spoke. Ben soaked his handkerchief with well water.

"Here, hold this against your head. Gosh, it's a dangerous world without ice cubes."

Loverian did as he was told. He was in no hurry to stand up. Still, it could have been worse. Everett was surprised someone hadn't already beheaded him for disabling the knight. He looked around for the prince and saw him hanging back under the poplar.

"I'm sorry, Your Highness," Everett said, running over to him. "I wasn't trying to kill him."

Avery stared at him, his face a mask. Was he angry? Afraid? Impressed? "I—I just did the best I could. Sire." It seemed a good time to bow.

"Peace, Everett. Thou hast done what I have asked." Avery took a deep breath, and his features relaxed. "Thy magic is formidable."

"Ben's looking after him, I think he'll be all right. See, he's already come round—"

"The knight is not my concern." The prince held out his hand, and Everett, understanding at once, handed him the wand. "It puzzles me. It is naught but wood." Avery turned it over in his hands. "Thou wilt best every knight at the tournament, Sir Everett. And when the Adept comes, we shall follow her into the wood and she will lead us to this Other Place." He fell silent, then spoke again, as if to himself. "I was told magic was foolish, a fairy tale. But such wonders *do* exist. I have long dreamt of magical worlds such as thine, but they were always denied me. The hours I spent studying my father's nautical maps have come to nothing. I am not permitted even to travel the seas of my own world." He slipped the wand carefully into his own pouch and fixed Everett with his blue eyes. "I have never tasted freedom. At last shall I see someplace beyond the walls of this castle. And thou, Sir Everett, shalt take me there."

Chapter 34

Forging the Wand

Everett may have thought that magic rained on Holly like so much confetti, but she didn't feel that way at all. Even now, as she prepared to forge her wand in the late-morning sun, the idea of being a real Adept made little sense to her. She was a bit frightened of the Wandwright, and not sure if even the others entirely trusted her. Ranulf seemed disappointed that Holly just wanted to use her wand to free the boys, not to overthrow the king. But perhaps once she had the wand, the Wandwright would initiate her somehow and she'd finally feel that she was ready to take on whatever task lay ahead.

She could not have been more wrong.

"It is vital," said Lady Belisanne, "that the Adept choose her own herbs. It is my task to formulate them, but yours to choose them."

Holly and Jade stood with the Wandwright in the jumbled garden behind the cottage, where trees grew

CLAIRE M. CATERER

nearly as thick as a forest. Belisanne had consented to Jade's presence, because he was Holly's familiar, and Áedán's, because he was bound to her. Almaric and Ranulf were not allowed.

"One herb is chosen for each of the four elements," said the Wandwright. "The stone, representing the fifth element, I have chosen myself. We begin with fire, as this is its season, and it is an element well suited to you." She indicated the ground at Holly's feet. "In fire's garden, the herbs include blackthorn, gorse, juniper . . ."

They all sounded prickly and difficult, Holly thought.

"All suited to Her Ladyship," Jade commented.

". . . and the holly."

"Shouldn't that be it, Jade?" It was the only plant she recognized. "I pick this one."

The Wandwright handed her a drawstring pouch made of black silk, and a small pair of silver scissors. Holly clipped a sprig off the bush. "Is this enough?"

"It is the choice of the Adept."

She took a deep breath. "Okay then."

The Wandwright led Holly into another section of the garden. "Here dwell the herbs of the water."

Holly snipped a long stem from a plant with tiny purple flowers. "Curious," the Wandwright said. "Heather's blooms do not oft appear before the sun's zenith." Holly took this as a good omen.

They walked on to two more gardens. For the element of earth, Holly chose two pointy leaves and a yellow flower from the mugwort plant. For the element of air, she picked a long sprig of lavender, which the Wandwright called elf leaf. The farther they walked, the darker the forest grew, as if it were expanding with their every step. They stopped in a small clearing surrounded by a circle of seven trees. They looked like people frozen in a contra dance.

"Wands are forged from wood, Lady Adept. Choose the wood with care." The Wandwright stood aside and let Holly enter the clearing alone.

She walked around the circle of trees. Her neck prickled where Áedán clung to it. Though the air was still, the trees' leaves rustled. Holly placed her palm on one thin, sturdy trunk. The smooth bark swelled, then shrank, under her fingers. The change was small, but Holly recognized it: The tree was breathing.

The seven trees clustered close enough together that Holly could reach out to touch the next before letting go of the first, and in this way she made her way around the entire circle. But how to choose? Some were very tall, others hardly more than a sapling. They all seemed to speak to her, but who was she to hear them? She'd have to just pick one and trust it to be right.

Holly stood in the middle of the circle, closed her eyes, and listened. She heard nothing but the leaves of the trees rustling, but then the warmth in her chest spread to her limbs. She reached out her right hand and opened her eyes.

She was pointing at an evergreen tree at the edge of the circle. It was at least thirty feet taller than all the others, and its bark was a rough reddish hue. Holly frowned, stunned for a moment. "Is that . . . ?"

"It is the Redwood," said the Wandwright behind her. "A very young specimen. Because it reaches such heights, it draws the powers of heaven to heal the earth."

"But . . ." How could a redwood tree grow here, on the moorland? But Holly knew there was no answer that would satisfy a herbologist or university professor.

"It offers protection, endurance, and survival. Its province is great wisdom and experience, which shall serve you well, Lady Holly." Belisanne held out a very sharp, black-handled knife. "Cut a thin switch with great care, so as not to harm the tree."

Holly hesitated with the knife raised to the Redwood tree. Then quickly—like ripping off a Band-Aid—she sliced off a small branch. She closed her palm gently over the wound.

The Redwood needles rustled in response.

"The trees understand you, Lady Adept. They shall be your friends in your hour of need."

Holly stretched, feeling dizzy. "I'm sorry . . . Is there much more to do? I'm just so tired."

"Come and rest."

Holly's limbs dragged as she followed the Wandwright back to the cottage garden, where Almaric sat talking with Ranulf. Belisanne walked to the sideboard under the eaves of the cottage and pulled out supplies, mixing something in a tall earthenware pitcher shaped like a tulip.

"This is the nectar of the fireblossom," said Belisanne, pouring Holly a cup from the pitcher. "It shall restore you. Sit and drink, but do not tarry long. The process cannot be interrupted."

Before Holly could take a sip, Jade thrust his whiskered face into the cup and sniffed. He glanced up at her and nodded, then withdrew. "Fireblossom."

Holly blushed, hoping the Wandwright wasn't offended, but she only gave one of her almost-smiles. "Your familiar is most loyal," she commented, and waited for Holly to finish the drink. It was cool and sweet going down, but once in her stomach its heat was almost painful. Still, that lasted only a moment, and the fatigue seeped from her bones.

CLAIRE M. CATERER

"Are you quite ready, Lady Holly?" Almaric asked, laying a wrinkled hand on hers.

Holly had no idea how to answer, since she wasn't sure what she was getting ready for, but the Wandwright nodded. "Come. We do not have the luxury of time." As Jade leaped down from the table, Belisanne raised her hand. "I am afraid none but the salamander may join the Lady on this journey," she said, and Holly cast a wistful glance back at him as she followed the Wandwright. She felt safer, somehow, with the black cat at her heels.

The Wandwright led the way back through the garden into a forest glade. At first, Holly thought they had come back to the wandwood grove, but this circle contained only five trees, and they grew so dense that their intertwined branches blocked the sun overhead. The Wandwright laid a hand on Holly's arm.

"Lady Adept, together we shall forge the wand that is to be yours. The task is complex and dangerous. I cannot give you advance instruction, for this ritual is a guarded secret, and part of its trial is how well you adapt to it. Take my hands."

The Wandwright faced her at about arm's length and held both of Holly's hands in her own thin, cool ones. Belisanne closed her eyes, breathing deeply, and Holly, not sure what else to do, imitated her. As she breathed, a hundred thoughts raced through her head. What would everyone expect of her when this was finished? That she'd lead them into battle? Rid the kingdom of the hated Sorcerer? How would she get the boys out of the castle when it was overrun with tournament knights? But when she sensed the Wandwright's breathing had eased, she opened her eyes.

"Once traveled upon, this road cannot be retread. The ritual must be followed exactly. You shall come to no harm . . . if indeed you are a true Adept."

If.

Together they entered the circle. It was dark and cool within. As they stood, it grew darker still.

"Is it a storm coming on?" Holly asked.

"It is the forging of an Adept's wand," said the Wandwright. They stood in the center of the ring near a low tree stump. The Wandwright took the Redwood switch Holly had cut along with the pouch of herbs and placed them in Holly's left hand. Holly stepped back. She felt like the center of a large clock.

The Wandwright's voice deepened until it was nearly unrecognizable. "Look thou to the elements, Adept, for each serves thee, and thou shalt return their service." The Wandwright approached one of the trees. At its base lay a cut log.

"From the element of Fire, we seize passion and

strength," said Belisanne as she retrieved the log, then moved clockwise around the circle. She took a log from each tree in turn. "From the element of Water, we take clarity and intuition. From the element of Earth, the fertility of birth and death. From the element of Air, intellect and wisdom."

The Wandwright cradled four logs in her arms now, and stood before the fifth tree. "And from the Power of the Aether, we call up the magic of the Adepts, that most ancient of races, and we ask that power be granted to this initiate."

Lady Belisanne opened her arms. Holly waited for the logs to fall, but instead they floated in midair, then flew to the tree stump in the center of the circle, settling around it in a teepee shape. The Lady stood opposite Holly on the other side of the stump and bowed low to her. Holly bowed as well.

"And now commences the Forging of the Wand, by the powers of Deas, Iar, Tuath, Airt, and Aethyr." The Wandwright reached long white arms to the sky, and as she spoke, the tree stump burst into flames. Holly blinked at the bright golden light. As she watched, the fire's core changed from red to orange, to green, blue, and a deep indigo, then back to red. It hurt her eyes to look at it.

Through the flames, on the other side of the stump,

Lady Belisanne lowered her arms and spread them out to Holly, as if embracing her.

Clearly, this was Holly's cue, but what was she to do? She looked down at the branchlet and pouch full of herbs in her hand. Was this the test, that she was supposed to figure out the next step? "What do I—?" she started to say, but the Wandwright brought one finger to her lips. Asking wasn't allowed, then.

Belisanne started to walk around the tree stump toward Holly, and something told Holly that she should walk too. The two of them remained opposite each other, like spokes on a wheel. Holly gazed into the flames. Áedán's sticky feet clung to her neck. How had she called him out of his fire? She had just listened to it; she'd heard a song. The moment the memory crossed her mind, she heard another song.

She was quite sure the song was not in the air, but in her mind. Or in her body. That tugging, simmering part of her that called to her wand, crackled in her rib cage. Then she knew what she had to do next, as if the unborn wand itself was telling her.

Cradling the switch and the pouch of herbs in her left palm, she opened the drawstring with her right hand. She reached into the bag and pulled out one of the sprigs she had collected: the holly. She continued to walk clockwise around the circle, the Wandwright

CLAIRE M. CATERER

visible through the flames. Holly took a breath and cast the green sprig into the fire.

The flames shot into the air. They broke through the crown of the trees in a burst of red and orange. She waited for the trees to catch fire, but of course they didn't.

"Holly branch of Deas, grant this Adept protection on her journeys," the Wandwright chanted.

Holly reached again into the pouch. She drew out another sprig and cast it into the fire.

A shower of blue sparks erupted, illuminating the glade like moonlight. "Heather of the Iar, grant this Adept the good fortune that is thy province," chanted the Lady.

Holly closed her eyes, her fingers plying the bag until they closed on another leafy branch. As it fell into the fire, the flames burst forth again, deep green like a pine forest.

"Mugwort of the Tuath, grant this Adept the Sight of the mind that is thy power," said the Wandwright.

Nearly done. Sweat trickled down Holly's neck. She reached for the last time into the pouch and drew out the final plant. She cast it.

"Elf leaf of the Airt, grant this Adept the love and peace that are thy gifts."

The flame shot up once more, this time bright

yellow. Holly let out a deep breath. Her heart thumped loudly in her chest.

She stopped walking. The Wandwright stopped opposite her, and the fire calmed, burning very bright but low upon the tree stump. The logs looked untouched, but the stump itself was turning white, like ash. Holly winced as the Wandwright reached a hand directly into the flames. Resting in her open palm was a single purple stone. Holly laid the switch from the Redwood tree in the Wandwright's hand.

As soon as the Redwood branch connected the two of them, Belisanne withdrew and let it fall into the flames, along with the stone. Holly let go too, still clutching the empty silk pouch.

"Now call to the Aethyr!" The Lady threw her head back, her arms open to the sky. "Call to the Aethyr to forge the Wand of the Adept!"

The fire between them gathered itself into a ball. It writhed like a great cat in front of Holly, its haunches bunching, and then it leaped forth with a roar.

Holly skipped back against the trees. The fireball exploded, licking around the circle. She closed her eyes, willing herself not to run. Áedán huddled close to her neck. The inferno poured over her body like a hot shower, licking through her insides and out her eyes, but still she kept them tightly shut. She could feel it coming now: the most difficult and painful part of the ritual.

The Aethyr, whatever that was, circled her like a whirlwind and churned inside her head. It was a little like when the Wandwright had entered her mind: Her thoughts opened, then poured forth unbidden, uncontrolled. But they weren't pictures of her world. They were pictures of *her*, of all the things she wished she could forget: her third-grade teacher scolding her for drawing on another student's paper; her mother's disappointed face as she perused Holly's grade card; a group of the more popular girls huddled together and whispering as she passed them on the playground; and worst of all, her fingers brushing Ben's little white hands as Fleetwing swung her away from the castle and she fell to the earth, having failed to save him.

All that she could not be, had never been, welled up inside her.

The glow in her heart cooled, growing dim.

And then Holly fought back.

She thought of how her father had framed one of her drawings and hung it in his office; how one of the fourth-grade teacher's aides had called her a "creative soul"; how good it felt to make the long journey to the Wandwright's home, to free Áedán and save Jade from the knights; the wonder of holding the key, and then the wand, in her hand, and how it spoke to her heart and received a reply.

The fire within her glowed fiercely and she opened her eyes, tears streaming out. She was aglow, bright and hot, even strong and firm. But opposite her, Belisanne's dress billowed in the updraft. The flames licked up her torso; her arms glowed white with heat. Her voice rose in pain.

The Wandwright was burning.

Chapter 35

The Unlocking Spell

Holly screamed.

She couldn't see the Wandwright anymore, just a tall, humanoid form wrapped in fire. A moment later Belisanne's limbs melded into a white column of light. Holly looked away. The inferno sputtered out. The beam of light solidified into the Wandwright herself, alive and whole, standing between Holly and the tree stump.

"You have done well, Lady Adept. Retrieve your wand."

Belisanne stood aside and Holly saw a thin stick floating a few inches above the tree stump.

"Is that . . . Is it really mine?"

Holly grasped the wand by its broad end. The wood was a deep red, like the Redwood tree, and the handle was thick and curved to fit her hand comfortably. Set into its base was a round, violet stone that nestled into her palm. Carvings decorated the shaft, runes and pictures of circling flames, stars, and planets. The longer she gazed at it, the more pictures she saw, and the more real they became.

"Take care, my lady. It is untamed," said Belisanne softly. "Time grows short. Are you ready to begin your training?"

Holly glanced up at Belisanne's unchanging porcelain face. "Yes. I'm ready."

Almaric rose from his chair in the back garden as Holly and Belisanne approached. Holly smiled and held out the wand. The others crowded around to see, exclaiming over Holly's skill and the wand's beauty.

"It is exquisitely crafted," Almaric said. "Lady Belisanne, what are its properties?"

"It is forged from the Redwood tree and the holly, which offer protection. From the mugwort, to grant the Sight. The heather, for strength of mind. The elf leaf, for she will bring peace. And finally, the amethyst stone, to give her authority and connection to all living creatures."

The little group fell quiet.

"And what of the Adept's training?" Jade asked at last.

"We must not mistake the king's might," said Ranulf. "Neither Fleetwing nor I was able to deter his knights for long. Her Ladyship must make a show of strength. If she were taught the Banishment—"

Jade glanced up at the centaur. "The Banishment is beyond Her Ladyship's powers. She is not of our world. She has not the elemental connection to secure the spell be permanent."

"Wait," said Holly. "The Banishment—that's what Bittenbender was talking about the other day. What is it?"

Almaric patted a chair for her to sit in. "'Tis a most powerful spell, my lady. It was used in days past to rid the land of evil. But Jade speaks rightly. It is not for our purposes."

Ranulf pawed the ground. "But Her Ladyship could free us from the king—or even Raethius himself."

Holly felt the blood drain from her face. "You mean the Sorcerer."

"The very one, Lady Holly."

"If I could . . ." Holly's mind wandered for a moment. She saw herself in a scarlet cloak, her wand raised. Facing her was the thin, hooded figure of Raethius as she had seen him in the vision she had shared with the Wandwright. At her words the Sorcerer dissolved into mist with a shriek. Every creature in Anglielle clustered around her, their eyes round and voices hushed.

"But you cannot," said Jade flatly.

"Someday, perhaps, Lady Holly," said Almaric. "For now, Raethius is unimportant."

"Unimportant!" snorted the centaur.

Almaric ignored him. "A useful variant is called the *Vanishment*. It would serve to transport you and the others away from the king's castle to the forest, whence you can return to your own land."

"A tall enough order," Jade muttered.

A stirring of worry tugged at Holly. "Why? Is the— the Vanishment very advanced?"

"It is one of the more challenging spells," Almaric admitted, but then brightened. "But quite up to Your Ladyship's skills. For most Adepts, it takes a week, even a fortnight, of practice to learn. But I'm sure you could easily master it in four or five days."

"But we don't *have* four days!" said Holly, her heart quickening.

"Do we not?" The magician looked flustered. "I was sure the tournament was . . ."

"The day after tomorrow," Holly said. "Ranulf, how will we get back in time?"

The centaur shifted from hoof to hoof. "'Twill be a hard journey, even if we depart at daybreak," he admitted. "We must collapse a two-day journey into one."

"And the boys' time is running out," said Holly. "We should leave now, before it's too late."

"But when will you learn the Vanishment, my lady?

The Wandwright's knowledge would be valuable in your training," Almaric said.

"I don't know, I can't . . ." How could she take precious time trying to learn a spell that was probably too hard for her anyway? She clutched her wand, which felt so warm and easy in her hand. This was hers, she had proven herself worthy of it; it couldn't all be for nothing. It was a part of her, even more so than the one Mr. Gallaway had given her.

Mr. Gallaway.

"Keys are for unlocking things," she murmured to herself.

Jade and the others exchanged glances. "My lady?" said Almaric.

"Keys are for unlocking things," she repeated, getting excited and talking too fast for them to understand. "My wand—it used to be a key. That's what it was good at, that's what *I* was good at—unlocking things, like the oak tree, and the veil at Darton Castle, and the prince's language. I didn't even have to try!"

Ranulf, Almaric, and Jade all looked bewildered, but the Wandwright nodded. She went to her sideboard and pulled out a small iron chest. It had a keyhole in the center. The Wandwright tried to pry open the chest, but the lid wouldn't budge. She gestured to Holly.

Holly swallowed and took a deep breath. She

gripped the handle of her wand, the cold amethyst stone smooth against her palm; then it pulsed warm, greeting her. She felt her core of energy respond. She pointed the wand at the keyhole and closed her eyes, focusing, seeing it open. A word flashed into her mind and she uttered it.

"*Osclaígí!*"

She heard a click and opened her eyes. The clasp of the lid on the chest had popped open—it had actually worked! Holly grinned at Almaric, who gaped at her.

"This wand knows you, my lady," he said finally, sounding proud. "Even better than the old. Why, you could not open my own cottage door not two days gone!"

"The wand forged by an Adept is her strongest weapon," said the Wandwright. "And this lady, while of Anglielle, has forgotten our ways, and needed time to recall them."

"And how is it that you know the Old Tongues as well?" asked Ranulf.

"I don't even know what I said, or where that came from," Holly admitted. "But you see what this means? I won't have to do the Vanishment, Almaric! All I have to do is open their cell or dungeon or whatever. That's got to be easier, right?"

It was a moment before anyone spoke. "Her

Ladyship would have to enter the castle itself," Ranulf said uncertainly.

"It would be a great risk," Jade agreed.

"But I could do it," Holly went on. "All those knights will be there for the tournament, and they'll all have squires, right? If I just blended in—"

"The castle guards will surely not know *every* squire," Almaric said.

"And I'll just slip in like one of them, find the boys—"

"Spring them from their prison—"

"And lead them out *how*, exactly?" Jade broke in.

"I'll need help," Holly said, her mind brimming with plans. "Ranulf, could you get some of the Exiles together again? All they'd have to do is keep the knights busy while I got the boys to the woods. We could ride from there on a horse, if we could find one—"

"You shall have mine, Lady Adept."

Everyone had quite forgotten the Wandwright, who closed the lid of the little iron chest with a satisfying click. "You will take two of my own mounts, who are faster than the wind itself. They will aid you in your journey back to the Elm this day, and they will guide you and your charges to your portal in the Northern Wood as well."

Holly broke into a smile. Her plan was going to work. "Thank you, my lady. We can do it, Ranulf, can't we?"

"Of course," Almaric answered for him, but the centaur measured his words after a moment's thought. "We shall need the Exiles, my lady, as many as we can find. Their allegiance will be difficult to acquire, but in light of recent events . . ." Ranulf smiled at the wand in Holly's hand. "They may be easier to convince than I had feared."

CLAIRE M. CATERER

Chapter 36

Message from the Dvergar

While Ranulf and Almaric gathered supplies, the Wandwright brought two squat, white horses to Holly's side from somewhere behind the cottage. "Trust these horses to find the safest path to the Northern Wood," she said. "They will return of their own accord. And one more thing you require, my lady." She fastened a thin leather belt around Holly's waist. A finger-shaped pouch hung below it. "An Adept's wand must have a proper scabbard."

Holly blushed, suddenly shy. What could she say to this lady? "I wish I knew how to thank you. There's no way I could save Ben and Everett, or take us home, without your help," she said.

"It is I who should thank you, Lady Adept," said Lady Belisanne in her cool, studied voice. "It is many an age since I have plied my trade, and I am gladdened to do so again."

Holly thought of the iron chest she had unlocked.

"I didn't get to see what you keep in that box," she said.

The Wandwright lowered her eyelashes and nearly smiled. "No, Lady Holly. That is for another time."

The white horses bowed to allow Almaric and Holly to climb up on them. Jade leaped up to sit directly in front of Holly, and Áedán nestled against her shoulder.

The Wandwright laid her cool palm against Holly's cheek. "Farewell, Lady Adept. Use your tools wisely."

The Wandwright inclined her head, turned, and walked back into her cottage. At once the little house seemed to fade. The flowers turned dun-colored against the moor; after a moment, they were hardly noticeable, shaded despite the sun. The little group turned toward home and left the Wandwright behind them.

Belisanne's horses, like Ranulf, did not tire easily. Although the hills were hard climbing, they galloped across the open moorland. They camped a few hours' ride from the Elm, and by midmorning the next day, they had arrived back at Almaric's cottage.

Holly spent hours practicing her spell again, using as many different locks as Almaric could produce. She had only one day left before the tournament and she was determined not to waste it.

"Only take care, my lady," said Almaric, as Holly unlocked his bedroom door. She turned the latch and immediately tried again with her wand, but her head was spinning and the lock held fast. "Doing spells depletes your resources. They cannot be repeated a moment later without great risk." He leaned forward, catching her arm before she stumbled.

"You mean like draining a battery?" Holly sank onto the little bed and put her head between her knees. The dizziness eased.

"Er . . . if you say so, my lady." The magician tilted his head to see her face. "Is this posture helpful?"

"Her Ladyship has many unusual habits, whether or not they be helpful," Jade observed from the window-sill.

"I just need to get this right," Holly said crossly. "If I don't, the three of us will be lucky not to be killed on the spot."

"Skill is required, but also patience," Almaric said. "And there is another consideration that the Wandwright failed to mention."

"Oh, great," Holly said. "Now what?"

Almaric sat beside her. "Your kinsman, Lady Holly, will be fast in the tower. This much we know. The door will prove easy for you. But . . ."

"But?"

He smiled nervously. "If the lads are chained, the matter is a bit more tricky. I wouldn't advise you to try breaking manacle locks."

"Why? What's the difference?"

"Please don't misunderstand me." Almaric patted her hand. "You are a most apt student. But your power is still unfocused. It takes a great deal of skill to dissolve the locks of an iron bracelet without . . . that is . . ."

"What Almaric is trying to say," Jade cut in, "is that Your Ladyship is likely to dissolve the bones of your kinsman as well as his bonds."

Holly's head swam all over again. "What? His *bones*?"

"Now, Jade!" Almaric waved away the concern. "Yes, Lady Holly, it certainly could happen. Bones, you see, are locks as well, and if your spell were to go just the least bit awry—"

"And it likely would," said the cat.

Her stomach lurched. She might end up killing Ben. "Be—be honest, Almaric. Would it? Would the spell go awry? I've been practicing so hard."

The old man shrugged, his eyes flitting nervously back and forth between Holly and the cat. "Well . . . to be honest . . . yes, my lady, it is quite likely. But not to worry! Surely there will be no chains involved.

Let us take some tea, and then you might practice more."

Holly tried to follow Almaric's advice and convince herself that she wouldn't have to bother with dissolving any manacles, but the thought kept creeping back into her head, chilling her skin in the hot sun. She was nervous and irritable. She missed Ranulf, who had disappeared as soon as they arrived, saying he would not return until after teatime. It was nearly dark before she heard his familiar hoofbeats outside the cottage window. She ran outside.

"Ranulf, where've you . . . ?" she started to say, then halted.

Standing in the twilit clearing with Ranulf was Bittenbender of the Dvergar, shouldering his ax. He gripped it when he heard Holly approach, then relaxed. "Lady Adept," he said quietly, and nodded to her.

"Bittenbender, right?" Holly didn't know whether to shake his hand, so she only nodded as he had.

The small man sat down on a tree stump and motioned to the grass as if inviting Holly to join him. Ranulf's chest rumbled, as horses' do, and Holly guessed the Dvergar wasn't showing her the respect Ranulf thought she deserved. But she sat down anyway.

"Is it true ye've met the Wandwright?" said

Bittenbender. His voice was tight, as if struggling to keep patience.

"Yes," said Holly. She sat up straight and looked down at the man's squinty eyes. He wasn't going to scare her. "I forged a new wand—I mean, she helped me to." Holly pulled the wand from its scabbard. Bittenbender recoiled a fraction.

"So ye have." He held out a grubby hand. "May I?"

Holly started to hand it to him, but something in Ranulf's stance made her reconsider. "Sorry, but it's mine. I had to work pretty hard to forge it. It's very powerful."

The Dvergar grunted. "Ye've learnt well, my lady. There's a new sort of look about ye. Ranulf came to us today, singing yer praises, callin' fer an army of Exiles— those what lacked faith in ye not three days gone." He pulled a dagger from his belt and turned over his boot, scraping mud from the heel. "I was amongst them."

"I know," Holly said. "And what do you think now?"

Bittenbender shrugged. "I think it still be a fool's errand. But we'll join with ye."

Holly remembered the host of creatures she had met—the stags, centaurs, and others who had doubted her. "And Fleetwing? Will he come too?"

Bittenbender shrugged. "A leogryff does as he likes. And what he likes is to be paid in kind."

"I don't understand. What changed your mind?" she asked.

The little man grinned. "I an't changed a thing, lass," he said. "We'll join ye, I say—but we wants something in return, do we. Fleetwing, too."

Holly shivered, as if a breeze had blown between them. She had seen Raethius in her vision at the Wandwright's cottage. "You want me to Banish the Sorcerer."

"Ranulf, but she's quick, this one!" crowed Bittenbender to the centaur. Ranulf swished his tail but said nothing. "Aye, lass. We want the Banishment."

"I already told you. I'm not ready to do that yet. Maybe someday, but—"

"Aye. *Some*day. That's all we's asking."

Holly's heart lifted. "You . . . You just want a promise? A promise that I'll come back and help?"

"The word of an Adept's meant to be binding," said the Dvergar, "but I'll be needing a bit more than that."

He rifled in his tunic—which Holly saw had a dozen different pockets—and drew out a small silver dagger. It was thin and triangular, like an arrow, and along one edge ran a hundred jagged teeth, while the other edge was beveled smooth and sharp. Bittenbender turned it over by its gilded handle and Holly saw a rune etched in the steel.

"What is that?" she asked. Áedán nestled close to her, but she felt no warmer.

"One of the tools that *we* forge, we the Earthfolk," said Bittenbender in a whisper. "With this we take a blood oath, one which ye can't easily break."

"You mean, I'd swear it?" Holly glanced at Ranulf. Did he think this was a good idea? The centaur returned her gaze, then finally nodded.

"Ef ye *can* return, ye *must*. That's what the oath says." Bittenbender pulled a small scroll of parchment from another pocket. Holly tried to read it, but the language wasn't English, and the wand wasn't helping her translate it.

"I have read it, Lady Holly," Ranulf spoke up. "The Dvergar speaks truth. You may trust him."

But she didn't—not really. She might believe what the oath said, but the Dvergar's shifty eyes didn't encourage good faith. "I want to come back anyway," she said defensively.

"Then signing this oath should be easy, lass." Then, with an uncomfortable glance at Ranulf, he added, "Yer Ladyship."

"What do I do?" Holly asked, trying to still the trembling in her fingers. She'd have to be brave for this; she was asking the Exiles to risk their lives— again.

"Hold yer right hand still, and I'll make a wee cut. Yer blood on this parchment will be yer oath from this day forward." The little man brandished the dagger. "Are ye ready, Lady Holly?"

"Yes," she said, before she had more time to think about it. "Just do it." She looked up at Ranulf and kept her gaze fixed on his wide brown eyes while the sharp point slashed across her palm. She couldn't help emitting a gasp, but she didn't scream. She was proud of that.

"That should do it," said Bittenbender, rolling up the scroll and standing, all business now. "Until the morrow, Yer Ladyship." He tipped his ax like a hat and swaggered into the wood, whistling tunelessly.

Holly stood up. Ranulf's tail swished as he gazed after the Dvergar. "I hope I did the right thing," she said. She pressed the tail of her tunic into her palm, trying to stanch the blood from the shallow cut the dagger had made.

"An oath goes both ways, Lady Holly," said the centaur. "You have earned the protection of the Exiles. That is no small gain."

She gazed up at the stars. Everything was different here—even the moon, swimming large and yellow near the horizon. She couldn't quite see the features of the man in its face.

THE KEY & THE FLAME * 379

Ranulf laid his heavy hand on her shoulder. "They are as old as time itself," he said, following her gaze.

Holly wanted to say that didn't make any sense, since some of the stars were much older than others, but she only nodded.

"There, in the south." The centaur's long arm pointed halfway up the bowl of the sky. "Do you see, Lady Holly? The transit of the Lion's Tail."

Even among the blaze of constellations, Holly picked out a large ball of a star, bigger than Jupiter, with a sparkling tail behind it. A comet?

"It comes but rarely across our skies. It foretold your arrival."

"I don't see how. It could mean something else— anything else. Me coming here, it was just an accident."

"The Mounted do not believe in accidents," said the centaur.

Holly sighed. "Everything that's happened seems like a big accident to me."

"How so, Lady Holly?"

She thought a minute. "It's hard to explain, Ranulf. My world's so different from here. Nothing really special ever happens to me. I'm kind of a failure, really. I mean, Ben's the one who's so good in school and does what all the teachers like. He's in advanced math and he's into robotics and programming, and he's got cool ideas on how to design new computer games. I've got a compass and some climbing gear. And I'm good at reading, I guess. I know that forging the wand was something really special. But I can't help feeling like I've fooled you all into thinking I'm somebody I'm not."

The centaur was quiet, shifting his weight from hoof to hoof. "I cannot speak to your position in your own world, my lady," he said at last. "I can only tell you of your place in this one. You have a purpose here."

"And what purpose is that?"

"You were given an Adept's wand in your world, where there be no Adepts. That wand was lost, and you, the last of that mighty race, forged a new one at the Wandwright's hand. You come from a distant realm, and yet you forge and train like our Adepts of old. Do you not see purpose in that?"

Holly shrugged off a chill. "I don't know. Yes, of course. I mean, it seems like . . ." *Like I belong here.* But that was ridiculous.

"I believe that one day you will rid us of the evil that has befallen us."

She glanced up at him. "The Sorcerer?"

"Raethius of the Source. You must know him, name him, in order to Banish him. This much I know of Adept magic."

"But Jade said there's no way I could learn that

spell. And anyway, there's no time. I have to find the boys and get us all home safe."

"The hour is not yet at hand. But it will come. You will return one day to Anglielle." Ranulf gazed back up at the stars. "Of this I am certain."

CLAIRE M. CATERER

Chapter 37

The Return of the King

While Holly was busy forging a wand and signing blood oaths, Everett had spent two days training for his jousting tournament. Once he had acquired the red scarf—what Sol had called his "lady's favor"—everything had changed, both for him and for Ben.

His initial bumbling with the wand had been forgotten. He was a knight now, and everyone in the castle turned out to watch him practice. Even Lord Clement, the king's adviser who had nearly severed Holly's hand in the forest their very first day, arrived on the pitch.

"Your station is much improved, lad," he noted dryly. He was watching Everett throw firebombs at shields positioned around the pitch as targets. He rubbed his stubbled beard and regarded Everett with dark eyes.

Everett shrugged. "It's Avery's doing, not mine," he said. Clement's pockmarked face hardened. "I—I mean, His Highness. He's the one who said I should use the wand."

"Wands are tools of Adepts and traitors," Clement said.

Prince Avery, who had been fencing with Loverian, tossed his shield in Ben's general direction, ignoring him as he cried, "Hey! Watch it!" He walked up to where Everett was practicing. "Sir Everett is no Adept, my lord Clement," he said easily. "We have dubbed him 'the Mage.'"

"And the difference, Your Highness?"

Avery shrugged. "He is not of our land and poses no threat to the kingdom. He is not the magicfolk we hear tell of in stories. He has only a happy talent for illusion, as have our court magicians."

"It's all just trickery, my lord," Everett put in. "You know, like a show."

Ben came up to Everett and handed him a cup of water. "I've seen it before where we come from," he said. "Nothing magic about it, really."

Clement scowled. "Look upon yon castle, Your Highness. What see you? A fortress built on trickery? Nay, we are *men*, not mages, not Adepts. It be by our own strength that His Majesty's castle stands. And what of our good knights? There be not a mage nor merman amongst them. If this lad uses trickery, how may he compete in fairness against them?"

Avery smiled. "None shall assume Sir Everett to

compete for a true prize," he said. "This display is but for our royal amusement."

Lord Clement *humphed* and strode away, still frowning.

"You know, he has a point," Ben said. "Isn't everybody else going to think the same thing? Won't they hate Everett because they'll think he's a whatchamacallit, Adept?"

"Squire, thy speech is likened to the wind," said Avery dismissively, turning to Everett. "What thinkst thou, Sir Everett?"

"Ben could be right, Ave— I mean, Your Highness."

"Hmmm. The opinion of a knight is to be considered." Avery threw an arm around Everett's shoulders. "Let us think on it, thou and I, over luncheon."

Together they walked to the wide poplar tree at the edge of the lists. Behind him, Ben called, "Oh, sure! When it's a *knight's* opinion, you have to think on it!" Everett heard Dart say something about the horses, and Ben replied, "*Okay*, I'm coming."

Everett felt a stirring of guilt walking away from Ben, but he knew that the closer he got to the prince, the better off they all would be. He could hardly refuse. And he could always apologize to Ben later.

After lunch, though, Ben refused to speak to him. His face was blotchy and swollen, and Everett asked if he'd taken his medicine. "He has, my lord," Dart volunteered, when Ben stalked off to the other end of the tilt. "But I did come upon him weeping not an hour gone."

"Here, take Buttercup a moment, can you?" Everett slid off the horse and handed the reins to Dart. He picked up the well bucket and followed Ben.

"Looks like you could use a wash," he said when he came within earshot. "I brought some water."

Ben turned away and walked around the pitch, setting up the shields in the dirt for more practice. "I guess *luncheon* was good," he said finally, not looking up. "You took long enough. I've been in with the horses all afternoon."

"We were just talking," said Everett. "You got Avery worried. You were spot on about the magic. But Avery's got a good idea. He's going to post notices all over the village about a mage and a show, so it all looks staged— like we're making sport of Adepts, not trying to be one—"

"That's great. Glad I could help you and *Avery*." Ben sounded anything but glad.

"It's helping you and me, Ben. It's not like I'm enjoying this." And he wasn't. Not much, anyway.

"Oh, come on!" Ben threw down one of the shields and turned on him. "You're throwing around lightning bolts and jousting and feasting and calling him Avery. What am I doing? Brushing horses! And it *smells* in that stable. And I'm allergic, in case you forgot! Now, all of a sudden, you're best friends with the guy who was ready to chop our heads off two days ago."

"Look here, I've got to play along, haven't I? How else are we going to get out of this, by making him the enemy?" Everett lowered his voice. "I'll try to get you out of the stables, all right? But we've got to trust each other."

Ben sighed, and kicked one of the shields for good measure. "It's just . . . I'm tired. I want a real bed and my computer and normal food. I even want to see Holly, even though she's bossy and annoying." His voice thickened and he swiped a hand across his nose.

"I know. Me too. Let's just get through it, yeah? We've got a tournament to win. And I need your help, Ben." Everett patted him on the shoulder and led him back to the other end of the tilt.

He felt another twinge of guilt, remembering his promise to Sol. She wanted him to deliver Holly to her, but for what? Surely the fairy wouldn't hurt Holly; she'd done nothing but great things for Everett.

The night before, he had lain awake on his straw pallet, thinking while Ben snored next to him. He couldn't very well just give Ben's sister over to Sol, no matter what the reason. But he was clever enough to engage Sol's interest, wasn't he? Clever enough, he thought, to outwit her. He would use the lady's favor, all right. He only needed to get through the tournament. Then he and the others could escape, and Sol could have her token back; he wouldn't need it anymore. He pulled it out of his sleeve now and wrapped it around his free hand. In truth, it was all the help he needed. He didn't need Ben at all.

It wasn't hard for Everett to keep his promise to Ben. Everett had gained the trust of nearly everyone in the castle, and the squires and pages all argued over who would bring him his horse and hand him his lance. Ben had little to do but stand around and look impressed with Everett's skill. The prince's attitude didn't change much, but at least he allowed Ben to eat meals with them.

Relieved of squiring duties, Ben appointed himself chief medic of tournament practice. Knights were constantly being thrown from horses or lanced in the gut, and Ben found that crumbling a Tylenol in a stein of ale cured most ills. The other squires respected him, and he even looked a bit stronger. The fresh air and exercise were doing him good, and he blushed and smiled when the knights praised his efforts.

CLAIRE M. CATERER

Everett continued to work all the next day, though now he seemed to need no more training. With his lady's favor wrapped around his hand, Everett threw sparks and fireballs at will, and Buttercup obeyed every command like a prize stallion. Every man in the castle challenged him in turn, some eager to see his displays, others sure they could best him. Everett conjured phantoms with long faces that spooked horses and knights alike. Once, a flaming yellow bird flew from the wand and set fire to one of the pennants flying over the grandstand. As the pages scurried to pull down the flag, Everett peered through the smoke and saw a tall, slender lady with fiery red hair sitting alone at the top of the berfrois, watching him, her porcelain face as still as a doll's. He blinked as the sun caught the circlet on her head.

The queen?

For a moment Everett was distracted as the pages shoved him aside, stamping out the flames before they spread on the grass. When he looked back up at the berfrois, the queen was gone.

The training recommenced. Servants neglected their duties to sit and watch. Even the knights Pagett and Gervase forgot their own practice and cheered for Tullian as he galloped through Everett's purple fog, eyes shut, thrusting with his lance. But one flick of

Everett's wrist sent the lance flying over the knight's head, landing upright in the soft turf beyond.

Meanwhile, the castle bustled with preparations for the tournament. Knights from all over the kingdom began arriving. Avery's notices had spread the word about the strange young knight and his magic, and everyone wondered what the king would say. The knights whispered among themselves that whatever His Highness pretended, Everett's feats looked like *real* magic, not a show. And hadn't the two youths appeared in the forest from nowhere? Did His Majesty know what Avery was about, that he had captured an Adept and was setting him against the king's own champions?

But of course the king knew nothing of the sort. He had been off on a hunting party the last two weeks. And even in the midst of all the cheering and praise that Everett was earning, in the back of his mind—like looking forward to a very hard exam or a flu shot—was the idea that soon the king would return to the castle and find out exactly what they were up to.

At that afternoon's luncheon—in fact, the same afternoon that Holly made her mad gallop back from the Wandwright's cottage—Prince Avery sat both boys next to him at the high table, and he commanded a toast be drunk to Sir Everett and his prodigious skill.

CLAIRE M. CATERER

They ate well, even if the food was a little strange—
venison and cygnets and boar's head and eel pasties.
Even Ben seemed to be getting used to it. Dessert was
custard tarts flavored with honey and cinnamon and
some other spice Everett couldn't identify. It was just
as he turned to Avery to ask him what it was that it
happened.

First came a gasp from the far end of the Great Hall.
A young woman, the daughter of one of the nobles,
pointed to the arched doorway and shrank away from
it. In the doorway stood something—a ghost, Everett
thought.

And why not? If this place had magic wands and
flying panthers, why shouldn't there be ghosts, too?
The figure was a girl, transparent, but at turns almost
solid, as if she were a film projection just out of focus.
Her hair was in long braids, and . . .

Everett felt the blood leave his face. The ghost was
in blue jeans. And glasses.

Ben glanced at him. "What the—?" Then he stood
up so fast he knocked over his goblet of juice. "That's—
Holly! It's Holly!"

"It can't be," Everett whispered.

"Don't you touch her!" Ben cried, but Grandor, who
had been standing just to one side of the high table,
had already leaped off the dais.

The phantom figure held out a hand, as if trying to reach them.

Grandor charged forward, his sword drawn. Avery, speechless, sat with his mouth open. The knights and ladies stampeded toward the dais, and Grandor pushed against them as if swimming upstream. "Stop!" he hollered. "In the name of the crown!"

Too late, Everett thought of going to help her. It would be impossible to push through the crowd now, and from the dais he could see Grandor's hand reach out to grab Holly as he brought the sword down.

But, just as suddenly as she had appeared, she vanished.

"Where did she go? Is she okay?" Ben was babbling. But she hadn't run away; she had simply disappeared, like a TV turned off, like . . .

Like Holly's living-museum people, back about a hundred years ago.

Everett grabbed Ben's sleeve and pulled him down on the bench. All around them, men and women were talking in panicky voices, Grandor was bellowing, and Avery was trying to shout over the commotion.

"She was here," Ben insisted in a low voice.

"No, she wasn't," said Everett. "At least, not really. Remember that day in Darton Castle? When she kept saying she saw the people in fancy dress? When she said she saw *you*?"

Ben's eyes grew round. "No way—"

"She said someone came at her with a sword—a big dark-haired bloke, remember? At a party, with you sitting at the high table? She was *here*, Ben!"

Ben grew pale, and he looked like his eel pasty might be making a return appearance at any moment.

And then Everett's stomach did a somersault too, for he heard a sound that, without realizing it, he had been listening for all day: a round, full series of trumpeted notes.

"What's that?" Ben asked.

"The king," said Everett, feeling a cold fist around his heart. "The king is home."

The trumpets only threw the Great Hall into further chaos. Clearly, the feast was over. Loverian seized the boys and led them out of the hall to their room. Avery didn't glance at them twice, but seemed busy conferring with Lord Clement on how best to track down the Adept. Before the boys were even out of the Great Hall, they saw Gervase bound up to Avery. "His Majesty has returned and would see you at once, Your Highness."

"I knew it," Ben said gloomily as the door banged shut behind them. "There goes any chance we have of getting out of here. The king's never going to let you use the wand, Everett. We'll be lucky if they don't kill us tonight. They probably think we let Holly in somehow too."

"Shut it," said Everett, but he knew Ben was right. "They might not even have noticed she'd come in if you hadn't stood up and pointed at her."

"It was because of everybody *else* pointing that I saw her in the first place!" Ben said, his face reddening.

Everett shrugged, by which he clearly meant, *If you say so.* It was unfair—untrue, even—what he'd said, but he was frightened now, and it made him irritable. He thrust a hand into his pocket, clutching at the red silk scarf, hoping it would calm him. But it didn't. The last few days, all the practice, all the cozying up to Avery, was getting them nowhere. He didn't feel right without that wand in his hand. It gave him a power, a feeling that he was right and good, which justified whatever else he might say or do. What Ben didn't understand is that sometimes you had to make sacrifices to do great things, things like perform flawlessly in a jousting tournament to save your friends.

Of course, it was really Holly who had tried to save them, and he was counting on her to come back and rescue them again, as Sol had said. But it was *him*, Everett, who was doing all the work. And Holly would probably come dashing in and take all the credit.

CLAIRE M. CATERER

Ben heaved a sigh and flopped onto his pallet. "We went to that castle days ago. How could Holly be in Hawkesbury and here at the same time?"

Everett thought a moment, trying to still the irritation that burned in his chest. "I don't know, exactly. But she said the key unlocks places and times. Maybe just being there at Darton Castle, holding that wand— that key—it's like she looked through a veil, like Gallaway said." He shrugged. "I mean, if it *was* a few days ago. If she *is* still here."

"What do you mean, if? Where else would she be?"

Perhaps it was the lady's favor that he wrapped so tightly around his hand that the fabric cut into his knuckles, or maybe it was just the fear rising in his throat now that the king was home, but something prompted a rather awful thing to come out of his mouth. "Maybe she found a way home and left without us."

Ben stared at him for a moment, then said tightly, "Take that back, Everett."

"And how's she going to rescue us?" Everett went on, unable to stop himself. "Those Adept powers of hers didn't look so brill the other night."

"Holly doesn't even *need* powers!" Ben shouted. "You don't know her! She's supersmart and knows all about animals and fossils and weird myths and stuff, plus she's a wicked rock climber and she's brave and she *does* things! She knows how to plan and think and strategize—well, okay, not in computer games, but in real life, anyway. And she's *loyal*. She'd never leave without us, even if she could."

"How do you know?" Everett countered. "She got out of the castle somehow, but she didn't take us with her, did she? She's off making friends with flying cats and centaurs and all!"

"*You're* making friends with Avery!"

"I didn't notice *you* turning down any of the food today!"

The two of them stood about a foot apart, breathing hard, faces red. Ben looked like he wanted to hit Everett, but instead he turned away and rubbed his eyes.

Everett threw himself down on his own pallet and turned his back on Ben. He shouldn't have said that about Holly; he didn't really believe it. Or maybe he did. He didn't know her that well, and anyway, it seemed like these Adepts and their friends were bent on taking over the kingdom, like they'd tried to do before. Maybe Holly's whole rescue plan was more like a cover for a castle siege. Ben's view of things was skewed; he'd gotten kind of a raw deal, even Everett admitted that much. He was so sure Avery and his lot were in the wrong, but hadn't they done what anyone would have, finding poachers on their land? And hadn't Avery been a pretty regular bloke since then?

But what *was* Everett going to do when Holly came for them? Sol would be unhappy—no, furious—if he didn't give Holly up to her. But what could she really do to him? Sol couldn't touch the wand—she'd said so. She needed Everett to make it work. So there *was* something special about him, whether or not he was *of the Blood*. His wand could perform feats that Holly could only dream of. He would make sure the rescue wasn't botched. Unlike Holly, he knew what he was doing.

After a while Everett heard Ben begin playing a solo game of Battleship on his side of the room. The shadows began to lengthen, made late by the impending solstice, and finally Everett admitted to Ben that he'd been out of line and of course Holly hadn't left them stranded in Anglielle. Ben took to checking his watch every fifteen minutes and announcing the time like Westminster. No one brought them either news or food. Surely by now the king had discussed matters with Avery.

"Maybe the queen will help us," Ben suggested. "She gave the order to hold our execution. She seems nicer than anyone else."

"But she's never around, is she? I saw her one time

in the berfrois—at least, I *think* it was her—but she's not even at the feasts."

"I never saw her up in the—thingy," said Ben, pouting a little. "What's she like?"

"I don't know—pale. Avery says she's often ill or something."

"The king's probably got *her* locked in a tower someplace," Ben said.

"No worries. I'm sure Avery's putting in the good word," said Everett.

"If he's not stabbing us in the back, you mean."

"There you go again. Look, just because he and I've gotten to be mates—"

"He's not your *mate*, Ev. He's a prince. And now his dad's home. You think he's going to take your side over the king's? What choice is he gonna have?"

"But he's sort of a prisoner too, isn't he? He made it sound like he never gets to go anywhere, except hunting for poachers."

Ben sighed. "I just wish this was over."

There wasn't much else to say after that. Ben tried to get Everett to tell him how he'd got the wand working so well, but Everett didn't dare tell him about his agreement with Sol. Besides, she had chosen Everett, not Ben, because of his—well—special gifts. Like Mr. Gallaway had chosen Holly.

CLAIRE M. CATERER

They lapsed into a bored silence as the room darkened. It was well past midnight when a key finally rattled in the lock. Dart scurried in, holding a tray with some leftover meat and a flagon of mulled wine.

"What's going on?" Ben asked. "Is the king mad? Is Avery okay?"

Dart was out of breath. "Apologies, my lords. We are much occupied with preparations for the tournament. The vespers has already begun, wherein the squires compete. The king is hosting a feast with the knights and ladies, and more arriving all the time, all needing rooms, and food and drink—"

"That's all right," Everett said. "But stay a moment, can't you? Do you know if the king's been told about us?"

Dart set down his tray and sat on one of the pallets. "He and His Highness were closed inside the king's chamber for a long while. And at the feast, whispers travel up and down the trestle, telling of thy feats."

"Oh." Everett felt a bit queasy.

"The king said naught of you in my hearing. He talks only of his hunting party and the tournament to come." Dart stood up. "I beg your leave, my lords. I have duties."

"Sure," Everett said. "Go ahead."

Dart gave a little bow before running out, as if the boys weren't prisoners at all. They picked at the food. Occasionally they heard a loud cheer from the Great Hall below, and sometimes the voices of the castle guards who patrolled the grounds. The moon rose, high and full in the sky. Ben muttered that no news was good news. But Everett wondered if the king had dismissed Avery's idea outright without giving it another thought. After all, an execution might make an interesting addition to the tournament's entertainment.

Chapter 38

His Majesty's Knight

Not long after dawn Everett startled awake and sat up on his pallet. He had heard a key turning in the lock.

This time it was Avery himself who came in and sat next to Everett. Ben stirred.

"What's going on?" he said, rubbing his eyes.

"Do not fear," whispered the prince to Everett. "The king will permit thee to compete."

Ben sat up. "And he knows that Everett's going to be using the wand?"

The prince glanced away. "I had . . . other matters to discuss with my father."

"You mean you chickened out," said Everett.

"Thou art fortunate to be alive," Avery snapped. "Have I not told thee what I wouldst do to see thy world? We shall escape as planned. I have spoken with His Majesty's advisers about the wand. They assure me all will be well."

"Oh well, *that* ought to be good enough." Ben scowled.

THE KEY & THE FLAME   * 401

"It's the only plan we've got," said Everett. "Are we together?" He held his hand out and Ben laid his on top. After a moment, but firmly enough, Avery covered Ben's hand with his own.

It was the sort of spectacle that would have been great fun to watch if you weren't afraid of being shot at, arrested, or gored with a knight's lance. The berfrois was draped in banners of red and gold, and scarlet pennants flew from every corner. The stands were full of people. Young ladies-in-waiting, their hair woven through with gold ribbons, waved handkerchiefs from the upper boxes. Silken veils flew from their tall conical hats. The knights had hung their shields all around the berfrois. Each was different, rampant with lions or eagles or swans, but all were emblazoned at the top with the king's emblem—the black raven holding crossed swords.

Everett clambered up on Buttercup behind the berfrois at the end nearest the castle, surrounded by the king's knights on horseback. He was hot and itching in places that he couldn't reach, and his palms sweated inside leather gloves. He'd been outfitted with odds and ends from the king's armory that morning, and wore a chain-mail shirt that hung to his knees and two mismatched, clunky leg pieces. His helmet

CLAIRE M. CATERER

was round with a horizontal slit that kept slipping below his eyes.

The older knights chuckled when they saw him. Their own gleaming armor was covered by surcoats decorated with their emblems. Even their horses wore silk housings in bright colors, and they pawed and snorted, eager to race onto the lists. Buttercup, who'd had to make do with a cursory brushing, sniffed the dirt and looked bored.

Next to Everett, Loverian held his helmet in one hand and Buttercup's reins in the other. Suddenly he lurched toward Everett as someone shoved him from behind. His jaw tightened. Grandor edged up beside them.

"My pardon, Sir Loverian, I beg you. I only wish to see that our newest knight of the realm not try any tricks." He sneered at Everett.

"I have charge of him," said Loverian. "He knows well that should Their Majesties fall into danger, his life is forfeit."

Grandor's hot breath tickled Everett's neck. "It shall be forfeit in any case. That is *my* oath to you."

The trumpets sounded, and the horses jostled each other. Everett could see Lord Clement pacing the lists. He raised one arm and shouted: "Hear ye, hear ye! Well met, Your Majesties, Your Royal Highness, lords and ladies from all corners of the realm of His Most Royal Majesty King Reynard! Here shall ye witness feats beyond imagining, bravery and skill ne'er before witnessed! Your welcome, I bid you, to His Majesty's Royal Tournament of Skills! And now I give you His Majesty's knights!"

The horns trumpeted again, and Pagett, at the front, cantered his horse out, his squire trotting alongside. He circled the tilt, reared the horse, and galloped back the way he had come, passing the others. Close on his heels rode Grandor, who had somehow pushed his way to the front, and then Gervase and Tullian. Then it was Everett's turn.

The sunlight dazzled him for a moment. Loverian rode with him, leading Buttercup around the tilt. It was broader than the fence he'd practiced with, and draped in banners like those on the berfrois. As they cantered down the other side, Everett glanced up at the gallery.

He spied Avery first, wearing a silk surcoat and a heavy, brocaded cloak; the circlet on his head sparkled. Next to him sat the tall, pale woman Everett had seen before. She wore a dazzling white gown, and her hair caught the sun like a flame. She stared down at him without expression. Beside her was the king.

If Everett had expected to see a fat, jovial-looking

fellow sporting an oversize crown, he was disappointed. The king was thickly muscled, tall, and hard. His jawline looked chiseled from stone, his eyes dead in his face. His crown was short and heavy, studded with a very large, white-blue stone like a diamond. Everett could almost see his thoughts: *Everything and everyone belongs to me, to do with as I please.* But it didn't look like much pleased him. His eyes stayed fixed on Everett until he and Loverian cantered off the lists. Everett let out his breath as they retreated behind the berfrois. Sweat trickled down his back.

"Ev, are you okay?" Ben handed him up a waterskin, from which he took a long pull.

"I'm all right," he said, but he was trembling as he dismounted, the armor clanking like the Tin Man. "What about you?"

Ben's face was blotchy and starting to puff up. He'd been standing in the knight's line for a long time. "I just took some medicine. I'm okay."

"Come on," Everett said. "It's not our turn till the end of the first round."

Several pavilions, which were like small brightly colored circus tents, had been erected for the knights to relax out of the sun. They walked inside the nearest one. Loverian went with them and sat on a low cot to take off his breastplate.

"I was talking to the other squires," Ben said. "First up is Gervase. He's jousting with some guy from the northern end of the kingdom, called Adémar. Then it's Pagett against Sir Somebody . . ."

"Sir Rocelin," Loverian supplied.

"Yeah, Rocelin. And then Tullian fights Anselm, I think it was . . . Anyway, there's seven jousts ahead of you. Then whoever wins those is paired up again, so we'll be down to eight guys in the second round, then four, and two in the end."

"Who's my knight again?"

"Jordain." Ben sniffed. "Everyone says he's easy. He was a squire last year, still pretty green. You won't have any trouble with him."

Everett grasped the wand. He had the feeling trouble was exactly what he was going to have.

Chapter 39

Lady in Waiting

The morning of the tournament, Holly woke with the sun. All the cottage was asleep. Folded on a chair next to her bed were her original clothes, jeans and all, which had somehow been washed and dried. She slipped into them gratefully. Even her tennis shoes had been cleaned of mud. Around her waist she fastened the belt with the scabbard the Wandwright had given her.

She had to look like a page or a squire, though. Over her ordinary clothes Holly slipped on the tunic and leggings she'd worn the day before. She wove her hair into a single braid and tucked it inside the tunic's hood.

Áedán blinked at her from the mirror's reflection, half hidden beneath her tunic. Holly had gotten used to his warmth on her shoulder, but what would happen to him today? She couldn't bring him home; her mother would, well, freak out. And he'd hardly make it through customs back home to the States. But the Wandwright had said he could hibernate until she returned—which she would, as soon as she could. She touched the cut on her palm. Bittenbender had seen to that.

While Holly was picking over her breakfast, too nervous to eat, Hornbeak the falcon arrived to go over the plan with her and the others. She would need to lose herself among the boys at the tournament and try to fit in with them. Hornbeak had seen Ben and Everett just the night before being led to their room, which was on the lower level of the east tower. Jade, who had been to the castle before, could guide her, but the Exiles would need to do their part to draw the guards away from the prisoners.

"I would expect the guards to be redoubled," said Hornbeak, who had seen many a prison break. "These lads were near rescued once already."

"But if someone's storming the castle, won't everyone go to defend it?" Holly asked. They'd better, or she wouldn't be able to get the boys out. Everything depended on the castle being thrown into confusion.

"We shall have to hope 'tis so, my lady," said Ranulf. And after that, there wasn't much left to say.

Almaric fitted a saddle and bridle to one of the Wandwright's white horses. He gave Holly a new bow and quiver and helped secure them behind her back-pack. Ranulf helped her to her mount. Jade and the falcon leaped up in front of her. "Hornbeak shall be your eyes and ears, as well as our own," Ranulf told her. "He will signal us when you have gained the castle. And should any harm befall you, the Golden Salamander will protect you, my lady."

Holly remembered the ring of fire Áedán had con-jured when he'd thought Ranulf was a threat, back at the Wandwright's cottage. Her shoulder glowed with the salamander's warmth beneath her cloak.

Almaric embraced Holly briefly, then blushed and backed away, bowing. "Lady Adept, it has been an honor."

A tight lump grew in Holly's throat. "But I'll be seeing you before I go, won't I?"

Almaric glanced down and coughed, fiddling with his walking stick. "I had thought to await Your Ladyship in the wood, but Ranulf . . ."

"It will be for Almaric's own safety to remain, Lady Holly," said the centaur gently.

"Yes, yes, best all round, should something go awry," the magician agreed, wiping his eyes. "But in any case, my lady . . . Well . . . I would have you know how grate-ful we are to you."

"But I haven't done anything. I've just . . ." Tears

pricked behind Holly's eyes. "I've put everybody in danger."

"You have given us hope, Lady Holly," said Ranulf, looking into her eyes. "That is no small feat."

"But I will come back," she said. "I'll see you all again."

"Let us think only of our task ahead," said Ranulf. "It is enough to concern us."

Holly's white horse followed the path through the Northern Wood and out onto the meadow. Seeing the castle in the distance, Holly felt very small. They could be attacked at any moment. Her only comfort was that Hornbeak was keeping a lookout from above.

"The knights will all be busied about the tournament, Lady Holly," Jade said, reading her thoughts.

As they approached the castle, she spied the grandstands set around the tournament pitch. The king's banners flapped in the wind. "I hope you're right," she whispered.

She entered from beyond the lists, and here a dozen different things took her attention. Clusters of blue-cloaked musicians piped tunes on recorders and strummed mandolins. Several men juggled bright flags, swords, and burning torches. Villagers competed in their own archery contests and horseshoe games.

Winners took away mince pies and round cakes that smelled of honey. Children scampered every which way, waving toy wooden swords and burlap flags painted with the image of a raven. Village women clustered in groups, weaving on large wooden looms and selling some of their wares. Silversmiths hawked medallions and goblets.

Holly led the horse along the fringes of the fair. "I don't understand, Jade," she whispered to the cat. "I thought the king was a tyrant. These people look happy."

"The king's peasants are granted only a few days of gaming and feasting at Midsummer," Jade said, looking straight ahead so as not to appear to be speaking. "But look more closely, my lady."

Holly peered into the crowd and her breath caught.

"Let fly the arrow! Who of you can best the Adept?"

The crier stood below a wooden scaffold heaped with hay and firewood. Standing on it was a kind of scarecrow in a long gown, a crude stick tied to one arm like a wand. As Holly watched, a villager stepped up and, after paying a coin, shot a flaming arrow into the heart of the scarecrow. The effigy smoked; another arrow flew. The straw woman caught fire and the crowd cheered.

"Death!" chanted the people. "Death to the Adept!"

Now Holly could see the true nature of the games. One woman sold pies said to be made of centaur meat. Children caught butterflies in nets and tore their wings, crowing that they'd killed a fairy. On a stage nearby, a man and his daughter demonstrated how the king had slain the Wandwright's apprentice ages ago. The crowd cheered as the child clutched her belly and feigned death.

"Their fear of the Exiles is as great as their fear of the king," Jade told her. "But look sharp, my lady. We must secure the horse."

Holly nodded, feeling ill. She took a deep breath and walked the horse alongside the grandstand until she found an opening in the long banner covering it. They slipped inside.

It was close and dark underneath. Quickly she tied the horse to one of the wooden posts. She and Jade returned, blinking, to the sunlight.

"Look, there's Hornbeak!" The falcon dipped lower and landed on her arm. Holly ducked back under the berfrois banner to talk to him.

"I come with news from the falconers, Your Ladyship," said the bird. "They say the youth of the wood is to compete in the king's tournament of skills."

"You mean *Everett*?" asked Holly.

"Aye, my lady. The elder is to joust with the king's

knights, the lad to be his squire. The prince has offered the lives of the prisoners in exchange for a victory."

Holly and Jade stared at each other. "It sounds too good to be true," said Holly. "Why would the king let them be in the tournament?"

"His own amusement, Lady Holly," said the falcon. "Of course, Reynard expects them to be killed in the contest. Perhaps he has even planned it so."

Holly gasped, but Hornbeak held up a wing to calm her. "It is not exactly a match of skills. The youth is to show a bit of sorcery meant to confound his opponent."

"Sorcery?" said Holly, confused. "How? Does the prince know magic too?"

"Not as you know it, my lady," said Jade. "The king's court has kept mages for many a year. They use trickery and illusion to scoff at true magic."

So some kind of stage magician would be helping Everett? Holly couldn't quite picture it.

"Sir Everett competes late in the joust," Hornbeak said. "I have seen it on the boards. Count the competitions, Lady Holly; his shall be the eighth."

Sir Everett?

Holly turned to Jade. "If the boys are out in the open, all we have to do is let them know I'm here. Then we can all ride away to the wood together."

"With a full complement of the king's knights after you," said Jade.

"Not if the knights are diverted by the Exiles," the falcon said, taking flight. "I fly now to inform Ranulf and the others." He disappeared through the slit in the berfrois covering.

"Find yourself a seat on the lower benches, my lady," said Jade. "I shall find your kinsman and his companion. Await me here." He streaked out from beneath the berfrois, and Holly was left alone with Áedán.

Chapter 40

Jade's Message

Inside the boys' pavilion the air grew stuffy as the sun climbed, and Loverian opened the flap to admit the breeze. Everett could see a bit of the lists from their position. Gervase, the first to compete, easily unseated Adémar, who took a direct hit to the chest and lay still as death on the ground. The crowd roared in response.

"I wouldn't fancy my chances against him," Everett said.

Loverian glanced at him. "Gervase is not even the best jouster in the kingdom. That honor lies with Grandor, despite his lack of chivalry."

Everett pulled out his wand, studying the markings on it. Sol had not appeared yet to claim Holly. He still had the lady's favor, and a lot of time before his turn.

"Will we get through two rounds today, do you think?" Ben was asking.

"Aye," said Loverian. "One round, followed by

luncheon and the lesser competitions. The day ends with the second round. The third round is reserved for the morrow, with the championship on the third day, afore the ceremonies."

And when would Holly get here? Everett wondered.

"Oh no." Ben held his handkerchief to his face. "They're worse than horses."

"What are?"

Then Everett noticed the sleek black cat who had walked in through the open pavilion flap. Loverian jumped up and edged toward the entrance, walking parallel to the cat's path. "It bodes ill, Sir Everett," he warned.

"That's just a superstition," Everett said, forgetting who he was talking to. But a moment later the cat seized the wand in its mouth and raced off with it.

"Hey!"

Loverian drew his sword.

"Let me go! I've got to get that wand back!"

"I'll get it!" Ben dodged Loverian and raced out of the pavilion. The knight cursed and glanced after Ben, then back to Everett. "You had best pray thy companion return."

"He will." *And fast, Ben.*

But several minutes slipped by, and Ben still had not come back. Loverian glanced outside the pavilion, uttered a curse, and took a chain and padlock from a trunk at the foot of his cot. "I shall search for the squire," he said, taking Everett outside. He looped the chain around Everett, securing him to a nearby tree. "Stay fast," he said, and disappeared into the crowd.

A moment later Ben dashed up. "What're you doing chained up?"

"Loverian went looking for you. What happened?"

"Lots of stuff! That cat—he's Holly's! And he *talks*!"

"Where'd she find a talking cat?"

"Never mind, I have to tell you what he said before Loverian comes back. Holly's got a horse hidden at the north end of the bleachers—"

"*Berfrois.*"

"Whatever. Anyway, when you make your first run in the joust, that'll be toward the south end. But don't finish him off, okay? When you turn around to do the second run, you'll be heading toward the north end."

"Right."

"So on your second run, ride past him and follow Holly—she's on a white horse at the top of the hill. She'll be heading for the forest."

"What about you?"

"I'll just have to jump up on Buttercup behind you. There won't be much time."

"But Avery's supposed to meet us, yeah?"

"Forget about him!" said Ben. "The point is to get out of here."

Everett didn't like the sound of that. Avery trusted him, and didn't he need rescuing too, in a way? "He's counting on us. We can't just leave him, Ben—"

"Do you want to get home or not? Let him find us. He'll be up with the king and queen, and there'll be a lot of confusion. Holly's friends are going to divert the knights."

"*Divert* them? How?"

"I don't know, but we should be able to get a head start. And Holly can protect us. Jade said she's got another wand and she's learned all kinds of stuff."

Just as Sol had said. "Who's Jade?" Everett asked.

"The cat."

"Huh." Everett paused. Sol had said nothing about a cat, nor any other friends of Holly's.

"Oh, and there's one more thing," Ben said, turning red. "They've changed the contestants around a little."

"What do you mean?"

"You were supposed to joust with Jordain. I don't know how it got changed, or whose idea it was . . . well, but I bet I *do* know . . ."

"Ben! Who am I competing against?"

Ben quieted, swallowing. "Grandor."

"*What?*"

"Look out, here comes Loverian." Ben stood at attention as the knight strode up, his face dark red. "Good fortune is thine, squire," he said, unlocking Everett's chain. He pushed them, none too gently, into the pavilion. "Ye shall keep your lives this day."

"I'm sorry," said Ben, "but I had to get the wand back. Everett would be dead without it."

Loverian snorted, pulling his hand through his curls. "He shall be like to die in any case."

"I wish everyone would stop saying that," Everett muttered. His heart dropped, settling around his belly button. Grandor: the best jouster in the kingdom.

When it was time for luncheon, Loverian led the boys outside and chained them to the same tree where he'd secured Everett before. He left them a platter of food and went to join the other knights for the midday feast. Between the high sun and the heavy food, Everett started to feel drowsy. Next to him, Ben had already dozed off. He closed his eyes.

But at that precise moment, a bright light flew out of the tree's canopy and onto Everett's knee, startling him. "Sol!" His stomach tightened into a knot. She couldn't know he was going to break his promise—could she? He lowered his voice to a whisper. "I—I didn't expect you quite so soon."

"There is little time, my lord," she said urgently. "I have heard the Adept's plans that the squire hath told thee. It is all to our greater good." She smiled at him, her golden body glowing. "When the joust be finished, you must ride to the Adept's side and seize her wand. I shall be with you. Ride with me into the forest; the Adept will follow you as the bee to the hive. But take care! We must arrive at the firenest. Only there can the Adept's destiny be realized."

"Um . . . yes, right. Okay," Everett said, wondering what destiny that might be. Sweat trickled down inside his chain-mail shirt. He glanced at Ben. "But what if Holly doesn't want to go with you and get her . . . destiny? She might just want to go home." In fact, he was quite sure of that.

Sol gave a low hiss, baring two rows of very sharp teeth. "I have granted you power," she said. "Do you wish to face the knight without it?"

"No, of course not!" Everett said, feeling panicky. "I can do it, I can bring her!"

"See that you do," whispered the flaming creature. And with that, she vanished.

Everett let out his breath in a shaky sigh. What would Sol do when she realized he had double-crossed

CLAIRE M. CATERER

her? Beside him, Ben shifted in his sleep. A bit of drool dribbled out of his half-open mouth. Maybe he should've told Ben about Sol from the very beginning. But it was too late now, and it was all up to Everett. He couldn't let down Holly—or Sol. He would just have to work it out. Somehow.

Chapter 41

The Joust

For Holly, watching the jousts was a bit like sitting in the dentist's office waiting to have a cavity filled. She couldn't still her fluttery heart. She kept twisting a piece of her tunic in her hands. She had found a seat in the berfrois, close to the ground, and Jade sat in her lap. He kept turning to frown at her every time her legs jiggled nervously. At least he had found the boys. Knowing this, picturing Ben alive and well and chatting with a black cat (and sneezing, likely as not), filled Holly with a strange sort of pride. Her dorky little brother was making do, being brave, and she was going to get him out of here.

Still, for all of these hopes, the next moment all she could think of was that Everett might be hurt or killed. How had he managed to get himself a place in the tournament? In two of the contests she watched, one of the knights had been knocked unconscious. Jugglers and musicians roamed the lists, entertaining the villagers between jousts. Sometimes a lady stood by to hand a knight his helmet. Holly kept count as each contest commenced. At last a squire announced the seventh joust, between Sir Jordain and Sir Osgood the Seafarer.

"Everett's next," Holly whispered. She slid off the bench and walked around the berfrois. Jade followed. Once out of sight, they slipped underneath the banner.

She untied the white horse and led her around the fairgoers to a hill at the northern end of the meadow. She sat tall in the saddle, feeling a tickle as Áedán poked out his head to see. Holly put on her glasses. Too bad she hadn't any binoculars. She could make out the jousters but couldn't tell who was who, especially with helmets on.

Another roar went up from the gallery; Osgood had unseated his challenger.

"Everett's turn," she whispered. "Oh, Jade, I hope this works."

The knight Grandor was introduced first. Holly's stomach turned over. How would Everett ever survive *him*? His squire was a tall, thickset boy of about fifteen, with squinting eyes and a crooked nose that had probably been broken in a fight. He cried loud to the gallery, extolling Grandor's virtues. The knight's scarlet cloak billowed in the breeze. He drew his sword and saluted the royal box. The crowd roared in response. Grandor cantered his horse to the southern end of the tilt, facing Holly. Then a small figure scurried onto the lists and hollered up at the crowd.

"Jade, look! It's Ben!"

She could just make out his squeaky voice. "Hear ye, hear ye! Announcing His Majesty's newest knight, straight from"—a pause—"straight from parts unknown! Other places! Better places! A knight with powers beyond belief! With skills . . . er . . . well, they're wicked awesome! I give you the Mage, Sir Everett of the Wand!" He scampered back and grabbed the reins of a short, yellowish horse who trotted along with Everett on her back.

He sat straight in the saddle, and although his armor was odd looking, it gleamed impressively in the afternoon sun. He didn't have a fancy cloak like Grandor, but he lifted his chin and waved to the crowd as if he wasn't worried about a thing. He was almost . . . arrogant. Some of the crowd snickered until Everett's horse reared. He kept his seat, waving and smiling, and a few cheers went up. He rode out to the end of the tilt nearest Holly.

The fairgoers hushed and settled on the hillside to watch. Holly had a clear view of Everett as he trotted in her direction. He gave no sign of having seen her, but she supposed that was best. He wheeled the horse to face his opponent.

Ben stood next to Everett's horse and glanced back toward her. She raised a hand. She thought he nodded back, but it was hard to tell.

But wait—Ben had forgotten something. Grandor's squire handed the knight's lance and shield to him. Where were Everett's? Ben didn't seem to notice his mistake. Everett bowed to his opponent, then held out his hand.

Ben presented something small and thin to Everett. An excited murmur spread through the gallery.

What could they be up to? Was Everett just that stupid? He was facing a *trained knight*, he could hardly—

Everett lifted his right hand over his head. Holly squinted to see what he held, and then the sun hit it just right, and it gleamed.

A wand?

Everett took a deep breath. "I can do this, I can do this," he muttered to himself. Hold off Grandor long enough to get to Holly. Then do *something* about Sol. Maybe he could throw away the lady's favor just as he rode off toward Holly. Sweat trickled down his face inside the helmet. He pulled the red silk scarf from his sleeve and wrapped it around his palm, gripping it so tight that the fabric strained against his knuckles. The wand looked small and weak in his hand.

Grandor's visor went down. He spurred his horse.

Everett did the same.

The crowd held its collective breath.

Grandor came at him much faster than had Loverian in training. The point of his lance glinted in the sun. Everett took a deep breath. He had to survive this charge in order to wheel around and face Holly waiting at the northern end. He hadn't chanced a look backward; he only prayed she was there.

The space between the knights closed. Grandor's lance swept down over the horse's shoulder.

Everett raised the wand over his head.

He swallowed. The lance was only a foot or two from his chest.

Everett didn't bother with the lasso move. Inspired, he flicked his wrist as if wielding a whip. Purple smoke blew from the wand and enveloped the lance. Everett smiled; the lance would fall in the next moment.

But it didn't. The smoke obscured Grandor's vision and the lance glanced off the tilt barrier. Grandor cursed, but he kept hold of his weapon. The horses passed each other, gained the far end, and swung around.

CLAIRE M. CATERER

Gasps and cheers rose from the gallery—at first a muffled cacophony and then three syllables, chanted together from the far end of the berfrois:

"*Ev-er-ETT! Ev-er-ETT! Ev-er-ETT!*"

His name. They knew his name.

He raised a hand to the audience. They cheered.

"Ev, get going!" Ben yelled from the sidelines.

Grandor had taken the chance to urge his horse forward. Distracted, Everett kicked Buttercup, who charged ahead. In the distance, Everett saw Holly, a brown hooded figure on a white horse. She was waiting.

He would throw Grandor, grab Ben, and keep going. And keep Sol away from Holly. Somehow.

Grandor shouldered his shield, swung the lance to his opposite hand, and at the same time pulled his sword from its scabbard. It flashed in the sun as he swung it over his head. Over the crowd, Everett heard Ben's voice:

"Everett, look out! He's got a sword!"

And then a soft *umph* from Ben's direction.

Everett took a breath to focus on what he thought the scarf was telling him to do. He raised the wand and circled, once, twice, three times.

The lance and the sword slashed as one, Grandor squeezing the horse's flanks with his knees.

Everett struck at the knight's breastplate.

A threefold tongue of flame burst from the wand in red, orange, and yellow. The yellow strand leaped for Grandor's right hand, wrapping around the sword; the red streak burst into bloom on the breastplate; and the orange flame ripped the lance from his left hand, throwing it into the air. Buttercup reared in fright; Everett only just managed to keep his seat. Grandor roared in pain as the flames enveloped his armor. Everett wheeled to watch as the black horse sped by. The fire whirled around the armored knight like a cyclone and then elongated, stretching out into a great maw with ears on either side.

"It's a dragon," Everett whispered.

He could see Grandor in the midst of it, slashing the sword back and forth at the beast's head, but it engulfed him in its mouth until it finally pulled him off the horse. The dragon's head blew skyward then, roaring in triumph, until at last it extinguished about forty feet above the knight.

But, incredibly, Grandor still stood.

He had been frightened, but not harmed, and he clutched his sword in his fist. Everett turned to look back at Holly.

The white horse was galloping toward him.

And in front of him, a tiny, fiery creature appeared

　CLAIRE M. CATERER

before his eyes. "Now is the time, my lord," said Sol. "The wand and the Adept, the both, as per our accord."

Desperately, Everett watched Holly approach, willing her to turn around. Why was she riding this way? She was supposed to wait for him, and now . . .

He took a deep breath. "I'm sorry," he said to the little fairy. "I can't do it. Holly wants to go home, and so do we."

Sol blazed, the heart of a small fireball, and stretched out long fingernails toward his face. "Dost dare to betray me, mortal?"

"No, wait! Here! You can take my wand!" He held it out in front of him. "It's just as good as hers, honest!"

"Fool!" hissed the Elemental. "Do you think I can touch the wand, even a thief's? It must be the Adept!" She raised a white-hot hand to his cheek and slashed across it, burning a long mark across his face. He shielded himself, tears springing to his eyes, and struck at her with the wand. The flame that leaped from it grazed her.

"If it be so, mortal, then face your fate on your own power!" cried the fairy. She flew to the wrist holding the wand, and yanked the silk scarf away. It fell free in a great scarlet flourish. Everett watched as it climbed, as if on the wind, into the sky.

"No, please! Bring it back!" he cried.

"You shall see it anon!" called the fairy. "It goes to one who is more worthy than you!"

In the next moment, Sol and the silk scarf vanished.

And standing in front of Everett, looking dazed but unhurt, clutching his sword, was Grandor.

Chapter 42

The Vanishment

"Ben!"

Holly saw what Everett had been too busy to see: Grandor's burly squire had pounced on Ben when he cried out his warning. Holly gasped when the older boy drew his sword, but instead of slashing at Ben, he turned it and butted him in the gut with the hilt. That was the *umph* that Everett had heard.

Ben fell without another sound, and through the tangle of swords and horses' hooves, Holly saw the squire kicking Ben in the head and ribs. Her brother would never get up on Everett's horse now. She urged her own horse forward.

"Lady Holly! We are meant to wait!" Jade cried.

"I know!"

Everett gaped at her, then wheeled around. Grandor's sword clanged uselessly against his armor. Everett waved the wand over his head again—*where* had he gotten it?—and the knight skipped backward. But his time, the wand did nothing.

And then everything seemed to happen at once. Knights poured onto the lists; the crowd stampeded from the berfrois; and with a screech and roar, Holly's allies spilled from the forest. Behind her came the thundering of centaurs' hooves—Ranulf leading the charge—and the beating of wings as Hornbeak and his falcons screamed over her head. Bittenbender and a few other Dvergar charged forward, waving daggers and battle-axes. A small bird flew in their wake, then in a flash, popped into the form of a leopard. The changeling! Two stags galloped by, kicking dust into her face, and the knights, most of them lacking helmets, turned white. Swords and shields came forth, and Ranulf bellowed something about freedom for the Exiles. She couldn't see Ben or Everett through the dust and chaos. The Wandwright's white horse reared and Holly clung to its mane. The black cat yowled.

"I can't see Ben, Jade!"

"Use the wand!"

Of course. No point in hiding her identity any longer. She pulled out the wand and it warmed in her palm. She knew no enchantments besides the unlocking spell, and she couldn't think how that could help.

But she pointed at the path in front of her, focusing on the stampeding horses. *Clear the way.*

It is a good deal easier to wield newfound power in practice than when dust and screaming and blood explode on every side. Still, a falcon who had flown into her wake screeched and wheeled above her, and for a moment a clear path appeared on the trampled grass. But the next moment, the knight Gervase staggered across it, dragging Bittenbender by his long beard.

"Let him go!" Holly cried, waving the wand without thinking. Gervase cursed and dropped the Dvergar, grasping his stung wrist. The knight's eyes found hers.

"The Adept." He turned his sword on her. "Lay down your wand, lass, and see none else harmed this day."

"Get out of the way!" The white horse reared again and Holly started to slide off.

Gervase lunged forward and brought his sword down on the horse's neck.

Holly screamed.

The knight vanished.

"There, my lady!"

Jade pointed at the sky. Fleetwing the leogryff had swooped down, dodging arrows, and grabbed the knight in his claws, bearing him off across the lists. Several knights noticed too and fled toward the castle. In a moment Holly's path was clear.

Ben lay crumpled against the berfrois. Holly jumped off the horse and ran to him, ducking as one of the centaurs galloped past. She shook Ben's shoulder. "Ben, wake up! Can you hear me?"

He slumped over. She tugged on him, but he was too heavy for her. She would never be able to hoist him onto the horse's back. "Jade, what can I do? Where's Everett?"

An arrow whistled past her ear and landed in the dirt. Holly glanced up at the gallery; the king's archers were shooting at her. Holly crouched against the lower benches, shielding Ben with her body. "Everett!"

But it was Ranulf who appeared. She almost didn't recognize him with his chain-mail shirt on. "Lady Holly, you are not safe here," he said.

"Ranulf, help me with Ben! I don't know where Everett is."

An arrow pinged off the centaur's armor as he lifted her brother with one arm and sat him on the horse. "He must be wakened afore he can ride."

"I can hold him up." Holly scrambled up behind Ben. "Is he all right?"

"He does not appear wounded. Here, my lady." Ranulf took his own shield and threaded Holly's arms through the straps so that it lay across her back. "You are too fine a target. Now make haste!" Ranulf galloped off down the length of the berfrois, shooting his own arrows into the gallery as he went.

Holly glanced wildly around for Everett. One of the stags was down, with an arrow in its neck; the female centaur clashed swords with one of the castle knights; a volley of arrows rained down from above, though somehow they fell in a circle around Holly's horse.

"Ranulf's shield offers some protection, but 'twill not last," Jade told her. "You must go."

"But I can't leave Everett! What if he's hurt?"

She wheeled the horse in every direction. Bittenbender, free again, was dueling with the young knight Jordain, who cursed and fell as Bittenbender jabbed his dagger into the knight's knee. Fleetwing wheeled over the king's box and knocked several archers from their stance. Then out of the dust appeared another knight, who had regained his black horse and swung his sword above his head as he bore down on her.

Grandor.

"Sorcery is nothing against the king's champion!" He closed the distance between them, bringing the sword down.

Holly screamed.

Then came a clash as Grandor's sword met another's. It was Loverian, the dark-haired knight, who had run up on foot between the horses. He aimed a thrust at Grandor's unguarded side.

"Will you betray king and realm, Loverian?" Grandor snarled, answering with a parry.

"Are you a killer of squires and maidens?" Loverian asked.

Holly backed her horse away, then shied as another arrow flew past her. She pulled her own bow from her back and shot an arrow into the crowd of archers. She couldn't see if she'd hit a mark.

Grandor locked swords with Loverian and pressed down on him from upon the horse, their faces only inches apart, until Grandor disengaged with a mighty shove that sent Loverian sprawling. The burly knight leaped from his horse and drew back his sword at Loverian's neck.

"No!"

Holly galloped her horse at Grandor, knocking him down. Loverian scrambled to his feet. Grandor wasn't badly hurt, though, and this time he charged at Holly.

She reached again for an arrow.

But before she was able to fit it to the bowstring, a wall of flame erupted around her in a great circle. Grandor cursed and fell back; Loverian gaped at her.

"'Tis the salamander, my lady," Jade whispered.

"Lucky for me," Holly breathed. Beyond the flames the two knights backed away from her, and the path to the woods opened up as the centaurs and remaining stag drove the fighting toward the castle. "Enough, Áedán," she whispered. "We're okay now."

The flames died at once, leaving her eyes dazzled. The villagers screamed and stampeded away from her, and even the king's archers disappeared into the crowd. She wheeled once more and gasped. Galloping toward her on a black stallion, his embroidered cloak flying behind him, was the prince. And right on his heels—finally—was Everett.

"Everett, look out!" Holly pointed her wand at Avery. A thin spark flew from its tip and grazed his arm.

"Peace, Lady Adept!" cried the prince, and Everett came up even with him.

"Don't, Holly! He's helping us!"

"He's *what*?" Everett must've gotten knocked in the head. *Helping* them?

"It's all agreed, he's all right—"

"I mean thee no harm, my lady—" the prince added.

"Oh, never mind, just come *on*!" Holly turned her horse again toward the Northern Wood and urged the beast forward. Whatever Everett was up to, she had to get them to the woods before it was too late.

She didn't look back. She clutched Ben with one

arm as she held the reins and her wand in the other hand. She rode hard, closing the distance to the woods. After a moment, a terrific sneeze dampened her hand.

"Ben! Are you okay?"

"Holly?"

He tried to turn around.

"Yes, it's me. Just face forward."

"My head really hurts—and my stomach—"

"One of the squires attacked you."

"But where's Everett?"

"He's right behind me. But so's the prince. Hold still, I told you! We're almost there."

By *there* she meant the edge of the wood. The fairgrounds were empty now, the grass trampled and the people scattered. Holly wheeled the horse and looked down into the valley.

The villagers had poured into the fray, some screaming in fright, others awed by their first glimpse of a centaur or leogryff. Fleetwing wheeled above the lists, plucking up knights where they stood. A moment later Everett and Avery joined her.

"Be quick!" the prince ordered. "Perform thy magic!"

"Everett, what's he doing here?"

"He's coming with us," said Ben.

They couldn't be serious. "What are you talking about? He's not going anywhere!"

"We have to take him! He's helping us escape," said Everett.

A roar went up from the valley and Holly turned back, scanning the crowd. She caught sight of Ranulf fighting bitterly; two men from the village had fallen on him, beating him with sticks as he swung his sword back and forth.

"Jade, we have to go back and help."

"Nay, my lady," said Jade sharply. "Ranulf would not want it so."

"But what if he's captured?"

"What if Your Ladyship herself be captured? We must follow the plan."

Avery nudged his horse closer. "Does the *cat* speak?"

"Silence!" Jade hissed. "Lady Holly, we have no agreement with His Highness. Leave him."

Avery seized Holly's arm, his fingers crushing her wrist. "Your kinsman swore it, Adept."

"Look!" Everett cried. "It's Grandor!"

The knight had broken free from Loverian and remounted his horse. He shouted something behind him and galloped full on toward the forest, head down, sword drawn. In a moment he would be upon them, and a host of knights on his heels. They had lost their advantage. Holly couldn't worry about Avery; they would deal with him in the woods. She gripped the wand. What good was her talent for unlocking anything now? She would have to try the Vanishment. It was their only chance. She closed her eyes and tried to visualize the beech tree they had entered by—the portal.

But she didn't know the spell.

Her heart drummed against her chest. What difference did it make what words she used, anyway? Hadn't Ranulf said she knew the Old Tongues, somehow? There must be a word, a phrase. . . . Or maybe she could just *think* it. . . .

The ground shook as Grandor's stallion approached.

"Lady Holly! Act quickly!" said Jade.

"Come on!" Holly said. "Everyone get close together, grab hold of my horse. And you all have to be very quiet."

The prince edged closer to Holly's left side, and Everett pushed up behind him, grabbing a piece of the white horse's bridle. Holly took a deep breath. The picture of the portal focused in her mind. The air grew quiet and still. She brandished her wand. Then her mind opened, and she saw the word as if written in the trees.

"*Hurry, Holly!*" yelled Ben.

"*Adepts and traitors!*" Grandor roared.

"Imigh!" Holly cried.

One moment Holly felt the hot breath of the knight's horse, heard the rasp of his chain mail as Grandor raised his sword; and the next, all was silent. The forest in her mind compressed in a blur like a fine green shower all around them. Though she couldn't see the others clearly, she heard them *oooh* and gasp until the green mist began to clear. Slowly the forest came into focus like a photograph developing, the dense canopy of leaves above, the soft moss beneath the horses' hooves . . .

But then, next to her ear, came a bright, slicing noise, steel rasping on steel. Was someone else drawing a sword? The forest scene grew muddled, as if Holly were seeing it through rain-streaked glass. The white horse lost purchase on the ground and whinnied; and then, for a horrible moment, everything went black, as if a heavy curtain had been thrown over them. What had she done?

"Holly?" came Ben's voice ahead of her.

Then other sounds crowded in, demanding her attention: the cries of the villagers; the falcons' scream; the knights' roar. They were going back, fading out of the safety of the forest. "Quiet, all of you!" Holly cried. She couldn't let this happen; she could already feel her energy draining, just like Almaric had said it would. If they ended up back on the hill above the battlefield, she'd never be able to perform the spell again. She just didn't have the *strength*, the power that the others thought she had—who was she to wield a real Adept's wand? She was just playacting, she didn't even belong here. Even Jade had said so. . . .

The cat's voice came out of the dark, as if reading her mind. "Think not on it now, my lady," he whispered. "You *are* the Adept. The only one left. Perform the magic."

All the training, the fighting, forging the wand, even Áedán, gripping her shoulder with his sticky feet—none of it mattered, not really: She was doing this for Ben, for Everett, to get them home. Because if she didn't . . .

"Imigh!" she cried again, gripping the wand. At once the darkness cleared; the battle noises died away. All she could hear was the horses' snuffling, and Ben's labored breathing; and then, abruptly, the air brightened, the green mist appeared and focused, the soft ground solidified below, and all around them was the quiet Northern Wood.

She had done it.

They had not quite landed at the portal, but on a small rise above, but that was all right: Holly could see the beech tree clearly in the valley below. Ben gave

CLAIRE M. CATERER

a feeble cheer, and Holly turned to smile at Everett behind her. But before she could do so, something seized her horse's reins and jerked her around the other direction.

Holly winced as her right arm was squeezed in a firm grip. "What—?"

But she stopped, midquestion. She saw at once what she had done. She had Vanished them, all right: herself and Ben, Everett on his yellow mare, the prince on his black stallion, and, his sword drawn and pointed at Ben's throat, the king's knight—Sir Grandor.

Chapter 43

In the Woods

It took a moment for everyone to realize what had happened, but not nearly as long as it takes to tell it. Holly, astride the white horse, froze for a split second at the sight of Grandor and, before she regained her wits, he wrenched the wand from her hand. Her palm stung as the wood slipped from it, and her stomach buckled as if he had stolen a bit of her own soul. Then just as fast, he seized Ben under the arms and pulled him onto his own horse, knocking Jade to the ground, who spun and snarled.

"Holly!" cried Ben, reaching out to grab her as he was yanked away.

"Silence!" cried Grandor, turning his sword to Ben's throat. "Now shall we see the mettle of this Adept. Where be thy power now?"

"Grandor." Prince Avery's black stallion approached calmly. "That prisoner and the Adept's wand. They be the property of the crown."

Holly glanced at Everett. Was it true? Was Avery really helping them? Everett nodded, almost imperceptibly.

"As you wish, Your Highness," said Grandor sullenly, shoving Ben onto Avery's horse and handing him the wand. Ben nearly hugged Avery in relief. *Now,* Holly thought desperately, watching the prince for some signal. But he didn't look at her, only twirled the wand in his fingers, watching it catch the sunlight.

"Hold him fast, Your Highness," Grandor said. "The better for me to secure the Adept. She would not see her kinsman harmed, nay?" He leered at Holly. Avery, shrugging, wrapped one arm around Ben's neck. Whatever he said, whatever they did, Holly would have to go along. At least until she got Ben free—somehow.

Grandor pulled a length of iron chain from his belt. He clapped manacles around Holly's wrists and held the chain fast. "And the Adept herself, Your Highness? It is time to rid our land of this pestilence, once and for all."

"No!" Ben cried. Avery's arms gripped him harder. He coughed. "Everett, do something! The wand!"

Grandor smiled slowly, laying the flat of his sword blade against Holly's neck. The steel was cold and she could feel the sharp edge angled slightly toward her skin. It would take only the smallest force to slice across her neck. She didn't dare move, but Áedán, still safe on her shoulder beneath the cloak, stirred restlessly. "Wait," she told him softly. Grandor was too close; if Áedán tried to protect her now, Grandor would be encircled in the protective flames alongside her.

The knight smiled as Everett drew out the wand. "Indeed! I would be glad to finish what was begun on the lists." He jumped off his horse, pulling Holly with him. The manacles bit into her wrists as she fell. Grandor yanked her to her feet and rummaged in his saddlebag until he found a padlock. Then he dragged Holly to a tree at the edge of the clearing and wound the chain around the trunk, locking her there.

Beneath the cloak, the salamander's sticky feet burned on her shoulder. Áedán trembled.

A moment later, something silky brushed her ankles. Jade had emerged from the trees so silently that no one else noticed him. Grandor had drawn his sword. Everett had slipped off the yellow horse and held out his wand, facing the knight. He looked very pale.

"Go on, Ev! You can take him!" Ben cheered.

"Just hang on a second," Everett said, almost choking on the words. "We don't have to duel. Avery here— I mean, His Highness—he can take us back to the castle. You can go, Grandor. I've got no fight with you."

"You have no fight indeed," said Grandor softly. "Pray, show us the magic, lad. You are so proud of it."

Holly stole a glance at the prince, who sat impassively on his horse, one arm around Ben, who was nudging him and whispering furiously. She waited for Everett to strike with his wand, but nothing happened. Everett flicked his wrist with a trembling hand, but the wand only fizzled like a Fourth of July sparkler.

"What be the problem, sir knight?" asked Grandor in a mocking tone, closing his circle around Everett. "Has the magic run out of your wand, like spilt wine?" He raised his sword.

"Avery! Do something!" cried Ben.

"Halt, Sir Grandor," came the prince's voice. He didn't sound especially concerned. "I believe Sir Everett seeks something to even the playing field."

Holly bit her lip. "He's not with them, Jade," she whispered. "This whole thing's a trap."

Grandor glanced at the prince but did not lower his sword. "And what might that be, Your Highness?"

"What's going on?" Everett asked, his voice shaking. "Avery, what're you playing at?"

"I'll tell you what," said Ben. "He's double-crossed us, that's what!"

"Silence!" cried Avery, tightening his forearm around Ben's neck. Ben gagged.

"Leave him alone!" Everett cried. "You're supposed to be helping us!"

"Helping you?" Avery laughed bitterly. "I have *played* you, the both!" His voice broke; he sounded like he might burst into tears. He pointed Holly's wand at Everett. "*Sir* Everett! Thou thinkst me vain and stupid!"

"No, I don't," said Everett. "Honest, I don't!"

"Then why wouldst thou promise what thou canst never deliver? To take me to other lands, other worlds? Bribe me with false stories of such wonders?"

"They weren't false stories," Ben cut in. "We'd have done it, if you'd only let us. We still could. It's you who's betrayed us!"

"No," said Avery softly, "never betray. But *learnt*. I was led astray in the king's absence. My father helped me see clearly what I had become, a puppet to outlaws, a slave to the magic of another. Did ye think I would allow an Adept to leave Anglielle, someday to return? Ye think I have no knowledge of magic, that I fear it. But I have watched thee, Everett of the Wood. Watched thee with thy stolen magicks. That wand will do naught lest it be aided by this, thy lady's token." With a flourish, Avery pulled from his sleeve a silken red scarf.

"What lady?" said Ben, glancing at Everett.

"She took it!" Everett said, sounding tearful. "She just *took* it and left me to get killed!"

CLAIRE M. CATERER

"*That's* what made the wand work?" Ben asked. "The handkerchief?"

"It was child's play to discover the secret," said Avery. "He guarded it too closely, even from thee, squire. To take it is to strip this mage of all his magic. And somehow, it appeared in my hands, just as the Adept uttered her spell." Avery wrapped the scarf around his hand as if binding a wound. "I believe this is how it is done?" He took Holly's wand in his bound hand and pointed it at the turf. A wide spark erupted from it, making a small explosion at Everett's feet. Even Grandor leaped back.

"But Everett, why'd you need that?" Ben asked, forgetting Avery for a moment. "Why wouldn't it just work?"

"Because he stole it," Holly said suddenly. She looked at Everett, remembering. "You did, didn't you? You stole it that day at Mr. Gallaway's!"

"He *gave* it to me!" Everett said. "Do you think you're someone special? *I've* known him for ages! And I can do a lot more than that rubbish you do! You couldn't even rescue us!"

"Hey, she tried the best she could!" Ben shouted. "At least she didn't go making friends with the enemy, like some people!"

"I didn't have much of a choice, did I? At least I was doing something!"

"Enough!" Grandor's roar silenced even the birds in

the forest canopy. "I have heard all I care to from this traitor." He lunged at Everett, grabbed him by the arm, and threw him to the ground. He snatched the wand from his hand and planted one boot on Everett's back, pinning him there. "As it should have been from the beginning," snarled the knight, raising his sword. "For the glory of the kingdom!"

"No!" Holly cried.

"Wait!" Ben shouted.

But before Grandor's sword could do its royal duty, a great thundering came down the forest path and the knight was knocked to the ground. Ranulf, still clad in chain mail, slashed at Grandor with his sword.

"Now is the time, my lady," muttered Jade, and streaked in a blur of black fur across the clearing.

"Halt! In the name of the king!" cried Avery. His horse, startled by the centaur, shuffled back and forth; Avery brandished the wand. A broad fireball burst from it but missed Ranulf by a good margin. Instead it set a nearby tree ablaze from crown to roots.

Grandor was on his feet again, dueling with Ranulf. The two swords flashed back and forth so fast that Holly was blinded as the sun glinted off of them. She cried out as Grandor cut a long slash in Ranulf's flank, but the centaur ignored it, pushing the advantage of height and weight. But where was Jade?

CLAIRE M. CATERER

She peered through the dust and horses' hooves at Avery's black stallion. She could see the prince waving the wand wildly over his head; Ben was struggling with him now, kicking and elbowing him. A great roar went up as the wand struck another tree and it lit up like a giant candle. The fire began to spread, and the smoke thickened. Holly coughed, her eyes stinging; then Avery screeched.

Through the haze she could make out Jade, like a black weasel, scrambling up and down Avery's back. The prince howled as the cat's claws raked over his face. *Crack!* went the wand again, and a pinwheel of flame spun down the hill into the valley.

Their valley.

The beech tree.

Holly pulled on the chains, her wrists straining against the manacles. But the iron cut into her skin, holding fast. The tree . . . They had to get to their portal. . . .

Then she heard a yell. It was Ben.

"I got it! Let's go!"

Together he and Everett appeared out of the smoke at her side, Ben waving the wand over his head. "Holly! I bit him! I bit him! I've got the wand!"

"But what good does that do?" Holly cried. "I need to unlock these chains! I can't get loose!"

Everett looked at the wand longingly. "Can't it . . . I don't know . . . become a key again?"

"That's not how it works!"

"My lady!" Jade fled through the smoke and appeared like a ghost, his fur covered in ash. "The knight has fled, and Ranulf after him. You must hurry to the portal!"

"But *how*? What about what Almaric said? The bones—"

"Lady Holly," said Jade, "recall what you told us—keys are for unlocking things!"

Ben thrust the wand into her hands.

But *could* she do it? The energy had drained out of her like air from a balloon from the strain of transporting herself and the boys, along with Avery and Grandor. She pointed the wand at the manacles. It shook in her hand.

"'Tis only one lock, Lady," Jade whispered. "You have the power for that."

If she didn't take off her own hands while trying. The thickening smoke stung her eyes; her head ached and her knees trembled. She *might* have the power, but what about the focus Almaric had talked about? She touched the wand tip directly to the irons and closed her eyes.

The heat pressed in on her. She smelled live trees burning, a sick scent somehow different from the odor

CLAIRE M. CATERER

of autumn bonfires. But she couldn't think about that. Jade was right; this was *her* spell, the one she had felt in her heart from the beginning. She would have to make it work. She took a deep breath, envisioning the iron chains lying broken on the forest floor, her hands strong and whole and free. Just one lock. That's all it would take.

"*Osclaígí!*"

Holly knew at once it had worked; the irons trembled as if made of silk and fell apart. Holly broke away from the tree, staggering, dizzy from the effort. She turned to Jade.

"You have no time for farewells, Lady Holly." The cat's voice was raspy with smoke.

Holly felt tears pricking her eyes. "Just go, Jade, before the whole forest catches fire."

"Holly!" said Everett. "The tree!"

"I know, I know." But she couldn't help it; she scooped Jade up in her arms and kissed him, in a most undignified manner; he struggled for only a moment, then allowed her to set him down. He bowed. "Until we meet again, Lady Adept."

"Holly, come on!" Ben was tugging at her hand. She glanced back at Jade and blew him a kiss, then turned back to the valley.

But the valley was in flames.

Chapter 44

Through the Fire

Avery's fire had roared through the wood like a wild animal released from a trap, igniting one tree after another until their path was completely blocked. The smoke rolled in a black cloud through the valley. Holly could only just make out the beech tree. The fire was pulling closer to it.

"We'll just have to run for it," she said in a low voice.

"There's no way!" said Everett.

"We can't stay here forever!" cried Ben.

"We won't have to. Áedán, I need you." Holly reached under her cloak and pulled out the little salamander. "Can you do it? For all three of us?"

The golden creature gazed up at Holly with his bulbous eyes. She felt Áedán's strength gathering in his tiny body, like a cat about to spring. "Wow!" Ben breathed. "That's cool! What is it?"

"It's the Golden Salamander," said Holly. "There's no time to explain. Just stay close to me, both of you!"

CLAIRE M. CATERER

The boys huddled around her and the three joined hands. Holly glanced up and saw Avery—impossibly, not gone, not fled—stampeding through the smoke. "It is too late, Lady Adept!" he shouted. "Your portal has been destroyed!"

"Avery, don't be daft!" Everett said. "Get out of here before you burn up!"

"Who cares if he does?" Ben countered.

But Holly was peering through the smoke into the valley, hearing a great crash as trees fell, igniting others, and then she saw that the prince was right: The beech tree was in flames. "Now, Áedán!"

She spoke none too soon. In the same instant as the leaves at her feet began to burn, ignited by sparks carried on the breeze, the warm curtain of flame rose up around the three of them like a golden balloon. She could hardly see through the gauzy flames, but she could make out Avery's silhouette, his stallion rearing in panic, and his voice choked with smoke, crying out to them. Holly turned to the valley. Rabbits and chipmunks streamed out of the underbrush in every direction; flocks of birds burst from the canopy. Everything was ablaze, but surely Áedán could protect them; wouldn't fire best fire? The little group began to move as one.

"Faster, Holly!" said Ben. "The tree's already burning!"

The three began to run, borne over the burning leaves by the fire curtain. In front of them, a tree crashed to the ground and they hustled around it, pushing through the smoke with their eyes shut, until, moments later—though it seemed like much longer— they reached the beech tree at last. Holly's heart sank. How could the wand possibly work? The tree was in flames.

"Just try it!" Everett cried.

She pulled out the wand and pointed it at the burning tree trunk. A faint light glimmered, but the tree broke only halfway apart with a weak crackling sound. The branches at the top of the tree creaked, then fell, raining fire all around them.

"Áedán, we have to leave you," Holly said desperately. She blinked away tears, remembering what the Wandwright had said. Áedán would hibernate, safe in the flames, until her return. *If* she returned. She plucked him from her shoulder and he gazed at her with his bulbous orange eyes. Did he nod?

"We can't go through there without him!" Ben said.

"We'll have to. He'll be all right. Come on, everyone together!" Then all at once, Áedán's fire curtain fell away and the heat from the forest fire engulfed them. Holly couldn't tell if the tree trunk had broken apart because of the wand or the flames; would it even work now that it was nearly burned to a cinder? The beech looked like nothing magical now. She put a foot through the crack as the flames licked up her legs; she tightened her grip and pulled on Ben's hand, which pulled on Everett's. Holly squeezed through and she was aware of two things at once: the impossibly hot flames on her skin and the sickening smell of burning hair. She jumped.

At the same time, the earth shook and everything went black. Smoke choked her lungs and she coughed; everything was so hot; they weren't going to make it. But a moment later, she collapsed on damp grass, her clothes crackling with flame. She rolled, still pulling on Ben's hand, and the fire smothered beneath her. Before she could call out to them, Ben and Everett fell through on top of her and for a moment they were all a tangle of arms and legs and feet in one another's faces. When they were finally sorted and the flames stamped out, they looked back at the beech tree they had entered by. It was a twisted, blackened hulk. As they watched, its branches closed in on themselves and the tree dwindled down, shrinking into ashes.

Chapter 45

Teatime at Number Seven

But it wasn't only the beech tree that had disappeared. When Holly righted herself in the cool grass, she saw that the keyholes in all the other trees had vanished.

Or perhaps they had never been there in the first place.

She ran around to the other side of the oak tree—there was no need to step back through it. Clearly, they had emerged from Anglielle back into England, not into that bright place between the worlds.

Behind her, she heard Ben ask, "What happened?" And then a *shush* from Everett. Holly ignored them.

In her hand, she clutched the key—for it was no longer a wand—and held it up to the knothole in the oak's trunk. But the metal plate had shriveled and twisted like molten iron. The key no longer fit.

Holly didn't know where else to go. Of course, she took Ben home first. Everett walked with them as far as

Hodges Close, and then turned down the block to go to his own house, giving a silent wave. No one spoke. It seemed to be midmorning, and as far as Holly could tell, it was the same day they had left, since her father, who was busy at his computer, hardly glanced up when she came in the door. She and Ben took turns showering and putting on clean clothes, which felt more wonderful than clean clothes ever had before. Ben went straight to his computer.

Holly would have loved to have gone to bed, to curl up with her own things—or as much as that was possible, seeing as her own pillow and blankets were thousands of miles away, very close to the exact center of another continent. But instead she walked out of the house again and wandered down the street to Number Seven.

She found Mr. Gallaway puttering around on his screened porch, repotting plants. Holly knocked on the door.

The old man looked up, startled, and opened the door. He took her by the elbow, led her into his kitchen, and set the kettle on. He said nothing, though he winced at the bruises on her wrist where Avery had grabbed her. Then, when the tea things were ready, Mr. Gallaway carried them on a tray into his sitting room, motioning her to follow.

A sudden lump grew in Holly's throat. She realized, looking around at the comfortable chintz-covered chairs and settee, how like Almaric's cottage this room was. Mr. Gallaway didn't comment when she swiped the back of her hand against her cheeks, though he did pass her a handkerchief. And when at last he had poured the tea, his ancient face crinkled into a smile below his deep-set blue eyes.

"Now, sit down. You must tell me everything."

And Holly did. She talked until her voice sounded raspy. Several times during the telling of her story, her throat thickened, and more than once she blew her nose into the handkerchief. Never did Mr. Gallaway say anything like "Don't be ridiculous" or "That couldn't possibly have happened." Holly would have been very surprised if he had.

"And now?" he prompted, when she seemed to have finished. "You seem unhappy."

"I miss Áedán. He didn't come through the portal. He'll die without me."

"Oh, I should think not. Salamanders, even golden ones, sleep quite happily in their nests until their keepers return. Or so I have read."

Holly didn't ask where he could have read such a thing. "If I ever can return. Or maybe I'm crazy. Maybe none of it really happened."

Mr. Gallaway snorted. "Come now, Holly. Even children younger than you know the difference between real events and imaginary ones."

"But I stayed for days in Anglielle."

"I don't understand. What has that to do with anything?"

"Well, where did all that time *go*?"

"You're quite a clever girl. I expect you know exactly where it's gone." The old man sat back and sipped his tea.

"I traveled somewhere. . . ."

"Did you?"

She frowned. "No, not *traveled*, exactly. I went *through* to somewhere, though. Everett said we were still in England. But we couldn't have been."

"Holly, unlike yourself, I've spent very little time in classrooms." Mr. Gallaway hobbled over to a bookshelf. "Never found them to be very useful. Books, on the other hand, are a different story." He took down a leather-bound volume and handed it to her.

The Nature of Quantum Matter and Alternate Worlds by Anthony Krendall. "This looks kind of hard."

"I assure you it is not. As I say, I am not an educated man. But I do know that there is much that *none* of us knows. Including Dr. Krendall."

"You think we went to some kind of alternate universe?"

Mr. Gallaway shrugged his gray eyebrows. "I know very little of such matters. But that is a fascinating book. I would like you to have it."

Holly laid the book beside her. "So I would have come back to the same time and place that I left."

"It appears you have done, whether or not we understand how."

Her face fell again, and the old man said, "Something else?"

"It's just that . . . I didn't *do* anything, did I? I didn't defeat the king or Banish the Sorcerer. I might even have made things worse. The king will probably hunt the Exiles down, and when Raethius gets back, who knows what he'll do? Nothing's changed. I haven't helped at all. And I *promised*."

"A promise, as you say, that binds you to that place."

Holly glanced up from her teacup. "Do you think there might be a way to get back?"

"Oh, I wouldn't have any idea."

"Mr. Gallaway, I know you know more than you say. You gave me the key. You have a whole trunkful. You got them from *somewhere*."

"Keys, like wands, are forged. It is a simple matter. Ask any ironmonger you like."

Holly searched his blue eyes. He raised the teapot. "Another cup?"

Holly drifted through the week, staying indoors as the weather turned rainy. She wrapped her key in a piece of muslin she found in an empty drawer and closed it inside its wooden box, which she tucked in the bottom of her suitcase. Every now and again, when she felt a chill, she reached up to her shoulder where the Golden Salamander had nestled. She spoke very little, to the point that her mother insisted she see a doctor, who pronounced her fit and in need of some sort of activity. The family went to London that weekend.

Another weekend they went to Stonehenge, and another to Paris. Holly saw vast cathedrals and ate mussels and croissants and learned a few words of French. But none of it mattered very much to her.

When they returned to England, Holly spent most of her time exploring the village of Hawkesbury and the fields and hills on its southern side. She stayed clear of the castle and the woods. She was glad after a few weeks when she realized they would be going home soon. It was on one of these last days that finally, just to say good-bye, she found herself walking through the woods to the clearing where the oak tree stood.

She had not brought the key with her. She sat on the grass near a cluster of primroses, gazing up at the twisted knothole in the tree trunk.

A rustling.

Holly sat up, her neck prickling. She tensed, waiting, until Everett and Ben poked their heads through the trees.

"We saw you go into the wood," Everett said by way of explanation. They sat down opposite her, forming a little circle.

Holly had hardly seen him in the last few weeks. She disappeared into the garden when he came over to play Planeterra Five with Ben. It seemed awkward to sit with them now in the forest, afraid to disturb the silence.

"You've not been round much lately," Everett said at last.

Holly shrugged. "We went to Paris."

"I know."

"This is weird," Ben said finally. "We should be *talking* about it. I mean, as far as I know, we're the only three who's ever had anything like this happen to them for real."

"Ben, we're leaving in two days. What difference does it make?"

"Aren't you—" Everett paused, and coughed. "Aren't you ever coming back to Britain again?"

"I don't see why we would." Holly had a sick, hollow feeling in her stomach. She had made a blood oath to Bittenbender and the others. If she could come back, she must—but how could she?

"That's all you know," said Ben.

"Why? What do *you* know?"

"Just what Mom told me," said Ben. "When I *asked*. Like you should be doing."

"What did she say?" Everett said.

"She said that the office in Oxford really likes her. That we'll probably come back here again—maybe lots of times. We could even move here someday. I said no way, it's nice and all, but the electrical system is all bizarro and my computer doesn't always work right, plus what's the deal with all the *rain*, and it's kind of cold, too—"

"Ben!" Holly cut in. "Is that what she said? That we'd come back?"

"Well, if you ever paid attention, instead of moping around all the time, you'd have heard."

"But if we came back," she said, her stomach feeling lighter, "maybe we could get back to Anglielle, too. Maybe we could really help them next time, instead of just being—I don't know—a burden."

"I don't see how," said Everett. "The beech tree burned down."

"But there's lots of trees."

"Do they all go to the same place?" asked Ben.

"I don't know. We can't get in through the oak tree, but there must be some other way."

"Holly." Everett took a deep breath. "You did the best you could. You were . . . well . . . brilliant, you know."

Holly gave a real smile for the first time in weeks. "Really?"

"I thought Avery's head was going to come off when that centaur showed up!" Ben exclaimed.

"That was brilliant, biting Avery to get the wand," said Everett.

"I think that Loverian really wanted to help us."

"Oh, don't be so thick. He's the king's *knight*. . . ."

"Mr. Gallaway said Áedán would be fine, just hibernate in a kind of fire . . . like he was when I found him. . . ."

"Yeah, where did he come from, anyway? Without him we would've died!"

"I still don't see how you got the whatsit, the lady's favor, Everett. . . ."

"I just found it, that was a bit of luck, is all. . . ."

"You should've seen me with the horses! People kept falling off and nobody had any *ice*. . . ."

"I had to learn to joust. That wasn't easy. . . ."

"That's nothing, I had to ride on a leogryff and shoot arrows at the same time!"

"Sorry I screamed and all. . . ."

"Grandor would've killed you for sure if he'd got the chance. . . ."

And so finally Holly began to believe she wasn't quite crazy, and the three of them rehashed everything they'd been through, filling in the blanks in one another's stories and reassuring themselves that of course the Shepards would come back to England, and they *could* get back to Anglielle, if they just put all their heads together. They talked about Mr. Gallaway, and how was it he had the keys ("I don't think they came from Ace Hardware," Holly said); and about the queen, and why had she stepped in to help them ("She's like the king's slave," Ben said); and of course, about Avery, and how he'd betrayed them ("He seemed like such a regular bloke, too," Everett said).

Holly realized she *was* sad to be leaving, that she really did like Everett, though there was something about him that still bothered her a little. She felt quite sure that he *had* stolen the key, whatever he said. But they exchanged e-mail addresses, though Holly admitted she didn't e-mail very often, and Ben said he would teach her, and Holly said she *knew* how to do it, she just didn't *choose* to do it, and Ben said she was a computer neophyte, and Holly didn't like being called that, whatever it was. They were still arguing when Everett waved good-bye to them as their little car trundled down Hodges Close back to Heathrow, and although he didn't know it, they were still arguing on the plane back to the States. Their parents rolled their eyes and were glad after all that the children's seats were several rows behind their own, and Holly and Ben made a good show of sounding like their old selves.

Except, of course, that they were anything but.

Acknowledgments

I would be ashamed to send *The Key & the Flame* into the world without acknowledging the hard work and encouragement of those who helped me give it life. My heartfelt thanks go to:

Sally Caterer, who supported me in more ways than one through the writing;

Margie Caterer-Clark, who believed in me when my own faith wavered;

Melanie Bohling, whose beautiful heart cheers me when I'm down;

Dr. Peter Grund of the University of Kansas English department, who lent me his expertise in Middle English;

Chris Richman, agent extraordinaire, whose enthusiasm fuels my own;

Ruta Rimas, editor supreme, who loves my characters as much as I do, and the marvelous team at Margaret K. McElderry Books;

Leigh Blackman, Megan Foote, and the women of SMOAUF, for being my cheerleaders;

Eloise and Sawyer, who gave up many a walk when deadlines loomed;

and Chris Bohling, who lets me work behind closed doors, chases the gremlins from my computer, and loves and supports me in all that I do.